Go Slowly, Come Back Quickly

by

DAVID NIVEN

BOOK CLUB ASSOCIATES

London

First published in Great Britain 1981
by Hamish Hamilton Ltd
Garden House 57–59 Long Acre London WC2E 9JZ

Copyright © 1981 by Marulto AG

British Library Cataloguing in Publication Data

Niven, David
   Go slowly, come back quickly.
   I. Title
   823′.914[F]   PR6004.I/
   ISBN 0-241-10690-7

Typeset by Western Printing Services Ltd Bristol
Printed in Great Britain by Redwood Burn Ltd, Trowbridge, Wiltshire

To
'PHANTOM'

Author's Note

I asked a friend of mine, a world-famous author, if he had any hot tips for writing a novel.

If I had surprised him on the steps of the Russian Embassy with his arms full of blueprints of the latest Trident missile, he could not have become more reticent. 'Well' he said, 'you could perhaps try . . . giving it a beginning, a middle and an end.'

I am grateful for his contribution.

I am also grateful to another friend, the painter William Feilding, who donated the leg on the jacket.

David Niven
Candolin
Goa
India

PART ONE

The Beginning

1

Stanislaw Skolimowski was six feet two inches tall, the possessor of a magnificent athlete's body, blond all-American good looks and slanting green eyes. He also had an erection and it hurt.

The erection was an anticipatory one and it hurt because it was constricted within a heavily reinforced jock strap (or 'cup' as sports stores prefer to list these uncomfortable safeguards of minimal efficiency).

Carole, the gorgeous seventeen year old reason for his arousal, was seated directly behind him in the packed stadium, clad, despite the cool late Fall afternoon, in a pink and silver crotch-length sequin outfit. Her long, golden legs tapered down provocatively into high boots of white calf leather – she was the most dazzling cheer-leader within living memory at Alwyn High.

His 'cup' was part of the standard equipment of the Alwyn Football Squad. The team was now locked in mortal combat; the closing minutes of the game that would decide whether they or Rosemead would be proclaimed State champions for the year 1938.

Stani, as Stanislaw was known to his friends, pressed down on the top of his 'cup' to try and relieve his discomfort.

With a renewed surge of his loins, he envisaged the pleasure that would soon be his, once this deadlocked game had finally crunched to its close. Carole had a key to her mother's little white house on Chestnut Street and her mother had unwittingly contributed to the success of the forthcoming proceedings by choosing this particular weekend to visit some relatives in San Francisco.

From his seat on the bench, Stani glanced impatiently at the

11

big electric clock above the scoreboard at the end of the stadium. Alwyn had the ball on their own forty-yard line. There was time for only two more plays. 'Thank God', thought Stani. In the lengthening shadows he snuggled beneath his blanket (decorated with his number 39) and contemplated with pleasure the fact that his uniform was still spotless. His team mates on the bench, to a man, would have been ashamed of displaying a spotless uniform at this stage of the game – dreadful proof that Coach had not seen fit to enlist their services during the long, hard-fought battle. But Stani was made of different stuff. He had a highly developed sense of self-preservation and a very definite repugnance to getting hurt.

Carole and the other cheer-leaders leapt high, flourished pom-poms and cavorted about, exhorting the massed faithful in the stands to a last frenzied encouragement of the gladiators.

Mat Matussian, Alwyn's beloved quarter-back, with the best throwing arm in High School football, adjusted his shoulder harness and barked out a complicated play. The rampaging enemy defensive unit crouched ominously with ham-like fists implanted on the surface mud. The play failed in a bone shattering collision. Matussian was dumped, caught in the pocket, thrown for a five yard loss, and Pete Bernstein, the Alwyn star end receiver, was taken away on a stretcher with a broken pelvis.

Now there was only one play to go; the big game was almost over. Despite the tension around him, Stani smiled to himself and took another lascivious look at Carole's hour-glass figure. A nice warm shower, he promised himself, some careful distribution of the Eau de Cologne that Carole had given him. And the 1938 football season, the last of his ignoble athletic career at Alwyn High, would end in a blaze of glory in the house on Chestnut Street.

He received a thump on his back. 'Get in there kid,' Coach yelled. 'It's all yours . . . tell Mat it's the same play.'

In a daze, Stani sloughed off his blanket, picked his helmet off the turf, and, his erection a thing of the past, cantered out to midfield, adjusting his chin strap as he ran.

'Same play,' he panted, as he broke into the huddle.

The quarter-back, still dazed from his collision with a two hundred pound human tank, stared at him blankly for a

12

second, then nodded and croaked out the order as before.

Most of the spectators were now on their feet. A cacophony of sound made all thought impossible. Stani rehearsed in his mind what was expected of him . . . a lateral run of twenty paces to the right, a quick shift and a zig-zag of twenty yards towards the goalposts, followed by a diagonal sprint to the corner flag; then, if all went well, he would look over his left shoulder (still at full gallop) and there at the end of its long flight the ball would hang, for him to grab out of the air. He would plunge over the line for the golden touchdown. The play had worked beautifully in practice and it now worked beautifully once more – except that when Stani looked over his shoulder he saw, not the ball, but the dazzling orb of the setting sun.

The pig-skin projectile, beautifully fired, was right on target, but it eluded his groping fingers, hit him on the helmet and ricochetted into the arms of a charging rhinoceros in the Rosemead colours. Other pachyderms submerged him beneath a mud-spattered, blood-stained heap. Dimly, he heard the final whistle blow.

His popularity in the post-game dressing room was not marked, nor was his welcome at the little house on Chestnut Street too enthusiastic, at first.

'Oh boy!' Carole said as she opened the door, 'you really blew that, didn't you.' But a few minutes later all was forgotten and with the enthusiasm of healthy uninhibited youth, an exquisite programme of time-honoured practices, with imaginative experimentations, unfolded in various parts of the little house.

The next morning, Stani received a cable from England:

HAVE JUST MARRIED ENCHANTING SAILOR
COME AS SOON AS SCHOOL IS OUT
LOVE MOTHER

Stani's mother, from the time she had been a golden Californian beach girl, had always been disorganized, so he waited patiently for elaboration, and more precise instructions. Eventually he picked up the tickets she had ordered at the travel agency and in Los Angeles boarded the Santa Fe Chief for

13

Chicago; it would connect with the 20th Century Limited to New York arriving in time for him to board the *Europa*, which would sail him into Southampton two days before Christmas.

His mother's second cable had said: *Charles and I will meet you at the dock. Wear your overcoat.*

Carole volunteered to drive him down to the Union Station in her mother's convertible. She arrived in plenty of time, looking gorgeous; so gorgeous that a last picnic in a shady cul-de-sac in the Hollywood foothills developed uncontrollably on the back seat, and the trip ended in a mad dash through the suburbs of Los Angeles to head off The Chief at a passenger stop in Pasadena.

Stani enjoyed The Chief enormously. He had a small sleeping compartment to himself (his mother never economized on travel or illness) and found the ministrations of the black sleeping car porter, the observation car barmen, and the dining car waiters (all with starched white jackets, black bow ties and indulgent smiles) far more attractive than their white overseers, who wore rimless glasses and specialized in heavy hints for tips.

He particularly enjoyed the presence of a Hollywood actor and a script writer who were permanently encamped in the bar. The actor was in a very nervous condition because he had made a film test for an important role and was awaiting the outcome.

'My agent,' he confided to Stani, 'told me to play it unconcerned, said the only way with those Studio guys is to show 'em you don't give a damn whether you get the part or not, that's why he put me on this train. He's told 'em I'm sick of waiting and I'm on my way back East to consider a big Broadway offer. He says it never fails and as sure as hell at Albuquerque, New Mexico a telegram will be delivered to the train telling me the part's mine and to come on back! I've only booked that far. I hope to God the studio falls for it!'

The script-writer was much more relaxed.

'I've got me a free ride to New York,' he explained. 'A lot of people who suffer the loss of a loved one far away from home don't like the idea of the body travelling all alone to the funeral. Well, I've found this undertaker in Gardena and when there's a corpse to be shipped back East he gets me the job to make sure it gets there. My family's in Scarsdale.'

'Are you . . . er . . . with somebody now?'

'Yea, there's an old broad in a box back there in the baggage car. I have to drop her off in Mount Kisco, won't take me long to get home from there.'

No telegram was delivered to the actor at Alberquerque so the script-writer persuaded him to stay on board till the Raton Pass. Nothing was there, but whisky raised his hopes enough to continue to Dodge City. After drowning his disappointment there, at Lakin and at Hutchinson it was decided that Kansas City would surely be the repository of good news. When he drew blanks there and at Galesburg there was nothing for it but to stay aboard till they pulled in to Chicago. The two days and nights of disappointment and Dimple Haig had taken a heavy toll and both men were a sorry sight on arrival. They tried hard to persuade Stani to join them on a side trip to Miami and the last he saw of them they were making arrangements for themselves and the writer's silent travelling companion to spend a few days by the sea.

A well-favoured lady of thirty cunningly lost a hundred and forty dollars to Stani playing gin rummy between Albuquerque, and Kansas City, and invited him to take her to a cosy luncheon on the proceeds, during the long afternoon stopover in Chicago, but, with a major miscalculation, she pumped herself so full of dry martinis that he had to carry her aboard the 20th Century Limited and the well constructed third act was ill-attended. In New York the next morning, she kissed a welcoming husband hello and cut Stani dead. Apart from those diversions, during his three and half day ride from Pacific to Atlantic, he spent many hours staring at painted deserts, red foothills, distant Rockies, giant cacti, dust storms, vast herds of Herefords, peaceful farm lands and the sordid, decaying slum belts around big cities.

He had ample time to imagine what Charles, the nautical man his mother had provided as replacement for his Polish diplomat father, would be like. He also tried to evaluate himself, and had been half shocked, half amused to realize what a mongrel he was. His father had decreed that he should study in the schools of the countries to which Warsaw had sent *him*, and his mother had counter-insisted that only English be spoken in

15

their home (wherever *that* might be). So Stani held a Polish passport, was fluent in six languages, but could not utter a word of his father's tongue. Also, except for a few mosquito-mottled, little boy's forays, he had only hazy recollections of the Skolimowski family estate at Mielnik, on the banks of the aptly named River Bug. When his father had been sent to the Polish Embassy in Washington, on a five year assignment, Stani had felt some roots going down, but these had shrivelled up when his mother had dropped her bombshell about divorce and he had been bustled off to distant cousins in Santa Barbara, and to Alwyn High.

He had never really understood his parents' divorce. Typically, his father had shouldered all the blame, saying that he had spent too much time on his job and not enough with his beautiful, if scatterbrained, wife. But Stani remained unconvinced that it was entirely the fault of the quiet, aristocratic, ex-cavalry man and guessed that it had also been tied up with his mother's enthusiastic rejection of approaching middle age which had increased her restlessness, sharpened her oft-expressed intention 'not to leave a stone unturned', and sped her on to her frequent European travels. He loved them both, deeply. But some bizarre paper work by the Californian attorneys had arranged matters so that he saw much more of his mother than he did of his father. This saddened him. He missed his father very much. He had hoped to see him when he got to New York, but he had been called back to Poland for consultation.

Aboard *Europa*, Stani had a small cabin in the tourist class. For his age he was certainly an experienced traveller, but not so sophisticated that, starting off for the first time, alone, on an Atlantic crossing, he did not feel rising excitement at the breaking of the umbilical cords of paper streamers between dockside and decks. Nor, at the sight of a tangerine sunset acting as backdrop to the breathtaking silhouette of the receding New York skyline. He stayed on deck a long time, until the glow behind the skyscrapers faded to deep purple. When the pilot clambered down a rope ladder on to the attendant cutter and the great ship shuddered, gathered speed and headed eastward into the gathering darkness, he shivered within his overcoat and went below.

A voyage aboard *Europa*, while of average interest to Captain and crew, was one of pure self indulgence for Stani. The food was splendid, the service maharajal, and the company, Europe-bound for Christmas, a splendid mixture of disapproving elders and eager youth. The time passed all too quickly. Aside from a mid-Atlantic gale of alarming proportions which produced mountainous waves, hand-ropes on the stairways, much lashing down of pianos and widespread seasickness he enjoyed every minute of it, games, movies, dancing, the fun of meeting new people, the sense of adventure and the excitement of changing continents. The Captain's Dinner, complete with champagne, was held on the last night.

Stani's constant companion by that time had become a raven haired beauty from Miss Charlotte's School for Girls in Ashville, North Carolina: of much the same specifications as Carole, an adventurous girl en route to spend the holidays with her parents in Paris. She had looked adorable in a cork life jacket at Boat Drill on the first day.

'We have to find a way to get up to the First Class tonight,' she said. 'It's okay down here in Second but the real action'll be up there.'

Since elaborate efforts to produce fancy-dress costumes would be made and the air would be filled with balloons and paper streamers, they spent the afternoon planning to crash the class barrier accordingly. First they asked a steward to produce a copy of the First Class Passenger List, 'because,' they said, 'they wanted to send a note to a friend.' Then they selected a very First Class passenger for the next step in the plot:

Mrs. P. Mellon III and maid
The Lord Beaverbrook and valet
Miss Amelia Astor and nurse
The Duke de Primo de Rivera and secretary

were the final contestants.

Miss Amelia Astor got the nod because, as the girl said, 'She's either a kind old lady who'll understand if we get caught, or she's sick and won't know what the Hell's going on.'

The forgery was elementary, a note on the ship's writing paper addressed to themselves inviting them to dinner in her cabin that night and signed by Amelia Astor. The girl did the forgery in her best Miss Charlotte's School for Girls script, adding the correct Cabin Number, M.23. Sharp at eight, dressed approximately as an Egyptian belly dancer and a black-face French sailor, they presented themselves and their note to the steward barring the connecting door to the First Class. A steward on the far side of the door had not been bargained for.

They stayed close together like a brace of nervous partridges as he led the way through immense carpeted saloons and up a soaring staircase of mahogany with walls of priceless marquetry. Stewards and other crew members were evident in great numbers, tidying, sweeping and preparing; but the passengers had not yet surfaced for the evening.

The steward knocked loudly on the door of M.23 and a nurse in starched apron and headgear appeared. She spoke with great severity.

'Go away at once! The baby's just gone off to sleep. If she sees you she'll cry all night.'

The steward was good about it 'Walk about and take a look; I don't think you'll enjoy it though, you'll have much more fun down in Second.'

They settled themselves in the empty main saloon and ordered drinks of appalling expense. Gradually it filled with elderly people in evening dress, jewels flashed warning signals and, in Stani's case particularly, looks of alarm came their way; they evacuated.

In the long bar their appearance caused a silence to fall and lorgnettes to be raised. A ship's officer wearing wing collar, black bow-tie and short white jacket, with four gold stripes on the epaulettes and miniature medals upon the lapels, detached himself from a group of marked distinction. He explained much more loudly than necessary that in the First Class, paper hats would be distributed after dinner. Aside from that no fancy dress would be worn; he added that in his opinion they should return whence they had come.

As they slunk away beneath the pitying eyes of barmen and waiters the girl was seized by a fit of the giggles.

'That old goat's the one who's giving the party!'

The steward had been right, it was much more fun in the Second Class. As the class barrier closed behind them the average age dropped twenty or thirty years, everyone was in

18

costume and the dancing didn't stop until four o'clock. So much fun was it, that Stani and his belly dancer did not realize till they reached her cabin how greatly *Europa* was rolling.

Perhaps Miss Charlotte had seen to it that her charges were less advanced in certain directions than the students of Alwyn High. In any event the evening ended in a long, standing kiss in the middle of a very restricted area. The steady tilting of the floor propelled them, glued together at the lips, back and forth like tango dancers richochetting off bunks, basins and cupboards.

The next day, at Cherbourg, a swarm of voluble, blue-smocked porters swarmed aboard with the last stained inches of Gauloises wobbling from claret-coloured faces; his belly dancer cried when she said goodbye and waved from the tender till *Europa* turned to the open sea and set course for Southampton.

During the short cross-Channel trip Stani packed and coped with a stream of cabin stewards, dining room and deck stewards, baggage handlers, head waiters, barmen, lift men and shoe cleaners, all pointedly wishing him a *very* happy Christmas. As *Europa* rounded the Needles off the Isle of Wight he got his first view of Britain – not a very inspiring one. In a clammy mist, she sailed slowly up Southampton Water between long lines of rusting freighters and tankers, dejected reminders of better days in the Merchant Navy of the Island Kingdom.

Stani adored his mother and had missed her sorely; he spotted her standing in the crowd at dockside. Far above her he looked down from the boat-deck as the mighty midget tugs, bullied and coaxed till deep window-rattling blasts from her foghorn announced that *Europa* had officially arrived. As he came off the gangway, he was proud that she looked so good. Blonde hair peeked out from beneath a headscarf, hazel eyes shone with excitement and her still remarkable figure was neatly silhouetted within a belted, white raincoat. She hugged and kissed her son – and then she introduced him to his sailor step-father.

Charles Rainbird was a tall, ruddy complexioned man of fifty with direct blue eyes. He was oddly dressed, Stani noted, for a retired Captain of the Royal Navy, sporting an outfit of twill breeches, cloth gaiters, brown boots, a long waisted tweed

19

jacket topped by a deer-stalker; the whole ensemble was garnished by a shepherd's crook.

'Damn glad to meet you, young feller,' boomed the Captain with a charming smile. 'It must be strange for you to have me suddenly dumped in your lap, but I'm sure we'll get along splendidly once we've had a shake down cruise. Now let's get your tackle.' They did, and then off they went to Captain Rainbird's little house at Lauriston.

They reached the house by ferry across the Solent and then by the Royal Isle of Wight railway. Lauriston harbour was at the end of the line, and Stani, on arrival, watched fascinated as the engine, detached from the elderly train, puffed itself on to a circular turntable where it was manhandled by the driver and fireman into a complete about face.

Rainbird's house, at the entrance to the tiny harbour, was pleasant and incredibly shipshape – silver gleaming, brass brilliant, china lined up carefully, pictures straight, towels ironed. And in the window of the living room was a large telescope through which Captain Rainbird refreshed his memories and polished his nostalgia when the ships of the Royal Navy steamed in and out of Portsmouth Harbour, six miles away across the Solent.

In 1916, Rainbird had fought in the Battle of Jutland. During this encounter, fourteen British and eleven German ships had been sunk. A lamentable lack of information had hampered the British Admiral, Jellicoe, and some of his orders had been so peculiar that Sub-Lieutenant Rainbird (on the bridge of the destroyer *Spitfire*, at midnight, and travelling at twenty knots) had the nasty experience of seeing the huge German battleship, *Nassau*, coming straight at him. The helmsman had spun the wheel and *Spitfire*, amid showers of sparks and the rending of metal, had scraped along the entire length of the charging monster, finally escaping into the darkness with a mass of German plating decorating her forecastle.

Ten years after this episode, Charles Rainbird, now a Commander, had fallen victim to the 'axe' when grateful Government after grateful Government rewarded the gallant wartime Navy by cutting it to the bone. He had been put on the beach permanently, with a pension of a few hundred pounds a year and the rank of Captain. Since then, to sustain himself, he had

20

been the secretary of the Lauriston Sailing Club, in command of three boatmen – and two dozen twenty-two-foot, clinker built, half-deck sloops with rust red sails. The summer season being short, the Captain had little to do the rest of the time except look through his telescope and hope that one day the Navy would need him again.

Virginia Skolimowski, visiting sailing friends the previous summer, had hit the Captain in his finest hour and had promptly fallen in love with the handsome club secretary, in his summer finery of yachting cap, black reefer jacket and white flannel trousers.

Stani liked the simple sailor very much. He was an uncomplicated man of transparent honesty and if not of blinding intelligence, was obviously devoted to Stani's mother and she to him.

Lauriston in winter was a damp, dreary, windswept place. The inhabitants moved around semi-congealed, awaiting the arrival of the high-spending summer residents and the less welcome appearance of 'day trippers' who would come tottering ashore after a nasty crossing from Portsmouth aboard a top-heavy paddle steamer, known in the Sailing Club as the 'Sixpenny Sick'.

The one hotel was closed, the boarding houses were empty, no buckets, spades, beach balls or shrimping nets were displayed outside the village shop, and, with most of the boats pulled out of the water for refitting, the harbour, which smelled at low tide, looked grey and empty. The Sailing Club, the hub of the summer social wheel, was locked, with its three boatmen out of sight in a row of sheds, busy rejuvenating Captain Rainbird's little fleet.

Stani enjoyed Christmas 1938 very much, but before 1939 came along, he was bored out of his wits. His step-father produced an antidote for his 'cafard'.

'Young feller, you will take sailing lessons.'

Stani's accent was basic English with overtones of French, German, Spanish and Swedish, but his answer to this startling announcement was pure American: 'Sailing lessons! For Chrissakes . . . who *needs them*?'

His stepfather looked pained. 'Once you have learned to sail a boat, you'll never forget it – it's something you will enjoy for the rest of your life. It brings you close . . . to nature. It may,' he added wistfully, 'bring you great peace. Tomorrow. Jervis Matthews is your man. I don't altogether approve of the feller but he's the best seaman on the island.'

Jervis was a sailor who earned his livelihood by his knowledge of the changing sea. He had great knowledge of the creatures which dwelt beneath its surface, and was known for the strength with which he propelled his sturdy twenty foot boat heavily laden with lobster pots, nets and tackle. This boat, was emerald green above the water-line, white below, and Jervis rowed standing straight and facing forward, the oars crossed before his chest. He rowed effortlessly, mile after mile, feathering his oars as beautifully as the stroke of a university crew. Jervis lived aboard a converted Motor Torpedo Boat, a left-over from the Great War, which lay half beached in the harbour. When the spring tides of the full moon came, she was completely afloat. At other times, her stern remained fast upon the muddy shore. She was accessible by a wooden plank.

In the winter when the great storms roared in from the west, Jervis repainted the boat, repaired his lobster pots, made good his tackle, and, on quiet days, gave occasional sailing lessons. With his ready laugh, warm good humour, flashing eyes and magnificent physique, he was a popular, if controversial, figure. He was the most highly decorated member and coxswain of the lifeboat crew.

Every year, on the first day of May, Captain Rainbird would enter the Sailing Club and survey with satisfaction the winter handiwork of his three boatmen – the shipshape ensemble of the manicured gardens, the immaculately painted superstructure and balconies, the gleaming brass work of the telescopes and the bobbing symmetry of the racing boats with their club burgees bravely fluttering. Then he would stiffen and avert his eyes because at the far end of his domain, like a beached whale, lay Jervis's unsightly houseboat. Sometimes a clothesline would display a flapping assortment of long, grey, woollen underwear; quite certainly, flying at her masthead and in ironical deference to the opening of the class conscious Sailing Club, would be a red flag embossed with yellow hammer and sickle. Jervis was the only Communist in Lauriston.

Captain Rainbird, with senior rank authority, beat upon the

gangway with his shepherd's crook.

'Jervis! I have a pupil for you – my new stepson.'

Jervis's brown face appeared.

'Come aboard, sir,' he smiled, 'I was just brewing up.'

Below decks, the M.T.B. was warm, homely, and cluttered with the orderly untidiness of the seaman. Oilskins, sou'wester and seaboots for the lifeboat were nearest to hand. The bunk was neatly made up and everywhere lay the paraphernalia of the fisherman's trade – weights, hanks of line, hooks, floats, spinners, and over all, a delicious aroma of tar. There was a large number of books on the shelves, some photographs of the owner's days in the Royal Navy, and, proudly displayed, his decorations for gallantry in the Life Boat Service.

'Now then,' said Jervis. 'How about a tot of rum in your tea today, gentlemen, just to keep out the westerly?'

Stani liked Jervis on sight, and with care and patience in the days to come, Jervis taught him to sail, much about the sea and instilled in him a healthy respect for it. He taught him to fish, with hand line, net or spinner, took him, chattering with cold at sunrise, to pick up his crab pots; and, up to their armpits in giant waders, showed him how to catch lobsters by hand out among the big rocks uncovered by the spring tides. Stani speared vicious conger eels below the chalk cliffs, and, on black stormy nights when the rockets had summoned the crew from their beds to rescue poor souls from being pounded to death far out on the notorious Ledge, Stani warmed himself with the villagers before driftwood fires and lent a useful hand on the frozen lines hauling the returned lifeboat out of the tumultuous sea.

The potentially dull and lonely days at Lauriston were thus transformed for Stani by his new friend. Jervis was ten years his senior but neither had been exposed before to anything quite like the other and each, in his own way, was a sophisticate. If their approaches, for instance, were different, their objectives were often the same.

'I like the one in the corner in the yellow dress,' whispered Stani at a village dance. 'But she looks so innocent. Do you think I could get anywhere with her?'

'Move right in and help yourself, mate,' said Jervis, 'she's seen more stiff pricks than she 'as hot dinners.'

Europe was making no move to stop Hitler and his rampaging troopers from taking over Austria and Czechoslovakia, and the United States was busy turning to the sports pages in a determined effort to disregard the British and French ostriches as they stuffed their much more vulnerable heads into the sand. Jervis enjoyed dispelling the foggy illusions in Stani's non-political mind. One blustery day out sailing, he said, 'You mark my words. Everyone's goin' on about 'ow clever old Chamberlain was when 'e come back from Munich, waving that bit of paper and spouting about pluckin' somethin' out of that fuckin' nettle danger. But 'itler's got us on the run and we and France and even your Dad's country will all be in it afore long . . . I 'eard in the village today that some blokes in the Reserves have been called up already.'

'Will you go back to the Navy?' Stani asked.

Jervis looked away. 'Can't do that,' he said. 'I was slung out after Invergordon.'

'Invergordon?'

'Yeah – I wos one o' the mutineers an' they slung me out.'

'I never knew there'd ever *been* a mutiny in the British Navy.'

'Well, it was eight or nine years ago. Nothin' much 'appened – not like the old sailing ship days when they put their officers over the side into the longboats an' told 'em to find their own way 'ome from the middle of the Pacific.'

'What happened at Invergordon then?'

Jervis refilled his pipe as he spoke.

'I'd been sent to *Rodney*, a big battleship. I dunno what started it all but some bank went bust in Austria and that old twat with a beard at the Bank o' England, Montagu Norman, got panicky and we wos told that our pay had been cut ten per cent. Well, orf we went on several weeks' exercises an' you can imagine 'ow the lads felt when we dropped anchor off Scotland an' got all them letters from 'ome. Specially the married blokes.

'There was a meetin' in the Band Room of *Rodney*. I kept me mouth shut but I could see the lads meant business. Someone gave me a paper to sign an' I found I'd become a member of the Communist Party!

'Ashore, I went to a meetin' at the canteen. The shore patrols come but we locked 'em out, sang the Red Flag an' some poor bloody officer got beer thrown all over 'im. There wos

24

some fightin' too. The next day the Admiral ordered the whole Fleet to sea to cool off. A few ships put out in good order but most of 'em refused to up anchor. The crews just hung around the forecastles refusin' to work. Some 'ot 'eads tried to get the lads to go ashore, leave their officers aboard and march from Invergordon to London to the 'ouses of Parliament. We didn't do that but it worked an' we won – Government took off the pay cuts but they didn't arf come after the ringleaders!

'I'd never opened me trap mind but they found out who'd joined the Communists and that did it for me . . . I got a nice little letter from the Admiralty saying that me services were no longer required! No, I could never get back in the Navy.'

'Are you still a Communist then?'

'I've been to a coupla meetin's over at the dockyard and me name's still on that list, I suppose, but I'm not plannin' to blow up Buckingham Palace!'

Stani was not too excited about leaving his mother and Rainbird, and going back to Alwyn High. He had half made up his mind to go to University in Europe – preferably to Heidelberg. But the final decision about his future was made for him one January evening when he came into the kitchen of Captain Rainbird's little house proudly bearing half a dozen lobsters which he and Jervis had tickled out from under the rocks off Sunset Point.

Freezing cold, he headed for a hot bath. The suspect wiring in Captain Rainbird's house had that day been adjusted by one of the boatmen from the Sailing Club. Stani leaned over the bath and turned on the taps. The shock he received was so great that his back arched like a crossbow and he was flung into the air. He fell into the bath but either going up or coming down, he hit the handle of the shower and lay unconscious with scalding water playing on his naked back and buttocks till Captain Rainbird found him and with some sixth sense warning him of electrocution, closed the shower lever with his shepherd's crook.

Stani's burns were bad enough to put him in hospital, but his youth and health overcame the shock and the painful dressings and by early spring, he was convalescing at Captain Rainbird's house.

There, from his bed, Stani enjoyed an uninterrupted view of the village pond, an insanitary little lagoon, the happy hunting ground of small boys catching tadpoles, tiddlers and various infections. One day, shrill cries brought the patient to the window. A wild swan from the marshes, making hostile noises, was circling at a very low altitude, scattering the alarmed youngsters in every direction. Badly miscalculating the length of the pond, the big bird came in for a landing, and although it lowered its flaps to the utmost and applied to the maximum the brakes of its upturned, black feet, it ended up an undignified heap in some bulrushes. Cries of joy greeted this effort and the boys closed in gleefully to taunt new arrival. The swan was more than their match and with fearsome hisses and alarming charges by land or water, demonstrated its domination of their playground.

During the days that followed, Stani grew fond of the swan. He felt they had much in common – he confined to bed, the bird trapped on a small expanse of water from which it could never again hope to take off.

He watched the swan cruising back and forth, checking the possibilities of escape. He saw it make countless efforts to become airborne, but each time, after tremendous flapping and pedalling, it would fail, and, braking frantically at the last minute, would collapse once more into the bulrushes. After each failure, he was saddened to see the once proud arch of its neck take on an increasingly dejected curve.

He became convinced that if the pond could be lengthened by a few yards, the bird could become airborne, so, with the help of Captain Rainbird and Jervis, he planned the swan's getaway. His stepfather volunteered to move some rose bushes and two sections of wooden fencing to accommodate the new waterway, but after several trips to the Marshes, to watch take-offs and landings, he announced that they had under-estimated the situation. Jervis then undertook to soften up the next door neighbour, and after an historic night at the Pilot Boat Inn, the village baker gave his consent to the temporary removal of his rock-garden.

In the village that March, hopes ran high and while advisers propped up the bar of the Pilot Boat, others beneath the cold, disapproving eyes of the swan busied themselves in blustery, chilblain weather, arranging for the bird's bid for freedom.

On the great day, with a freezing north wind blowing over close-cropped bulrushes, and with a congregation of mauve villagers watching from various vantage points, Jervis and Captain Rainbird opened the sluice gate and flooded the extension of the pond. The swan cruised down the new waterway, inspecting it with an expert eye, checking the depth, exposing its feathered bottom in the process; but was haughtily unappreciative and the odds against early take-off lengthened in the Pilot Boat. After a week of declining interest, the village gave up hope and the baker made pointed enquiries about the re-assembly of his fritillarias, campanulas and bog orchids.

Finally, only Stani witnessed the swan's departure. A cold wind raged across the Solent and rattled his bedroom window; he awoke and looked at his watch . . . seven o'clock and still very dark. He lay thinking of Alwyn High and Santa Barbara, of its sweetly scented orange groves, hibiscus, flowering eucalyptus and all those lovely, long, golden, suntanned legs. Then, as the first grey streaks of dawn appeared, he heard it – the 'flap-flap-flap' of pedalling feet and of giant wings on water. He leapt out of bed, and watched the huge bird, ghostly grey in the half light, neck strained desperately forward and frantic feet drumming the surface, clear the remains of the bulrushes by a few inches and fly on, just skimming the sand-dunes. Gradually, it gained height until it became a black speck above the whitewashed horizon.

He felt it should come back and gratefully circle the village, even do a victory roll, but it didn't, and he went back to sleep. He never forgot the swan.

During his stay at Lauriston, Stani, probably for the first time in his life, really became close to his mother. She had changed greatly and on long walks over the Downs, he discovered a new depth in her. She told him how much she still admired and had once deeply loved his father but how she had come to feel so intellectually inferior to him and so socially inadequate, that the split had become inevitable.

'I really was wrong for him, darling,' she said, striding out along the cliff paths. 'He was very patient with me and I was so proud of him – but somehow I could never relax and be myself.

And I don't really believe he missed me very much when I started travelling. I was running away, I suppose.'

Stani glanced at her glowing cheeks and clear eyes. She looked ridiculously young.

'Was it a terrible shock for you?' she asked.

'No,' said Stani gently. 'I knew for years that you were both acting parts for me . . . I just hoped it wouldn't happen, because . . . well, it seemed a shame to let it all fall apart when it had once been so happy. And I was selfish, I guess.'

There was a long silence during which Stani's mother held his arm tight. Then, after a while she laughed. 'Charles is a wonderful person – so easy and thoughtful, and he's always *there* . . . he makes me very happy. I am very lucky.'

Stani didn't look at her because he sensed a hint of desperation. After a moment his mother changed the subject.

'You see those things on that hill over there?'

She pointed at a cluster of high steel masts knitted together by cables and wires. A barbed wire fence surrounded them. In the middle was a small hut.

'Charles explained it all to me one day. It's terribly secret, he says! It's called radar and they're putting them up all round England so that when the war comes, we'll be warned if the Germans send bombers over.'

'Do you think war will really come?'

'Of *course* not! The Germans are much too nice. Remember what fun we all had in Berlin? I thought they were divine. And *so* good looking!'

'What about Charles?'

'Oh, he's always popping over to Portsmouth and seeing his old buddies in the Navy, he gets all steamed up about it. He even had me press his uniform the other day, in case he gets called up. I think he rather hopes it will come – he misses the Navy dreadfully.'

By April, Stani's immediate future had been decided – he would indeed go to University in Europe, not Heidelberg, to Cambridge, but in order to pass the entrance examination, he would first study with a 'crammer' in London.

'Got you all fixed up in a very nice little basement flat in South Audley Street,' Captain Rainbird said. 'The landlady is an old flame of mine, still damned attractive by the way – she'll keep an eye on you.'

By May of that 1939, Stani was installed in South Audley Street, and by mid-June, Captain Rainbird was joyously flourishing the result of months of badgering – a document from the Admiralty announcing that he had been recalled to the Royal Navy!

'Darling! It's come!' he called to his wife. 'I'm a bit old for the motor torpedo boats but maybe I'll get a destroyer!'

In July, Stani received a letter from his father. 'War is coming quite soon', his father wrote, 'and I shall join my old cavalry regiment. It is very sad but for some time it has been inevitable, Hitler is quite mad. No country wants to attack Germany so when it *does* come, the world will at least know where to place the dreadful responsibility for the slaughter that will follow. Look after your mother. I miss you both very much.'

In August, Captain and Mrs. Rainbird departed for Paris, she clinging to a conception of war that went little further than handsome wounded officers falling for beautiful nurses, and conquering heroes receiving ticker-tape welcomes down Fifth Avenue, and he manfully making the best of his new appointment as supernumerary Naval Attaché at the British Embassy.

Before they left Stani spent a weekend at Lauriston. On the last night they had a farewell dinner in the Sailing Club.

'They want me for the job because I learned the lingo in school,' the Captain told him. 'Always got on well with the Frogs too, rather suspect seamen I always thought. Maybe it's the shape of their caps – they look like engine drivers. Anyway, I'll soon be at sea!'

His mother was sad at parting but made brave efforts to be lighthearted; she had little idea of the vagaries of the French and British telephone systems. 'We'll only be a few miles away from you, darling, we'll call each other every night.'

Captain Rainbird sought to submerge his lack of experience as a surrogate parent beneath several glasses of vintage port, and became quite flushed.

All in all it was a nervous and troubled evening.

When Stani was first confronted by Mrs. Quansett-Fowles, she was twenty years past her prime. At seventeen, when she had first come to 'Auntie's Bar', she had possessed a voluptuous body atop spectacular legs, and topped off by baby-blue eyes and a pouting red mouth in a nicely structured face. A luxuriant growth of corn-coloured hair was customarily held back on one side with a blue bow. If she had been unlikely to win a scholarship to the Massachusetts Institute of Technology, she had nevertheless always been good company – 'a good sort' who was fond of people and had a natural warmth of heart which the sex-starved ship's officers who frequented the place found irresistible, when their vessels, after long periods at sea, finally dropped anchor in Malta's Grand Harbour of Valletta.

'Auntie's Bar', a red plush establishment of great popularity, was presided over by an avaricious lady from Yorkshire who produced a seemingly inexhaustible supply of well-shaped and talented 'nieces' who came to visit her from various European capitals. She presented Amy Bowen as her 'niece' from Cardiff and before Amy had been carried off triumphantly at the age of twenty-two to be the bride of Lieutenant Quansett-Fowles of the Royal Navy, she had been the supreme favourite of the customers.

Carefully schooled by 'Auntie', Amy had been extremely parsimonious when it came to the distribution of her favours, and a host of admirers had been left panting with unrequited sex, when the well-heeled Lieutenant claimed his prize. Some were churlish enough to hint that 'Auntie' had collected a percentage from the takeover.

Amy had not been too well received by Quansett-Fowles' parents. 'Nouveau riche' themselves (they had coined a fortune making hob-nailed boots for British Tommies in the Great War), they had none of the splendid security of Amy, who was proudly and devoutly 'common'.

After the marriage, the Lieutenant left the Navy and shortly thereafter died of a surfeit of pink gin, in a leather chair in the Naval and Military Club. Amy had genuinely mourned his passing and becoming increasingly lonely and depressed at Chalk Hill Manor at the foot of the Marlborough Downs, sold the main house, kept the Home Farm, and moved to South Audley Street in Mayfair.

To start with she cried a great deal and drank large quantities of champagne, but once she had recovered from the demise of Quansett-Fowles, she entered with enthusiasm into the London scene, quickly accumulating many friends and a short but impressive list of lovers. Incurably sentimental, she remained faithful to each paramour in turn and her affairs with a portrait painter, a Duke, a rag-trade millionaire, a racing driver and an ambitious Junior Cabinet Minister had been followed avidly by readers of the glossy periodicals, but pavement artists with war medals or elderly donkeys with heavy loads still made her cry.

When Stani presented himself to the house on South Audley Street, the door was opened by an attractive Danish girl, one of two working as 'au pair' for Mrs. Quansett-Fowles.

Amy had been crying and was dabbing at her eyes as Stani was announced in her cheerful drawing room on the the first floor.

'So you're Charlie Rainbird's stepson!' she exclaimed between sniffs. 'Come and sit down, dear boy – and have a glass of "shampoo".' She filled a goblet with champagne and brightened considerably as she looked him over.

'Well! Charlie was the best looking man in the Navy when I first met him and you don't look too bad yourself! By the way, I'll not have you trying any slap and tickle with Ingrid and Brigitta.' She made some cosmetic adjustments with the aid of a gold compact as she spoke, a hint of the Welsh valleys still in her voice.

'Sorry you caught me like this, luv, I've just had some bad news – Jason's been shot.'

'I'm so sorry – where?' asked Stani.

'In the arse,' said Amy. 'He barked at a poacher who was after my ducks and the bugger shot him. Look, I can let you have an occasional bird or an egg or two and maybe a little butter now and then because the rations are nil for someone living alone. Or perhaps you'd like to muck in with the three of us and pool everything – but first let's see how you get on. Did Brigitta show you the flat?'

'Not yet,' said Stani. 'It's very good of you to let me have it.'

'Oh balls!' said Mrs. Quansett-Fowles. 'We're only too happy to have a man about the place and one more for fire watching practice – a proper pisser that is, by the way. Come

31

on, I'll show you your hole in the ground. We have to go outside to get to it.'

The basement flat at the bottom of a flight of stone steps was tastefully decorated and consisted of a bed-sitting room, a bathroom and a minute kitchen. There was a telephone and through the solitary window Stani could see feet, legs and an occasional flash of underwear in the street above.

'It's great,' he said, 'thanks so much.'

'Here's your work bench,' said Mrs. Quansett-Fowles, pulling back the covers of a divan and unveiling a three-quarter size bed. 'Now come back up and have some more "shampoo".'

In the next few weeks Stani became very attached to his landlady and during the early days of his tenancy, she made it plain that there was no need for him to be frustrated.

'Let me know if you're not getting your greens regular,' she said, flicking back her hair, which was dyed orangutan orange. 'There's plenty of it around and the threat of war does wonders for the sexual urges. In fact the hedging and ditching season is now in full swing.'

Stani had a feeling that she would be more than happy to arrange things personally, if the need should ever arise, but she did not press the matter and during the ensuing weeks, so demonstrated the sterling qualities that had once made her the toast of Auntie's Bar that, awash with champagne or bathed in tears, she became his friend, confidante and counsellor. Some women see their love affairs disintegrate into acrimony and mutual recrimination; a large proportion watch them fade away in indifference, alcoholism or aching sadness. But a blissful minority somehow manage to preserve the friendship of ex-partners when all else has gone, and Amy, with her good heart, her generosity, her humour and her earthy common sense, was one of the fortunate few. Her first floor sitting room was filled, every evening, with old friends, new acquaintances and the lonely of both sexes. All were very cognisant of the rigours of rationing, so her bar and larder were constantly replenished by her guests. Stani had a permanent invitation when he returned across Hyde Park from his long day of toil with Mr. Halliday, the crammer, and on special occasions, he would find a note slipped under his door – 'Sholto Douglas coming tonight, Head of Fighter Command – very interesting'.

Or, 'A French General for drinks, need your help'. 'Two lovely girls from Bobby Howes' show and some of the Crazy Gang tonight – don't miss it'. Or 'a nice American from the Embassy has given me a ham – bring a girl for dinner'.

Stani's studies with the crammer, and his life in South Audley, were rudely interrupted early in September. On the first day of the month, and without a declaration of war, Germany attacked Poland. On the third day, Britain and France, honouring their pacts with Poland, declared war on Germany. Two weeks later, Russia treacherously invaded a reeling Poland from the rear and Stani, having received word that his father was a prisoner of war, captured near Lwow, found himself with the world falling apart and nobody from his immediate family to turn to.

One night, a great wave of loneliness and desolation swept over him and, not for the first time, he felt the stomach-lurch of fear. He had experienced it before in boxing rings at various schools, but one episode he could never erase from his memory, and it came back to haunt him now. It had taken place in Uppsala when he was nine, when the whole school, with Swedish thoroughness, had been required to demonstrate escape drill before the local fire chief. Stani's room had been on the third floor and the boys were required to whizz, head first and on their backs, down a canvas chute. It was imperative to keep heads low because the top of the chute consisted of wooden rungs down which the hard pressed could clamber. Stani had long perceived the extreme unattractiveness of the whole operation and had resolved never to go down that chute unless flames were the spur; so, on the morning of the fire chief's drill, he had fake-fainted in the lavatories and watched the bumping and bruising of his classmates from the safety of the matron's window. But, deep within himself, he knew that his courage would ever be suspect.

Now, in his lonely flat, his imagination got the better of him. London blacked out and air raid wardens drawing loud and abusive attention to the smallest chink of light reminded him that, although so far no bombs had fallen anywhere in Britain (except one on some sheep in the Shetland Isles) at any minute they might rain down upon the city. The thought of being buried beneath his landlady and several hundred tons of rubble

33

brought him up into the street.

It was after midnight and he walked aimlessly along Piccadilly and through Soho. The streets were thronged with hurrying, jostling figures and there was much laughter and bonhomie as the after-theatre crowd cannoned into one another or tripped over sandbags in the darkness. In the faint glow of the headlights of a passing bus, he noticed that gas-masks in square boxes, slung like bandoliers, were very much 'de rigueur'. He longed to talk to someone.

On the corner of Wardour Street, a flashlight was pointed straight into his face and a cheerful, cockney voice said, "allo 'andsome, want a little fun to take yer mind off the war?" The whore then directed the beam upon herself, illuminating a black-rooted blonde of thirty busy summers. Her hopeful smile displayed what appeared to be gutta-percha teeth, but her eyes were rather fine in their challenge.

'This is what you get for three quid,' she said, 'but as you're so luvly, I'll let you 'ave it for two pound ten.'

Stani looked at the proffered bargain while the whore smiled enticingly into the flashlight.

'Come on 'andsome, I'll give yer yer money's worth.'

'I'll buy you a drink if you like,' said Stani, hesitantly.

'You'll have to pay for me time,' said the whore. 'It's the rush hour now yer know.'

'All right. Where do we go?'

'To me club,' she said, taking Stani's arm. 'It's not very posh but at least you won't get poisoned.'

She steered him to Greek Street and stopped at a door marked 'Ponce's – Members Only'. The whore rang the bell. A wizened little man in a sleeveless pullover greeted her. "ullo Glad, c'mon in.'

Down a flight of stairs, they entered a room lit by candles. A bar was at one end, a piano against a wall, a wood fire blazed cheerfully and groups of tables and chairs were dotted about. About twenty people were present.

'Look who just picked me up!' said the whore loudly. 'Prince Fuckin' Charming!'

Good natured laughter and a few whistles greeted this announcement and Stani looked around at the club members. Fringe theatre folk, he judged, bright young people, a sprink-

34

ling of intense gentlemen with beards and woollen scarves and a brace of bull dykes with short cropped hair drinking rum.

'I'm an actress meself in me spare time,' giggled Gladys, settling at a table. 'But I don't bother wiv it too much. I've got me Equity Card though. That's 'ow I got to be a member 'ere, but of course I'm not allowed to solicit on the premises.'

The wizened little man brought beer for Stani; Glad ordered a large port and lemon for herself.

'Tell you wot, 'andsome – and my Gawd you are – give me a coupla quid, buy me some of Charlie's rabbit pie and we can sit 'ere in the warm for a while. But me regler boyfriend expects me to 'ave at least six quid in me bra by mornin' so I'll 'ave to get back to work before too long. Wot line are you in, dear?'

Stani enjoyed the beer, the cosiness of the club and Gladys' companionship. She used a dreadful perfume which made his eyes water and he was considering how he could tactfully suggest a change in her toiletries when a spate of new arrivals clattered down the stairs, four boys and two girls.

'I know that lot,' Gladys said. 'They're all in Sid Field's show over at the Prince o' Wales. Sid's ever so funny, don't you think?'

Stani looked at the boys, three of whom had not removed their stage make-up and were swishing around the room outrageously. The fourth was in sailor's uniform.

'Look at 'arold,' one of the boys screamed to the club members. 'She's been called up into the *Navy*, lucky girl!'

'Look at 'er *feet*,' shrilled another. 'Wot *HUGE SHEWS*!' He saw the whore, kissed her on the cheek and appraised Stani.

'Glad darling, where *did* you find *that*! You *must* tell me what you *do*!'

Stani's embarrassed eyes followed the two girls as they made their way to a table. One was perhaps a little dumpy but she had a pretty, open face. She took off a plaid coat. The other stood with her back towards Stani, removing a blue reefer jacket and shaking, long, blonde hair free from a silk scarf.

Her figure was superb; dark slacks were lovingly moulded to the lower part of it and Stani half hoping she would not spoil everything by turning around, braced himself for the coming let down. When at last she faced towards the room, he gaped at what he saw.

The blonde hair framed a high-boned face of perfect proportions. The eyes were huge, grey and cat-like, the small nose delicately sculpted. Her skin in the candlelight was flawless and the mouth a marvellous mixture of the humorous and the sensuous. All these attributes did not of course register themselves with one click of Stani's mental shutter, but rather he discovered them one after another during a series of what he fondly imagined were well disguised inspections. The last possibility of disillusionment was removed when her plump companion said something and the blonde girl laughed, displaying dazzlingly perfect teeth.

He could not take his eyes off the girl, and fell into nodding vaguely as Gladys prattled on. She waved to Charlie for another port and lemon.

'Of course, two nights a week I can't work full time because I'm on fire watch. I spend 'alf the night on the roof, dear, waitin' for the bombers to come over and drop their incendiaries. They never come, thank Christ, but the fire chief gives me a bucket of sand and a bloody great douche bag to put out the fires with once they start. We don't 'alf 'ave some larfs up there. Some of the wives in our street don't take to their 'usbands spending' all night on the roofs wiv me and one or two other girls in the same line, but they don't 'ave to bother becos we don't give nuthin' away for free and we're particular who we sell it to anyway. Now some fellers 'igh up in the regular Fire Brigade – they're different. There's one geezer what pays well and 'elps 'imself, right up there among the chimney pots. 'e likes it that way in 'is 'igh leather boots, and 'is shiny buttons wiv a fuckin' great brass 'elmet on 'is 'ead . . . you're not payin' attention are you dear?'

'Who is *she*?' Stani asked.

Gladys followed his nod.

'I just told you,' she said, a trifle ruffled. 'They're all wiv Sid Field across the street. Want me to fix you up?'

'No,' said Stani.

'No offence I'm sure,' said the whore forking up the last mouthfuls of her rabbit pie.

Stani was suddenly anxious to be rid of Gladys's company. He stood up to leave and the blonde girl casually flicked an eye in his direction. Then at the sight of his companion, she whispered to her friend, giggled and turned away.

'Let's get out of here,' said Stani abruptly. 'I have to get up early and you have to go back to work.'

The whore looked at him for a moment, then, with tattered dignity, gathered together her poor belongings.

'Suit yerself, dear,' she said. 'I only wanted to 'elp. It's been nice meetin' you.' She smiled a little sadly. 'Give us a kiss.'

Stani obliged with a peck on the cheek, looking at the same time over her shoulder. The blonde girl seemed oblivious to his presence.

For the next two days his mind was divided unequally between a prison camp in Poland, the British Embassy in Paris, a crammer near Holland Park and the Prince of Wales theatre. On the morning of the third day, a Saturday, he purchased a seat in the dress circle for the matinee performance.

Sid Field, London's favourite comic, was in top form and gales of laughter greeted his inspired renderings of the spiv, the queer photographer and the half-wit golfer. While the mirth piled up around him, Stani waited, holding his breath, for the first appearance of the blonde girl. He carefully checked the chorus line but throughout the first act he caught no glimpse of her. Had she been shielded, perhaps, by the hat of the lady immediately in front of him, a basket-like receptacle with a tulle compôte of various fruits and vegetables? Throughout the show her escort, a gentleman of purple mien, wheezed loudly and issued penetrating evaluations of various performers.

'Luvly bit o' stuff, that Zoë Gail,' he pronounced, 'wouldn't mind givin' 'er the best of three falls and that's a fact.' Later he objected to the leading male ballet dancer's conformation.

'Got a cage of budgerigars in 'is tights, if you ask *me*.'

The neighbours shifted uneasily in their seats. The lady, beneath her plums and radishes, stared stonily at the stage as a steady stream of observations wafted her way. Just before the interval, however, her companion went too far.

A white-tied and tailed tenor was singing (hopefully) about the end of the black-out. 'When the lights go on er-gain, all ov-er the worrld . . .' he warbled.

'Why don't yer show us yer cock?' the man enquired loudly.

The lady's hat quivered and then, with massive disdain, she rose from her seat. 'Yor *breath*', she said, and jerked her thumb towards the exit.

Their departure opened up an unimpeded view of the stage and Stani did not have long to wait for his patience to be rewarded. The blonde girl entered bearing a vase of paper flowers and unimaginatively dressed as a secretary, in a dark skirt, white blouse, severe hair-do and horn rimmed spectacles, but her great beauty and spectacular figure stilled the rattling tea cups and drew a murmur of appreciation from the matinee audience.

Stani was riveted as the sketch unfolded. The girl seemed wonderfully poised on the stage, her voice was clear, her smile radiant, and he knew without a shadow of a doubt that he must somehow find out all about her but could it be possible that such a delectable creature was not married, engaged, or 'involved'?

After a rousing musical number utilizing most of the cast, the first act curtain fell. Stani remained in his seat, planning his assault on the citadel. He looked at the cast list.

> The Secretary . . . Pandora Bryce

He headed to the stage door and was told by a suspicious, military-looking character wearing a houndstooth jacket that the curtain would come down about five-fifteen and would go up again at seven sharp; providing members of the company who wished to leave the theatre with little more than an hour in which to grab a bite to eat.

'Who d'you want to see anyway?'

'Pandora Bryce.'

'Got an appointment?'.

'No, I . . . er . . . collect autographs.'

'Young men like you ought to be in the Army,' said the man, and turned away.

By a quarter past five, Stani had joined a knot of teenagers and adults forming outside the Stage Door; stage hands and electricians were hurrying out, heading for their favourite pubs or cafés. The musicians came next, finally a few actors and actresses. The well-known among them smiled at the faithful and signed programs, the others bustled by, chattering and laughing, their heavy stage make-up garish in the northern evening light.

Stani's overall strategy depended on two things: the decision of Miss Bryce to leave the theatre, and an urge to refresh herself during the short period at her disposal. At the last minute she obliged on both counts and accompanied once more by her plump friend, scampered off down the narrow alley in the direction of Soho.

Stani trailed them through the drab streets, and watched them go to ground in their theatrical burrow. He allowed a few minutes to elapse before he followed them in. At the bottom of the stair the wizened Charlie again barred the way.

'Good evening,' he said. 'You're not a member, are you?'

'No,' Stani answered, 'but I've been here before as a guest . . . of . . . er . . . Gladys.'

Charlie scrutinized him. 'Yes, think I remember you.'

'I'd like to join the club, if that's possible.'

'Should be two names on the application form,' said Charlie, handing him one. 'It's not that we're exclusive, if you know what I mean, it's for the police really and their bloody licensing laws but you must get a couple of names on it. Got two quid for subscription, have you?'

Inside, the club was almost empty. The girls were seated by the fire; two young men were with them and another group was nearby. For a moment Stani hesitated, then he crossed to the blonde girl's table, his application form in his hand.

'I wonder if someone would be good enough to sign this for me?' he asked.

Four pairs of eyes checked him over.

'We have a five year waiting list, you know,' one of the young men laughed. 'What's the name?'

'Stanislaw Skolimowski.'

'Ah! Irish! cried the dumpy girl.

'Or a German spy!' said the second young man, pointing to a poster on the wall of a sinking ship and the words 'CARELESS TALK COSTS LIVES'.

The blonde girl, who had been looking at Stani with curiosity, broke a short silence. 'Why don't you sit down and join us,' she asked, patting the seat next to her.

The boys, dancers in a rival show, were friendly enough and before they left one of them signed the form and pushed it across to the blonde girl.

'Here, darling, make him legal and don't give him the pass-

39

word when he's filled you with champagne.'

The girls' short break seemed to Stani to pass in a flash and soon they were due back at the theatre. He had sensed something defensive about Pandora Bryce, and a slightly mocking glint in her beautiful eyes warned him not to rush his fences, he could feel her cool appraisal and restricted his bursting curiosity to one question. 'Do you come here often?'

'On matinee days and sometimes for a drink on my way home at night,' she answered.

'Home' she had said. Stani's imagination behaved like a slide projector during a travelogue. 'Click!' She came out of a block of luxury flats and was helped into a sports car by a magnificent young male animal. 'Click!', same luxury block but this time a gleaming Rolls Royce and an elder, shorter, fatter and obviously richer male animal. 'Click!' (and here a clutching hand grabbed his intestines), she came out of a rose-covered cottage with a baby in her arms; a healthy-looking husband was digging potatoes in the background.

Pandora cut short Stani's private showing.

'Sorry!' she said as she stood up. 'We have to get back to work.' She held out her hand.

Stani tried to steady his fluttering nerves. What the hell was the matter with him? Back in California the girls had been all over him. Some, it was true, were reputed to have 'round heels – one little push and over they went – but he wasn't looking for *that* with this girl. Or was he? This surely was different, this was special, this feeling of champagne in his knee joints had never happened before.

'Oh!' said Pandora, 'I almost forgot. Here's your membership form. We really must rush.' She smiled at him sweetly. 'Why not give it to your friend Gladys – I'm sure *she'll* fill it in for you. Goodnight.'

Stani watched her beautiful rear end twinkling up the stairs, and curbed a strong desire to kick it.

2

During the remainder of 1939 and well into 1940, Stani settled down, like most of Britain, into the deadening routine of the 'phoney war'. As an increasing number of ships were sunk, rationing of food, drink and clothing became ever more stringent. Petrol for pleasure became a thing of the past and on village greens, small boys built rusting dumps of kettles, saucepans, bicycles, ploughs, railings and gates which the authorities promised would be rendered into tanks and destroyers. The Royal Navy was fully employed keeping the lifelines of the non-self-supporting Island open. But the Army, in an extension of the much vaunted defences of the French Maginot Line, remained immobilized on the borders of neutral Belgium, and the R.A.F. was ordered to bomb German soldiers with leaflets telling them not to be silly and to go home before they got hurt.

Stani slaved on at the crammer and, like most people with whom he came in contact, began to believe that, one day, he would wake up to find the War had gone away.

His landlady, forever solicitous of his well being, continued to invite him to join her upstairs, and questioned him closely.

'Getting plenty, Stani? We can't have you coming out in spots, can we?'

In fact, Stani had been getting very little. London, with its false gaiety and air of unreality, made him feel very much the outsider. A short-lived and, on paper, low risk affair with the wife of a B.B.C. radio announcer had come to a nasty climax when, thrashing about in supposed safety during her husband's reading of the nine o'clock news, the bedroom door had opened to unveil a closely kept military secret – the nightly bulletins were recorded several hours prior to being broadcast.

However, Mrs. Quansett-Fowles did her best to fend off any

eruptions of his skin by inviting attractive girls to her evening parties of young officers, politicians and service 'brass'. Many of these ladies appeared in the uniforms of the three services and one stunning red head showed up clad in her own creation, a very snazzy outfit on the shoulders of which she sported the letters S.L.O.T.S. – standing, she confided to fellow guests, for 'SEX LIFE OF TROOPS'. Though rebuked by an admiral named Haddock, the red head was complimented by Mrs. Quansett-Fowles who announced that frustration led to masturbation which in turn undermined courage. 'The boys *must* get their greens,' she announced firmly.

While Stani was most appreciative of his hostess's selections, he could not forget Pandora Bryce: nor was Mrs. Quansett-Fowles deceived when he mentioned ever so casually his two encounters with her. She immediately insisted on being taken to a performance at the Prince of Wales theatre. During the show she praised the astonishing looks of the girl and as soon as the curtain dropped she went into action.

'Now we'll go backstage, and find out all about her.'

Stani followed obediently and was confronted once more by the hostile hound-toothed doorkeeper.

'Sid Field, please,' said Mrs. Quansett-Fowles loudly and added her name with such authority that the man immediately announced it over the phone.

'He says you're to come up at once, it's across the stage, dressing room No. 1.'

Stani had never been backstage before and padding along behind his leader, he found himself in a whirlpool of colour and organized chaos. Long-legged chorus girls hurrying for their dressing rooms were unhooking each other's scanty clothing bent on keeping dates or catching the last bus home. Stage hands were shouting, property masters were swearing, backdrops, scenery and furnishings were being hoisted, shifted, lowered or arranged for the next day's matinee. With the curtain now raised and the house lights on in the empty auditorium, he beheld a small army of middle-aged ladies, scarves on heads, Hoovers and brooms in hand and cigarettes dangling from mouths, collecting programmes, emptying ashtrays and generally making the place presentable for the morrow. He had a sense of loneliness as he looked up at the tiers of seats disappearing into the gloom of the roof; was surprised at the slope of the stage towards the footlights and very pleased indeed that he was not an actor.

Sid Field's dressing room was already full of people and during the few minutes they were in it, a stream of friends from the audience came to say hello, to kiss and congratulate him; members of the cast popped heads in to say goodnight. As the changing crowd eddied around him, Sid Field, in a terry-cloth bathrobe stained orange with make-up, dispensed drinks and friendliness with prodigal generosity. His sad, heavy-lidded blue eyes twinkled with pleasure at the compliments that were heaped upon him.

'It's a load of old rubbish, this show,' he told one and all, 'but it's fun to do because the audiences are so great. Have another.'

Mrs. Quansett-Fowles managed to corner the hero for a couple of minutes by pinning him against his washbasin, but when she signalled Stani that it was time to leave, she was ill-satisfied with her investigations.

'Your girl,' she said on the way home, 'seems to be a very cool number. She works hard, keeps herself to herself and there is a rumour that everyone in the cast has tried to get her into the feathers but no one has succeeded yet. No sign of a steady boy friend but no talk of her being a 'les' either. That's all Sid knows but I'll keep after it. She really is a dish – you've got good taste, dear. And it's funny, she didn't have much to do up there on the stage. But I couldn't take my eyes off of her! Not because you asked me to check her out, not for that face, those legs or those boobs – she's just got something *special*! I looked around, it wasn't just me, everyone in the place was doing the same thing. She just *makes* you look at her, and that's a great gift in the Theatre. Anyway, leave it to me, I'll have something for you soon.'

Stani did not spend hours in his lair below stairs pining away from unrequited love, in fact, so vivid was the memory of his urge to boot the ass of Pandora Bryce that he tore up his application for membership of Ponce's. When Mrs. Quansett-Fowles next summoned him to one of her 'evenings', Stani found the mixture much as before. Among the twenty or so present, a startled man from the American Embassy was being attacked on all sides because Ambassador Kennedy had just recommended President Roosevelt to 'forget about Britain – because Germany is bound to win the war'.

'What a beastly thing to say,' said a slim girl in the crisp naval uniform of the WRNS. 'I thought he and his family liked us.'

'He wants to go home,' sniffed a blue-veined wine merchant who was now a Major of Hussars, 'because he's got his hands on the United States import licences of a couple of our best Scotch whiskies.'

Stani paid little attention to the attacks on the American who, incidentally, had contributed a leg of lamb and two bottles of Burgundy towards the success of the evening. He fell to pondering on how handily the Wren[1] scored, in her trim navy blue outfit and black nylons, while the two girls in the WAAF uniform lost a head start provided by their well-cut powder blue outfits because of unfortunate slate grey, cotton stockings. His imagination boggled at the thought of the nightmarish undergarments that were reputedly issued for compulsory use by all three services; he questioned Mrs. Quansett-Fowles on the subject. She loudly gave it as her considered opinion that if uniforms, male and female, induced horniness in the opposite sex, then it was up to the interested parties to find out what lay beneath them.

'Anyway,' she added, 'you forget about the uniforms tonight. I have something special in civvies coming in later.'

Shortly after dinner, Mrs. Quansett-Fowles, smirking like a cat with canary feathers still attached to its whiskers, crossed the room towards Stani; behind her was Pandora Bryce.

Stani rose from the sofa upon which he had been making no progress with the Wren and mumbled incoherently when he was introduced. Pandora, after a moment of non-recognition, bestowed upon him her dazzling smile and said, 'Oh! Yes, I think we met once. You were with Lady Trollope.'

If the reunion got off to a shaky start it improved later when he sidled up to her and said, 'Why are you so bitchy about your fellow club member? She only says the nicest things about *you*.'

For a long moment the grey cat's eyes bored coolly into his, then she smiled. 'I've had a long, hard day at the office. I could do with a drink.'

[1] Members of the WRNS were known as Wrens.

44

Around two a.m. with the wine merchant major intoxicated on his own contribution of brandy, the girls in uniform paired off with Fighter Pilots, newspaper men from New York or sailors back from North Atlantic convoys, and Mrs. Quansett-Fowles locked in her pink satin bedroom with the nice man from the American Embassy, the guests began to melt away.

Stani had not exactly monopolized Pandora but he felt that sufficient progress had been made to warrant an offer to see her home.

'Where do *you* live?' she asked.

'In the basement.'

'Well, it's very sweet of you, but I'm sure I can get a lift from someone who's going my way.'

She waited for him to light her cigarette, then said, 'You live in the basement of this house?'

'Yes, I am a paying guest. I'm studying for my Cambridge exam.'

'How dull,' she said, and giggled. 'I thought you might be Amy's lover.'

Stani was still trying to think of a witty rejoinder, when people, in the fashion of the times, started making their travel arrangements. 'Who's for Chelsea? I've got room for a couple.' 'Anyone going North of the Park?' 'Fulham for me, any offers? I can spare a coupon.' Etc.

Pandora got herself a lift with a group heading in her direction and held out a slim hand to Stani.

'It really has been nice, I hope I see you again.'

'Where can I find you?' asked Stani, trying to sound conversational.

'At the Prince of Wales theatre for six nights a week with matinees on Wednesdays and Saturdays,' she laughed. Then she was gone.

Before Stani composed himself with difficulty for sleep he resolved not to appear too keen and to let at least forty-eight hours elapse before he made further contact with Pandora, but events dictated otherwise.

Mr. Halliday, his crammer, decided that Stani should accompany him forthwith to Cambridge to spend a few days doing preliminary tests at college level. He also wanted him to be interviewed by various provosts, deans and tutors who

45

might help, and advise and, hopefully, facilitate his acceptance into the University.

Stani had not been in Cambridge more than twenty-four hours before that noble seat of learning ground to a halt, stunned like the rest of the country by the news that the Phoney War had gone up in smoke and all hell had broken loose on the Continent. The Germans had invaded Holland and Belgium and, after a thousand dive bombers had decimated the French defenders at Sedan, hordes of tanks had rampaged into France.

The Dutch surrendered, followed ten days later by the Belgians; then Prime Minister Reynaud ordered the French Government to leave Paris and the British Army was concentrated to evacuate.

Stani and Mr. Halliday had hovered about in Cambridge before returning to London to watch helplessly with the rest of Britain while Hitler's 'Blitzkreig' netted him a million prisoners in three weeks, and then to rejoice when a massive miscalculation on his part, aided by a miracle of good weather and inspired organization, allowed a quarter of a million men to be rescued from Dunkirk.

3

An eerie lull followed the storm of Hitler's successes. For months now Stani had made the same round trip, between his lair in South Audley Street and his crammer's modest house behind Kensington Palace Gardens. He was in no great hurry and the late June evening was displaying 'the lungs of London' at their most beautiful.

The Germans might be in Paris buying pictures of the Eiffel Tower, but after the incredible salvation at Dunkirk, despite the fact that Russia was still an ally of Germany, France about to collapse altogether, the rest of Europe either occupied, defeated or resolutely neutral, many Britons seemed to believe that their war effort had suffered nothing more than a temporary dislocation. Stani was less optimistic, in fact he experienced a strong urge to be back in California. On the Round Pond, ducklings and cygnets were taking indignant avoiding action as intense gentlemen with long, padded poles redirected their graceful model sloops and schooners across the water. The Serpentine played host to a regatta of sailing dinghies and row boats. Everywhere children fished or played, woodpigeons cooed in the trees, people distributed edible largesse to ducks, geese, swans and moorhens and the only reminders on that tranquil evening of the Second World War were the silver barrage balloons at the end of steel cables, swaying like monstrous, bloated toys two thousand feet overhead, hoping to keep marauding bombers at a respectful distance.

Stani had voiced his misgivings to his crammer before starting his walk home.

'I really don't understand the British. 'They don't seem to be worrying.'

Mr. Halliday had puffed on his evil-smelling pipe. He

seemed so stolid and so unflappable that Stani was a trifle surprised to hear him say, 'Don't be taken in by us. We are all deeply disturbed, full of doubts and dreads, but we have been taught from childhood not to display emotion, "not to make a scene." The weather has a lot to do with our character. It's so awful most of the time and always when we need it to be good, it's bad! As children we look forward for weeks to a picnic, and then on the day, it pours with rain and the picnic is cancelled. Later a cricket match goes the same way because the pitch is waterlogged. Or a football game cannot be played because of fog, our favourite race meeting is scratched because the ground is frozen, and it's *always* pelting down for Trooping the Colour, Henley, Ascot and Wimbledon. So you see, as a race we have been inoculated against disappointment. Dunkirk? . . . well that's just a big disappointment, something we'll have to overcome.'

Stani had been intrigued but not persuaded, and now, as he moved past the bandstand and across the open green expanse towards Park Lane, he took in the sunbathers lying on the grass, staring up into the blue and – for the moment – unthreatening sky. He glanced at courting couples entwined beneath clumps of trees, at older people in deckchairs reading newspapers or dozing, and a sense of impending disaster settled upon him more strongly than before. It did not lift when he left the Park and passed a newsvendor on the corner of Curzon Street arranging his newly delivered evening papers in neat piles upon the pavement. Paper shortage was already acute so the delivery of display sheets bearing catchy headlines had been abandoned and with cockney inventiveness newsvendors had provided themselves with chalk and blackboards upon which they emblazoned the news they thought most likely to stir the interest of passers-by. The announcement this man had selected stopped him in his tracks.

FRANCE FALLS . . .
NOW WE'RE IN THE FINAL!!

Stani had heard no word of any sort from his mother and Captain Rainbird since the evacuation at Dunkirk had been completed, almost three weeks before. He had telephoned the Foreign Office and had been told by a soothing voice that though the British Embassy had left Paris, the personnel were

48

moving to another location, according to plan.

At the sight of the chalked-up headline, a surge of panic gripped him and he quickened his pace towards South Audley Street. More than ever he felt desperately alone and longed for someone to talk to. Someone who might perhaps calm down his over-active imagination, advise him and soothe him. Mrs. Quansett-Fowles had been crying a great deal lately because so many friends had been taken prisoner or killed at Calais and St. Valéry, others had been shot down or dreadfully burnt in the skies over Dunkirk, and, perhaps nearest to her heart were the losses in the Royal Navy, but, though he had an unreasonable longing to talk to Pandora Bryce, it was to Mrs. Quansett-Fowles he was to turn. He clattered down his stone steps and was pleased to find a 'special summons' under his door: *Come at once, urgent.*

The evening sun was slanting into her happy room when Stani entered, Mrs. Quansett-Fowles was dabbing at her eyes with a handkerchief. 'Here – have a big glass of shampoo,' she said. A tall, drained-looking man in filthy clothes stood with his back to the window.

'This is Mister Blakestone. He . . . he has something to tell you.' Suddenly, the champagne forgotten, she rose from the depths of her sofa, flung her arms round Stani's neck and pressed her tear-stained cheek to his. 'Oh, you poor, poor boy!' she sobbed. 'Oh! The bastards! The dirty, rotten, stinking bastards!' Then she fled from the room.

Stani looked towards the bedraggled stranger, and the man crossed from the window to put an arm around his shoulder. He smelled dreadful, a mixture of filth, sweat and oil, he spoke slowly from some deep well of exhaustion, dredging up his words with difficulty and punctuating them with heaving sighs.

'I have dreadful news for you, my boy, the most dreadful news you can hear.'

Stani stared ahead blankly, unable to speak; he sensed of course what was coming.

'Your mother is gone. She's dead, son. I came as quick as I could.' Stani felt suspended, in shock. 'The Captain is gone too.' Blakewell added. Stani groped his way to the sofa, Blakewell sat down beside him.

'Oh my God, son, I wish I didn't have to tell you this but we promised each other we would, if anything . . . went wrong.'

'What happened?' asked Stani, and he was surprised that his voice sounded steady.

'We were all in the Embassy together,' said Blakewell slowly. 'Ten days ago, I think it was, the Ambassador called us in and told us that the end for France was coming. He said a small skeleton staff would remain behind in Paris to burn papers, destroy equipment and so on, and then go with him somewhere South – he didn't say where. The rest of us were to try to make it to the Atlantic coast, to Brest, Lorient or St. Nazaire, about two hundred and fifty miles away . . .'

'How did she die?' Stani interrupted. 'How did my mother and my stepfather *die*? . . . Please tell me everything.'

'Oh God, son – I'm so sorry, but I'll tell you as best I can. You see, I had my little Peugeot two-seater all ready. I had filled her up in case of emergencies some time before, so we just piled in, the three of us, and headed for Brest. Traffic was jammed up all the way out of the city and the roads, even the little back ones to the coast, were chockablock with people – men, women, children, on foot, on bikes and in farm carts, all streaming away from Paris, carrying what they could. French soldiers too, lots of them, trying to get home. We kept to the back roads because we were told they were machine gunning the traffic jams on the big ones but even so, after three days, in a lane near Mayenne, they strafed us. A lot of people were hit, some killed. We lay in a ditch and were all right, but the Peugeot was wrecked – burnt out.

'Your mother was wonderful, never complained, kept cheerful all the time, and we set out to walk the rest of the way, over a hundred miles. Everyone was looking for food. The farmers kept us away with pitchforks and shotguns, so we slept in fields and tried to forget our hunger. We caught up with some R.A.F. ground personnel who said Brest and Lorient were destroyed and rescue ships would be at St. Nazaire. They were all exhausted, they'd been marching for days, all the way from Rouen in terrible heat. We got your mother on to a farm cart that day because her feet were so raw and bleeding and finally, three days ago, we made it into St. Nazaire.

'The whole place was in flames and it was teeming with British soldiers, some Belgian and some French too but things seemed well organized and we were put on a tender and it pushed out into the Loire estuary. We could see ships of various sizes lying outside the mouth of the river. They were being bombed, one was hit and went on fire, destroyers were pumping up anti-aircraft fire, there was a lot of smoke and noise. But your mother was marvellous, said it looked like the Fourth of July. We were taken alongside a big liner about three miles off St. Nazaire, the *Lancastria*, and put aboard. The troops from all sorts of regiments were very well disciplined. There were many women and children too, canteen workers, ambulance drivers, Red Cross people and so on. The stewards on board were very calm and we were even allotted a cabin with three others and given sandwiches and tea. They wore their white jackets and told us that we would be sailing at once and that there were over six thousand people on board. We were beginning to feel safe at last in spite of the racket outside.

'Suddenly there were three or four terrible explosions and we knew we'd been hit. We rushed out of the cabin and found the passageway outside jammed with troops heading up on deck. There was no panic. The ship heeled far over almost at once and people fell on top of each other, then it righted itself and went over even further the other way. Captain Rainbird more or less carried your mother up on deck. She was wonderfully calm and even joked. 'Maybe we're going to swim to England', she said.'

Blakewell faltered and passed a hand across his eyes, infinitely weary. 'Shall I . . .'

'Yes,' said Stani quietly, 'please finish.'

'On deck,' Blakewell continued, 'life jackets were being distributed, but of course there weren't enough. Captain Rainbird got one for your mother, then he said to me – 'Look after Virginia, I must report to the bridge to see if I can help'. We didn't see him again. A steward told us that one bomb had gone down a funnel and another into an open hatch and blown a hole in the side.

'Then the loudspeakers told us to abandon ship. She was heeling further and further over and it was impossible to lower the boats. Your mother and I waited for a few minutes for Captain Rainbird. While we were waiting a woman with a little girl was begging for a life jacket. Without a moment's hesitation

51

your mother took off hers and gave it to her. 'I'm a good Californian beach girl', she said, 'I can make it to shore anytime'. I persuaded her to climb over the rail and follow people sliding down into the water. The ship was almost on her side by this time. We slithered down the plates and they were quite hot, from the fires inside, I suppose, and there was a nasty drop as the side curved away. We couldn't see the water but your mother never hesitated. We both hit the water at about the same time – it was covered with fuel oil. When I came up I found a deckchair floating right beside me and I grabbed it. Your mother was only a few yards away and was struggling towards me when a plane came over, machine-gunning people in the water. I think she must have been hit in the head or heart because she just rolled over and in a couple of seconds she was gone.'

Blakewell shook his head in utter despair. 'I did my best, son, to find her, but you see – I can't swim.' He paused for a long silence, his journey completed.

'During our days on the road,' he said, 'we promised each other that if things went badly for one family, the other would . . . well you know. I'm just sorry I took so long to get here, a destroyer picked me up and landed me at Falmouth. I haven't been home yet.'

Another silence was broken by Blakewell whispering, 'It all happened so fast. *Lancastria* sank only ten minutes after she was hit. They reckon four thousand went with her. Hundreds of soliders were down in one hold and when she heeled over so quickly, they couldn't get out. I saw a young priest or padre in R.A.F. uniform lower himself down into that hold on a rope. He said something about 'going to comfort them'. When your mother and I were in the water, they started singing, those boys down there and the last sound she heard was "Onward Christian Soldiers".'

Then he broke down completely and the quiet room on that summer evening was filled with his distress.

For days, Stani was unable to comprehend the loss, unable to grasp the meaning of what was happening to his life. Mrs. Quansett-Fowles and the two Danish girls were endlessly kind but he was swamped by grief and despair. He hardly dared to think of his father, what might be happening to *him*. Prodded finally into action because she thought it better for him to be doing *something*, Mrs. Quansett-Fowles prised from him the name of a London lawyer who had been sending him his small monthly allowance from his mother. He went to the offices of Butterworth, Jilkes and Butterworth, which were gloomy but warlike. There was an air raid shelter igloo of sandbags in the basement, the window panes were criss-crossed with adhesive tape; a bucket of sand, another of water and a stirrup pump stood on the threshold.

'A tragic loss, my dear boy. What terrible times we live in. Please be patient while I look up your particulars. My younger partner, Jilkes, and my son have both gone off to the Army, most of my staff have been called up and I've sent the greater part of the files down to Chalfont St. Peter – they're in my garage. We're in a bit of a mess here as you can see but I have quite a good idea where everything is.'

Stani was brought a cup of tea by a spotty girl with pebble glasses who looked at the windows and said, 'It's ever so dreary in here with all that stuff on the glass. Mr. Butterworth's worried about the bombing but I don't think they'll *dare* to come over, do you?'

Mr. Butterworth returned. 'Yes, I have everything, all right,' he said. He was carrying a slim file covered in dust. 'But I'm afraid your mother's will and other documents are in my garage. I'll look them out tonight when I go home. I do remember that Captain Rainbird bequeathed his cottage and any capital to his sister and her children, your mother insisted on that as I recall, and I am quite sure that her bequests to you will be advantageous. Though I don't want to give any sort of estimate until . . .'

'Look, sir,' said Stani. 'What I really wanted to find out is if there was anything she wanted me to do after she . . . you know . . .'

In a somewhat vague fashion, Mr. Butterworth was quite efficient and in the next couple of weeks wills had been found and read and a meeting arranged at Lauriston with Captain Rainbird's sister. A brisk, pleasant-faced chain smoker, herself the wife of a Destroyer Captain serving in the Mediterranean, she had a down-to-earth, no tears approach to her brother's demise, in fact to death in general.

'Charlie would have wanted to go that way,' she announced after several pink gins in the Pilot Boat. 'He hated being on the beach – the Navy was his whole life. He was miserable out of uniform. Give the potato chips a fair wind, will you?'

The business of the cottage was quickly concluded and the disposal of personal belongings arranged.

'Might I take charge of Charlie's telescope?' she asked. 'My boys loved looking at the ships with him.' Some hasty nose blowing at this point was hurriedly explained away: 'Bloody hay fever – get it every summer.' Her briskness soon returned.

'Look here, what the hell do we do about a funeral service? I mean, we know now, officially, that they both . . . er . . . bought it, but we can't do much more than say a few prayers for them, can we? Let's go up to the vicarage and have a word with the Sky Pilot.'

The vicar was charming but deaf and referred to the deceased as the 'Brainbirds'. A private service was arranged for a couple of days' hence. Stani's stepfather had many friends and admirers in Lauriston and during the short months of her occupancy as mistress of his house, Stani's mother's charm, beauty and American directness had noticeably swelled the number.

The day of the memorial service dawned cloudless and windless; the Solent was like glass beneath a heat haze. The bell tolled solemnly from the little church upon the hill, and up from the houses and the harbour below toiled a stream of fishermen, lifeboatmen, landladies and their families and Naval cronies over from Portsmouth. Stani stood beside Captain Rainbird's sister feeling rather out of it all, but he returned the self-conscious little smiles and nods directed his way.

The village had greatly changed. The big houses were shut, the small ones housed no holiday-makers; the young men and women were away in the Services. As in the rest of Britain, barbed wire and scaffolding covered the beaches and the village knew that if invaders headed inshore, underwater pipelines somewhere further out to sea would turn the surface of the Solent into an inferno of blazing oil. Stani looked out to sea; the hot sun had burned off the early mist and he found himself thinking of the kindness he had received from these simple

54

people, and how happy he had been here for a short time; of the swan trapped on its pond; and then, with a greater pain, of his mother, and her gallant sailor. And somewhere, but oh God where? . . . his father.

In perfect 'V' formation, a flight of wild swans from the marshes flew overhead as the honest burghers of Lauriston filed past, murmuring their condolences. The little church on the cliff top was bathed in the warming sun, flowers were everywhere, and below, the sea shimmered.

Suddenly, the quiet was shattered by the sharp rattle of machine-gun fire. The mourners surged towards the cliff to watch the spectacle of a German bomber, its black crosses plainly visible on wings and fuselage flying below them, a few feet above the wave tops. It was trying to shake off two R.A.F. Spitfires. One fighter, attacking from dead astern, was hit by the bomber's tail gunner, and pieces flew off it, but it disengaged, banked and climbed steadily away towards the mainland. Then the second fighter launched a slanting attack from above and the bomber, almost at once, plunged into the water, disappearing in a mighty eruption of flame and spray. The mourners cheered heartily and a voice at Stani's elbow said, 'Got the bastard! Look! They're dive bombing the docks over at Portsmouth.'

He turned; beside him, in the uniform of an Able Bodied Seaman of the Royal Navy, stood his old friend Jervis.

Their reunion could hardly be described as joyful, but once the mourners, fascinated by a front row view of the Stukas hurtling down on the Naval Base and several thrilling dogfights far above their heads, had departed with apologetic glances in his direction, he gratefully accepted Jervis's gruff invitation to drop down 'for a little something to take your mind off it'.

'Yes,' said Jervis as he poured two hefty tots of rum, 'I'm back in the Navy. I changed me last name of course, kept the Jervis for luck, but I couldn't stay out and I'm glad I'll be able to 'ave a go. Sorry about what they done to your Mum and the Captain, Stani. That's bad, real bad.'

Stani stayed with Jervis for most of the day; the rough, salty common sense of the man was both balm and beacon, and by the time he tottered down the gangplank, he had made a big decision . . . he too would get into uniform. Because of a tendency towards seasickness, he would avoid the Royal Navy; and Jervis had painted the Army in unflattering colours. 'It's most important to 'ave a nice, dry bed and not a waterlogged trench before or after a battle, that's wot my Dad always says.' So influenced by the spectacular success of the Spitfires which he had witnessed that day, he decided to do his best to save the world from the pilot seat of an R.A.F. fighter.

4

Mrs. Quansett-Fowles produced an Air Vice-Marshal who, she was confident, would 'do the necessary' if Stani wanted to join the R.A.F. Flattery and spirits were pumped into the bemedalled officer and he became most helpful.

'I'll talk to my opposite number on General Sikorski's staff in the next day or two and put him in the picture,' he said. 'After the Russians stabbed your country in the back, a large number of Polish troops and airmen fought with the French. Now many of them have escaped from France and come over here. Under Sikorski, as head of the Polish Government in London, they will be forming Polish squadrons in the R.A.F. and divisions in the British army – several units of your Navy have already joined the Royal Navy so it shouldn't be too difficult.'

The Air Vice-Marshal was as good as his word and by the middle of October, after a cursory medical exam and a security check conducted by a Colonel Zamowski who had known his father, Stani found himself posted to No. 5 R.A.F. Officers' Training Unit on Salisbury Plain, no wings as yet on his uniform but proudly on each shoulder was displayed a flash – POLAND.

Before he left London, Stani wanted to impress Pandora. Although he had not seen her for much too long, she had never been far from his thoughts and somehow he felt she might be pleased with his progress; anyway he reckoned he had nothing to lose, she might refuse to see him but until he tried he would never know.

He polished his shoes and headed for the Prince of Wales theatre. He wanted to see her once more from the audience before he made his approach via the awful doorman; he half-hoped that she would look so different from his mental picture of her that he would be purged of his great longing to be close to her. He bought his ticket for the dress circle, settled down, and opened his programme. A printed announcement was clipped above the cast list:

Until further notice the part of the Secretary will be played by JANE PUMBLY.

The doorman told Stani that Pandora was 'recovering from flu' and was away with her family.

When he reported to Andover he found that his fellow trainees came from every walk of life, garage mechanics, undergraduates, stockbrokers, farmers, bank clerks, factory workers and crane operators. Few had any flying hours to their credit but all were consumed by an urge to emulate the exploits of the heroes of the Battle of Britain which had so recently and so gloriously been on display. Their ages were between nineteen and twenty-two. Their instructors were sergeants of great experience and fluctuating patience and if the nights were spent drinking heavily in the local pubs and chasing the few available local girls, the days consisted of sitting in Nissen huts listening to lectures on basic flying procedures, followed by harrowing attempts to put them into practice in Harvard Fighter Trainers. The instructors sat in the rear cockpits issuing streams of warnings, oaths and prayers and, occasionally, grabbing the dual controls to save their own lives as well as those of their pupils.

By the spring of 1941, Stani's uniform had sprouted wings and as a fully fledged Flying Officer, he was moved to an advanced officers' training unit at Grangemouth, near Falkirk in Scotland. There he was indoctrinated by battle-hardened 'aces' into the art of flying, and fighting a Spitfire.

The front line was becoming alarmingly visible. Soon, he would be taking his place in an operational squadron, fighting alongside dedicated Poles far from their families and their country, doughty warriors filled with vengeance who had already become a legend, famous for sailing into the attack against appalling odds with almost lunatic heroism. He was less than fascinated by the prospect. Several Poles were also in training at Grangemouth but apart from his proud shoulder flashes, he had little in common with them and when they discovered that he was unable to converse in their mother

58

tongue, they retreated behind the language barrier and peered out at him with a thinly veiled suspicion, especially when they heard him jabbering away in French and German to the Belgians and Dutch who were also on the course. The Polish pilots were a square-jawed, indomitable, hard-drinking lot, much admired by the local Scots, but their English, of necessity the language used in the R.A.F. for the giving and taking of orders, was apt to switch to instant Polish in moments of stress. So quite early on Stani determined to leave no stone unturned to avoid fighting shoulder to shoulder and wing tip to wing tip with these devil-may-care gladiators.

Whenever he went off the station, however, the 'Poland' flashes on his uniform attracted attention and he was the constant recipient of heartfelt congratulations upon the legendary exploits of his compatriots. Zdzislaw Krasnodebski, Miroslaw Féric, Stanislaw Karubin, Witor Urbanowicz, Jan Daszewski, Zdzislaw Henneberg and the others had performed miracles of daring during the entire period of the Luftwaffe onslaught and the British public was in no doubt as to their contribution nor of the magnitude of their sacrifices. He received these plaudits modestly but became increasingly nervous about his future.

Owing to a certain timidity at the controls, he was far from being a star pupil, and his first solo flight in a Spitfire left him weak in the knees, bathed in sweat and smelling mightily. He had misjudged both landing and propeller pitch, and had pancaked in a sewage farm at the end of the runway. Eventually, as he became less afraid of the awesome power of its Rolls Royce Merlin engine, he derived a certain enjoyment from the Spitfire, although night flying and close formation work still scared the pants off him and the feeling of claustrophobia from having his head encased in helmet, goggles and oxygen mask was acute.

The exercises that he hated the least were the high altitude dog fights with other pilots of equal calibre, or occasionally with one of the battle-hardened 'aces'. During these encounters Stani noticed that when it was his turn to chase – getting into up-sun position, or breaking off the attacks at the last split second – he was somewhat less effective than when he was taking avoiding action or finding cloud cover in which to hide;

but he kept this knowledge to himself and tried to push to the back of his mind the fact that by September he would no longer be playing hide and seek with acquaintances, he would be eyeball to eyeball with markedly hostile strangers.

The autumn of 1941 came early to Scotland; the heather was a purple blaze on the hillsides, the glens and lochs were misting over in the late afternoon chill, blue smoke from peat fires was curling from the crofters' chimneys. With two weeks' leave Stani was on his way to spend the first few days with a fellow officer who lived at Arisaig. He was savouring the wild beauty of the landscape from the passenger seat of a rattling and rusting sports model Riley. News from the war fronts could hardly have been worse but he was relieved. He had found a way to avoid a future with his gallant countrymen. He had volunteered to be a Catafighter.

A naval officer in 'The Thistle', his favourite pub in Grangemouth, had alerted him to the existence of this highly experimental force. 'I don't know what the hell they do,' he had said, 'but it might make a nice change from an ordinary fighter squadron. I know a couple of Fleet Air Arm characters who are in it and they say they have a wonderful party. Every now and then they disappear, wrapped in secrecy. A few weeks later they're back with armsful of nylons from New York, bloody great Virginia hams and cases of Canadian Club whisky. If you're interested I'll find out who you have to see about it. It's a volunteer show but for some reason there don't seem to be too many takers.' The man did not forget and shortly thereafter, Stani had been interviewed by a senior naval captain in Liverpool, a huge, pink man of horrid heartiness.

'As you can see, it's a fairly risky business,' this officer concluded happily, after a vague description of the role of the Catafighters. 'I can't tell you any more for obvious security reasons but at least now you know something of what you're letting yourself in for! We've had quite a measure of success with our little toys and I'm sure we'll find room for you. I've had you vetted by MI5 and by General Sikorski's headquarters – the transfer can be made very easily. In the meanwhile, keep your mouth shut and remember this whole operation is TOP SECRET. I think you'll enjoy yourself.'

'Thank you very much, sir,' Stani had said. 'How long will

the training for my switch-over to Hurricane take?'

'That and the special training involved, six weeks of concentrated work,' the Captain replied. 'I'll send a signal to your Station Commander at Grangemouth and fiddle you a few days' leave before you report here. Welcome aboard, young man!' he boomed, then added, 'you're not married, are you?'

'No, sir.'

'I'd leave it that way for a while if I were you,' on which ominous note Stani withdrew, wondering if he had been stupid enough to jump out of the Polish frying pan into the Royal Navy fire.

For the rest of his leave he returned to Mrs. Quansett-Fowles' house. On arrival he received a rapturous welcome and the sight of his wings prompted Amy's observation that 'he looked like a friggin angel'. Outwardly, the scene in South Audley Street had changed little; the 'shampoo' still flowed and the long, chintzy sitting room was filled with hearty laughter. But faces were drawn and grey from the long, sleepless nights of the Blitz and several of the younger habitués were gone forever, cut down in their prime, in the desert, sky, sea or in the City itself. But the hostess remained indomitable, pouring scorn and ridicule on 'Corporal Schickelgruber and his mates', 'that old queen, Goering', 'the mad midget, Goebbels', 'fat old fart-face, Musso', and 'Himmler, the pouf with pince-nez'.

A leak-prone under-secretary at the Foreign Office confided to Stani a grim rumour circulating among the London Poles. It seemed that several thousand of their brother officers, taken prisoner in the early days of the German-Russian onslaught on their country two years before, had lately been wiped out – massacred by the Russians near Smolensk.

When Stani heard this, he retreated to his little apartment below stairs and sat quietly, all alone, in the darkness for a while, weighed down by loneliness and desolation, feelings not quickly dispelled by the wailings of an air raid alert. When the bombs started falling, he surfaced and carried out his original plan for his first night in London. He groped his way in the blackout towards the Prince of Wales theatre.

It was a heavy raid that night and not many people were abroad because, in addition to the bombs, shrapnel from the anti-aircraft shells was also raining down. In the banging, whistling gloom, he noticed that the doormen of the Mayfair and Ritz hotels had substituted steel helmets for their customary top hats, and that the railings round Berkeley Square had been removed to be fashioned into tanks. Fire trucks and ambulances clanged past him, headed towards Leicester Square. When he arrived at the theatre he saw why.

Across the street, a bomb had shrieked through the roof of the Café de Paris, exploding on the packed dance floor, killing or maiming the entire band and most of the customers. The dead and dying were being dug out of the rubble when Stani arrived, shocked survivors were wandering about asking for relatives and friends.

The Prince of Wales theatre had been rocked and shaken by the explosion, much plaster and glass had fallen, and the lighting system had been knocked out for a few seconds. But following the Blitz-time procedure of all London theatres, the audience and performers had remained quietly in their places till order had been restored. Then the show, like a film 'frozen' at the touch of a switch, had gone on from where the animation had been suspended.

The events of the night and the presence of danger had softened the stage doorkeeper's behaviour towards his fellow men; he accepted a pound note and undertook to deliver a message to Pandora Bryce. It was a scribbled note enquiring if she would like the help of the Royal Air Force to get her home after the show. When he came back, Pandora was with him.

'Oh! It's *you*,' she cried, and, pointing at his uniform, added, 'my goodness! I had no idea you were one of the Brylcreem Boys!'

There was genuine admiration in her voice when she used this description which desperately tired and defeated soldiers back from the hell of Dunkirk had once muttered on seeing news photos of clean, well-groomed young fighter pilots. Stani pressed home the advantage.

'I've only got a few days' leave,' he said, acutely aware that 'Houndstooth' was listening to every word. 'It would be a great contribution to my war effort if you would have supper with me after the show – that is if there is anywhere left standing, by that time, to have supper in!'

'Of *course*,' smiled Pandora and Stani had never seen a smile so dazzling. 'I'd love to.' She hesitated and glanced at the clock. 'The show'll be over in half an hour . . . Charlie, can I take my friend in – I'll see he's not in the way?'

'Well,' said Charlie, 'it's against regulations, Miss, but seeing as how the gentleman is on leave, I think we can blink an eye this once.'

'Thanks, Charlie, you're a darling.'

Stani was stationed in the wings and watched fascinated as the orderly backstage chaos swirled around him. The West End seemed to be getting special attention that night, the theatre rocked, scenery and arc lights swayed and much of the dialogue was lost. But the show never faltered and the audience, grateful to have its mind taken off the nasty possibilities, reacted with gales of laughter and ecstatic applause to the antics of Sid Field and his company.

Pandora appeared briefly in one more sketch towards the end of the show, then lined up with the rest of the company for the curtain calls. Stani could not take his eyes off her. He had never seen anything so beautiful. When the curtain fell for the last time, the smiles were wiped from the faces of the performers as if by magic, and there was a general stampede towards the dressing rooms. Those who couldn't get home to a distant suburb, on a heavy night such as this, would grab a blanket and pillow and spend the night on the cold, draughty platform of a nearby underground station. Pandora was in no hurry. She linked an arm through Stani's and led him to a box-like dressing room which she shared with three other girls.

'They'll probably be flashing their boobs and bottoms by now,' she said cheerfully, 'but I'm sure they'd love to meet you.'

The girls were in various degrees of undress when they entered.

'Take cover,' she said, 'I've got a real live pilot to show you.'

Stani did look rather magnificent in his powder blue uniform and his entrance into the little room was greeted by wolf whistles from three long-legged beauties.

'Eunice, Toni and Flo,' announced Pandora.

'Pleased to meet you,' chorused the girls.

'What's it like out there tonight?' asked one, slapping cold cream on to her face.

'The Café de Paris took a direct hit,' said Stani, 'and I heard that a lot of stuff was dropping round Waterloo Station and the docks.'

'Oh! No!' said another girl. 'I won't be able to get home if they've hit the lines.'

'I 'eard that "Lord 'aw 'aw" on the wireless from Berlin during the interval an' he was telling the Jews to watch out because they're going to flatten 'amstead 'eath tonight,' said the third girl in a rich cockney voice as she eased a skirt over her hips. 'The silly bugger don't even know most of us live in Whitechapel. I'd like to get me 'ands on that bastard though, 'im with 'is smarmy voice an' all. I wonder wot got 'im turned round like that in the first place. I suppose we'll 'ang the fucker when we gets to Berlin.' She slipped into a well-worn coat and knotted a scarf under her chin. 'Well, I'm off! G'nite Pandy, nite Tini, nite Eunice, and g'nite you beautiful man!'

'Goodnight, Flo,' chorused the others.

When Toni and Eunice had completed their dressing they said their goodnights and rushed off together, obviously bursting to discuss Pandora's latest acquisition.

'I won't be long,' she said when they had gone. 'The make-up I'll leave on and hope you'll take me to a dark place, so if you'll just turn your back for a second, I'll slip out of this thing and change my knickers.'

Unaccustomed to the possibilities provided by theatrical dressing tables, with their interplay of mirrors, Stani turned his back as ordered but found he was in a perfect position to watch the unveiling of the glorious globes of Pandora's behind. She wriggled out of her costume, worked it over her head. Secure in the knowledge that his back was indeed turned towards her, he made no move to miss a flash of her perfectly shaped breasts and the exquisite positioning of garter belt, gunmetal grey nylons and high-heeled shoes. Too late he realised his silence had betrayed him and as a short pleated skirt was lowered into position, obliterating this tantalizing spectacle, Pandora said casually, 'You've been very quiet – were you having a good look in the mirror by any chance?' The blood rushed to his face and he stoutly denied the accusation but when he was bidden to turn around, he knew from her open smile that she did not believe him for a moment and also that she was not all that unhappy to have provided him with a glimpse of herself.

When they stepped out of the stage door, the underside of the clouds was reflecting the glow of many fires to the East and South of the City, dull angry red for the most part, but brightening ominously to yellow as gasometers or oil tanks exploded. There was a lull, no bombs were falling and the anti-aircraft guns were silent; but the long, one-note wail of the 'All Clear' had not been sounded and as they picked their way along rubble-strewn streets, Pandora, more raid-wise than Stani, said, 'I suppose the swine have gone back to France to load-up again so they can keep it up till morning. I mark a little calendar – this is the eighty-fifth consecutive night that we've been bombed. I wonder how long they can keep it up?' But as ambulances and fire engines careered past them, both were wondering how much longer Londoners would be able to stand it. In Soho, the pubs were doing a roaring trade and most restaurants were open for business. They chose 'Au Jardin des Gourmets' because Pandora insisted it still had a good stock of wine.

They pushed open the door and, for a brief moment in the darkness between the door and the blackout curtain, their bodies touched. Stani felt a surge of excitement between his legs and an intense desire to crush the girl to him at last. But she pulled the curtain aside, smiled at him, and led the way to a table. The restaurant was packed and as waiters busied themselves tidying things up, he marvelled at the gaiety of the scene. Aside from a sprinkling of uniformed customers and gas masks hanging among the overcoats, there seemed little hint of a war going on outside. Glasses were emptied, forks paused mouthward as jokes were made, and laughter was everywhere. It was as though the clientele had decided to leave their fears and sorrows in the streets with the broken glass, the smashed houses, the falling ash and the mangled bodies.

Despite his years amidst the golden casual youth of California, Stani had never found it easy to relax with the opposite sex, in the first rounds of a relationship. And now the proximity of his spectacular companion, the woman he had dreamed about so long, coupled with her aura of self-assurance to inhibit him completely. He was losing his nerve! He was also acutely aware that he was receiving signals on his sexual antennae.

As he had followed her through the crowded room, he had

not failed to notice that a large proportion of the male eyes in the room had swivelled in Pandora's direction. Consequently, try as he could to think of something to say, he was unable to open the conversation. Even his two pre-dinner dry martinis did little to loosen him up. Pandora gave a much better performance, making little jokes about the food shortages and dazzling the head waiter into confessing that he had partridges which he was keeping for very favoured customers. Then she suddenly turned her enormous eyes upon Stani and said, 'I think war is an aphrodisiac, don't you?' Stani, who had been toying with the idea of opening the proceedings along rather more traditional lines, could only manage a reply of minimal distinction. 'I suppose we all feel we should enjoy ourselves while we still have time,' he said. 'Hmm,' said Pandora. 'Tell me about yourself. Why do you have a Russian name, a slight American accent and an R.A.F. uniform? Are you a spy?'

He told her about his nationality, and over some potted shrimps and a bottle of Montrachet, he filled her in on his upbringing, travels and schooling. Halfway through his partridge and the second bottle of wine, he told her about his fears for his father, and with difficulty about his mother and Captain Rainbird. When he finished there were tears in Pandora's eyes. She held his hand.

'You poor, poor darling, you must be so lost and lonely. Who's looking after you? Do you have many friends in England?'

'No,' said Stani slowly, 'no – I don't. I have well, a fisherman in the Isle of Wight and I suppose Mrs. Quansett-Fowles, my landlady.' He paused. 'I'm sorry to have unloaded all this on you. That wasn't my idea for the evening at all.'

Pandora smiled, twirling the pale, golden wine in her glass. Their intimate silence was shattered by the terrifying, metallic concussion of what was obviously a very big bomb very close. Everyone – diners and waiters – froze. They all knew that bombs fell in sticks of three or four, with about fifty yards between them; much, therefore, would depend on what happened in the next couple of seconds. With the familiar whistling shriek, the second bomb exploded. The building swayed crazily but practised ears knew that the bomb had fallen further away than the first. Relief, conversation and laughter flooded back

66

into the room, and waiters bustled about once more. Stani realized Pandora still held his hand.

'I feel bad about it, but when I hear that horrible, rustling whistle coming down, I pray that the bloody thing will fall on somebody else instead of on me,' she said. There was a tiny pink lamp on the table and her skin looked creamy.

'Tell me about you, now,' Stani said. 'I've done all the talking.'

'My story is not very original,' she sighed. 'I've always been stage-struck. My one ambition in life is to be a great, big Hollywood film star one day. But I haven't got very far and I've been at it for three years. Oh, I've been in a couple of touring companies, quite nice parts too, but in dreadful places like Sheffield and Bolton, living in theatrical digs with gorgons for landladies. But I love the people in the theatre. We laugh a lot and help each other out and cry and get hysterical and earn no money and live on cups of tea and sausage rolls and lose our figures and have mad love affairs with all the wrong people.' She paused. 'Anyway, now at least I've got into a show in the West End which is supposed to be the big next step. So now I'm just waiting for Alexander Korda or someone to come back-stage with a bunch of red roses and a big fat film contract!' She smiled and added rather wistfully, 'Daddy has never seen me on the stage. Acting is still not looked upon as a very reputable profession by Englishmen of his class and generation, I'm afraid.'

'What class is your father?' asked Stani, but added hastily, 'That sounds very rude. I mean is he an officer like my father or what?'

'He was an officer once,' said Pandora, 'in the last war. But then all sorts of people become officers in war time, don't they? Oh! My Lord,' she laughed, 'now that sounded very rude of *me*! Let's not talk about my family. Daddy's a darling, very lonely, I'm afraid, since my mother died. He lives at Hawksmoor in the country and I go down there when I can.'

She took a long swallow of wine signalling that conversation about her background was at an end and they sat silently for a while listening to the noises outside – the lethal storm seemed to be passing and the detonations were further away but ambulances and fire engines still rushed past continuously.

'I wonder if this bloody war will ever end,' Pandora sighed. 'Are you afraid of being killed? What's it like killing someone?'

'I haven't killed anyone yet because I haven't been in action,' said Stani. 'I don't know how I shall feel about any of it.' He looked away as he spoke and tried to sound casual. 'I expect it all happens pretty quickly, perhaps one doesn't feel anything much at the time. Most people I've met in the R.A.F. seem to think that everyone else will get knocked off but they'll be all right themselves. I'm not so sure that I feel that way though. I'm in a bit of a muddle about the whole thing, actually.'

'Are you in a fighter squadron with all those wonderful Poles?' asked Pandora.

'Well,' Stani replied, 'I'm not in anything at the moment. I've just finished my training and I've been posted to something which I'm not allowed to talk about. I'm not all that sure that even *I* know what it is! I've got a few days of my leave left before I have to report somewhere near Liverpool.'

'I see,' said Pandora thoughtfully and fell silent. Then she said, 'I'd love a brandy, do you have any in your place or shall we have it here?'

Stani felt a lightness of head, a tightening of his stomach muscles, and he turned to search her face for a clue; but he was met again with that Mona Lisa smile and direct gaze from her huge eyes. He hesitated.

'It is war time, you know,' Pandora said.

After paying the bill, Stani stood up. He had a feeling of giddy excitement mixed with new confidence. The head waiter bowed them out and this time, between the blackout curtain and the door, Stani did not hesitate. There in the darkness he put his arms around Pandora's slim waist and pulled her unresisting body to his. Her mouth was soft; they clung together. She pressed herself against him and moved her hips subtly when she felt his hardness. He probed with his tongue and she responded eagerly, her breath coming more quickly. He could feel her breasts and the warmth of hers against his and as his mind was reeling with the magnitude of his good fortune, the blackout curtain was unceremoniously flung aside and a matronly figure cannoned into them.

'Terribly sorry!' said a woman, 'I had no idea! But it *is* a funny place to be doing it, isn't it?'

'We were not *doing* it,' said Pandora. 'We were just *thinking* about doing it.'

'Oh! I see . . . jolly good show,' said the lady, and passed into the street followed by a man with a gas mask slung across his chest.

'I *told* you war is an aphrodisiac,' Pandora said.

At the bottom of Wardour Street, they gazed with sadness upon a beautiful Sir Christopher Wren church which had been reduced to a pile of rubble and stained glass. The bomb, probably the first one they had heard when they entered the restaurant, had fallen on some houses directly across the narrow street, demolishing several, and the blast had blown the little masterpiece to smithereens. Blast from bombs was notoriously erratic in its behaviour and this time, its major destruction completed, it had slammed on up the street, sucking out windows, doors and removing roofs. One house of three floors had been denuded of its entire facade, with apparently no damage to the inhabitants who were now bared to the public gaze, gingerly getting together what small valuables might be removed without disturbing the balance and bringing the remains of the structure crashing down. Firemen were erecting ropes to keep pedestrians out of range of falling masonry. One weary man, his blackened face lined with fatigue, had a mug of tea in his hand. He was yelling advice to an old lady on the top floor who was groping about under a brass bed.

'You can't bring *that* thing out, Missus,' he yelled.

The old lady removed her head from beneath the bed, looked down and said with dignity, 'I'm looking for my false teeth.'

The fireman shook his head. 'Cor blimey!' he muttered then yelled back. 'Wot d'you think they're dropping around 'ere . . . sardine sandwiches?'

It took Stani and Pandora almost half an hour to cover the short distance to South Audley Street. Frequently, they had to duck into the nearest solid-looking doorway when they judged a bomb was falling too close or when the clatter of shrapnel on roofs and porticos became too heavy. There they kissed and fondled each other with increasing urgency. Crossing a deserted Berkeley Square, they watched fascinated when, high above their heads, a Dornier bomber was picked out by a single searchlight. Other beams immediately joined in, framing the intruder; like a little white moth, it turned, twisted, swooped and dived, trying to escape. Greyish bursts of anti-aircraft fire followed it relentlessly up and down the beams and, finally, it happened. The bomber seemed to stop dead, glowing in the sky, then, like an autumn leaf from one of the giant plane trees among which they were standing, it fell, twisting down in a long, slow spiral until it disappeared behind the rooftops. A smattering of polite applause like that accorded a firework display, came from the darkened windows of the Square.

When they finally reached the sanctuary of Stani's basement flat, Pandora wasted no time. She turned on the bedside light, kissed him long on the lips, then, turning her back to him, whispered 'undress me.' Slowly he peeled off her dress, bra, garter belt, shoes and stockings, then lifted her off her feet and placed her gently on the bed. As the hours passed, he was intrigued by her imaginative love-making, by the great expertise she displayed, by the variety of her demands, amazed by her instinctive compliance with any unspoken whims of his own and flattered by her screams of delight. Not to put too fine a point on it, Pandora was a four-star, fur-lined, ocean-going expert in the noblest art of all.

The remaining days of Stani's leave passed in a haze of love-making and laughter. Pandora fetched some clothes from the little flat in Chelsea which she shared with her plump girlfriend, and moved in with him, an arrangement greatly approved of by Mrs. Quansett-Fowles. Apart from the time Pandora spent at the theatre, they were inseparable. When he told her that he had fallen in love, she lined up her glorious body alongside his, giving him the full benefit of her satiny skin, and sounded a warning note.

'Don't do that, darling. I'm nothing but trouble. When you know me better you'll find out. I'm not really to be relied on. Let's just enjoy each other while we can. I do have a lovely time with you, but . . . I don't know . . . wartime romances are dangerous, aren't they?'

'*I* don't think so,' said Stani firmly. 'I think things just come into focus quicker when everybody's future is one bloody great question mark. Anyway, I just know that *I've* never been so happy and I want it to go on for ever.' He sighed. 'Do you think it might?'

'It might,' she said slowly. 'Yes, it might. But I've got a lot of things to straighten out first. Things are in quite a shambles really, and I am too.'

'What's this shambles you're in anyway? I thought you told me you weren't involved with anyone special.'

'I'm not, darling, but you may have noticed that I love making love! In fact, I love it so much that sometimes it worries me. I mean I do get involved, and I don't want to hurt anyone, but sometimes I do and I don't want to hurt you because you're special. Also I want to go to Hollywood and be a great big, glamorous movie star! Now, stop talking and let me get on top so I can see your face.'

Stani's next remark was drowned in kisses. Later, they dressed and walked hand in hand to the theatre.

By the time Stani left for Liverpool, he was obsessed by Pandora. On a wet afternoon, she came to see him off, radiant even in the dingy gloom of the terminus, the bloom still on her cheeks from their farewell encounter. When the train took the first bend, his last view of her was obliterated. Miserable, he sank into his corner seat in the unheated compartment.

As the crowded train gathered speed through grimy, glistening North London made more depressing by gaps of destruction in rows of tenements, he hugged the memory of Pandora to himself and tried to face the future with some kind of enthusiasm. It was a brave effort but any relief from his gloom provided by twilight views of the beautiful Buckinghamshire countryside faded rapidly when it was replaced by the darkened, smokey horror of Birmingham, Wolverhampton and Stoke.

He loved her so much and already missed her so desperately, but her strange little warnings unsettled him and he turned over her words again and again. 'I'm nothing but trouble . . . I'm not to be relied upon . . . you'll find out!'

Of *course* she could be relied upon, he'd trust her with his life, but what would he find out? Whatever it was it couldn't be *really* bad . . . he just wished she hadn't said it.

To cheer himself up, he broke his word. He opened a little box from Asprey's, something Pandora had given him and made him promise he would not open until he got into bed.

Nestling in cotton wool he found a thin gold chain, attached to which was a small golden disc. It was inscribed in her

71

handwriting with these words:

He hung it round his neck.

On arrival near midnight at Liverpool, Stani presented his pass to the Railway Transport Officer and was recommended to 'amuse himself for a couple of hours' till a truck that was heading for Speke airfield could be fitted with a new back axle, the original having disintegrated when the machine fell into a bomb crater the night before.

In the early hours of the morning, he reported at a remote, rainswept airfield and fell asleep beneath sheets apparently made of sailcloth and a grey blanket with the texture of a Turkish carpet. The small room he could call his own was indistinguishable from the one he had lately vacated in Scotland but the bleakness of it was relieved by a photograph of Pandora which he set up beside his narrow iron bed.

The weeks of training passed quickly and his companions were congenial; there was less pressure because all were working towards the same technical perfection. There was no schoolboy-type competition to see who would do the best in the final exams and qualify for the elite R.A.F. Fighter Squadrons instead of having to fly Lysander bi-planes with Army Reconnaissance. Furthermore, the pilots in training were mostly professionals from the Fleet Air Arm, with a sprinkling of R.A.F. veterans from the Battle of Britain, and all were unfailingly helpful to the half dozen 'amateurs' among them. Stani, the only foreigner, received much kindness. He found the switchover from the Spitfire with its bird-like silhouette to the more rugged hump-backed Hurricane not too difficult, and his fellows showed him many hard-earned tricks of aerial combat. But the knowledge of where he might be called upon to display those tricks gave him sleepless nights in his narrow iron bed.

Telephonic communication with Pandora was a nightmare of frustration. A four hour delay was normal and, because of the hours of their respective jobs, it was almost impossible to make contact from a switchboard which, except for national emergencies, closed at 9 p.m. However, telegrams and letters finally arrived, chopped to pieces en route by censors on the Isle of Man because of the heavy cloak of secrecy in which Stani now found himself wrapped.

Three times Pandora made the dreary all-night train journey to Liverpool to spend Sundays with him in the Adelphi Hotel. On the first occasion, the fog from the Mersey, mixed with yellow industrial fumes, was so dense even inside the hotel, that they had to grope their way around the cavernous lobby to find the receptionist and sign in. With much giggling, they registered as 'Pilot Officer and Mrs. Quansett-Fowles'.

The second visit by Pandora coincided with a full moon and, consequently, with an all-out air raid on the port, a prime target, the receiving end of the life-line between the New World and the Old, the point of arrival for hope-giving convoys of food, fuel and steel. As they had on the first occasion, Pandora and Stani ignored the war and made almost continuous love in a Victorian suite of dark red, over-stuffed horror, with only occasional breaks for food and drink.

'The night of the Grand National!' said Pandora softly during a period of battery recharging.

'What about it?'

'Wonderful! Every year we'd come here, parties in all these dreadful rooms, champagne everywhere and no doors locked!'

'Who's *we*?' Stani enquired.

'Mind your own business,' she giggled. 'I'm not asking what you did before. Let's just enjoy ourselves and each other. Are you happy?'

'Totally,' said Stani. 'I love you – in case I haven't made it quite clear.'

She sealed his lips with a kiss. 'Shss! Let's just enjoy each other,' she whispered and moved her long, lovely body against his. Their love-making had become so perfect, so wonderfully orchestrated that it amazed them both.

'I can't believe it,' Pandora murmured. 'There's never been anyone like you!'

Then she said, 'I have some bad news for you, my darling. Not bad really – but odd.'

'What?' asked Stani, propping himself up on an elbow and

73

staring into her cat's eyes, heavy lidded now with total relaxation.

'My father is an Earl!' Pandora announced.

'Well tell him not to bother about it, and also tell him I am obscenely in love with his daughter. What does that make you, by the way. A Marquesa?'

'I'm a Lady.'

'Lady Bryce?'

'Lady Pandora Bryce, *if* you please!'

Stani pondered this.

'Would it be all right if I made an indecent suggestion to Lady Pandora Bryce?'

'Not *again!*' Pandora giggled happily.

Later he asked for more information about her family.

'Does that title of yours get in the way of your acting career?'

'It certainly would have before the war because of all the gossip columns and Society papers,' said Pandora. 'I'd have been made to look stuck up and a fool. I don't think I would have been accepted at all. But now it's different, nobody knows or cares. I hate the word but there is no such thing as Class any more; everyone in this country is in the same boat, we're all subject to the same 'call-up' for National Service, up to sixty-five for men and fifty for women. Same ration books, petrol coupons, clothing coupons, same bombs and bus queues, same enemy. It's really very healthy! Of course my father is happy that nobody bothers about my being an actress, he'd hate to have his name in the papers.'

'Bryce?'

'No – Hawksmoor.'

'I though you said that was the name of your father's house.'

'Yes I did. Well, the house is named after him, or the family was named after the house, I forget which. Anyway it's all too complicated.' Pandora paused. 'Will you promise me something?'

'Anything.'

'When you get your next leave – spend it with me, all of it. And I'll take you to Hawksmoor – you'll love it and you'll love Daddy too; he's fallen on his head so often out hunting that he's a little peculiar sometimes but I adore him. Will you come?'

'Of course,' said Stani. 'Now, will you promise *me* something?'

'Ask me.'

'Marry me.'

Pandora hugged Stani, then pushed him away and looked right into his face.

'I adore you,' she said. 'You know I do. I could easily be in love with you, but I don't *know* yet. Another thing, I believe we can all be in love several times in our lives. I've thought I've been in love three times already, but each time it turned out to be sex and nothing else, so each time it fell apart. Because when the sex side of it gets less important, and God knows you and I can't keep *this* up for ever – there has to be something pretty damn good to fall back on. Don't you agree?'

'I love you,' said Stani, 'and don't you forget it.'

The occasion of the third visit was a one-sided affair. Pandora arrived but Stani did not meet her at the staion. At the Adelphi the elderly receptionist shook his head.

'Mrs Quansett-Fowles,' he said, 'your husband left suddenly last night. He tried to stop you coming but we couldn't get through. He seemed very upset.'

While Pandora spent a lonely day in the almost-empty hotel, Stani was enduring slithering discomfort in an aluminium bucket seat in a converted four-engined bomber. It, too, was almost empty except for some men wearing Homburg hats and huddled in dark overcoats against the numbing cold, they looked like spies, or politicians. The plane was headed for a remote airfield in Eastern Canada.

5

The voyage from Halifax, Nova Scotia, back to Liverpool had, so far, been memorable only for boredom and bad food. Now, it was half completed. It was the day after Stani's twentieth birthday and he was shaking like a leaf.

Although he had celebrated the night before with an overdose of rum, it was not the hangover that made his tongue stick to the roof of his mouth, nor was it the cause of his sweating profusely, on a freezing February morning. The reason was fear – pure, unadulterated terror.

'The scourge of the Atlantic', Winston Churchill had called the giant four-engined Fokker-Wolf Condors. In the past four months, they had sunk a hundred and thirty British merchant ships. They had also directed wolf packs of submarines toward the lumbering, sparsely protected and desperately needed convoys, more than two million tons of which had been torpedoed in the same short period. So it was decided that the Condors, prowling the North Atlantic at will from their French lair at Bordeaux-Merignac, with a range of two thousand miles, had, somehow, to be eliminated.

Necessity may be the mother of invention but she has also, on occasion, given birth to some exotic solutions to current problems. So it was not long before the Admiralty came up with the idea of erecting catapults on the forecastle heads of selected merchant ships and projecting, with rockets, fighter aircraft into the mid-Atlantic sky. Each convoy, they reasoned, would thus be provided with its own private Hurricane, to make up for the absence of an escorting aircraft carrier, and to gloss over the fact that the merchant ships' only armament against aerial attack were World War I Lewis and Vickers Mark IV machine guns, antique fowling pieces, of minimal effectiveness.

76

Stani, aboard *Mersey Marigold*, an eleven thousand ton grain carrier, was being strapped into his Hurricane by a solicitous R.A.F. rigger, while a naval torpedo man fiddled about making last minute adjustments to a cluster of thirteen rockets which, they hoped, would propel him down a seventy foot rail with sufficient speed to be airborne by the time he came to the end of it.

If two or more rockets in the cluster failed, Stani knew that he would 'woosh' over the nose of the ship and die, horribly, in her churning propellers. If all went well (and he was superstitious enough to wish that there could have been twelve or fourteen rockets) he would soon be in mortal and lonely combat with a giant Condor, armed with three 7.9 machine guns and two 20 millimetre cannon. If by any lucky chance he should survive that St. George and the Dragon confrontation, his future prospects were equally unattractive, the convoy was still six hundred miles from land, far beyond the range of the Hurricane, and he knew that he would have only two choices: to risk ditching his plane in big swells close to a ship, or go to the head of the convoy, wag his wings to attract attention, climb to three thousand feet, bale out, inflate his rubber dinghy and pray. He wished with all his heart that he had not been so intent on avoiding his courageous Polish countrymen.

The Hurricane, perched on its trolley, had been exposed for the past five days to a constant buffeting and soaking in foul weather. A slippery rime of salt had attached itself to its skin and God alone knew how much rust was inside the gun barrels, nor what corrosion might be in the firing circuits, plugs, contact breakers or engine mags – in the whole electrical system, in fact; even the trolley wheels were suspect. There had been little time to check because the sea had suddenly subsided, the sky had partially cleared and a greenish-grey Condor had been reported skulking about on the horizon, shadowing the convoy of forty-nine merchant ships wallowing along at the speed of the slowest – seven knots. Spread over many square miles, protected by only three destroyers and two corvettes, it represented a family of sitting ducks for the bombs of the Condor or the torpedoes of packs of submarines which, with their superior speed, the bomber could easily summon to lurk in the depths ahead.

In a daze Stani tested the R/T link with the fighter direction officer, swung the rudder back and forth, waggled the stick, looked at the ailerons, switched on petrol, checked oxygen, gun firing button and sights, and when the nervous torpedo man signalled that the rocket cluster was ready to ignite, he started his engine. The Rolls Royce Merlin roared into life. The locking pins were removed from the front of the trolley, the catapult directing officer made sure that the flight path was clear and that everyone was under cover in the blast shelter; then he signalled the Captain on the bridge that all was ready for launching.

Stani looked down that tiny little runway, dimly registered with a ghastly lurch of his stomach that the end of it was rising and falling about twenty feet with the swells, prayed that the people responsible for his departure would improve his chances of survival at least by pointing him up instead of down, and fumbled desperately to touch Pandora's little gold disc. The catapult directing officer raised a blue flag. Like a dog watching a snake, Stani waited for him to rotate it, the signal for him to open his throttle right out, jam himself back against the seat and headrest and wait for the flash and bang of the rockets.

After an eternity, with his muscles tensed like a steel cross bow, there was indeed a flash, but the blue flag was lowered and a red warning one waved frantically instead. He throttled back, delighted at his last minute reprieve; then he saw what had happened. Half a mile away on the starboard quarter, a big tanker, full of high octane gasoline, had been hit and had exploded in a monstrous, billowing ball of flame. A voice crackled inside his headphones – 'Launch delayed to pin-point Condor. We don't want him to see you take off.'

Half a minute later, the blue flag was up again and this time, after another gut-wrenching pause, it was rotated. Stani gave himself maximum revs, locked the throttle, braced himself anew, closed his eyes and clenched his teeth. Nothing happened. He was on the point of opening his emergency panel and refusing to die when someone banged on his canopy with a spanner and he looked up to see the startled face of the torpedo man. He cut the engine, the radio inside his helmet cracked into life again.

'Sorry, Stani, rockets failed to ignite. Looks like a broken circuit or faulty safety link. We're checking. Couple of minutes, no more.'

He had heard that people being hanged at dawn outside Wandsworth Prison were allowed to go free if the rope broke; surely now his executioners would let him off the hook. No such luck. Up went the little blue flag a third time, it was quickly rotated and this time there was a tremendous 'bang' and, with a jerk that practically tore his head off his shoulders, he was sent hurtling towards the sharp end of the ship.

To his surprise, instead of finding himself being chewed to pieces beneath his grain carrier home, he realized he was airborne and climbing gently at about eighty-five miles an hour. He raised his flaps which had been at 30° and teased his Hurricane along, getting the feel of her. He started routinely checking his range and wing span indicators, adjusting propeller control and switching on sights. At fifteen hundred feet, he disappeared into cloud and heard the voice telling him that the Condor was located, with bomb doors open, in position to attack another tanker on the other side of the convoy. At two thousand feet he came out of cloud and below him, about three miles ahead, was the Condor circling menacingly round her next victim, lining up for a lethal low level attack at mast height.

It must have come as a horrible shock to the Condor pilot to see a fighter above his head in the middle of the Atlantic but he was also very alert and he spotted Stani at precisely the same moment that Stani saw him. He turned quickly away, climbing for cloud cover, dropping his dirt harmlessly in the sea as he went. Stani saw three big bombs explode, spouting up great geysers of water, and as the Condor carried seven all told, he guessed that the other four had been responsible for all those poor wretches from the first tanker being blown to pieces or struggling in the flaming water, spewing out their guts and dying with lungs full of oil. The thought of them injected something into Stani's spine. He put his own button on 'fire', pushed the stick forward and dived after the Condor.

His plan was to come up underneath him if possible and fire a long burst from his eight machine guns at the soft under-belly which he had been confidently taught was poorly armoured and housed all the fuel lines.

79

He levelled off about five hundred yards astern and was shocked to realize that the Condor was shooting at him! He had imagined that his Hurricane would be opening the proceedings.

Tracer from the rear gunner was leaving the Condor slowly, almost lazily, seeming to curve harmlessly away. Stani watched it in suspended time, then, alarmingly, it curved inwards much faster, and whipped just past him. The Condor was climbing quickly and presented Stani, for a split second, with just the target he was waiting for; then it disappeared into cloud and he lost it.

Confused instructions as to its whereabouts now poured into his ears so he levelled off at a thousand feet and did a slow turn to starboard, flying blind. He reckoned that he had been moving about a hundred miles an hour faster than the Condor when he entered the cloud so he throttled back and hoped to see him again on the other side of it. The German pilot must have made some very sophisticated moves inside that cloud because when Stani emerged from it, the huge four engined machine was coming straight for him.

The forward gunner and Stani both opened up at the same instant and the Hurricane shuddered as Stani squirted off his burst before he kicked over rudder and stick and dived to avoid a head on collision. He just scraped under the wing tip.

A great deal of hide and seek now took place in and out of the clouds and he got in a few ineffective bursts. That Condor had a hell of a pilot! He threw that big machine all over the sky, jinking about like a startled hare, and when he disappeared periodically, Stani never knew at what altitude or going in which direction he would next see him. However, he got in one longish squirt from four hundred yards dead astern, closing to a hundred and fifty, and saw white smoke pour out of one engine. As he climbed away to starboard, he was pleased with himself, till several holes appeared in his own port wing and there was a loud bang as something went through his canopy.

During training, the great South African fighter ace, 'Sailor' Malan, had repeated again and again, 'Get in fast, hit hard and get out quick.' Stani knew well that his bursts so far had been too long and too tentative and he resolved to give it one more try. More by good luck than anything else, he found himself

80

once more beneath the Condor and sprayed its underside on his way up – his original plan. This time he saw white, dusty-looking puffs as he knocked off chunks of fuselage and one engine cowling flew away as the big bomber disappeared into cloud. Stani entered the cloud and hoped he would not see the bomber again; after all, it was harmless now, its bombs had been jettisoned. So, in a way, he had done what he was supposed to do – he had neutralized it; but coming out of cloud, he spotted it once more. The white smoke from the damaged engine had changed to a dirty black and the plane was trailing a lot of muck behind but it was still flying strongly and still looked extremely menacing. He climbed away and entered another cloud.

The whole action had lasted only a few minutes but now, for the first time, Stani realized with crystal clarity what he had been doing and longed to be far away. He started to shake and his teeth chattered. For the first time since he had flashed into the air, real fear was taking the place of reflex actions mixed with a sort of lunatic excitement and he wanted no further part of the desperate game in which he had become involved. He could not have much ammunition left anyway so all he had to do was follow the routine as laid down – find the convoy, make sure they saw him, then bale out ahead of one of the escorts. His stomach was in mid-lurch at the thought of the impending bale-out when, much sooner than expected, he shot into a big, clear patch of sky and there below him, in perfect position for a beam attack, was the Condor.

In one last uncontrollable reflex action, he found himself diving and opening fire from maximum range and full deflection, with the pale sun behind him. Closing to a hundred yards, he emptied everything he had into the Condor. Tracer from all eight guns slapped into it, then there was a hiss of compressed air as he ran out of the stuff. For several seconds all seemed normal aboard the bomber, then everything happened at once. First a dull glow inside the fuselage and a muffled explosion, then a second engine burst into flames. The hydraulic system must have gone too because the wheels came down and the bomb doors opened. Then the whole tail section just fell off. Stani climbed away, watching with a mixture of amazement and horror the havoc he had wrought. Then he remembered

81

that he had so far made no report to the fighter directing officer and, almost in disbelief, he said into his mouthpiece, 'I've got him . . . he's going down!' But even as the great plane was turning slowly over on its back, someone, probably the cannon gunner in the gondola on the underside, was still firing at him. There was an explosion and Stani's instrument panel disintegrated in front of him. Then his right foot was nearly knocked into his mouth. It felt as though it had been hit by a sledge hammer. Black smoke poured into the cockpit, glycol and hot oil slammed into his face. He tried to wipe his goggles and started to retch. It got very hot and there was a smell of burning rubber; no flames yet but they had to come and, with the coolant gone, it was only a matter of seconds before the engine would seize up solid. So, with leaden controls, he climbed while the propeller was still turning.

Many pilots remember exactly what happens in emergencies. Stani had but the haziest recollection of much of what went on but he must have gone through the correct motions of ripping off his helmet, pulling the pin out of his straps and yanking out the W/T plug. Later he remembered that the aircraft had seemed to hang quite steady for a long time before he realized it was flipping over and over on its way down. Vividly he remembered trying to open the canopy but it was stuck firm and would not budge. He was sobbing and shouting as he struggled with the emergency panel but that too refused to open. Flames now were darting into the cockpit. He received a hammer blow of searing pain on the right side of his face and, with the superhuman strength of terror, he tugged again, desperately, at the handles. The canopy came away unexpectedly and with the Hurricane plummeting straight down in a screaming dive through cloud, he pulled himself out. But the force of the wind was so great that he was trapped half in, half out. Struggling, kicking and fighting, he got free, tumbling end over end and fumbling frantically for the ring of the rip cord. The parachute opened with a jerk that nearly castrated him and he found himself swaying gently down just below the cloud base. There was no sign of the Condor, nor of his Hurricane and none of the convoy. The wind must have freshened because the black sea, a thousand feet below him, was ominously streaked with grey. He inflated his Mae West and put frantic hands on his harness release.

The cold water and the impact together took his breath away and his parachute, filling in the stiff breeze, towed him for a while, turning him over and over like a mackerel spinner till the release worked and he got free of it.

He inflated his dinghy from the CO_2 bottle on his Mae West and tried to get into it. In training he had practised this a couple of times in a swimming pool in swimming trunks and even that had been difficult. Now, in sodden flying jacket and fleece-lined boots, and with apparently only one serviceable arm, it seemed impossible but, somehow, he struggled into his little coracle and lay gasping and blubbering, face down, in six inches of water, blood and vomit.

Somewhere along the line, he had wrenched his left shoulder half out of his body but it was the pain in his right foot which first bored into his brain. He struggled to get his boot off and discovered that his big toe and much of the ball of his foot were missing. In shock, he gazed at the gaping hole; pieces of wool and leather were embedded in it. Then he realized that the right side of his face and down over the jaw had no feeling. He touched it. Blood and shards of flesh came away on his fingers and he knew he had also been burned. Then he blacked out.

When he came to, he looked at his watch; it was less than half an hour since he had been blasted off the *Mersey Marigold*. With difficulty, he opened the small first aid pack and stuffed the dressing into the hole in his foot. Then he removed the silk scarf from his neck and twisted it around just above the ankle as tight as he could and propped the leg up on the side of the dinghy. He didn't dare touch his face.

Just before the voyage, he had packed his own parachute and dinghy so he knew where to find the dressing. He also found a pint of brandy – he had forgotten about that. It was in the canvas bailer. His idea in putting it there had been to amuse the riggers with false bravado. He'd said, 'If ever I have to die on this job – I intend to die pissed.' The riggers had laughed and given him the thumbs up.

Now, he baled out the little oblong dinghy and settled down to wait. He had no idea where the convoy was – somewhere to the south he judged, but how far away he couldn't guess; he might easily have travelled sixty or seventy miles away from it

83

during his battle with the Condor, but he had been too busy to look at his compass and give a fix. Also, at that range, the chances that they could have followed his course on the R.D.F. were slim. His foot and now his face hurt terribly.

Visibility was getting worse and it was freezing cold, but mercifully the sea did not seem to be kicking up too much, though the wind was fresh. There was a ridiculous little sail in the dinghy which he hoisted, not that he thought that he would soon be skimming along eating up the six hundred miles to Western Ireland – he just decided that if anyone came looking for him, the sail might make him easier to see. It was a faint hope indeed but it buoyed him up during the remainder of that first awful day, and his eyes nearly fell out of his head straining to see a destroyer or a corvette. Nothing appeared and when darkness fell, he covered himself with the sail for protection.

The pain from his foot seemed to be spreading up his leg. He loosened the scarf because the leg was swelling and his wrenched shoulder sent electric shocks all over him when he moved. He shivered constantly and uncontrollably.

During the night the wind came up and the sea got worse. The dinghy slid up and down the waves and he hung on desperately, expecting it to turn over when white combers came hissing past in the darkness. He was very frightened and prayed a great deal.

During the night, three or four ships passed quite close. No lights were showing, of course, but he could hear the hum of their engines and the steady beat of their propellers. He yelled till he thought his lungs would burst and beat impotent hands on the sides of the rubber boat but their heartening sounds slowly faded away and as dawn slowly changed the black of night to ghostly grey, there was not a hull, a funnel or a mast in sight. He realized that although he had fallen ahead of the convoy, they had passed him in the darkness. He cried then, like a child.

By mid-morning, he was so thirsty and his foot and leg throbbed so unbearably, the salt on his face was such a torture, that he didn't think he could hang on. The wind was still strong and he was soaked with spray. He baled again, as he was sitting in water and blood; even the skin of his good leg was turning white and puckered. His hands looked greenish.

84

By early afternoon, he knew it would not be long before he drank some sea water in desperation, but he forced himself to remember the warnings of the survival expert who had lectured him during training. The man had probably survived nothing more dangerous than crossing Piccadilly Circus, but 'Never!' he had thundered, 'Never drink even a cup of sea water however strong the urge. If you do, your kidneys will take water from your body to flush away the salt and, in an hour, you will drink twice as much to replenish that, and so on till you die most unpleasantly.'

The icy wind blew through the zipper of Stani's flying jacket and he could not get into a comfortable position. He had cramp in his upper legs and back. He hurt all over.

From time to time, he lapsed into unconsciousness and once, when he came to, it was raining hard. He caught a little rain water in the sail and drank it down greedily but the sail was so impregnated with salt that, within an hour, he was more thirsty than before. Then the sea turned choppy with a different motion and he was sick, though nothing much came up.

After the rain came snow flurries and he lay with open mouth, hopeful of catching the flakes. He was cold, so dreadfully cold. Ice formed inside the dinghy. And now he could smell his foot.

By evening, Stani was floating in a sea of pain. He tried to bale again but could no longer manage it. He didn't really care much any more. He opened the pint of brandy and drank it; then he lay down in the water, blood and bile. He hardly felt the pain, or anything, now. He was barely conscious of his body. He stared up at the grey, scudding clouds and didn't even pray. In a mist and far away, he had a vision of the survival expert: 'One survivor,' the instructor said, 'saw an albatross sitting on the sea and when he saw it was drinking the water, he thought, ah! so can I, if I just find out how that bird filters out the salt; so he shot it with his revolver, pulled it to pieces and found it had a big padding of fat around its intestine, so he ate the fat, drank the sea water and survived for days.'

As night approached, Stani was having difficulty breathing but now he didn't feel the cold. The sky above changed colour and he watched the leaden grey give way to a colour he had never seen before – the sort of colour you never see in any shop window. He saw his mother and his father too, and Pandora and Mrs. Quansett-Fowles and Captain Rainbird. Then he saw the swan. The swan from the Lauriston marshes.

It was flying very high, its neck undulated and its wings made a squeaky noise. It circled lower and lower and he strained up to watch it. The swan landed right beside the dinghy. It hissed with rage, fluffed up its feathers and paddled aggressively towards him just as it had on the pond behind Captain Rainbird's cottage. Then the swan drank some water. He decided to kill it, eat the fat from round its intestine and drink some water too. He didn't have a revolver so he tried to kill it with the paddle. He struggled to a sitting position and flailed away at the bird with the last of his strength. Then he collapsed.

When Stani awoke, he was between cool white sheets. The Surgeon Lieutenant-Commander made sure he was being understood before he spoke.

'Well, young man,' he said, 'we've cleaned up your foot for you, your arm is back where it belongs and as soon as we get home, we'll get that plastic genius down in Sussex to give you a new face. You'll be as good as new.'

Stani tried to answer but realized that, except for his eyes, his face was swathed in bandages, so he weakly gave a 'thumbs up' with the one arm he could move.

'We were lucky to find you,' the naval doctor continued. 'We'd spent a long time looking for survivors from that tanker that went up – only a handful of the poor devils I'm afraid – then the Commodore gave us a spot about twenty miles west of where we found you where he thought you'd gone in. We looked for you for a couple of hours and had given up. The skipper had his foot right on the accelerator of this old basket to catch up with the convoy when the lookout spotted your little houseboat just before it got dark. The cox'un of the whaler that went to pick you up reported you nearly took his head off with a paddle.' The doctor smiled down on his patient. 'And perhaps you will explain to me one day how you managed to get as drunk as a skunk in mid-Atlantic in mid-February! Congratulations on knocking off the Condor, young fellow – that was a great piece of work – now go back to sleep. We'll look after you.'

As soon as the destroyer docked in Liverpool, Stani was transferred to a hospital where his mangled foot was given more specialized attention and the tannic acid which the Royal Navy had spread upon the burned areas of his face was looked at with some reserve. Designed to keep out the air, it had coagulated into a black crust with the consistency of tarmac and he was in considerable pain. The hospital telephoned Sussex for instructions and the great man there ordained that, with the greatest of care, it should be instantly removed as there was a very real danger of septicaemia beneath it and almost certainly they would find some exposed nerves. Saline compresses, he said, would be extremely painful but must be applied constantly until the patient could be moved south. Stani did not get a very clear picture of all this activity because aside from the morphia being pumped into him the well-meaning doctor in charge was prone to hearty anecdotes designed to keep up his morale and distract him from the agony of his dressings being changed.

'Gilles, the Army plastic man at Rooksdown,' the doctor said, 'had a case rather like yours – a soldier who'd trodden on a land mine. Wound up with a lot of his foot missing and part of his face gone too. Well, cleaning up the face, Gilles found the man's big toe – it was wedged in a hole in his jaw! Quite a shock for the old boy!'

The Wing Commander from his special unit at Speke visited him. He was kind and worried and told Stani that he had been awarded the Distinguished Flying Cross for conspicuous gallantry. He asked him how he could contact Stani's family but Stani said he didn't have one; he had decided he did not want Pandora to see him until he had seen himself.

In the Sussex hospital, he spent some weeks with his leg in a sort of tray, his head in a vice and his jaw clamped open, but the famous surgeon was a man of infinite charm, patience and encouragement and, indeed, when Stani came to know and was able to see the others in his ward (horribly disfigured pilots, burnt tank men and mutilated sailors) he realized how lucky he had been; and marvelled at his fellow patients' heartbreaking courage and determined gaiety. The foot required much time and many complicated operations but despite the fact that the two biggest toes on it and a large part of the ball had been blown away, he was given, by a miracle of grafting, something

87

upon which, in time, he would be able to put a shoe and to walk. The right side of his face, from cheek bone to jaw, was completely remade from a jigsaw of strips taken from the inside of his arms and legs. He had, indeed, been incredibly lucky, although nerves had been exposed and pain was his constant companion. His eyes, eyelids, nose and lips had escaped that awful tongue of flame so, compared to his companions, his disfigurement was minimal. 'Just a few honourable scars,' the super-surgeon had promised, 'which you can certainly wear with pride. But I'm afraid you'll have to wait till the war with Mars before they let you fly a plane again – the muscles and nerves of that foot won't be able to cope.'

Luckily Stani's face had been covered with gauze when he was given this news, because there was no way he could have controlled it sufficiently to hide his delight and relief.

He lay for weeks, being injected with drugs to ease pain, ward off infections or combat constipation; he was prepared for operations, suffered the torture of dressing changes and the indignities of bed baths and bed pans. As all this went on he decided that he had made his total contribution to the history of human conflict – no one would ever persuade him to take up arms again.

A whisky magnate of high financial and political proof owned a large Tudor-style country house in central Sussex and the major part of it had been turned into a convalescent home. A bed there was greatly coveted by those recovering from surgery. The place was extremely comfortable, beautifully run and the surrounding countryside was picture-postcard England. The wise genius of the hospital also used it as a mental rehabilitation centre for his disfigured patients; he encouraged them to walk the fields and lanes and enjoy themselves in the pubs, shops and cafes of the villages. Showing themselves in public for the first time could be a traumatic experience for the dreadfully disfigured, as the doctor well knew, but the grateful villagers soon became accustomed to the sight of appalling mutilation and saved the sanity of many a tortured young man with their earthy friendliness and common sense. The whisky magnate inhabited one wing of his sprawling mansion and every weekend the patients caught sight of a variety of beautiful or interesting guests. Carefully chosen because on Sunday mornings, after suitable briefing in how to eliminate shock, horror and, worst of all, pity from their faces, they were taken on a conducted tour of the convalescent wards so that the patients might have a chance to see them – the big noises conducting the war, or writers, painters, sportsmen, film stars and a selection of beautiful girls.

On one such Sunday morning, Stani was lying in bed. He had recently arrived from the hospital where the final grafts on his face had been completed. In a few days he would be taking the first tentative steps on his remodelled foot. He was suffering considerable pain in his missing toes, which he though grossly unfair, and the expanse of underarm which had provided the grafts also hurt a great deal. Apart from his eyes and mouth, his face was still swathed in bandages. Like Provençal wine, Stani did not travel well and the twenty mile trip from the hospital had left him cantankerous and lonely, like a new boy at school. The sister made her rounds, smoothing sheets, fluffing up pillows and sprucing her patients for the forthcoming inspection by the magnate's guests. Through the slits in his mask, he recognized from the newspapers a Field Marshal, a Cabinet Minister, a scientist who had invented Radar, an American movie actor in U.S. Navy uniform, and a Bishop. All paused at the foot of his bed, smiled encouragement and, seeing his mouth uncovered, asked how he felt. He felt awful but responded routinely with a thumbs up sign which appeased them and they moved to the next bed. Younger and less important members of the magnate's house party then followed but his interest had waned and he closed his eyes to save himself from being spoken to.

Perhaps he sensed the stirrings of increased interest among his fellow patients but, for some reason, he opened his eyes again just in time to see a gorgeous female form moving away from his bed. He caught a glimpse of maybe a quarter of her profile and blurted out her name – 'Pandora!' She turned in surprise and all eyes zeroed in on his bed.

Pandora glanced quickly at the temperature chart at the foot of the bed, hoping for a clue, but only got an impression of a long name followed by D.F.C. – it meant nothing. 'I'm dreadfully sorry,' she said with her lovely smile, 'I'm afraid I can't see who it is.'

89

The ward was now riveted with interest, so Stani whispered, 'Please come closer,' and showed her the little gold disc on the end of a chain.

'Oh my God!' Pandora cried, and one hand flew towards her mouth. 'What's happened to you?'

Well aware of the flapping ears in a suddenly quiet room, Stani underplayed his R.A.F. role in true movie star style.

'Had a little contretemps with some German gentlemen in their flying machine,' he said. 'They didn't seem to appreciate what I was trying to do to them so they put a match to mine, fried some of my face in the process and knocked off a piece of my foot.'

Pandora sat down on the edge of his bed and her eyes filled with tears. She took his hand in hers. 'Is it *very* bad?'

'No,' he answered, so low that only she could hear. 'Compared to most people here, it's nothing at all. All working parts are intact and I'll soon be able to walk. I'll probably limp, though,' he added.

They remained hand in hand and silent for many minutes; Stani was afraid that if he didn't say something soon she might float away like a butterfly.

'What's the party like over at the booze baron's?' he asked, and it sounded as superficial as her answer.

'The sort of people I normally avoid. But the beds are comfy; he still has good food and there are no bombs.' Another long pause followed. Then Pandora broke down. She kissed his bandaged forehead and laid her cheek gently against his bandaged face. Her tears flowed unchecked.

'I couldn't find out where you'd gone. I was miserable when I didn't hear from you'.

When she was calmer they talked low, trying to fill in the gaps since their last meeting in a foggy Liverpool hotel. Stani, acutely aware of the listening ears, gave sparse details of his exploits and Pandora, equally inhibited, mentioned that she had played in a cheap film about four girls of a Searchlight battery stationed in the docks.

'. . . a real quickie, total nonsense with everybody with not a hair out of place biting on the bullet and being madly brave, with bombs and bombers raining down everywhere. I just hope it never gets shown!' They were holding hands, totally engros-

90

sed in each other, when the Matron came over and said kindly, 'The others have gone across to the owner's wing but I'm sure the patients in the last ward would love a visit from you too if you have time.'

Pandora kissed his hand, looked at him with her huge grey eyes and said, 'Thank God I've found you.'

He watched her divine figure as she moved between the beds, pausing for a word at each and dazzling the occupants with her smile. At the door she turned and blew him a kiss. A mummified form in the next bed stirred. The terribly burnt tank commander back from the Libyan desert had lain motionless and silent most of the day with the pink, claw-like fingers of his two remodelled hands pointing towards the ceiling. Beneath his bandages were four new eyelids, a new nose and new lips. The metal of his goggles had melted into his forehead and cheek bones. Altogether he had been through more than two dozen operations.

'You lucky bastard', he chuckled. 'Is she as beautiful as she sounds?'

Stani's repairs took a long time; there had been nasty setbacks due to a painful staphylococcus infection of the skin grafts below his jaw line, and a grave danger of it spreading to those above and the physiotherapy on his leg seemed endless. Pandora, at her insistence, had several times been invited by the whisky magnate so she could visit him, and if her appearances in the wards were looked forward to by one and all, they were interludes of pure magic but of almost painful frustration for Stani.

On a quiet December day, the wards had been galvanized by the news that the Japanese had attacked Pearl Harbour and the maimed and mutilated young men who lay and listened knew that the United States, the most powerful ally their lonely nation could wish for, would now be standing at their side and, pray God, it would not be too late.

Towards the end of his stay, information of a more personal kind was brought to Stani by Colonel Zamowski, the Intelligence Officer friend of his father who had vetted his original entry into the Polish Forces. The Colonel and Stani walked

91

slowly about the gardens on a wet and windy afternoon and, sheltered from a shower in a hot muggy greenhouse, the Pole at last felt able to tell him the news. Confirmation from agents and refugees, he said, was unanimous – fifteen to twenty thousand Polish Officers, virtually the entire officer corps, had been taken prisoner in the first wave of the treacherous Russian invasion: they had been herded into a forest near Smolensk and slaughtered.

'We have heard what happened to your mother, my son,' said the Colonel, staring straight ahead and polishing an eyeglass. 'I am afraid there is little hope for your father, for Vladimir . . . I don't know how to comfort you.'

Stani, once again, shocked out of any reaction, said the first thing that came into his head.

'The only picture I have of him is in a box in California!'

'These reports are, unfortunately, very reliable,' the distinguished officer said. Then he put an arm awkwardly round Stani's shoulders, hunched his cloak over his own and they went out into the rain.

That night, when the main lights were turned out in the ward, Stani lay on his back, thinking of his father and of the last time he had seen him. His mother and father were still married, and his mother had rented a small house in Porto Ercole for Stani's summer vacation. But then she had dashed off on a trip to Deauville, and he had been surprised and delighted when he opened a telegram from his father which would have tested the decoding abilities of Mata Hari.

COME HAT OUNCE STOP HAVE SELLING BOAT
GREEK EYELIDS SEX WEEKS TELEGRAM EMBASSY
LOVE
        FARTER

A vintage tri-motor aircraft bore him from Rome to the Greek capital. The plane was neither sound-proofed nor heated and the stewardess, an elderly lady with a heavy cavalry moustache, crossed herself constantly while keeping the half dozen passengers topped up with 'espresso' from a giant thermos. She wore a thick blue overcoat.

In the golden evening light, the plane had flown over Athens, narrowly missed the Acropolis, skirted some hills and bounced

92

to a stop like a kangaroo.

Stani had not seen his father for three months and he took in with pleasure all that he saw. His forty-five year old body, well over six feet, was strong and straight. Thick hair was brushed straight back; the face, deeply tanned, was broad of forehead and square of jaw. The eyes the same green as Stani's own.

Memories of the days aboard *Symphonie* flooded in upon him and the pain-wracked ward filled with misty blue islands floating like clouds at dawn between sky and sea. He saw his father expertly executing slow, solemn dances at a village wedding on Siphos and remembered the boundless hospitality wherever they went. So hospitable had been the people of Pharos that in an olive grove with a mountain of pure white marble gleaming above him, Stani, aged fifteen, had lost his virginity to a sloe-eyed beauty of the same age as himself but light years ahead in experience.

How he had loved it! What fun it had been to share the golden days with his father. Stani had never before seen him so happy, so free from Embassy cares.

He turned in his lonely bed, stared at the dim ceiling and thought of a little white church high atop the fishing island of Skyros where Achilles (in drag for some reason) had been hidden by his mother. There he had noticed among the contributions from fishermen rescued from the sea below, a beautiful little silver boat with broken rudder and oars. Impaled in her side had been a marvellously worked silver swordfish. The village priest told them that, some hundreds of years before, the owner had been saved from a watery grave when his boat had been cast upon a rock. A passing swordfish, noticing his plight, had generously rammed its sword into the hole and plugged the leak. When his father had translated this piece of local lore, Stani had not actually laughed, but he had smiled in disbelief. His father told him, a trifle tartly, not to be too sure that miracles never happened.

'Don't worry, my son,' said the priest, speaking for the first time in English with a strong American accent. 'Young people often find it difficult to believe that particular miracle. But the sea is very mysterious and very close to God.' He had laughed at their surprised expressions. 'I lived and served our Lord for thirty years in Brooklyn, now I have come home to my beloved

Skyros to end my days. But I am very anxious about one thing – is there any truth in the terrible rumour that the Dodgers may be moving to Los Angeles?'

When the Meltemi wind put its mind to it, the ferocious Mistral of the Mediterranean seemed a gentle zephyr by comparison.

For three days in the Gulf of Corinth they sheltered from it in the lee of an island with the waves passing on either side like a giant mill race. The sky was an angry purple and the barometer remained alarmingly low. Then, as unexpectedly as it had struck, the wind dropped and sea and sky resumed their normal benign colours. When *Symphonie* re-set course for the Corinth Canal on the last leg of her journey the foaming combers had disappeared but the waves were still formidable.

It was then that Stani had spotted the fishing skiff. A man was kneeling in it head down, his chin upon his chest. Not until *Symphonie* was almost alongside did he look up, then he stared in disbelief and crossed himself.

Later, in the cabin, he had spoken slowly. 'I should have known the signs. I am very ashamed. I thought I could pick up my traps before the storm came. Then it blew me out into the Gulf. For three days and nights I have been fighting to keep from sinking, baling all the time. I had not eaten . . . I had no water. When you came to me I was finished . . . I had given up. I had no more strength to fight . . . I was praying to the Father to save me, to send me a miracle.' he paused, looked round the circle of faces and said simply, 'Yachts never come to these islands . . . He heard my prayers.'

Stani's father had smiled and whispered, 'The silver swordfish.'

Symphonie's last stop before tying up in Piraeus had been the tiny uninhabited island of Delos, the birthplace of the god Apollo.

To enjoy the sunset, they had toiled up to the summit of Mount Cynthus. The evening breeze was heavy with wild thyme and, at all points of the compass, misty and mysterious, lay the Islands of the Cyclades. It was a breathtaking sight and neither said a word till they had completed their descent. Stani sensed that his father was setting the scene for a disclosure of some import. In silence, he led the way through the eerie

94

remains of the streets of Apollo's Temple, the white marble 'Lions of the Naxians' crouched upon their pedestals and the crickets in the prickly grass had grown silent as they passed. Seated on a crumbling wall between the ghostly pillars of Cleopatra's house and facing the headless figure of the late owner, Stani's father spoke with great sadness.

'Your mother has asked me for a divorce. My poor Stani, I am heartbroken for you. I love you both very much.'

There had been a long silence. Twenty yards away little waves rustled against the shoreline and a gentle breeze swayed the long, dry grasses between the columns of Cleopatra's house. Stani had never felt so desolate. And now in the darkness, surrounded by young men who had sacrificed their limbs and their looks for Freedom, he wept soundlessly for his parents who had given all. The salt tears ran from the corners of his eyes and seeped into his scars.

6

By the time Stani was released for home convalescence and once more installed in South Audley Street, American service men and women were pouring into Britain, a blood transfusion for every walk of British life, from the beleaguered service chiefs and cabinet ministers to shopkeepers, taxi drivers, hoteliers and publicans, even to the whores shivering on darkened street corners. For Mrs. Quansett-Fowles, their arrival was a special bonanza, and coupled with her joy at Stani's return, her 'Salon' took on a new lease of life. Boundless enthusiasm and renewed confidence swept away old doubts and depressions; food, drink and nylons from the bountiful P.X. redecorated her scene.

On the first night Stani limped into her drawing room, the right side of his face pulled tight, still a multi-coloured patchwork from the numerous skin grafts, he was accompanied by Pandora, and it was then that he first met Major Charles V. Pesnick.

'Chuck', as he immediately introduced himself, pumped Stani's hand while checking over Pandora, and said he was 'on General Spaatz's staff'. As he was subsequently spotted dining in company with that illustrious airman at 'Les Ambassadeurs' (a favourite American haunt in Mayfair) this was possibly true. Some of his other claims proved more suspect, but he was a man of great goodwill and they both liked him immediately. For Stani it was a joy to be exposed once more to the cut and thrust of American idiom and humour and, as Chuck unveiled his pre-war activities, there were tantalizing glimpses for Pandora of the very world of which she longed to be part. Chuck had worked for many years, as he put it, 'on the publicity side of Hollywood'.

A man of boundless enthusiasm, he exuded confidence, and

sprinkled big names around like rice at a wedding ('Winston' and 'Ike' among them).

Stani, when he was cross-examined about what his future with the R.A.F. might be, mentioned the possibility of becoming an Air Traffic Controller. Chuck pursed his lips and shook his head.

'That'll never do,' he said firmly. 'Leave it with me.'

Ten days later, Stani, Pandora and Chuck gathered once more in Mrs. Quansett-Fowles' drawing room, the cocktail hour was at hand. They watched as the American unloaded gin, Hershey bars, cans of tuna fish, Lucky Strikes, nylons and a ham from the depths of his duffle bag.

'You're going into Public Relations', he told Stani. 'That's my racket and that's where you belong right now.'

Stani asked for clarification.

'Look. You're a good-looking sonofabitch. 'You've got a Distinguished Flying Cross, scars on your face and half a foot. What more d'you need? There's an organization in the States called 'Bundles for Britain'. It's run by Churches, charities and groups of Anglophiles, they're all over the U.S. They give dinners, dances, lunches and so on to raise money to send food and clothes over here. It's all strictly on the level. The way I see it, you could be a big help, standing up there, getting the word out. In a few weeks you'd raise an extra coupla million bucks.'

'What would I *say*?' Stani asked.

'Just tell 'em how rough things are over here,' said Chuck, refilling his goblet.

'I've got plans for Pandora too,' he added, and later over dinner at Les Ambassadeurs he uncorked them as well.

'That little movie you made about women at war. . . you know – where you were the girl in the searchlight battery who'd lost her boy-friend in the Battle of Britain –.'

Pandora gasped, 'I didn't know it had been shown yet. Where did you see it?'

'They ran it last week for the Trade,' Chuck replied. 'I took a peek at it because Mike Greenberg's coming over soon and he had his company put up half the dough for it.'

Pandora sat up. 'Mike Greenberg? *The* Mike Greenberg of Metropolis?' she asked.

'Mike *is* Metropolis,' said Chuck, a trifle defensively, 'and what's more he's right up there these days with Zanuck, Mayer and Sam Goldwyn.'

Pandora tried to sound offhand. 'What's he coming over here for?'

'Mike Greenberg,' said Chuck, 'is a Lieutenant-Colonel in the United States Army and he's coming over here . . . er . . . in the line of duty.'

Stani glanced round the long, rectangular room. The restaurant was packed. Ninety per cent of the men were Americans, lean, tough-looking paratroopers, air corps Generals, crew-cut youngsters straight out of Annapolis or West Point. Between them they seemed to have attracted the best looking girls in London. The much photographed, paunchy, movie mogul, Mike Greenberg, would look somewhat out of place here, thought Stani. Colonel of *what*, he wondered.

Their host too was an incongruous figure as a fighting man. Chuck was overweight, pallid of complexion and flat of feet. When dinner was finished, he drank a great deal of cognac, and explained at length that he was directly responsible for the success of the most spectacular films made in Hollywood during the preceding decade.

'I put those pictures over when I worked at Metro, and Paramount,' Chuck said. 'Now I'm selling the U.S. Air Force.'

While he talked, which was non-stop, his eyes were never still. They flicked from table to table; when two Generals walked in, he rose in haste.

'There's 'Tooie' and Mark,' he said. 'Excuse me, I'll be right back.'

The Generals, Spaatz and Clark, looked a trifle bewildered when he accosted them and barely paused in their purposeful march towards their reserved booth, but Chuck was unabashed on his return.

'Most days they're a barrel of laughs, those guys,' he said.

A Hollywood publicity man was a rare cog in the Allied war machine but, impervious to setbacks and unfettered by red tape, Chuck's Hollywood training stood him in good stead when it came to 'getting a little action'. He immediately went into high gear, visiting the 'Bundles for Britain' organization in London, who jumped at the idea of Stani as a fund raiser to tour the United States. Then, armed with a cable of request from the

'Bundles for Britain' head office in New York, he hot-footed it over to Brendan Bracken's office where a contact soon produced an approval signed by the Minister of Information himself. From there on it was a simple matter, with his network of buddies at the American Embassy, to arrange Stani's visa and transportation.

'It's all fixed, kid!' he exulted, forty-eight hours later. 'I talked to a guy at your Air Ministry and everything's okay as far as they're concerned. Here's his name,' he added, pushing across a slip of paper. 'Wing-Commander Clapp – God knows how he ever lived *that* down. But go and see him tomorrow. Also, he said for you to pay a visit to your Polish pal, that General what's his name – Ossobucco, something like that.'

'Colonel Zamowski,' said Stani.

'Yea, I guess that's it. Anyway, you're supposed to cover him from the Polish angle, then as soon as the group in New York have a little tour arranged for you – you're on your way. It'll be for at least a month!'

Stani was stunned by the speed of events though dubious of his qualifications as a fund raiser. Also, he did not fancy being separated from Pandora for a month. But the idea of returning to the country where he felt most at home and the prospect of a few weeks away from blackouts, bombs and, to himself he freely admitted, danger, was highly attractive.

When it came time for Mike Greenberg to arrive, Chuck changed: his self assurance vanished overnight, the wisecracks evaporated and he operated in a haze of anxiety.

'Colonel Greenberg is flying in tomorrow, Stani,' he said one day, 'it might be nice if you came along to meet him, and help.'

'Help with what?'

'Well, he's coming in to the R.A.F. station at Heston and I don't know what facilities they have there – you know for baggage handling and that. And of course he's used to the way they do things in Hollywood, he'll expect a limousine.'

'I don't think there *are* any limousines in England these days. Maybe the U.S. Army could lay on a jeep. Otherwise I'm sure there'll be a truck coming this way.'

'A TRUCK!' Chuck said, aghast. 'You don't get it. The Colonel won't stand for *that*."

It took all of Chuck's ingenuity to solve the Greenberg trans-

99

port problem. In the end a small Hillman Minx delivery van was promised by John Mills, the owner of Les Ambassadeurs.

'We have a chance to pick up a hundred skinned rabbits from a farmer down that way,' said Mills, 'so if you can swing me five gallons of petrol, we'll find room for your friend.'

'Jesus!' Chuck groaned, 'rabbit carcases yet. Greenberg won't go for *that* – he'll have my ass!'

In the end, Stani drove, a risky experiment with his bad foot, and Chuck sat hunched miserably in the passenger seat, nursing a large folder. On arrival at the farm, the farmer strung the rabbit carcases, head down, from wires crisscrossed inside the roof of the tiny van. The furry heads of the rabbits, with flopping ears and popping eyes, were still attached to their little pink bodies.

'The Colonel's not going to like this *at all*,' Chuck moaned.

When the Liberator touched down at Heston, the passengers, mostly in uniform, debouched from its behind down a ladder. The portly figure of Mike Greenberg was easily identifiable and the Colonel's uniform into which it was compressed did little to help, in fact it seemed to accentuate his bulges. His new brown shoes were lemon coloured thanks to an ill-chosen polish and, as he waddled painfully towards them, Stani noticed that the jaunty angle of his military cap was accounted for by tufts of grey hair seeping out on one side. Three brightly coloured medal ribbons adorned his chest; a grey stubble framed his very determined chin; bags of tiredness were beneath his eyes and his mouth was set in a thin, disagreeable inverted U.

'Hey, Mike! Glad to see you!' said Chuck with great heartiness, thrusting out his hand.

'Let's see that salute, Major,' Greenberg snapped out of the side of his mouth.

A shaken Chuck obliged as best he could but it was a doorman's effort. Stani's performance was more professional.

'You the driver?' Greenberg grunted.

'For the moment, yes, Colonel.'

'Okay, then. I've got a duffle bag and one large, leather suitcase, both with my initials in gold paint. Load 'em on quick so I can get me a hot shower and a Scotch. What a crappy aircraft *that* is,' he said, nodding disdainfully at the Liberator.

Then to Chuck he said briskly, 'While this guy's getting the bags, I'll take a look at those box office returns. You got 'em with you?'

'Sure, Mike. Er Colonel. Er Sir,' said Chuck. 'I have them right here.' He handed over the yellow folder.

During Stani's absence, Chuck steered Greenberg to the rabbits' hearse and must have absorbed the considerable blast which its appearance and contents occasioned, for he was a dejected punch-bag by the time Stani returned, squatting crosslegged on the bloodstained, sawdust-covered floor, with his neck arched uncomfortably forward to avoid contact with festoons of shiny little corpses. Mike Greenberg was leafing through the contents of the yellow folder, his cap on the back of his head, a cigar clamped between his teeth and his uniform jacket on his knee. Stani pushed the luggage into the back with Chuck and climbed in. As he leaned forward to switch on the ignition, he caught a glimpse of the tailor's tag inside Greenberg's jacket –

WESTERN COSTUME CO
HOLLYWOOD.

'Where to, Sir?' Stani asked.

'Claridges,' said Greenberg.

The drive to the hotel took twenty-five minutes, during which Chuck bobbed and weaved to avoid the flapping ears above him, and Greenberg grunted appreciatively as he totted up the totals of his box office receipts. He seemed satisfied and, as the van jolted to a halt outside the Brook Street entrance to the hotel, he stretched, belched loudly and said, 'The goddam Limeys are really going to the movies these days – don't they know there's a war on?'

Stani often thought about his fisherman friend, Jervis. Letters sent to Lauriston had gone unanswered and he had not seen him since the funeral service for his mother and Captain Rainbird. He was overjoyed, therefore, when he got back from the airport, to find under his door, a note from Mrs. Quansett-Fowles: *A man called Jervis came to see you. He drank gin like water and left his number. The Navy never changes!*

101

Their reunion was a great one, a familiar pattern – a pub crawl (bomb-free, luckily, as the industrial north was receiving the enemy's attentions that night). Their conversation was often hilarious, sometimes serious, and occasionally sad. In a saloon bar off the King's Road, Stani enquired about his friend's present status as a card carrying Communist.

'Well,' laughed Jervis, 'I've kind of let that lapse! I think wot finally pissed me off was them Commie shop stewards in the Ordnance factories telling the lads to go slow for more pay. And there was the Eighth Army bleedin' to death out there in Africa because they had no new equipment! Of course Churchill pulled a fast one on 'em and organized 'TANKS FOR RUSSIA' WEEKS. Doubled production right away, those bastards did, but I'll bet old Winnie didn't send many to the Ruskies.'

Stani told of his North Atlantic antics and in a Fulham free house. Jervis insisted on a minute examination of Stani's wounds.

'I won't be flying any more,' said Stani, trying to sound rueful, 'So I'm just reporting for my rehabilitation and waiting to see what they want me to do.'

'Lucky you didn't lose your eyes,' said Jervis peering closely at Stani's face. 'Lovely job they did on your map though, it'll hardly show when it's all settled down.'

'How about you?' Stani asked.

'I've been fuckin' lucky,' said Jervis, 'just finished six months of Arctic convoys in destroyers and I don't ever want to do no more! This last one, they stuck me on a big cargo ship. There was a gun crew of naval ratings and three of us signal men, the rest was Merchant Seamen. Wonderful blokes, middle aged a lot of them. Old Perce Murcell come with me from destroyers, signals too, bit of a lad old Perce – very small, a jockey from Newmarket in usual life.'

Jervis took a big pull at his whisky and looked at the flushed faces round the bar.

'Tanks for bleedin' Russia!' he said loudly and nearby people stopped talking. Then in a lower voice, 'Old Winston must have let 'em have a few because we was loaded down to the gunnells with 'em on that voyage bound for Murmansk. We even had 'em on deck – lashed together in rows like pork sausages. Their ammo was aboard too and with all that 'igh explosive about we didn't fancy being 'it by anything . . . not that it would 'ave mattered much because nobody could 'ave lasted in that water more than a couple of minutes – but we was thankful we weren't a tanker full of 'igh octane . . . whoosh! One on our starboard side took a torpedo off the North Cape and another astern of us got it from a Stuka. 'orrible sight they were when they went up. We lost a third of the whole convoy on that trip but we was a lucky ship, we 'ardly got touched. Submarines come at us off Iceland but somehow they missed us.' He took another swallow. 'Perce was unlucky really. We ran into a proper gale only a day out of Murmansk when all the action was over. We'd been 'it a couple of days before by one of them Stukas but the bomb went off on a big tank on deck – blew that apart, brought down the foremast and dismantled the rail . . . that's all. Perce was up forrard with a party cleaning up the mess and freeing the anchors – there was 'undreds of tons of ice on the foredeck, it covered everything, and the wind was blowing horizontal like, over eighty miles an hour the officer of the watch told me and the sea was like bloody mountains. I remember that officer's face, the spray had turned to ice and the skin had been stripped off like a rabbit's in a poultry shop.

'Well, suddenly, the old tub stuck her nose in a wave the size of Mount Everest. This is it, I thought, and it seemed kind of a shame after what we'd taken during the voyage. . . . I didn't see 'ow 'er bows could ever come up again but they did and about a 'undred tons of that ice water swamped the party on the foredeck. I didn't expect to see any of 'em again but some'ow they got washed against the tanks and didn't go overboard. All except poor old Perce, 'e just kept going on that ice. 'e grabbed at pieces of metal and ropes but 'e was grabbing at a skating rink and just slid slowly over the side amidships where the rail 'ad been. 'e never come up so 'e must 'ave gone in the props. Of course we couldn't stop to look for 'im becos of submarines.'

Jervis twirled his drink.

'Bit of a lad, old Perce,' he added softly.

'What happens now?' asked Stani, 'back to destroyers?'

'No, it's an anti-aircraft cruiser this time,' said Jervis, glancing to either side to make sure no one was listening. 'I'm joining her next week in Liverpool. My Dad's up there working for

Cunard 'trooping' aboard *Queen Mary* so I'll be able to see a bit of 'im – more convoy work I expect, a cruiser'll be a nice change though . . . a proper 'oliday in a floating 'otel after that Arctic caper.'

'What made us do it?' asked Stani.

'Do what?'

'Volunteer.'

Jervis thought a long time before his strong, honest face broke into a smile,

'I suppose,' he said, 'we just don't like being buggered about.'

When Jervis left for Liverpool, Stani went with him to the station. He humped the kit-bag and Jervis kept a tight hold on a small battered suitcase.

'Don't want to lose this,' he laughed, 'it's me books. Don't know where I'd be without me Dickens, me Keats and me Trollope. Matter of fact,' he added, as they pushed their way to a marble top table in the dimly lit refreshment room redolent of tobacco, coffee, beer and overheated serge uniforms, 'I want to write meself when this lot is over and in this 'ere little case is me notes for me epic contribution to the world of letters – you're in it of course.'

Stani guarded the table while his friend fought his way to the counter and came back, triumphantly, with two glasses of flat beer and a couple of ersatz sausage rolls.

'I called the roll,' Jervis shouted as he elbowed his way through the crowd, 'and the sausage reported absent.'

Jervis prattled on, dispensing good cheer, kindness and massive doses of common sense.

'How're things going with that lady friend you wrote about?' he asked, putting a half-smoked cigarette behind an ear and pushing back his round sailor hat on the ribbon of which was 'H.M.S.' but, for security reasons, no name of a ship.

'Fine, I think,' said Stani, 'but she has told me something which gave me kind of a jolt.'

'You mean she likes girls?'

'No,' Stani laughed. 'It's more complicated than that, her father is . . . well . . . he's an Earl.'

Jervis chewed for a while on his sausage roll before pronouncing judgement.

104

'It's 'ard for you to understand, Stani, but in this country not all titles are handed down from father to son. In the old days a bloke would do something brave on the field of battle and the King would say, 'Good show, Lancelot, now get off your fuckin' 'orse and kneel on the turf'. Then the King would whack him on the arse wiv his sword and say 'Arise, Sir Lancelot!' That's 'ow it all started and it was good to my way of thinkin'. A man became a knight for valour on the field of battle, see? Today a man can become a Knight or a Baron by owning the company that made the fuckin' sword; provided 'e gives away enough of its profits to the Party Funds the Prime Minister tells the King to whack 'is arse wiv it!'

'There must be more to it than that,' said Stani doubtfully.

'Of course there is,' said Jervis. 'Them Dukes and Barons at Runnymede, seven hundred years ago, did a great job taking the power away from the King and many of those old families on their estates are still mighty good people looking after their tenants when they're sick, givin' 'em a brace of pheasants at Christmas and all, but they're overbred like greyhounds now and don't have too much between the ears, but they're brave all right. They got slaughtered in the last war and you mark my words, they're being slaughtered again in this lot. They still believe they should 'set an example' to the people.'

Jervis glanced at the big clock over the sandwich counter. 'Got to keep an eye on the time,' he said. 'Yes, the class system in this country takes a lot of understanding. My Dad about had it weighed up. "The real top classes are good" he always said "and so are the real lower ones – but it's them buggers in between wot worries me".'

As they pushed their way through the smoky, hissing, gloom towards Jervis's departure platform, a silence fell between them. They knew that platitudes can only spoil private moments and both men sensed that a final handclasp and a nod would suffice. That done, Jervis heaved himself aboard and Stani watched him pushing his way along the corridor in a fruitless search for a seat. The train was packed with service men and there was little happiness among the womenfolk they were leaving behind. Jervis, finally wedged between two tough-looking U.S. Marines, gave him a thumbs up and Stani turned away as the train eased out. In the gloom, he faced a line of

105

white, strained faces. Some smiling bravely fluttering handker-chiefs, or holding up babies, some openly weeping and others, numbed and frozen with worry. By the time he reached the barrier, the air raid sirens were wailing like lost souls on the cliff tops.

7

Off to his beloved America, to crusade for 'Bundles for Britain', Stani flew to Toronto, another cold, bucket seat ride in a converted bomber, battling head winds all the way. After Toronto he savoured the comfort of a scheduled airline flight to New York, and the luxury of a hotel suite on Park Avenue. At La Guardia airport, he had been met by the representatives of 'Bundles for Britain' – highly attractive girls, tall and slim with shining hair, beautiful teeth and bright easy manners. He promptly fell half in love with both of them, and totally once more with the America he missed so much. For two days he was escorted everywhere, either by blonde Donna or brunette Fernanda. He was taken to lunch, cocktails, dinners, theatres, nightclubs; and never allowed to put his hand into his pocket, being constantly assured that 'This is on 'Bundles'. You'll pay soon enough!'. The one nagging worry was the wartime ban on personal phone calls to Britain and therefore no contact with Pandora.

The girls coached him in what he should say during his tour, arranged his itinerary down to the minutest detail and finally drove him to Stamford, Connecticut where, as guest of honour at a dinner-dance, he made his first 'appearance'.

It turned out to be much easier than he had thought, but even so his hands had been wet with apprehension when he clutched Pandora's little gold disc and headed for the microphone with the dance band launching into a blues rendering of 'Rule Britannia'.

After the initiation at Stamford, he was catapulted into the tour proper, and for four weeks, he criss-crossed the United States, consuming acres of steaks, mounds of apple pie, glaciers of ice cream and gallons of highballs. He appeared at luncheons, women's clubs, country clubs, Lions clubs, dinners, dances and in rented theatres and movie houses. His good looks, his uniform and the glamour of his wounds stirred a variety of emotions in the breasts of mothers and daughters; his modesty and evident courage impressed their menfolk. 'Bundles for Britain' were delighted by the financial results. It was all beautifully arranged. At each stop, he was met at the airport by his 'sponsors', usually a married couple who would put him up during his stay, entertain him royally and pour him on the plane the following day, supposedly well rested and ready for his next assignment.

It was, of course, totally exhausting. Stani's foot gave him pain in direct proportion to his tiredness. But he enjoyed every minute of America and perfected a way, after saying a few words of thanks for the 'Bundles', of encouraging questions from his audiences about the situation in Britain, and the impact of thousands of Americans pouring into that beleagured country. He visited Buffalo, Detroit, Chicago, Minneapolis, Cincinnati, Kansas City, Richmond, Miami, Fort Myers, Dallas, Phoenix, Salt Lake, Denver, Seattle, San Francisco and San Diego, finally ending up in Los Angeles. The girls had thoughtfully pencilled in a rest period there, so he could visit relatives of his mother, get his trunk and father's picture, and, of course, visit Alwyn High.

On his last day, he located Carole, 'the most sensational cheer-leader in the history of Alwyn High'. She answered the bell of a white frame house blissfully reminiscent of the one her mother had so trustingly left at her disposal several years before. She was still dazzlingly beautiful if a trifle more Renoiresque. A baby was in her arms and a little boy peered from between her gorgeous legs. Her face glowed with pleasure when she saw Stani. 'I don't *believe* it!' she shrieked. Then called over her shoulder, 'Jack! come here – hurry!'

A huge crew-cut Marine loomed up behind her.

All in all, it was a fascinating experience and Stani blessed Chuck Pesnick for arranging it. But the longer it lasted the more macabre it seemed that, like Cinderella, he would soon have to return to bombs, blackouts, pitiful rations and permanent apprehension. He also ached with missing Pandora. His pangs of jealousy occasioned by remembering her oft-repeated maxim that 'war is a great aphrodisiac' were not assuaged when he reminded himself that a 'Bundles for Britain' fund raising tour was no monks' convention either.

In Chicago, on the return trip, he was surrounded by Polish Americans, who forced him to make amends for his inability to speak their language by acknowledging many toasts in Polish vodka. So many, that by the end he couldn't even speak English.

In Salt Lake City, the Mormon stronghold, being dry, presented a different problem. The president of a big copper company produced a bottle. 'Stay close to me, kid, I'm the only Jew in town.'

In Kansas City, he had appeared in a movie theatre. The audience was particularly solicitous because, in addition to his limp and his burns, for a long time they were convinced that he was also blind. 'Always remember the gallery, Buster,' an old stage hand had advised him on the first days of his tour. 'They get sore as hell up there if you play too much to the stalls.' Blinded by a single, high spotlight of appalling incandescence, Stani had been unable to see the audience at all but, mindful of the old man's warning, he addressed himself mostly to those on either side of the beam, smiling and nodding as he did so. When the house lights went up for his question period, he saw that, in that particular movie house, there never had been a balcony.

At Fort Myers on the Western coast of Florida, after he had made his contribution to the evening, he accepted an invitation from a flushed dentist named Blackwell to go fishing early the next day.

'Whaddaya say we go catch us a mess of bone fish, sailfish and tarpon? Out in the Gulf tomorrow?'

'I'd love it,' said Stani. 'But I have to catch a plane at three o'clock for Dallas. Can we make it?'

'Don't worry about a thing,' said Blackwell. 'We'll get a real early start, they don't strike when the sun gets hot anyway. I'll have Mrs. Blackwell fix us some fried chicken. Bourbon suit you okay?'

At five-thirty the following morning, Stani kept his rendez-vous at fog-shrouded Parson's dock. His host was red eyed as were his two other checkered-shirted friends. Bud and Charlie genially shook Stani's hand.

'This mist will burn off by seven,' Bud said confidently.

'Yes,' agreed Charlie loudly. 'Gonna be perfect past the Point.' Stani reeled back from the onslaught of his three 'P's.

As the dentist powered the big day cruiser seaward, Stani reflected that it was fortunate for the man's patients that he had taken the day off and was not waving a high speed drill around the inside of their mouths, because with a jarring 'snap', a sizeable piece of his boat's after-rail flew into the air, still firmly attached to Parson's dock.

'Sorry about that,' said the dentist happily. 'Hey! Bud! Waddaya say we break out the Four Roses, sober us all up?'

Paper cups were filled, passed round, and the dentist opened the throttle.

'Can't see a goddamned thing,' he laughed. 'But I know this channel like the back of my hand.'

'Can I help?' Stani murmured nervously.

'Sure thing,' his host replied. 'Get up forrard and help Charlie pick out the Channel markers. Be real nice if you'd do that.'

The deck was slippery with fog and Charlie was hunched over his paper cup when Stani reached him.

'What do they look like, the Channel markers?' Stani asked.

'Small and white and a couple of hundred yards apart,' Charlie replied. 'There's one now – see it?' He pointed into the grey opaque curtain ahead and yelled to the dentist, 'Over there for Christ's sake! To your *right*!'

The dentist spun the wheel and the cruiser, doing about twenty knots, heeled to his touch. 'To starboard you mean!' he yelled back; they roared towards the marker, but their bow wave and their shouts proved too much for it and, with a shriek of displeasure, a herring gull rose into the air. A building and some trees loomed ominously through the mist and occasioned another abrupt change of course.

'Waddaya trying' to do for Christ's sake!' yelled Bud, appearing from the lavatory, 'go by road?'

After an hour of erratic manoeuvres, the fog was appreciably thicker and the dentist cut the engine.

'If I can hear the surf, I'll know where we are,' he announced.

Nobody heard anything so they decided to open a second

110

bottle of Bourbon and attack the chicken. Then they started off again.

'How about the compass?' Stani enquired. 'Where are we trying to get to?'

'If we can find the west end of Captiva Island, that'll put us out into the Gulf.' The dentist spun the wheel again as he spoke. 'That's where the surf hits. We'll feel the swells there too. That compass was no goddam good anyway. Some jerk in the boatyard took it to get it fixed. . . . I know my way okay, this fog should've lifted by now,' he added.

Half an hour later, the engine sputtered and stopped. 'Son-ofabitch!' said the dentist. Paper cups were refilled and with everyone giving advice, the spark plugs and fuel lines were located and inspected, then the overworked battery of the starter provided two last-gasp slow motion revolutions of the engine and gave up.

'Still don't hear that surf,' said Charlie in a conversational tone.

'Don't feel that swell neither,' ventured Bud.

'Sonofabitch!' said the dentist again. He refilled the paper cups. 'Tell you what. I've got this big Johnson outboard for emergencies so we'll just hang that over the stern and away we go!'

The heavy, sixty-five horse-power Johnson was unwrapped from its tarpaulin covering and, with conflicting advice coming from all quarters, was manhandled across the slippery after deck by Bud and the dentist and the delicate operation of clamping the huge machine into position got under way.

Stani was staring hopefully at a faintly lightening sky and Charlie was gathering together the remains of the chicken when they heard a splash. They looked towards the stern to find Bud lying full length on the fog-slick after deck, the dentist's rear end was draped over the after-rail.

'Why did you let go, for Chrissakes?' he wheezed.

'Because I slipped, Goddammit,' answered an aggrieved Bud.

A long silence followed the realization that, with the out-board at the bottom of the sea, their situation had not changed for the better. But they did not panic. Instead a staunchness of bearing manifested itself.

111

'Let's take another look at the Four Roses,' said the dentist and added a constructive command. 'Charlie, drop the anchor.'

Charlie eased his way forward and did as he was bid.

'Is it holding?' shouted the dentist.

'I think a mermaid's sitting on it,' came the reply. 'It's just swinging around down there.'

'Pull it up again.'

Stani was now looking at his watch a great deal.

For an hour or so, they drifted, leaving a trail of paper cups on the mirror-like surface of the water. In the grey sky faint signs of a cerulean blue underpainting were showing and they heard a couple of boats pass them in the mist. But there was still no sign of surf nor swell and their combined shouts brought no aid.

They decided to play gin rummy.

After perhaps another hour, with all but Stani engrossed in the game, there was a faint 'bump' and the normal movement of the boat became arthritic. Instead of an occasional gentle roll it seemed to jerk.

'That's a sandbank,' said the dentist without looking up, 'so we're just behind the Island. There's quite a few here. Charlie, put that anchor down again, will ya?'

Stani glanced at his watch once more and tried to keep alarm from his voice. 'How can I get from Captiva Island back to Fort Myers?'

'Easy,' said Bud, 'there's a causeway and a good road – taxis on the island too. You'll make it.'

Charlie returned looking relieved.

'Everything okay?' asked the dentist.

'Take a look,' answered Charlie. 'I think we've landed in Paradise.'

Standing beside the cruiser were two leggy blondes wearing tight T-shirts and the briefest of shorts. They had bicycles.

'Good morning girls,' said the dentist, 'wanna come aboard?'

The girls shook ther heads. 'What are you doing here?' asked one.

'Where *is* here?' asked the dentist.

'This track takes you to Parson's dock,' said the girl – pointing, 'about a mile down there.'

112

The girls left and the paper cups were refilled.

'Well, whadaya know,' said the dentist, 'it took us one hell of a time to go one mile.'

8

The winter of 1942 had hit New York early. When Stani arrived back there, at the end of October, Central Park was already dressed in russet and gold and the leaves were starting to fall. If the reservoir and ponds were not yet sheeted with ice, the wind that whistled through the concrete jungle that surrounds the Park sent honest burghers, homeward bound from their toil, scurrying eagerly down the steps and through the portals of their favourite watering holes.

In those fully stocked bars, as in restaurants, and other packed places of entertainment, it was hard to remember that less than twelve months before, the traumatic shock of 'a day that will live in infamy' – the treacherous Japanese attack on Pearl Harbor – had almost brought the most powerful nation on earth to her knees.

Stani hated goodbyes so he took a taxi to the Cunard White Star docks at the Western end of 49th Street. He wore his uniform and fended off the inevitable questions it occasioned from his driver.

'You a flyer or summin?'

'Occasionally – yes.'

'You British? You sound like it.'

'No, I'm a Pole.'

'Hey! No kiddin'! There's a Polak family lives on our block, name of Grabinski or Grabyourski, summin' like that . . . real nice folk. The old man's crocked all the time, he works in the sewers. Real nice guy – doesn't stink either.'

'Is that so?' said Stani, wishing the man would keep an eye on the darkened streets ahead instead of staring at him in the rear view mirror.

'Cunard docks, eh?' queried the driver. 'The *Queen Mary*'s

just come in – I seed her yesterday. She's carrying soldiers over to England. The poor bastards don't know what'll hit them when they get there. The way I see it, that goddam Roosevelt should never send them there in the first place – they're going the wrong way, for Chrissakes! Europe's finished, the Krauts are too goddam good for them. We should be takin' care of those little yellow cocksuckers in Japan instead of propping up those lousy Limeys and them chicken French.'

'You have a point,' said Stani and listened wearily until finally the man asked,

'Where d'you wanna get off – main gate okay?'

'Fine,' Stani said and busied himself with his documents for embarkation.

The sheds of Pier 90 were humming with organized chaos. Beneath a hundred arc lights, swarms of soldiers and long-shoremen filled the cargo nets of the giant cranes with tons of food, and mounds of equipment for the fifteen thousand troops already aboard the *Queen Mary*. Towering over the sheds were the skyscraper sides of the monster ship, and far above, silhouetted against the purple of the night sky, Stani could see her lofty superstructure and her three huge smokestacks. No longer were they a glistening and brilliant red. Now, like her hitherto shiny black flanks, all ninety thousand tons of her were painted a uniform, depressing, wartime grey. He shivered inside his greatcoat, took one backward look towards the roaring, happy-go-lucky, carefree city and contemplated with dread his return to whale meat, powdered eggs, drastic shortages, the curtailment of everything that spelled comfort or freedom of movement, and a nightly hail of high explosives. But if he felt any wistfulness at leaving total freedom, blazing lights, bursting stores, unfrightened children, much fun and no bombs, he also remembered with gratitude the humming American ship-yards and aircraft factories with their teeming round the clock shifts. Above all, he longed for Pandora. His absence from her had sharpened his love. At precisely 2 a.m. he presented himself as ordered to the Military Police Post at the bottom of the midships gangway. Suddenly all he wanted in the world was to get back and never be without her again.

A sergeant checked his papers and saluted. 'You've fallen on your feet, sir,' he grinned, 'they've given you a lovely single

115

cabin on the Sun Deck.'

'How many of us will be in it?"

'Not too bad,' said the Sergeant. 'Only four at a time. But there'll be three shifts for sleeping in every twenty-four hours, so I guess you could say there's twelve of you sharing S.11' He saluted once more and handed Stani a boarding pass.

'Looks like they've overbooked again, Sir. Enjoy your trip anyway.'

Aboard the ship, Stani struggled upwards, through an apparently endless series of decks and a seething mass of khaki. Duffle bags, rifles and equipment were piled everywhere. Officers and patient crew members were shepherding their flocks, out of the loud hailer system poured a constant stream of instructions. Nobody, it appeared, would be allowed on deck till the ship cleared the Ambrose Light: too many inquisitive eyes could be watching through high powered binoculars. Coloured cards were being distributed for the eating shift, the sleeping shift, and when at sea, for the shift that would be lolling or milling around the freezing upper decks.

Accents of all the States were heard – farm boys from Iowa, street-wise kids from Chicago and the Bronx, tall Texans and drawling Georgians. The crowd was good-humoured and the wisecracks flew thick and fast. 'Hey Joe! see you in the Turkish Bath!' 'I don't have a Tux for dinner tonight – Captain's table too!' The average age was no more than twenty; some of the boys had hardly started shaving.

It was hot in the crowded passageways, so Stani removed his greatcoat, unveiling his R.A.F. wings atop the blue and white diagonal stripes of his D.F.C. ribbon. Admiring glances came his way as he climbed ever higher towards the Sun Deck.

When he found it, a hard faced M.P. scrutinized his pass: the few cabins on the deck were for officers only. A fatherly steward in a white jacket approached. 'S.11, sir? Follow me please. Nice to have an R.A.F. officer aboard, sir,' he said, 'I'm afraid you'll find the cabin very crowded, sir. Four gentlemen are already asleep but they'll be getting up in a couple of hours, then it'll be your turn: it's very well worked out really – very good at organizing, the Americans, aren't they? But this trooping does make a lot of extra work, not that we mind it. We don't.

'Many of the young crew members went off to join the Navy,

volunteered like, but we manage to keep a full crew by taking on retired Company men like myself. The lifeboat drill in winter is a bit hard on some of us, and God alone knows what happens with this lot on board if we run into a torpedo! Here we are, sir – S.11. Lovely cabins up here in summer time, with their big windows and all. But we do get a lot of rolling in the winter, should be better in the *Elizabeth* if she ever gets finished. They say she's being fitted with these new fangled stabilizers . . . imagine, on a ship her size! That's one for the book, eh? Matthews, Charlie Matthews is the name, sir.' He had noticed Stani's limp.

'We have a little galley just there across the way, anytime you want a nice cup of tea and there's a deck chair stowed in there when you can't find anywhere else to sit down. We never know what time we'll be sailing but it's always at night so it can't be long now and you have to report to S.39 for instructions and so on.'

First Stani opened the door of S.11. He saw four recumbent shapes asleep in the double decker bunks.

'Get lost,' growled one of them. 'Come back at four o'clock.' Stani dumped his kitbag and greatcoat and departed in search of S.39.

Behind a mound of paperwork, sat a bespectacled Major with dark circles under his eyes. He was smoking a cigar. A soldier next to him concentrated on some noisy one-finger typing.

Stani saluted and presented his documents. The Major flicked them over and in the monotonous drone of a museum guide, outlined the shipboard rules and regulations and handed Stani an envelope containing his coloured shift cards and the faint outlines of a mimeograph map which he said would indicate the quickest way to his assigned lifeboat.

'Your life jacket will be worn at all times when at sea,' he advised. 'but don't pull the cord and inflate the goddam thing because we don't have room on board. Bring any liquor with you?'

'Afraid not.'

'Glad you didn't,' said the Major in the same monotone, 'because I'd have to throw you in the brig . . . that'll be all.'

Stani saluted and withdrew. The business, he reflected, had

been concluded with admirable dispatch.

During the ensuing five days, Stani discovered what it must be like to be a mackerel in a shoal. With the eleven other occupants of S.11 he exchanged monosyllabic greetings while making way for them or insisting that they make way for him during the shifts to sleep in the bunks. All were young and treated him with the awe that green and apprehensive troops reserved for 'battle-hardened veterans'.

Throughout the voyage, when tired of being compressed in the human shoal, many green-visaged with nausea as the liner rolled in the permanent swells, he fought his way upwards to the sanctuary of Matthews' 'little galley, the nice cup of tea and the comfortable deck chair'.

Matthews worried about *Queen Mary*.

'These American lads are ever so nice,' he said in his soft West Country voice, 'but I do wish they'd stop hacking the ship to bits! Have you seen those lovely teak deck rails, sir? Of course, there's nothing for them to do, so they stand about carving their names on the rails all day long. Another few voyages and there won't be no rails left – and don't they get a lot of medals, sir? Before seeing any action too! Good conduct medals, good shot medals, why there's a cook down below says he got the Purple Heart for chopping off a finger! Mark you, they're great lads for pulling your leg though aren't they? Terrible what's going to happen to a lot of them isn't it? It's easier for all of us with our families being bombed and all, but you really need to be angry to go to war, don't you sir? It must be so difficult for these lads to get angry so far from home.'

Once the American destroyers and aircraft that had protected *Queen Mary* outwards for three hundred miles had been recalled, she was entirely alone on the ocean, relying on her great speed and ever changing course to frustrate any mid-Atlantic submarines, but Stani wondered how, when she came closer to Europe, this huge target could avoid his old acquaintance, the Fokker-Wulf bomber.

Matthews was full of news. 'It's getting colder already, sir. That means we're going up towards Greenland. Of course, there's icebergs about up there at this time of year but the skipper knows what he's about. He was skipper last January when we had a terrible voyage. I've never seen such seas! We

118

was rolling to beat the band. One wave like a skyscraper hit us amidships and the *Mary* went right over almost on her side and seemed to hang there for ever with everything breaking loose all over the ship and the troops all piling up on top of each other in the scuppers. The skipper said afterwards he was sure she was a goner. She was right on her beam ends with half the decks awash and lifeboats coming off their davits and all. With fifteen thousand Yanks aboard it would have been the biggest naval disaster of all time. But somehow the old lady sort of shook herself free. You could feel her shuddering and hear her groaning as she struggled to get up again. That was a near go, all right.'

Stani was still thinking about those big four-engined bombers.

'Don't worry about them, sir,' said Matthews. 'After we've zig-zagged about south of the ice fields, we head down North of Ireland and then nip across into the Clyde where she was built. She always sounds her big fog horn when she comes home to the Clyde. It cheers the Scots up to know we've made another safe passage and brought another fifteen thousand good lads over to help them fight. The escort comes out to meet us between Greenland and Ireland, aircraft of Coastal Command first, then an anti-aircraft cruiser. Between them they take care of those bombers if they come after us and half a dozen destroyers join us to look after the subs.' The West Country voice dropped and the steward winked conspiratorially. 'Of course I'm not supposed to know, sir, but my son's aboard the escort cruiser that's been coming out to meet us the last few voyages. It's nice to think the family's taking care of the American lads!'

Matthews made sure no one was listening. 'My son's escort cruiser is the *Curacoa*. An old ship from the last war. I was in the Navy during that lot. I served aboard her for a while. Lovely ship, very fast in her day. She's a couple of knots slower than *Queen Mary* but we zig-zag astern of her and she can still give us good protection.'

Matthews squared matters with the Quarter Master and the hard-faced M.P. and Stani and his deck chair were installed at the base of the forward of the three towering smoke stacks. There he could find shelter from wind and warmth to combat the increasing cold as the great ship headed North, her four

119

thirty-five ton propellers, each twenty-five feet in diameter, thrusting her disdainfully through the swells at almost thirty knots.

He spent most of his non-sleeping shifts by his funnel. Haunted by Pandora's warnings of her 'unreliability' and longing for her with every moment, he willed *Queen Mary* to double her speed. When hunger or arctic cold drove him below, he presented his coloured card to an M.P. in a Mess Hall and hacked his way through another meal. But mostly he sat, swaddled in greatcoat, uniform, pullovers, his entire range of pyjamas, underwear and shirts and with his life-jacket illegally inflated for additional protection, alone with his thoughts of Pandora and aloof from the eddying mass of soldiery. He thanked God for Matthews. This admirable man frequently joined him for a smoke and a chat and his honest Devonshire face beamed as he rambled on about his wife, his cottage at Dartmouth, his cocker spaniel and, above all, his pride in his son in the Navy; like many others, he was dismayed that war had once more burst upon his unprepared country after a respite of only twenty years. 'Something must have been very wrong at the top, they must all have been asleep,' he said. 'How *could* the Jerries have got ready to start up again without anyone noticing? Makes no sense to me.'

For Stani the voyage seemed endless, but at last the weather became warmer and *Queen Mary* turned southward into increasingly calmer seas.

'Should be up the Clyde by tomorrow night, sir,' Matthews announced. 'Coastal Command's been out to have a look at us.'

The following day the old man was in a high state of excitement. 'It's *Curacoa* right enough!' he said happily, pointing out the silhouettes of half a dozen warships on the horizon dead ahead. 'She's about twelve miles away and the destroyers are out ahead of her. I'd know her anywhere! Visibility's perfect today sir! What a bit of luck! A beautiful day for a family get-together! Another three hours the way we have to zig-zag astern of her and we'll be up to her.'

Matthews continued to look out to sea. 'Know how they work out those zig-zags, sir? It's all done in advance at the Admiralty in London. There's a klaxon above the helmsman's head and every so many minutes it goes off: all he has to do is alter course hard a port or hard a starboard and hold her steady until it goes off again – he's got nothing to worry about. Now why don't you go below and get a bite to eat, eh? Soon after midday we'll be right astern of *Curacoa*. You can be sure I'll be back up here. As we pass his ship, if he's off duty my boy'll be on deck to wave to me even though he can't see me, of course. Being a couple of knots faster we'll gradually pull ahead . . . it's quite exciting really. We pass ever so close.'

Matthews' face was flushed with pride and excitement. Stani easily resisted the lure of the throng and stayed close to his funnel. At midday, Matthews reappeared.

'The American gentlemen have been told we'll be docking after dark tonight, sir,' he chuckled. 'Your cabin's a real sight – everyone seems to have lost everything! I'm staying out of there. Ah! doesn't she look lovely – the *Curacoa*? See that light coloured camouflage? That's new – it's for Arctic waters. Poor lad, those Russian convoys are very nasty by all accounts.'

The cruiser was less than a mile ahead of *Queen Mary* now as the big ship swung back and forth across the wake.

'Let's get forward, sir,' said Matthews. 'We'll have a perfect view.'

He led the way past huge ventilators noisily gulping down air for the decks below and threaded a path through a maze of heavy loading equipment.

'Here we are,' he said, 'right over the bridge – it's almost like we were steering! Funny how slow we go past, isn't it. Poor old *Curacoa's* doing her best but she's still a couple of knots slower. Can't be much fun looking astern at this great monster catching her up though. The top of our bow must be half-way up her foremast.'

Stani watched the cruiser gradually being overhauled on the port bow.

'How big is the *Curacoa*?' he asked.

'Just over 4,000 tons,' smiled Matthews as he stared ahead, 'with a crew of four hundred and thirty. And we're 90,000 tons with well over fifteen thousand on board!'

Matthews started frantically waving a white cabin towel which he had brought on deck for the occasion. 'My boy won't see me but it's just in case,' he said over his shoulder. His cries of 'Up here! Up here son!' were blown astern by the wind.

121

Stani had grown very fond of Charlie Matthews and was getting a great pleasure out of sharing a proud father's joy. He studied the old man's wrinkled face. As he did so he saw the expression on it change slowly, first to mystification and then to alarm.

'We're turning towards her!' Matthews muttered to himself.

Stani looked quickly at the cruiser now no more than a hundred yards off the port bow. 'What's happening!' said Matthews louder. 'Hard a-starboard, for Christ's sake!' he yelled, but the terrible razor bows of the liner were aiming directly at the middle of *Curacoa*. They were coming at her as high as a cliff and with the speed and deadly certainty of an express train.

'Oh No! No! NO!!!' shouted Matthews. 'Oh! Jervis! Oh! *JERVIS*!!'

Stani stood speechless as *Queen Mary* charged head-on into the light cruiser and sliced her clean in half. The collision sent only a tremor through the great liner; most of the troops on board never even noticed it.

Matthews grabbed Stani's arm and his strong old hands clawed into Stani's biceps.

'No! No! No! Oh God. No!' He whispered over and over. *Curacoa*, like a little toy broken in two halves clung pitifully to either side of *Queen Mary*'s vast bows. She remained there for several minutes, carried along by the awesome momentum and held by the pressure of the sea.

Matthews fell to his knees and pressed his forehead to the deck. 'Save him!' He was barely audible now. 'Oh! Please God save my son! Keep him out of the propellers!' Tears streamed down his face. 'Keep him out of the propellers.'

Stani was glad the old man stayed where he was because the two halves of *Curacoa* finally fell away, scraping along the whole length of the perpendicular grey walls of the liner's sides. The bows of the forward half came by first, pointed straight up into the sky with the guns of her forward turrets, like upstretched arms, appealing mutely to the sky for help. Black smoke poured from her two funnels and in her death agony escaping steam was an endless scream of pain. Stani turned his horrified gaze to the other side and saw the after half of the trampled warship pass below him. It capsized as it went, the twin propellers were still turning slowly in the empty air, then they stopped. Both halves of the gallant fighting ship continued their ghastly journey towards those four monstrous, churning executioners beneath *Queen Mary*'s stern. The old man's whisper at Stani's feet was barely audible, 'Save him, God! Save my Jervis!'

PART TWO

The Middle

9

From Liverpool Docks Stani managed to get a call through to Pandora, limited to three minutes, a stern operator informed him, but at least he heard her beloved voice. The conversation was a jumble as they both talked at the same time bubbling over with news and questions. But a plan emerged. Pandora was just leaving to see her father at Hawksmoor for the short holiday due her from Sid Field's show so Stani would join her there directly after reporting to his superiors in London.

'Whatever happens come for the week-end because you *promised*' she said, '. . . if you can't come down, then I'll come up to be with you. But *DO* try, darling, because I *long* to see you and I've missed you too much and I want you to meet Daddy . . . I *know* you'll love him.'

Kisses and intimacies were cut short by a stern 'Your three minutes is up' – CLICK.

Stani walked from South Audley Street to Paddington Station across Hyde Park. It looked forlorn and exposed. Miles of sturdy iron railings, which for a hundred years had encircled it, had gone to the armament factories. In the thickening dusk, he paused upon its bleak and windswept surface to gaze at newly installed anti-aircraft rocket batteries nestling in cocoons of sandbags and barbed wire. From other emplacements bulbous barrage balloons rose into the winter sky and, by the time he reached the terminus, the banshee wailings of the first air-raid alert of the night was signalling impending doom. To the east, over the Thames estuary, probing searchlights illuminated the cloud base, distant gun fire rumbled menacingly, and mole-like, grey-faced citizens hurried homeward to their Anderson shelters and sleepless nights amidst spam sandwiches, thermos bottles and frowsty blankets. It was barely four-thirty in the

127

afternoon. The bombing would continue till dawn, Stani felt relief as well as delight to be leaving at last on his first visit to Hawksmoor.

He was lightheaded at the thought of seeing and holding Pandora once more. Six weeks had been an eternity – never again!

In the darkened, sooty caverns of Paddington Station, he pushed his way through the rush-hour crowd and marvelled anew at the composure of the Londoners. Bombs were now crumping down ominously close, yet the patient travellers, continued to queue up for tickets, sandwiches, newspapers or lavatories. They knew full well that they were in a prime target for the Luftwaffe, but none showed apprehension or fear, and many, seeing his Distinguished Flying Cross and the scars upon his face, nodded a tired smile of gratitude and gave him a 'thumbs up'.

The train to Oxford was packed, so with his small suitcase at his feet, he wedged himself into the corridor between an elderly business man who talked non-stop and a girl with protruding teeth who munched buns out of a bag.

'I'm over sixty,' said the man. 'Of course, I've volunteered for everything, but they told me I'd be more help to the war effort by keeping my factory going.'

'What do you make at the factory?' Stani asked.

The man looked furtive.

'Rubber goods,' he whispered. The girl stopping munching and giggled appreciatively.

'Of course, I was in the last war,' the man continued, 'got gassed on the Somme. But it's an easier war, this one. Seen any action, have you?'

'Not much,' said Stani.

'I saw you on the platform,' said the girl, pointing to his uniform and covering a portion of it with a fine spray of dough-nut. 'Wot did you get that medal for, then?'

'Oh they have a list, they just pick a name out of a hat now and then,' said Stani, and changed the subject. 'Does this train go to Hawksmoor or do I have to change?'

Pandora had given him precise travel instructions so he was able to think of other things while the girl and the manufacturer gave him conflicting advice.

128

At Oxford, his companions wished him goodbye and disappeared into the darkness. Stani crossed the footbridge to the local train puffing fretfully on the branch line. This time he found an empty first-class compartment, settled himself comfortably in a corner, and by the blue, glow-worm glimmer of the reading light over his head, studied his evening paper; he was just able to read the headline, the rest was indecipherable so he fell to speculating upon his forthcoming visit. Pandora had painted such a loving portrait of her father that he had no apprehensions, but he wondered if he might come up against the usual suspicions of a doting parent. His train of thought was short-circuited by a tall, paunchy, pink-faced man in his sixties, who arrived with a white haired woman holding a grotesquely fat Pekinese and a fit looking fellow with a fierce moustache. Behind them, as far as Stani could see, was an attractive, slim girl with dark hair, dark eyes and very red lipstick. All wore well-cut tweeds and spoke in high-pitched upper class voices.

'Plenty of room in here, Archie,' said the pink man over his shoulder as he hoisted hand luggage and a gun case on to the rack immediately above Stani's head.

'It's a non-smoker, but it doesn't matter.'

'What a bloody bore this black-out is,' said the younger man as he hefted more suitcases and another gun case on to the rack. 'A porter just ran his trolley over Chrissie's toe, the silly sod.'

The pink man settled himself immediately opposite Stani and stretched his legs out, placing huge brown brogues between Stani's feet. His white haired companion put her Pekinese on the seat next to Stani. The dog sniffed at him disdainfully for a while, then curled up with its head in his crotch and went to sleep. All lit cigarettes.

Nobody seemed to notice him.

The branch line train had not been rattling along for more than a few minutes before Stani realized that his new travelling companions fitted perfectly the descriptions given by Pandora of his fellow guests at Hawksmoor for the weekend. The pink man must be Sir Hercules Hanford, a junior minister in the Government, and the Pekinese woman must be his wife. The young man was a captain in the Household Cavalry, accompanied by Christine Glenford-Bassett to whom Pandora said he was engaged. Chrissie was a friend of Pandora. Above the

129

barrage of snores that issued from the Pekinese, Stani listened with mounting unease to their small talk. 'What do you make of Brendan Bracken, Sir Herky?' the Captain asked.

'Personally, Archie, I don't believe he *is* the illegitimate son of Winston,' replied the Baronet. 'But he certainly has the inside track with the old man and gets away with murder. I find him a tricky devil at best but there's no question he's an able man.'

'I don't like him,' said the wife. 'He has green teeth.'

'I wonder who else is coming for the weekend,' Chrissie mused.

'I don't mind really,' said the Captain, 'as long as the chef is still there. He's the best in England but he'll wind up in the clink if old Cuckoo ever catches on that he's flogging his pheasants to half the restaurants in London.'

Without sound or warning, a dreadful, heavy smell left the Pekinese and permeated the compartment.

All eyes turned on Stani, who cowered behind his unreadable newspaper. The girl fanned ostentatiously with her hand.

'I hear Pandora has a new young man,' said the woman – 'I wonder who it is *this time*.'

'I gather he's some glamour boy from the R.A.F.,' said Archie. 'Probably fiddles petrol coupons for her from his Dad's garage.'

For this remark, the Captain received a hack on the shin from Chrissie, who had noticed Stani's uniform. He sensed curious but totally unembarrassed glances being cast in his direction. With his eyes watering from the smoke in the compartment, he remained behind his journal for an hour until the train slowed down at the little red brick station of Hawksmoor. The others chattered away as they prepared themselves for departure.

'Hope old Cuckoo remembered to send the brake,' said the Baronet. 'I wonder who he's got for a chauffeur now that Albright's been called up.'

'He'd better have plenty of cartridges,' said Archie, 'I had a hell of a job talking a hundred out of Purdey.'

'Oh, I expect he's allowed lots,' said the Pekinese owner, removing her hot and resentful charge from between Stani's thighs. 'After all, he *is* producing food for the country and he

130

has to keep down the vermin.'

After the group trooped out on to the darkened platform, Stani sat for a long moment, wondering if he could face them for a whole weekend. But the thought of Pandora banished any notions of defecting and instead of taking the next train back to London, he lowered his own battered suitcase and limped after them towards the waiting shooting brake.

An elderly chauffeur in livery touched his cap with his flashlight. 'Lady Pandora told me to keep an eye out for you, Sir. I recognized you from the uniform. Now I'll just put your bag on the rack if you'll take a seat inside with the other guests.'

The other guests, Stani noticed, were already seated facing each other on two long seats. He climbed in by the rear door, said 'Good evening,' which raised a grunt from the Baronet but otherwise no acknowledgment, and squeezed in beside Chrissie who made a token gesture of making room but immediately turned towards Archie and entered into a long conversation about the sex life of a mutual friend named 'Buffles'.

'I don't think he is actually a pansy. I just don't believe he does *anything*,' she said.

'Well I think he's as queer as a six pound note,' said the uncompromising Captain. 'And I'm damned glad he's been posted away as Gas Officer to a brigade in India.'

The shooting brake, which smelled of wet retrievers, was driven, despite its dimmed-out headlights, with great verve by the elderly chauffeur, and the five mile trip to Hawksmoor Park passed quickly, but, as far as Stani was concerned, in total silence. Pandora had warned him that his first exposure to an English country-house weekend might be rather up-hill in the early stages but, even so, he was fascinated to find himself faced by a sort of closed shop.

'Understand Chips Cumberland is thinkin' of opening his gardens to the hoi polloi after the war,' said the Baronet. 'Hope he knows what he's lettin' himself in for – I only kept them off *my* borders by putting up signs – "BEWARE OF THE AGA-PANTHUS".'

'Had a good laugh in Bindles last week,' said Archie, 'old Chips was sitting in the bar when some feller who's only been a member for about ten years spoke to him. You know how he hates strangers. Well, this feller asked him if he lived in London

131

and old Chips just glared at him and said 'No'. But the silly sod went on and asked old Chips if he lived in the country. After a long pause, old Chips said, 'I live so far *out* in the country that the owls come and rodger me chickens.' I thought that was awfully quick of him.'

Large iron gates were opened by a gatekeeper who issued from his lodge with a flashlight and wearing carpet slippers.

'Evening Bert,' he said to the chauffeur, ''is Lordship sent a message – you're to take it easy goin' through the park cos the deer is very restless tonight – they're all over the place – Lordship says it's the bombing up Rugby way – there's been a lot of planes goin' over.'

'Righty-o,' said Bert cheerfully.

'They must be after that ball-bearing factory again,' said the Baronet. 'I hope we shoot some of the shits down.'

'During the daylight blitz quite a lot of Huns bailed out over Kent,' said his wife. 'They fell in the hop fields and the hop picker women went for their eyes with their hat pins. The deserved it after what they's done to the East End.'

'If I ever come face to face with a Bosch pilot,' said Archie in his strangulated gargle, 'I'll shoot the bastard – then stuff him back in the remains of his plane.'

'Quite right,' said the Baronet.

A full moon – a 'bombers' moon, as the newspapers called it – was sailing through a clear patch in the clouds and Stani could see the silhouette of a magnificent avenue of elms flanking the winding driveway through the Park. Rabbits scuttered across in front of the brake and its feeble headlights reflected in the round, wondering eyes of fallow deer standing stock still under the trees. Thanks to carefully tailored black-out curtains, not a chink of light showed on the silvery facade of Hawksmoor as they turned in through splendid, wrought-iron gates and circumnavigated a hallowed circle of green turf before the steps and colonnade of the entrance. The brake crunched to a halt on the gravel and, followed by two men servants, the dignified figure of Powis, the butler, descended to greet the guests. While the footmen dealt with the suitcases and guns, Powis addressed the senior arrival.

'Good evening, Sir Hercules, I hope you had a comfortable journey. His Lordship will be back in a little while. He is out in the Park smoking down some pheasants.'

'What the hell is that, Powis?' chortled the Baronet.

'Oh! his Lordship is always on to something new, Sir Hercules. He's training a retired poacher to become an underkeeper now that we're losing so many staff in the call-up and this man is showing his Lordship how to smoke the birds down when they are up in the beeches roosting. It can only be done in the full moon it seems.' he paused. 'You and her Ladyship will be in the Kent suite as usual, Sir Hercules.'

After a while, the butler turned his attention to Stani.

'Welcome to Hawksmoor, sir,' he intoned. 'His Lordship is planning a shoot for tomorrow. You do shoot, sir, do you not?'

'Occasionally,' said Stani with truth, remembering his only exposure to the sport – two highly dangerous outings, quail hunting in the scrub covered hills of Santa Barbara County. 'I don't have a gun, I'm afraid, and also I have a bad leg so I can't do much walking.'

'His Lordship will be glad to fix you up, sir,' said the butler, who appeared not to have heard. 'If you follow me, sir, I'll show you to your room. Dinner is taken at eight-thirty and cocktails are served in the library beforehand.'

Where was Pandora? Stani wondered. He needed her badly.

In silence, he followed the butler across a hall with marble floor and terracotta coloured walls in which a log fire blazed, up a sweeping staircase, along an endless passage of squeaking oaken boards muffled by a beautifully woven strip of carpet. This in turn gave way to linoleum on the far side of a green baize door.

'These used to be the nurseries, sir,' explained Powis as they entered a gaily decorated, happy, chintzy room. A footman was laying out the meagre contents of Stani's suitcase on a four-poster bed.

'Henry here will be taking care of you, sir. I will inform Lady Pandora that you have arrived.' He withdrew.

The pasty-faced Henry returned Stani's 'Good evening' and posed a question. 'What will you be wearing tonight, sir? There doesn't seem very much here,' he added.

'My uniform, I suppose,' said Stani. 'It's all I have except for the jacket and slacks. What do you suggest – you know the form?'

133

'I'd be proud to wear that uniform myself, sir,' said Henry. 'I'm sure his Lordship will understand. Will you be taking your bath now, sir?'

'Er – yes – thanks,' said Stani, wondering if he was going to be soaped and rinsed by this man. The footman opened a door in the panelling, ran the bath water, squeezed some toothpaste on to Stani's toothbrush and laid it across a tumbler.

'Now, if you'll let me have your uniform, sir, I'll take it and give it a nice press.' Reverently, Henry held out Stani's tatty woollen bathrobe like a bullfighter's cape while the uniform was being sloughed off, then he wrapped Stani in it.

'I'll keep the fire going while you're downstairs, sir, but you'll find it quite cool in the mornings – Lordship's turned off the heating in this part of the house to help the war effort.'

When Henry had departed, Stani lay down in front of the fire and went through his daily exercises designed to strengthen the muscles of his lower leg and ankle. Just as he was finishing, the door flew open and Pandora, also in a dressing gown, flung herself on top of him. When he could take a breath, he told her about his trip with his fellow guests.

'Oh! aren't they *awful*,' laughed Pandora as she locked the door. 'Herky is a cracking old bore but he's all right really. His wife is a mean old bitch and I never could *stand* Archie. . . . Chrissie's sweet when you get to know her.' Pandora touched the light switch. 'And she thinks you're a dish, by the way, so just you keep your hot, sticky hands off her! Off dressing gowns!'

Pandora's beautiful body gleamed in the firelight. She held out her arms.

'Got any better plans?'

Later by the fire, Pandora told him her big news – Mike Greenberg had told her he was seriously considering signing her to a contract with Metropolis Pictures. She was ecstatic – Chuck, she said, was working on it.

After she had left there was a discreet knock on the door and Henry reappeared with the brushed and pressed uniform.

'A lot more bombers went over while you were resting, sir,' he said, apparently not noticing the bed which now resembled an explosion in a laundry. He busied himself refilling the bath with hot water, putting some logs on the fire and picking up

134

Stani's shoes.

'Mr. Powis said to remind you that dinner will be at eight-thirty, sir. I'll just give these a little rub.'

Stani had been instructed to collect Pandora on his way downstairs. Her room was on the smart side of the green baize door. When he knocked, she was ready, shiny eyed and lovely in a turquoise dress. He loved her so much it hurt.

'My knees are still wobbly,' she said. 'I think we ought to have you 'arranged' – you're a menace.'

In the vast library, six more people who Pandora whispered were 'neighbours', had arrived for dinner. To conserve their petrol rations, four had shared a car, the other two had pedalled five miles on bicycles. The women wore long dresses and the men dinner jackets – all except the seventh Earl of Hawksmoor, who wore a peacock blue velvet smoking jacket and blue velvet slippers embossed upon the toes in gold thread with his Earl's coronet.

He was dispensing drinks. Sixty-five or so, with a rose madder complexion, he was impish rather than imposing, of medium height and shaped like an avocado.

'Delighted, young feller . . . delighted!' he boomed when Pandora introduced Stani. 'What are you takin' for it? Whisky or the house martini? The gin's all right but the vermouth's finished, dammit; that wartime stuff called Votrix is made from pine needles by the taste of it so I use a dash of sherry – that can't harm you.'

Stani accepted the house martini.

'So pleased Pandora got you down here – I had a great friend up at Oxford who was a Czech.'

'Stani is a *Pole*, Daddy,' said Pandora.

'A Pole, eh! Well, it's much the same, isn't it? Here, drink this and you won't mind if you're a Greek, ha! ha! Met everyone here have you? Pandora, take him round. How do you pronounce that name of yours anyway?'

'SKOLIMOSKI,' said Stani.

'Oh, that'll never do – that's much too difficult,' said the seventh Earl.

'Call him Stani,' said Pandora, 'that's his first name.'

'Stani, eh!' said Cuckoo. 'Knew a feller up at Oxford called Stani. Black as your hat, but very decent really.'

135

Considering the stringency of the rationing, the dinner was magnificent; a few thousand acres, some well stocked streams and a good home farm made all the difference. Rainbow trout were followed by beautifully sauced strips of hare taken from along the back bone, succulent vegetables, a soufflé Grand Marnier and home-made cheese.

Stani sat between Pandora and one of the neighbours who wore a pink taffeta dress of mid-thirties vintage and sported a bouffant hair-do which made her look like a Shetland pony.

'Do you hunt?' she asked as an opening gambit.

Stani's return play of 'Hunt what?' went unnoticed.

'Poor Cuckoo, he's having a dreadful time', she continued. 'You know, of course, he's our Master here but fox huntin's off the menu for the duration, no fodder for the horses, nothing much for the hounds and all the hunt servants called up except the Huntsman and the First Whip who's only got one ball. It nearly broke Cuckoo's heart to put down most of his hounds but he's managed to keep about ten couples for breeding when things get sorted out. His own hunters get looked after by his farms. But it's a struggle, I can tell you.'

Stani had noticed that the dogs in the beautiful candle-lit dining room almost outnumbered the guests. Two greyhounds, a whippet, a couple of golden retrievers, two cockers, a King Charles and a cantankerous cairn had surged into the dining room behind the seventh Earl where, without a word of command they had deployed themselves like tigers at a circus, each on its allotted perch. The greyhounds and retrievers curled up in their baskets, the small dogs on chairs or window seats.

'What do *they* get to eat?' Stani asked.

'Oh,' said the Shetland pony, 'rabbit mostly. It makes them fart a lot of course.'

Unembarrassed by teeth apparently designed to consume apples through a tennis racquet, the lady leaned towards Stani and spoke conspiratorially. 'Poor old Cuckoo, salt of the earth really but everyone worries about his sex life these days ever since Eunice took that post and rail by the roots five years ago and broke her neck.'

'How come?' asked Stani.

'Surprised Pandora didn't clue you in,' whispered the lady leaning closer. 'Apparently in the full moon, Eunice used to harness him up in the pony trap and drive him all over the Park.'

'Did you ever see it?'

'No, but the blacksmith in Middle Parkhurst said that Cuckoo once made enquiries about having himself shod. Must say I'd have given a lot to see old Cuckoo trotting about with Eunice touching him up with the whip. I'd also like to see his famous tattoo . . . he got some Chink to do it in Shanghai years ago – designed it himself – starting at the navel, there's a pack of hounds in full cry and when Cuckoo turns round you can just see the fox's brush as it 'goes to ground' up his bum.'

Pandora attracted Stani's attention at this point by tickling the inside of his thigh.

'What's that awful woman going on about?' she asked out of the side of her mouth. 'You wouldn't believe it now but she used to be famous as the best fuck in Yorkshire – known up there as the Harrogate Hoover.'

Stani tried to concentrate on his strips of hare.

'Cuckoo! tell us about smokin' pheasants down out of the beeches,' boomed the Baronet down the table.

'Ah, that,' said the seventh Earl. 'Great sport! This little poacher feller's teachin' me the tricks of the trade. He has a bag of stuff and when he sees a bird roostin' up there with the moon behind it, he shakes this stuff out into a pile and lights it. If he judges the wind right, the smoke goes up and pretty soon the bird topples off its perch, then he hits it on the head.'

'What's the stuff consist of?' asked Archie.

'Ah!' said Cuckoo, '*that's* his secret. He showed me something else though, last night . . . how to catch partridge with a milk bottle and some raisins.'

General conversation died away and the guests leaned expectantly forward.

'When there's snow on the ground, the little birds get short of food. So, out in the stubble where the coveys shelter at night, under a bank or alongside a hedgerow, you just shove the milk bottle in the snow makin' indentations. Then you sprinkle the raisins around putting most of them in the hole. The birds find 'em, start feedin' and when they go for the last ones in the bottom of the holes, they topple in and get caught by the shoulders. All you have to do is pick 'em up in the morning all ready frozen for the game larder.'

Stani's mind wandered during these descriptions of the chase and he found himself surprised that no mention had so far been made of the headlines in the evening papers. He waited till the excitement over the ex-poacher's activities had died down before he asked, 'What was the news from North Africa tonight? Good or bad?'

A long silence followed. Knives and forks hung motionless in the candle-light and all eyes zeroed in on him.

Archie finally broke the spell.

'I don't know about you people in the R.A.F., but in decent regiments one doesn't talk shop in the Mess.'

A reinforcement came to Stani's aid from an unexpected quarter. One of the neighbours, a thin bespectacled M.P., cleared his throat.

'The point that Archie is making with the minimum of charm is that when we are invited to Hawksmoor, it is such an island paradise in the present, er . . . sea of troubles that our good host prefers us to try and forget about the war while we're here. Isn't that right, Cuckoo?'

'Er . . . yes,' said the good host with evident embarrassment, 'my fault, of course, should have warned you . . . er . . . tell me what's the shootin' like in Czechoslovakia?'

'Poland, Daddy,' said Pandora.

With the whole world flying apart at the seams, Stani saw little logic in Lord Hawksmoor's edict that war news should be swept under the carpet till Monday morning, but his host was in full spate.

'Trouble with these houses, built in the eighteenth and nineteenth centuries, is that a lot of the architects were Frogs and Eyeties,' said Cuckoo. 'Of course, they had no idea at all of hygiene – bathrooms and 'bogs' and so forth. After all, Versailles was only built to get the French Court away from the Palace in Paris in the summer because of the stench. *Those* people had to douse themselves with perfume and sniff pomanders because all winter long they'd been lettin' down their drawers and breeches behind the tapestry. Me Grandfather, here at Hawksmoor, luckily, was able to rip out some of the walls so we have plenty of baths and "bogs".'

'Very difficult,' said the M.P., 'adding lavatories in old

138

houses – your Grandfather was lucky, Cuckoo.'

'Yes, indeed. "Pingo" Marmesbury had a dreadful time – he had to fit in a "bog" under some stairs. He raised it up and disguised it as a wicker armchair. Quite comfy really once one was mounted but it was at the end of a sort of corridor, so narrow it was hard to turn round before gettin' into the saddle. I remember the first time I stayed at Marmesbury, Pingo directed me to his new "bog". Well, I forgot to lock the door and poor Dora Marmesbury – remember how fat the old girl was? – well, she knew the place well so she turned round *outside* – locked the door, lowered her bloomers, fluffed up her skirts and backed down the corridor towards me. I was in a dreadful situation – sittin' on that wicker chair fully engaged so to speak and advancin' towards me was me hostess's very considerable arse.'

'What happened, Cuckoo?' chorused the guests.

'Well, I toyed with the idea of flingin' meself sideways to the floor but I took off one of these slippers,' here the seventh Earl displayed his monogrammed footwear, 'and when it came into range, I whacked her hard on the right buttock. She uttered a cry and disappeared at full gallop I can tell you. Poor old Dora . . . it was a Friday night so all weekend she must have bin wonderin' which of the house party had seen her bum.'

The evening passed pleasantly enough with bridge, back-gammon and gossip about an assortment of highly bred animals. Finally, Pandora steered Stani upstairs and never before had her nursery witnessed such a variety of games.

They also lay for hours talking about the future. Both were determined that war or no war they would not be separated.

'Don't you ever go off and leave me again, darling. I was a zombie without you,' Pandora sighed. 'People thought I was ill, I missed you so dreadfully.'

Stani hugged her. 'I wish I wasn't so jealous. You never should have warned me about yourself. Tell me you didn't mean it, for God's sake.'

She smiled. 'I did *then* . . . I don't now.'

Sometime in the early hours, she must have slipped back to her room because, around six o'clock, mouse-like scuffles from the region of the fireplace alerted Stani to the fact that a housemaid was cleaning out the grate, re-laying and lighting the fire. The nursery was intensely cold and, through half-closed eyes, he watched the girl's billowing breath as she laboured.

At eight o'clock, Henry brought a cup of tea and a morning paper, each page of which had been ironed to ensure that cheap war time print would not soil fingers or sheets.

'Breakfast for the gentlemen is downstairs, sir. The ladies have it on trays. I took the liberty of laying out a nice warm shirt and a sweater of his Lordship's and a pair of thick socks and some gum boots for the shoot. There's a nasty east wind this morning; there was quite a frost during the night.'

Conversation was minimal at breakfast. A few 'good mornings' were grunted in Stani's direction as he seated himself at a round table in the hall. A log fire was blazing away and Powis presided over a sideboard laden with porridge, ham, scrambled eggs, bacon, sausage, kippers and cold partridge. Everything except the kippers came from the Hawksmoor estate. Stani ate heartily, trying not to think of the ration books which provided the average Briton with four rashers of bacon, two ounces of butter and one chop a week, and one fresh egg a month.

Soon after breakfast, the other 'guns' arrived – a farmer whose land 'marched' with Hawksmoor, a couple of local squires and an elderly Duke who considered that he was entitled to the best position at each drive. With Cuckoo, Archie, Sir Hercules and Stani, they numbered eight in all.

The fifty or so beaters, a mixture of soldiers home on leave and school boys playing truant, formed up on the sacred circle of turf in front of the house. All were equipped with long sticks of hazel wood and looked expectantly forward to a hot lunch with barrels of draught ale at midday and two pounds sterling apiece at the end of the proceedings. They knew that the Head Keeper would harry them mercilessly across fields, through vast expanses of wet, waist-high kale and over brown vistas of dead bracken, but, with excited cries of 'Cock over!' 'Hen back!' 'Hare forward!' and 'Woodcock!' they were apparently content to provide sport for the guns.

The activities started with a long walk over stubble with guns and beaters in a line pushing forward coveys of partridge for a later drive. Hares were plentiful and usually, with tiny hooves thudding, scampered away well ahead of the advancing line.

140

One, however, immediately in front of Stani, chose to lay back its ears, snuggle down in the stubble and hope for the best. A beater next to Stani whacked the ground behind the terrified animal and exhorted it to 'get oop ye lazy brute and join in't sport like other folk.'

Away went the hare in instant top gear and Stani, the focal point of all eyes, with his gun still on 'safe', missed the first chance of the day. But he was secretly delighted because he had seen the fear in the cowering; furry shape.

The first set piece was a drive of pheasants out of a large wood. To ensure high flying birds, the guns were strategically placed in a dell down wind at one end while the beaters, keepers and assorted dogs were poised to go to work starting at the other.

Cuckoo stationed Stani in a field behind the beaters.

'Save you a walk,' he said kindly, 'afraid those stubble fields were a bit much for your leg. Some old cocks will break back towards that plantation over there so you should get some shootin'. Old Tom will bring you along in the game cart for the next drive. I'll leave Solomon with you to help you pick. Sit!' he commanded a black labrador and pointed to Stani's feet. The dog instantly squatted as ordered and cocked its obedient head after its master as he strode off to join the others.

It was bitterly cold. An underkeeper offered Stani a silver flask from a cartridge bag.

''is Lordship's special brew, Sir – port and brandy mixed – 'e calls it 'is 'eart starter.'

After a long wait, three distant whistle blasts announced that the guns were in position and ready for action.

'All right, lads,' shouted the Head Keeper, 'in you go then – beat that bracken out good and proper and don't follow each other in single file like a lot of bleedin' Red Indians.' The beaters disappeared into the wood and soon whistles and calls of 'over' reverberated from its dense interior. Distant gun fire was heard. Solomon sat motionless. A few knowing birds flashed high out of the trees above Stani's head with their gaudy Chinese plumage a poor camouflage and headed gratefully for the plantation of firs. For form's sake, he fired a salute at them as they rocketed past but managed not to disturb a feather. Solomon looked depressed. As the beater noises re-

141

ceded deeper into the wood, stillness and peace descended upon Stani and he indulged himself in the beauty of the bronze and gold of the trees in the pale winter sunshine and the sparkling frost crystals on the grass beneath his feet. High above his head, a glint of silver and the sky trails of a flight of patrolling Spitfires momentarily caught his attention.

Suddenly, Solomon stiffened, got to his feet and, with hackles up and muzzle thrust forward, stalked something in a high pile of bracken just inside the wood.

'Oh! God!' thought Stani. 'Another hare.' He looked furtively around to make sure he was not being observed, then, to please the dog and with no intention of shooting the poor frightened little beast that was about to be flushed out of its hiding place, he followed, his gun still on 'safe'. Solomon stood immobile, his tail quivering, sniffing and 'pointing' at the bracken pile. Stani, the amateur, made noises to please the professional.

'Good boy!' he said. 'Go get it out then!'

Furious barking on the part of Solomon produced a movement in the bracken pile from something much larger than a hare and Stani found himself looking into a pair of pale blue eyes.

Slowly a man rose; leaves were in his blonde hair, his pullover and blue-grey trousers were torn and filthy. He was about nineteen years old, very cold and very frightened. He clasped his hands above his head and spoke with a heavy accent.

'For me the war is over,' he announced.

'Where did you come from?' asked Stani.

'I give only my name, rank and number,' said the boy with dignity. Stani saw he was close to tears.

Stani spoke in German. 'Put your hands down. I am an officer of the R.A.F.'

The boy obeyed but looked with fear at Stani's gun. He lowered it.

'Not war today,' he said with a smile. 'We are shooting pheasants.'

The boy stared at him without comprehending and Stani's mind flashed back to that moment when fate had put a Fokker Wolf into his sights in mid-Atlantic and his own fear-numbed fingers had automatically disembowelled it with a long burst

142

from his eight machine guns.

'I imagine you were shot down in the raid on Rugby last night.'

The boy did not answer.

'Do you have a contact in England you would have tried to make if the dog hadn't found you? You don't have to say anything except "yes" or "no".'

'Yes,' said the boy after a pause. 'A man . . . a man who my father helped to escape from Germany two years ago . . . a Jew. . . . Yes, I would have tried to find him, though I don't expect he would have wanted to help me.' He shrugged.

Stani heard only dimly the popping guns and the rural cries; he was no longer beside a quiet English wood, he was far away in mid-Atlantic, looking at a blazing bomber with its doomed crew of young men. He heard himself speak.

'Where is this man?'

The boy hesitated. 'In London.'

'Go by train,' said Stani. 'The station is two or three miles down that lane. If anybody asks, say you are a Pole. The British will believe it.'

The boy looked incredulous.

'Why?' he asked, 'why are you doing this? You are risking too much. . . . I don't understand. . . .'

'Neither do I.' said Stani, 'but get going.'

He pointed into the field. A patient carthorse stood between the shafts of an ancient vehicle containing the game so far shot, spare cartridges and a pile of gum boots and rain coats for the beaters. 'You'll find some clothes in that cart but the man will be back soon so get a move on. Here, you'll need this,' he added and shoved into the astonished young man's hand all he had in his pockets – a few pounds and some loose change. 'Good luck!' he said, 'Auf wiedersehn!'

The boy shook his head in disbelief, flashed a wide conspiratorial grin, then bowed stiffly and ran off.

When old Tom, the carter, appeared he was accompanied by Archie.

'Cuckoo sent me back,' said the Captain, rather sourly. 'How'd you get on? Anything to pick?'

'No, nothing,' said Stani. 'It was pretty quiet back here – a few old cocks came out very wide and headed for the plantation,

143

otherwise nothing.'

'Very little came out at our end either. Very odd,' said Archie as they climbed into the game cart. 'You didn't see anyone around did you? One of the underkeepers said he thought he saw someone go into that covert early this morning.' He looked directly at Stani who shook his head.

'Well,' Archie continued, 'whoever it was the bloody feller was worse than a fox.'

Conversation was stilled as the cart bumped and lurched down a rutted track so Stani had plenty of time to reflect on his quixotic gesture and the more he considered it, the more peculiar it seemed.

'Revenge,' he thought, 'does not seem to be part of my make-up. If I'd shot him it wouldn't have made me feel any better about my father, my mother, my foot or my face.'

'That's a very nice tweed you have there,' he said indicating the Captain's natty ensemble of cap, jacket and knicker-bockers, all of discreet grey-green with a large overcheck of purplish-brown. 'I notice that Lord Hawksmoor and the Duke have the same pattern as yours – is it made locally?'

'I wouldn't know where it is made,' said Archie pompously, 'but it's specially woven for past and present members of the Household Cavalry – that is the Life Guards and the Blues – no one else can wear it, I'm afraid.'

'It looks good on you,' said Stani, 'it goes well with your eyes.'

Archie looked nonplussed and changed the subject.

After several more 'drives' the shoot came to a halt and the guns were greeted by a farmer's wife who ushered them into her scrubbed and rescrubbed parlour where Powis, Henry and another manservant served an impeccable white-clothed luncheon. On a sliding scale of class distinction and diminishing comforts, the others ate elsewhere, the keepers in her kitchen, the chauffeurs in a barn and the loaders, soldiers, carters and school boys in a variety of draughty sheds or open ditches.

Pandora and Chrissie, looking very chic in head scarves, tweeds and Newmarket boots, joined the lunch party and afterwards, using the same distinctions, sat on their shooting sticks 'oohing' and 'aahing' at the prowess of the men folk, first behind the Duke, then Cuckoo, Sir Hercules, the others and finally, behind Stani.

'You're a bloody awful shot, darling,' remarked Pandora. 'I don't know how you ever managed to hit that bomber.'

After lunch, Stani, telling himself that he was helping to fill the national larder, dispatched a couple of hen pheasants and a rabbit for her benefit but derived no pleasure from it and was delighted when Cuckoo excused him from the remaining drives and ordered him back to Hawksmoor to rest his leg.

Henry was waiting to pour his bath. He produced an envelope marked O.H.M.S.

'I got my call up today, sir, from the Army. I go for my medical next week. I must say I don't fancy that life at all. I don't think I could kill a man if my life depended on it.'

'It's not easy,' said Stani. 'Training helps a lot, though.'

'I think I'd be more useful on the land or even in a factory,' said Henry wistfully. 'I've been in domestic service all my life and I'm just not cut out to be a soldier; perhaps I could get a job with ENSA entertaining the troops. I do imitations in the Servants' Hall . . . they go down very well.'

'People do all sorts of things to avoid military service,' said Stani, 'but that's breaking the law. I think the best thing is to join up and then get thrown out as an "undesirable".'

'How would one set about that, sir?'

'Well, one of the riggers in my outfit drank a gallon of water every night before he went to bed and let it all go a few hours later in his blankets. After a while they let *him* go because bed-wetters are not very popular in barrack rooms.'

'Thank you, sir,' said Henry. 'I'll bear that in mind. His Lordship says will you be riding with him after church tomorrow, sir? He likes to shake up his liver before lunch and it does the hunters good to get some exercise.'

Stani's riding experience was confined to sitting in comfortable Western saddles atop old plugs on the hillside trails or beaches of Santa Barbara County.

'No,' he said, 'I think I'll skip that. I wouldn't want to embarrass the horse.'

'I'm sure you'd never do that, sir,' said Henry. 'I'll lay out your uniform for church.'

Sunday produced a perfect winter's morning and the house party duly paraded at twenty minutes to eleven to walk, headed by Cuckoo, half a mile to the little Norman church of Hawks-moor. The pale sun was slowly dispelling an early ground mist but crouching stone lions on either side of the front steps still wore sparkling coats of frost. The distant church bells competed with the cawing of rooks in the high elms and under the golden beeches, rabbits and little knots of deer raised their heads to gauge the danger of the approaching hatted, tweeded and brogued procession. Stani thought of the sweating soldiers in Malayan jungles or African deserts, the numbed and frost-bitten sailors on Arctic convoys and, above all, of the airmen somewhere locked in battles thirty thousand feet above his head. And he wondered anew at his host's insistence that the subject of war should be taboo at Hawksmoor.

Inside the little church was a congregation of villagers and local gentry with a sprinkling of service men on leave. The atmosphere generated by the parson, an ex-Naval Chaplain who wore his World War I medals on his vestments, was a family one, with Cuckoo, who read the second lesson, a much loved father figure.

The house party sat in the private family pew tucked away behind the choir, warmed by a small wood-burning fireplace. Above the altar was a stained glass window of great beauty if somewhat erratic design, the result, Pandora explained, of villagers having taken it to pieces at the time of Oliver Cromwell and hidden it at the bottom of the river to save it from being smashed by the Dictator. Later, they had reassembled it from memory which accounted for two apostles with distinctly virginal faces and one sheep with a beard.

On the walls of the nave were reminders of members of the Hawksmoor family, many killed in battles fought by England since Agincourt. Again and again, Naseby, the family name, appeared upon marble plaques or beneath stone-carved figures in armour. One Richard Naseby, posthumously knighted by King Henry VIII on the field of battle for gallantry at Tournai in 1521, intrigued Stani, but a plaque in bright, white marble directly opposite the family pew caught his eye because it had been so lately fashioned.

In ever loving memory of
Flying Officer, The Viscount Naseby
aged 19

146

Slain in the Battle of Britain
September 13th, 1940.

Stani pressed his knee against Pandora and raised his eyebrows.

'My brother,' she whispered, 'the last of the Hawksmoors. Daddy can't bear to talk about it.'

10

When the pains first returned to Stani's foot he asked Mrs. Quansett-Fowles for some aspirin. When the swelling made it impossible for him to wear his improved surgical boot, he allowed her to bandage it heavily and sat for a couple of days in her drawing room with his leg on a stool and a drink at his elbow, as she put it . . . 'like some pissed old Duke in Whites a hundred years ago'. When he could bear it no longer she telephoned the R.A.F. Hospital Uxbridge. Apparently a splinter of bone had detached itself and was pressing against an extremity of the sciatic nerve.

'You've been using it too much' said the surgeon. 'Also there's an awful lot of decalcification in the whole movement area – I'm afraid we'll have to go back to the drawing board and remake your foot for you.'

It was a long job, brilliantly done, but Stani spent the greater part of the next six months in and out of various hospitals.

In September 1943 he was discharged by the R.A.F. doctors and given a month's convalescence leave before re-posting; it had been terribly painful but the results justified it – and – a major development, he had utilized the time taking an advanced course in photography. He found himself absorbed and fascinated and determined to pursue it if ever he had the chance.

Pandora had been a constant visitor. Shortly before he left the hospital she appeared at his bedside, her cat's eyes shining with excitement.

'I didn't want to tell you in case it never happened, but it's been cooking for months . . . Chuck has been a great help and finally it arrived . . . Signed by Hank Greenberg!'

'What?'

148

'A contract of course, with Metropolis Pictures!!! *Please* be happy for me . . . I've wanted it *so* much, for *such* a long time – to go to Hollywood, and now it's happened! . . . can you *believe* it?'

Stani felt a shock wave of apprehension, he tried hard to be enthusiastic but the wrong words came out.

'It's not very patriotic is it? . . . I mean going off in the middle of the War, leaving your father and everyone behind eating whale meat and powdered eggs . . .'

'Daddy *never* eats whale meat', said Pandora stoutly, 'and he wouldn't be seen *dead* with a powdered egg. . . . Anyway don't be so bloody-minded – the contract starts *after* the War is over!'

'I'm sorry' he mumbled, 'I just hated the thought of your going away.' Pandora kissed him. 'When I go . . . you're coming with me, aren't you? . . . Promise?'

He agreed of course, but if Pandora's news was a source of unease, a visit by Colonel Zamowski was a body blow. He arrived with final confirmation of his father's death.

'The Germans found the bodies, fifteen thousand of them, last month, buried in a wood at Katyn, they had been machine-gunned. The farmers accused the Russians of doing it and offered proof, then the Russians accused the Germans. The International Red Cross offered to investigate officially. The Germans agreed but the Russians refused to let them go near the place.'

On his next visit Colonel Zamowski produced an interesting idea, 'I have found a way to utilize your many languages,' he said. 'Soon the Allied Armies will be liberating the Continent. Nobody knows how many poor souls will have been forcibly deported from their own countries to work as slave labour for the Germans or to be locked up in Concentration Camps. The estimates are as high as twenty million. All these people will have to be collected, fed and looked after.'

'What's going to happen to them once they're collected?'

'It's being worked out now. Roosevelt, Churchill and Stalin will meet and a decision will be taken at the highest level but in the meantime we must organize so we will not be unprepared.'

'And me?'

'You will be invaluable to the Commandant of one of the Collection and Dispersal Units.'

149

Stani tried hard to persuade the Colonel that he was the wrong man for the job but finally found himself compelled to tell Pandora that he had to leave her once again. She cried and told him that she truly loved him, which made him even more unhappy, but he had underrated her patriotism.

'Of course you must go, darling, you'd feel awful if you didn't, and it won't be long . . . everyone says it'll be over by Christmas', she added hopefully.

The parting was a prolonged agony while he awaited his final orders and they both faced the dreadful cruelty of separation without any guarantee of communication.

On June 5, 1944 General Eisenhower locked himself in a room in his Headquarters in Southern England. Only he knew that when he emerged, he would have to give one of two signals. Either he would order five Divisions of American, British and Canadian troops to embark in gale-force winds and mountainous seas to cross the Channel to Normandy, in an attempt to breach Hitler's Atlantic Wall and open the door for the Salvation of Europe – or, he must announce the postponement of the entire Operation for a month, thereby inviting disaster because of inevitable leaks of information.

When Eisenhower, haggard and hollow-eyed, came out of the room, he gave the thumbs-up signal. Immediately the soldiers boarded their tossing craft, paratroopers blacked their faces and climbed into their transports, and the escorting warships primed their guns. The storm abated fractionally – and the rest is History.

While Eisenhower had been doing his agonizing, Stani and No. 36 C.A.D. Unit had been doing some agonizing of their own, trying to carry out his instructions.

'Proceed to the area Canterbury-Dover-Folkestone-Deal and keep all vehicles moving constantly along main roads till further orders.' No. 36 C.A.D., in concert with a motley assembly of thousands of other vehicles, was part of a master plan to bamboozle German Intelligence into thinking the Invasion was preparing to head for the Pas de Calais area. In reality, it was already being mounted a hundred miles to the West, preparatory to making the much longer crossing to the Normandy Peninsula.

For No. 36 C.A.D. the pre-Invasion antics provided a useful shake-down cruise. Stani was the only R.A.F. Officer, the hundred or so other ranks and N.C.O.'s were mostly Reservists with World War I medals, or recycled younger men like Stani himself, who had been wounded and patched up for further light duty. A slightly mad Sergeant Major from the Commandos named Monk, who had blown himself up in Tunisia was in charge of discipline; he insisted on the officers addressing him as 'Mr. Monk'. Three scholarly Lieutenants of sloppy appearance from Army Intelligence were in charge of interrogation and documentation. The Commanding Officer, a Major Glasebalt, known to one and all as 'Glassballs', was a round left-over Regular from a County Regiment, a man of total honesty and enviable relaxation. He was happy to be relieved of his job as R.T.O. (Railway Transport Officer) at Clapham Junction, where he had been bombed incessantly for three years.

'Glad to have you aboard,' he beamed, when Stani reported. 'Let me introduce you to Nell.' Nell was large and hairy and dribbling from the corners of her mouth. She was an Irish wolfhound.

No. 36 C.A.D. had little to do once the cliff-hanging operations in Normandy got under way; but in mid-July when the German Army was in full retreat across Northern France, they were despatched to the Continent. The Agreement reached by Roosevelt, Churchill and Stalin was deceptively simple. 'All Displaced Persons as soon as practicable will be returned to their countries of origin.'

No. 36 C.A.D. was called upon to implement this order for the first time when several thousand Polish miners, forced to work in the pits around Lille, came storming to the surface, brandishing Polish flags and demanding to kill Germans or Russians, whichever were nearest.

Stani persuaded them that they would soon be going home but did not have the nerve to tell them that many of their homes would turn out to be in the 30,000 square miles of Poland which Churchill and Roosevelt had handed over to Stalin.

'Good show, Stani,' said 'Glassballs'. 'You're doing fine.'

While Belgium, Denmark and Holland were being liberated, the infamous concentration camps disgorged several million

151

French, Belgian, Danish and Dutch prisoners and Italian, Czech, Yugoslav and Ukrainian slave labourers. No. 36 C.A.D., functioning within its designated areas and working overtime, followed behind the advancing Allies, sifting and rearranging lives, passing their share of a mass of human flotsam back to transit camps or to badly needed hospital treatment centres. Women and small children were in great abundance.

In Belgium the first of a series of complicated situations arose in the form of several hundred Latvians who in the early days had joined the conquering German Army to help rid their country of the hated Russians. After fighting bravely on the Russian Front with an S.S. Division, they had been trapped by the British army near Antwerp; they surrendered, wreathed in smiles, bearing flowers and happy to be back among friends. No. 36 C.A.D., sent for to deal with the situation, installed them in its already bulging confines and asked for a directive from Eisenhower's H.Q. in Versailles. It was a shocker: 'Russian Mission in Paris insists all Latvians be treated as Russians and moved forthwith to holding camps for repatriation to Russia.'

'What do we do about that, sir?' Stani asked. 'The Russians will chop them up, for fighting against them in the first place.'

'Hmm,' said 'Glassballs'. 'We have a tricky situation here. Let me give it some thought.' Later he handed down his decision.

'Stani,' he said, 'it's perfectly simple, clear as day in fact. Go down to their compound and explain to the Head Lat what this signal says. Make quite sure he understands it. Then tell him that those who *want* to go to Russia should stay here. Those who don't, should take advantage of the fact that our gates are always open. How many are there, by the way?'

'Four hundred and eighty, sir.'

'Splendid!' said 'Glassballs'. 'Good show!'

Overnight four hundred and eighty Latvians disappeared. When this became known to the Russian Mission in Paris, complaints were lodged at the highest level, and 'Glassballs' and Nell were last seen being driven away by a major of the Military Police.

Stani carried on as ordered: 'You will assume command of

No. 36 C.A.D. until replaced.' He became extremely proud of his command. 'Mr. Monk' remained eccentric and always addressed an area above the crown of Stani's cap, but the outfit itself developed a cohesion and teamwork under his hand, and the young Intelligence officers laboured like Victorian bank apprentices, hunched over their files from dawn till dusk.

Christmas 1944 found No. 36 C.A.D. in Belgium, dispersed among farm buildings near the village of Tubize on the edge of the Forest of Soignes. Frozen fog clothed the bare trees with beauty, ice and snow were underfoot. The location adjoined the hallowed battlefield of Waterloo. Some mail had finally caught up with them and the lucky ones had been reading and re-reading letters from their loved ones. Nothing had come from Pandora and Stani was thoroughly depressed. On Christmas morning he was addressing his men; beside him stood a Staff Captain from 21st Army Group; behind the Captain was a staff car and a truck.

'A bad situation has developed to our South,' Stani was saying, his breath billowing on the frosty air. 'The Germans have launched a major offensive through the Ardennes with the intention of crossing the Meuse, swinging North, reaching the Coast at Antwerp and cutting off the British and American Armies which are on the point of crossing the Rhine. Here we will be right in their path.'

The men looked uneasily at one another.

'The enemy has already made substantial advances,' Stani continued. 'They are spearheaded by paratroops wearing American uniforms and armoured units using captured American half-tracks and tanks. This officer tells me that the situation, because of fog keeping our aircraft grounded, is very confused but very dangerous indeed. At the moment the American 101 Airborne Division at Bastogne is holding up the German advance but if they break through there, No. 36 C.A.D. can expect to be in action at any moment.' Stani felt a wobbly sensation in his knees as the words put into his mouth by the Staff Captain sank into his own brain.

'Most of you have already seen action but of course we are not trained or equipped as a fighting unit.' He paused and turned to the Staff Captain. 'This officer has kindly brought us some armament. He says our job will be to find and destroy all

153

enemy tanks within our area.' As he spoke those ludicrous words and saw the utter disbelief on the faces of his gallant comrades, he curbed the hysterical laughter which welled up inside him. He turned to the Staff Captain. 'Would you care to say a few words?'

The Captain had a gargling voice that matched his pale face and weedy frame. He addressed No. 36 C.A.D. as follows:

'I have to be going, actually. We have a lot on our plate at the moment as you can well imagine. Your commanding officer will detail the defensive plan for your area. He will also arrange for the demonstration and distribution of weapons.'

Stani could hardly believe his ears at the idiot's parting words . . . 'and don't forget – the Bosche is no man's fool.'

When the Army officer had gone, the men stamped warmth into their feet and waited for Stani's instructions. With his limited knowledge of things military, he fell back on a time-honoured ploy.

'Mr. Monk!' he shouted.

'Sir?' came the answering roar.

'Tell everyone to fall out. Smoke, move about and keep warm . . . back in fifteen minutes!'

'Sir!!'

Alone with the Sergeant Major, he got down to basics.

'What the hell do we do?' he asked.

'Check the weapons and ammunition first, sir. Then call for volunteers who know 'ow to 'andle 'em.'

'What about the Intelligence Officers?'

'Under the circumstances, sir, with due respect – fuck 'em.'

In the truck from the 21st Army Group, they unveiled two heavy machine guns, a number of Tommy guns, hand grenades, two dozen bazookas, six anti-tank rifles and four cases marked: DANGER. ADHESIVE EXPLOSIVES!

'Them bazookas are the only thing worth a damn against armour,' said Mr. Monk. 'The rest is pissing into the wind, Sir . . . Wonder they didn't send us catapults and a bag of stones.'

'What about these Adhesive Explosives?'

'Never 'eard of 'em mesself Sir. Beg to suggest you ask if anyone 'as previous experience.'

No. 36 C.A.D. were reassembled. When Stani brought them

up to date, a wave of enthusiasm swept the ranks. Experts on the various weapons (mostly wounded veterans of desert battles or Commando raids) happily volunteered to lead tank hunting squads and to hold crash courses in training and communications. Mr. Monk's foghorn voice silenced the babel.

'Anyone 'ave knowledge of these 'ere Adhesive Explosives?'

Monk held aloft a brown aluminium object the shape and size of a small football; a six inch handle protruded from it.

'It looks like a Sticky Bomb to me,' said an educated voice, and a former bank manager stepped forward. 'They issued a few to us in the Home Guard just after Dunkirk – they were reported to be somewhat volatile.'

'Cut out that fancy language, Rifleman Cottesmore. Step up and show the Commanding Officer 'ow they work . . . smartly now!'

After some time with the former bank manager, Stani turned to Mr. Monk.

'I think we should demonstrate this weapon to the men. What can we blow up?'

''igh time the farmer got rid of 'is open air shit 'ouse . . . pardon the word sir . . . latrine. All rocks and cement, pongs to 'igh 'eaven . . . take a bit of knocking down, that will, you could stick one on that.' Mr. Monk, bent upon stage managing the forthcoming experiment, quickly gathered No. 36 C.A.D. in the vicinity of the noisome little igloo. A stream ran nearby. He handed Stani a Sticky Bomb and roared at the assembled soldiery.

'Pay attention now so you don't blow yourselves to pieces.'

Stani tapped the protruding handle.

'This handle is in two sections, held together by a locking pin. If I remove that pin the sections will spring apart, triggering the bomb and in seven seconds it will explode. At the moment I have no intention of touching that pin, so gather round and take a good look.'

Not without apprehension the men formed a close circle.

'The idea,' Stani continued, 'is to crawl up to a tank without being seen. Unfortunately they provided no Manual to explain how that is done!' (Scattered laughter greeted this remark.) 'Once alongside the tank, you open up this catch and peel away the aluminium covering.' Stani demonstrated as he spoke and the covering came away, revealing what looked like a giant toffee apple. '. . . and – there is your bomb! Two and half pounds of *very* high explosive!' He held it high by the handle for all to see.

'That yellow substance coating the bomb is an adhesive of great strength. The explosive itself can be moulded like putty. So once alongside your objective, you simply pull out the locking pin, jam the bomb on the side of the tank . . . and run like hell. Any questions?

For a while the pros and cons of the 'sticky bomb' were discussed, then Stani, unable to put off the evil moment any longer, called upon Mr. Monk to move No. 36 C.A.D. out of range.

'Down the bank of the stream! Smartly now,' he yelled. From the safety of the bank Monk continued: 'Watch carefully as the Commanding Officer prepares the bomb and approaches the latrine: when 'e places it upon the objective and commences 'is retreat you may get your 'eads down, 'ug the bank closely; any man who takes cover before the Commanding Officer starts running will be in trouble – got it?'

Although Stani had carefully noted the shortest route between the farmer's doomed privy and his own reserved place next to the Sergeant Major, when he found himself all alone with the sticky bomb his knees started clanking together like castanets.

'I am now approaching the enemy tank!' he shouted, and was alarmed by how high his voice sounded. Through tufts of frozen grass two hundred eyes watched his Quasimodo-like shuffle.

'I am now removing the covering!'

He did so and looked back at the head tops; they seemed a mile away. Suppose he slipped and fell on the icy ground. What if the Staff Captain had lied about the seven seconds? His tongue was becoming glued to the roof of his mouth; he had to force out the next words.

'I have removed the locking pin . . . I am still keeping my grip on the handle . . . I am about to place the bomb.'

With his arm slightly behind him Stani took one last look at the bank – it now seemed two miles away. He worked a finger through his shirt and touched Pandora's disc.

'Here goes!' he yelled and made the final lunge.

Nothing happened.

'MISTER MONK!!'

'Sir?'

'I'VE STUCK IT ON MY ASS!'

Sounds of confusion and consternation rose from his distant charges; but they were stilled by Monk's mighty bellow.

''ave you released the 'andle?'

'No!' Stani yelled back, and as he spoke his forearm muscles began to cramp beneath their awesome responsibilities.

'Stand up any man with a pair of scissors about 'is person!'

'I've got a knife, Sergeant Major,' someone shouted.

'Over to the latrine smartly now, and cut away the officer's trousers.'

Stani prayed that his rock hard muscles would not snap under the strain. The soldier slithered to a stop beside him, appraised the situation and made clucking noises.

'Afraid we'll have to take off most of the leg, sir – you might get it sewn on again.'

'Anything you say,' Stani breathed.

While he laboured at the seams the soldier indulged in calming Cockney wisdom.

'. . .'orrible stuff them 'igh explosives,' he said.

'Can't be too careful wiv 'em . . . never know what they'll do. Nasty incident down our way during the Blitz, sir. Poor old No. 19, they got a direct 'it. Luvly little kid they 'ad in that 'ouse, 'e was out in the street playing wiv 'is 'oop when it dropped. Stretched 'im out about fifteen feet long that bomb did. Very nasty stuff!' He showed Stani the remains of his trouser leg. 'There we are, sir! Lucky you didn't stick it on that nice flying jacket. Any message for the Sarnt Major?'

Stani held the sticky bomb in front of him; it was decorated with a ragged patch of Air Force blue.

'Tell him' he said, as calmly as he could, 'that I'll stick this bloody thing on the wall as soon as you get back.'

Once the man had rejoined them, the watching troops saw a flash of white buttock as their Commanding Officer leaned forward and jammed the lethal device against the rough wall of the farmer's sanctuary. When he turned and ran they ducked below the bank. Despite the ice Stani arrived on winged feet and flung himself panting beside Mr. Monk. The Sergeant Major was consulting his watch.

'Any second now, Sir,' he said, and pressed his face into the cold mud.

Five minutes later no explosion had occurred. After fifteen minutes it was decided to return to camp, following the course of the stream on hands and knees. As befitted his station, Stani led the way and No. 36 C.A.D. dutifully crawled after his exposed flank for several hundred yards. Half an hour later Stani was questioning Rifleman Cottesmore on the subject of defusing the weapon when with a BANG and a roar fragments of the farmer's distant toilet were flung a hundred feet into the air. The ex-bank manager shook his head.

'Very volatile,' he said.

Thanks to the extreme gallantry of the Americans, the attack by the German Sixth Panzer Army in the Ardennes was repulsed. After four weeks of heavy fighting, the Germans withdrew with the loss of a quarter of a million men, six hundred tanks and nearly two thousand aircraft; they reeled back towards the Fatherland. In March the Allies swarmed across the last great obstacle to victory – the River Rhine. By the beginning of May the long bloody war in Europe was over, but for No. 36 C.A.D. there was little relief.

For nine months they had been continuously on the move, like circus roustabouts, building and dismantling their compounds, feeding, sheltering and sorting thousands of Displaced Persons. When the Germans surrendered unconditionally, Stani settled his overworked troops in more permanent quarters in the pretty village of Feldbach, in Lower Saxony, only twenty miles from the River Elbe and the nearest Russians. By now between eight and ten million Displaced Persons were wandering all over Northern Europe and Stani's patrols, scouring his sector, returned all day long with truckloads of emaciated and starving humans found lying in woods, ditches and hedgerows, their feet bleeding and their heads on pathetic bundles of belongings, too exhausted and too hungry to take another step in their efforts to find their way home.

One morning Mr. Monk, with a stamping of feet, shattered the calm of the office Stani had set up in a windmill. In strict

158

chronological order he had been luxuriating in a delivery of twenty ever more loving letters from Pandora. The latest was seven weeks old.

'Instructions, sir, please,' he bellowed, 'An entire Regiment of Cossacks complete with 'orses 'as just surrendered to me personal-like.'

Stani shuddered. 'Where are they?'

'Camped down by the river, sir, swimmin' and singin' . . . very fine voices if I may say so.'

The Cossack Colonel was a magnificent man with a bristling moustache and turquoise eyes. He and his men were dressed in black fur hats, white blouses, baggy breeches and shod with high leather boots; they numbered five or six hundred, all had rifles slung upon their backs. The Colonel received Stani's salute and conversed in fluent German.

'We have come to you because the camps further North said they could not accommodate us.' He pointed to some trees; sitting patiently in the shade near a dozen horse drawn baggage carts were fifty or sixty women and children. 'Our families are with us,' he explained.

The Colonel and Stani sat on a fallen branch.

'We are Cossacks of the Don,' he said proudly, 'farming people. We have always hated the Bolsheviks and have fought against their oppression. When the Germans arrived in 1942 we looked upon them as our deliverers and willingly helped them. They were good to us and returned our property, stolen by the Bolsheviks. After the defeat of the Germans at Stalingrad we were afraid of what the Bolsheviks would do to us so we followed the German Army West. They were still good to us and settled us near Minsk. They formed us into a support Regiment growing food and supplying and training horses for their transport.'

'Colonel,' Stani interrupted, 'if you have come here to surrender, I must first insist that you lay down your arms.'

The Colonel frowned.

'You are a German Army Unit, Colonel,' Stani explained. 'And you surrendered unconditionally three weeks ago when Admiral Doenitz signed the documents.

'My men will not like to be separated from their rifles,' said the Colonel stubbornly.

159

Stani had a dreadful vision of having to lead his motley crew, assisted by Mr. Monk and the three Intelligence Officers, against a Regiment of Cossacks.

'If I accept your conditions,' the Colonel continued. 'What will you offer us?'

'Food, medical attention and what shelter I can until such time as I can arrange for your repatriation.'

'To Russia?'

'According to the Yalta Agreement – yes.'

The Colonel rose and looked down upon Stani. 'You would be sending us to torture and to our deaths,' he said evenly. 'We will be treated as traitors.'

Stani cursed the luck that had pitchforked him into this situation.

'Believe me, Colonel, I am very sympathetic – I am born a Pole and understand your problem. But I have to follow my orders.'

The Cossack shook his head.

'My men will fight the Japanese, they will do anything you ask, but they will never willingly return to Russia.'

Stani wished he could rub a bottle and a genie in the comfortable shape of 'Glassballs' would materialize. 'Glassballs'? Maybe there was a 'Glassball Solution'!

'One thing I can promise you, Colonel,' he said, 'is that so long as I am in charge here nobody will be *forced* to go back to his country of origin against his wishes.'

The Colonel's blue eyes misted over, he took Stani's hand in both of his.

'Thank you, young man,' he said. 'There have been terrible mistakes made. I will see that our arms are made ready for disposal immediately.'

Rumours of Russian agents infiltrating the Collection Camps having freely circulated, Stani, harbouring an entire Cossack regiment twenty miles from the Red Army, spent several sleepless nights. After three days he received an ominous message from Versailles: *Russian Mission requests information regarding your plans to repatriate immediately all Russian nationals under your jurisdiction. Treat as urgent.*

Experienced enough by now to muddy the waters of military bureaucracy in order to gain time, he replied thus: *Status of*

160

Tartars in Crimea appears unclear request Russian Mission official clarification of their position.

When the answer arrived from Supreme Headquarters. Stani hurried to the Cossack compound by the river. It was a cloudless day. Children were splashing in the water, men exercised horses or smoked in groups upon the lush grass, the women were washing clothes or cooking, there was a delightful family atmosphere and as he walked towards the Colonel's tent Stani received cheers from the men, smiles and waves from the women, children ran to greet him.

In his pocket were his orders. He had resolved to read them to the Colonel but the man's child-like trust sealed his lips.

'You have saved us,' said the Russian, his face shining with gratitude. 'We were all decided to kill ourselves with honour rather than let the Bolsheviks torture us, then shoot us like dogs.'

Stani excused himself as soon as he could and drove his Jeep at maximum speed to the nearest C.A.D. Unit in the American Sector some forty miles South at Klugendorf. His counterpart there, a lean bespectacled Major, in peacetime an attorney in Houston, Texas, was housed in great comfort in a Schloss with a trout stream running past the windows. Two or three thousand D.P.'s were lodged in a tent city in the Park, smart Military Police were everywhere, it all seemed much better organized and better run than 'Fort Glassballs'. Stani was given a real Texas welcome, then the American listened as he described his problem.

'I can see we both have the same idea here,' the Texan said. 'Screw Roosevelt, Churchill and Stalin! We're not handing anyone over to the Russians unless they want to be handed over . . . that right?'

'Right,' said Stani.

'So there's no problem then,' said Red Wyatt. 'We're not fixing bayonets and forcing people to go where they don't want to go – that's what we went to war to *stop* . . . right?'

'Right.'

'So . . .' said Red Wyatt, stretching, 'have another 'Wild Turkey' and come catch a trout.'

'It's not that easy,' said Stani, producing his orders. 'Take a look at this!'

161

'*Tartar problem does not concern you stop. Russians insist you immediately return Cossacks in your camp stop they are German Army prisoners of war stop Russians threatening to cancel repatriation of several thousand British prisoners they liberated from German prisoner of war camps stop confirm immediately*'.

'Sonofabitch!' said Red Wyatt. 'I guess the Russians have got you by the balls!'

Stani sipped his Bourbon. 'I was just wondering,' he said. 'Do the Russians have any American prisoners they liberated?'

Red Wyatt put down his drink. 'Let me check.'

Five minutes later he was back, a piece of paper was in his hand.

'We were lucky, all our guys were in camps west of the Elbe so they were liberated by ourselves or the British. No, they don't have any of ours. . . .' He paused and looked at Stani reflectively. 'Hey! I get your message! Let me think about it.' He paced the sunny, comfortably furnished room, then turned.

'You've gotta deal!' he smiled. 'We'll fix 'em up here. God knows where they'll wind up eventually, but they won't be going to Russia, that's for sure!'

When Stani told the Cossack Colonel that he must move his Regiment and dependants immediately to the American Camp, the man was transformed. His face became suffused, he grabbed Stani by the throat and brandished his whip.

'Judas!' he yelled. 'Liar! Dog! We never fought against you! Now you take our weapons and hand us unarmed to the Bolsheviks!' Officers came running and managed to pull their Colonel off Stani. He stood there waving his whip and shaking with rage.

'Scum!' he shouted. 'We cannot trust the British, they did the same at Lienz; they smiled and lied and promised, then handed over the Cossacks in Peggetz Camp to be slaughtered.'

When Stani could make himself heard, he asked for someone who could read English; a major with heavy side whiskers was produced. Stani showed him his orders and asked him to translate. The Colonel shook his head. 'A trick,' he muttered, 'we will all be murdered.'

Patiently Stani explained that for their own safety they must leave immediately. He told them of his meeting with Red Wyatt on their behalf and added for good measure that he was sending two truckloads of armed men under Sergeant Major Monk to ensure that they would not be picked up *en route* and herded into a Prisoner of War Cage. The Major and the other officers half believed him, the Colonel turned his back.

Two hours later the Cossacks moved off. The Colonel's place at the head of his men was taken by the bewhiskered Major. He ignored Stani's salute as he passed, the men's faces were masks of hatred or fear and the women were weeping. A few children smiled and waved.

Quickly Stani put volunteers to work, within an hour all traces of the Cossacks would disappear and their camp site be ready to receive the next batches of Displaced Persons. Suddenly cries arose from a willow thicket and Stani was surrounded by a tattered gesticulating group. He followed them towards the river bank and they fell back respectfully to let him pass.

Hanging from a branch like a broken doll, arms swinging at its sides and head lolling upon its chest was the body of the Cossack Colonel.

Stani had reckoned that it would be dawn before the Cossacks reached the safety of their American haven; he spent the night pacing up and down before his windmill. With the sunrise a message arrived.

'Your friends arrived safely – good luck – Red'.

By mid-morning an agitated corporal was looking for him.

'Staff car from 29 Division just pulled up at the gate, sir,' he panted. 'There's a Full Colonel and two Russian civilians asking for you.'

Stani presented himself and saluted the full Colonel, a tall languid officer with a pleasant sunburned face who was conversing with the others in fluent Russian. He was surprisingly young.

'Ah!' he said. 'Sorry to drop in on you unexpectedly like this. These gentlemen are from the N.K.V.D. They are concerned about the repatriation of your Russian Nationals.'

Stani nodded to the two unsmiling jerrycan-shaped characters flanking the Colonel and said nothing.

'As you are established in our Divisional Area I have seen copies of the correspondence between you and Paris,' the Colonel said.

'Yes?'

'Yes. The gentlemen want to know when they can expect delivery of your Cossacks?'

'I'm afraid I have no Cossacks to deliver.'

The Colonel raised his eyebrows and translated for the Russians. 'The gentlemen say they are talking about the Russian nationals referred to by Paris,' he reported.

'Referred to by Paris only – never by me,' said Stani.

After a conference with the Russians the Colonel said; 'The gentlemen indicate they would be most interested to make a tour of your compounds.'

'By all means,' said Stani. 'We're very overcrowded at the moment, I hope they'll understand.

'I'm sure they will,' said the Colonel.

Stani entered the captured Opel tourer and they drove slowly round the camp. As they progressed he called out the nationality of each group. When they spotted the Polish compound the Russians became very excited and the Colonel relayed their request to speak with the inmates.

'They think you have hidden your Russians behind the Poles,' he said.

Stani shrugged. The N.K.V.D. men approached the nearest Poles and spoke to them rapidly in Russian. As soon as they heard the language, Poles of every shape and size debouched from tents and huts. They surrounded the Russians shouting abuse, shaking fists, drawing fingers across throats and finally pushing and shoving.

'I think you'd better sort that out,' said the Colonel calmly.

As they drove away he translated the ruffled Russians' last request.

'For some reason they particularly wish to see your compound on the river bank.'

'No problem,' said Stani. 'There's a mixed bag of Turks, Yugoslavs and Dutch in there now, they'd been locked up in a forest making V2 rockets to be dropped on London.'

Slowly they toured the river bank site and the N.K.V.D. men scowled at the groups lining up for stew, washing clothes on bushes or lying in the sun.

As the staff car was preparing to leave, Stani saluted and the Russians nodded sourly. The Full Colonel smiled.

'A most interesting day, Mr. Houdini,' he said. 'Congratu-

164

lations!'

Being out of touch with someone you love is a major torture of
war. Stani had missed Pandora mightily. They had promised to
write to each other constantly but during the months of their
separation he had received only letters via the Army Post
Office, all thoroughly disembowelled by the censor. They all
told him that she still loved him desperately, so he prayed
there had been no change of heart in later undelivered messages. In mid-July, No. 36 C.A.D. was ordered home, the
stream of D.P.'s arriving in the camp had dried up, and amid
great rejoicing 'Fort Glassballs' was closed for ever.

Stani was standing by the lakeside watching his gallant
troops leave for home. Morale was at its zenith, it was a lovely
midsummer day, white cumulus clouds were sailing like majestic galleons in an azure sky, a last dip in the Oeyn See had just
been enjoyed by all. Mr. Monk materialized at his side and
whispered out of the corner of his mouth:

'That Full Colonel from Twenty Nine Div. is back again, 'e's
right behind you, sir.'

Stani turned and the Colonel, smiling as usual, returned his
salute.

'Glad I caught you,' he said. 'I wanted to say goodbye – you
and your people did a great job – you should be very proud.'

'Thank you, sir,'

'All victorious armies are prone to looting,' the Colonel
mused. 'Ours is no exception. There's been quite a lot of it
going on I'm afraid. I don't suppose your fellows indulged?'

'Oh no, sir,' said Stani, thinking of the Leica he had liberated
in Osnabruck, 'a pair of binoculars here and there perhaps.
Nothing big.'

Mr. Monk, who had moved to the rear of the Full Colonel,
suddenly fell to the ground writhing in agony, his eyes rolling
and clutching his private parts.

'Ooh! Ooh! EEE!!' he shouted. 'Somethin' crawled up me
leg . . . a wasp! . . . it's stung me in the knackers!! . . . AOW!!'
He got up, capered about, beating at his crotch, tried to salute
the Colonel, said 'Excuse me, sir,' and hobbled off behind a
clump of wild lupins.

'Poor devil,' said the Colonel, 'nasty place to get stung. Well

165

goodbye, young man, have a good trip home.'

Stani saw him to his car and hurried back to his stricken Sergeant Major.

'How does it feel, Mr. Monk?' he asked.

'Better now the Colonel's gone, sir. Didn't you see it?'

'What? The wasp?'

'No, that bloody great speedboat in the Cookhouse truck, them fuckin' cooks must 'ave nicked it orf the lake.'

11

Stani so arranged matters that as soon as he was back on British soil he went straight to London. He telephoned Pandora. From her flat there was no reply, and Sid Field's show was closed.

Mrs. Quansett-Fowles' number did not even ring. He called the Earl of Hawksmoor. There the voice of Powis the butler came over loud and clear.

'Welcome back, Sir, in one piece too I gather! His Lordship is growing vegetables for the War Effort these days, he has just left to take the onions to market. Of course Lady Pandora is still in hospital.'

Stani went cold. 'In hospital!'

'Oh yes indeed, Sir. She's better now I'm glad to say. She's been working in a concert party entertaining front line troops in India and Burma! She contracted some tropical disease. You can find her in St. Thomas's'

Stani, picking up a bunch of white lilac from a street vendor on the way, took the dangerous gamble of surprising a lady in bed. He found her in a little room high on the top floor overlooking the Thames; his heart was hammering at his breastbone.

'Come in,' said the voice he had longed so much to hear. He opened the door just enough to push the lilac into the room.

'Who *is* it?' Pandora laughed.

When she saw him she stared for a second in total disbelief, then turned her face into the pillows.

'You can't see me like *this* . . . I look *awful!*'

He crossed the tiny room in one giant leap and planted kisses in the nape of her neck; after a few perfunctory struggles she allowed herself to be turned round.

'See!'

She was bright yellow, eyeballs and all. She was also painfully thin.

'You look *beautiful*!' he said. They held each other very tight till Pandora ordered him to sit on the end of the bed; they just stared at each other grinning like idiots, then they both started talking at once, questions, answers and laughter were all pouring out. When at last they calmed down, Pandora asked if he'd heard about Amy Quansett-Fowles. 'She got blasted by a V2 rocket. The house was wrecked but no one was hurt. She stuck a notice on the railings: "Look what the F . . . ing Fuerher did to *me*!" She's moved to the Connaught Hotel.'

After Pandora had assured him she would be out of hospital within two weeks he begged to be brought up to date.

'I volunteered to go to the Far East with E.N.S.A. They put me in a troupe of six, three girls and three fellows; we worked up a repertoire: Noël Coward's *Private Lives*, some songs and sketches and bits of poetry. We were pretty mediocre because the actors were hard to find and out comic was really awful! "She was only a corporal's daughter, but now she's an officer's Mess". Or "Up your pipe King Farouk, Hang your bollocks on a hook". . . . That sort of stuff. Anyway, they got us some scenery, a truck and some costumes and fitted us out with light-weight tropical gear; we were all set to knock them dead in Bombay and Calcutta but where do you think they sent us? To the North of Scotland!! We nearly froze to death wearing pith helmets and mosquito boots, entertaining lonely searchlight crews, but finally they packed us into a troopship for Alexandria, we thought. Three girls and several thousand men! Believe me, I've never been safer! Well – we wound up in Cape Town! By that time everyone on board had seen *Private Lives* about twenty times!'

'How did you get to India?'

'Our ship went on to Egypt so we were shoved on another full of Australians and off we went to Karachi still playing *Private Lives*.' Her face clouded. 'Those poor men . . . so young . . . God knows what happened to them all.'

Pandora was tiring quickly and a disapproving nurse told him not to stay too long. He listened to a description of her trans-India trip in the truck to Burma and asked how near to the front line they let her go.

'When we got to Burma we must have been right in it. . . .'

Across the river the sun was setting on the battered city. She gazed out of the window and he could see that her thoughts were miles away, somewhere in the heat and weird noises of the jungle or close to the dreadful stench of death. She spoke again, very softly, watching the gleam of the last rays die on the dome of St. Paul's.

'After dark we were not allowed to make any noise because the Japs were so near – it was difficult to perform! There were some British somewhere at the end of the trail so we decided I should do some poetry readings alone and just talk about home. It was pitch black, a sergeant took me by the hand and helped me through the mud up onto the back of a jeep, then he said, "Don't speak too loud!"

'I asked where the stage was and he said "You're on it, Miss!"'

'Where are the soldiers?'

"All around you in the jungle – two hundred of them. They've been there for two hours."

'He told me they'd planned to use the headlights of jeeps to light me but it was too dangerous because the Japs are all around too . . . but there'd be half a dozen flashlights in the front row whenever I needed them.'

Stani asked no more questions; Pandora was worn out and when she spoke again her eyes were brimming with tears.

'At Imphal and Kolhma there were terrible battles. Night and day we could hear them going on, the jungle began to look like the end of the world . . . with the leaves and branches blown off the trees; we went to the hospitals. . . .' Pandora covered her face with her hands, 'Oh! God! darling, come and hold me . . . those wonderful, wonderful men . . . I can't get it out of my mind; I had no idea what war was all about . . . some of their bodies were completely shattered . . . a young boy, an Australian who'd been on the same boat with me going to Karachi . . . asked me to hold his hand and pray while he died . . . I held it and prayed – all night.'

Stani enfolded Pandora in his arms till her sobs had ceased. Across the river the lights of London, extinguished by war for six and a half years, were twinkling and smiling.

169

12

A grateful government sent Stani no letter of thanks for his services but it did give him:
1 suit worsted grey
2 shirts poplin white
1 tie striped
1 pr socks, woollen
1 pr shoes, leather black, and
1 hat Homburg brown.
But most important it gave him back his freedom.

With Pandora restored to health and beauty and the war over, he too became caught up in the excitement of her forthcoming Hollywood adventure. Metropolis Pictures was busy trying to arrange travel facilities, no easy matter, as victorious American fighting men by the hundreds of thousands had priority on ships and airplanes heading home to the United States.

In a dim tea-cup-littered office, Stani had a brush with the Inland Revenue.

'Now let me see,' said a pompous official, turning the pages of a file. 'You have applied to become a British Subject under the special dispensations granted to certain Polish nationals who were visitors to this country during the late unpleasantness. Am I correct?'

'I wasn't a visitor – I was *trapped* here, and joined up' Stani said.

The man ignored this.

'I see you have been drawing disability allowance. Had an accident, did you?'

'If you want to call it that. I got in the way of a German with a cannon.'

170

'I see,' said the man. 'Now of course you realize that before you can obtain a sailing permit to leave this country you must have a valid passport and clearance from me to the effect that you do not owe monies to the British Government who have been . . . er . . . shielding you, so to speak.'

Stani looked dumbfounded.

'In other words, you must show me the necessary documents to prove that you have discharged all your obligations, financial and otherwise, to this country.'

'What the hell are you talking about?'

The man looked pained. He passed nicotine-stained fingers through his greasy hair.

'As you have no dependants, you have to pay Income Tax at the full rate on your pay from the Royal Air Force for the past five years, for one thing.'

Stani could feel the cold clammy hands of bureaucracy closing round his throat. With difficulty he restrained himself from physical violence or even a blast of sarcasm.

'I shall need some help with all this.'

'The R.A.F. Welfare people would be your best bet,' said the man, and closed Stani's file, bringing the interview to an end.

Finally it was Mrs. Quansett-Fowles who turned out to be the best bet.

'You need a lawyer,' she announced.

Stani mentioned the firm who had sorted out his mother's will.

'They're a lot of old farts,' said Mrs. Quansett-Fowles. 'I know the bloke for you! Just been demobbed, he was with the S.A.S. – covered in bloody medals. He's back at being a lawyer, he'll straighten this out in no time, leave it all to me.'

Pandora took Stani to Hawksmoor to say goodbye to her father. He had aged a little but seemed happy enough.

'Don't think I'll ever live in the big house again,' he confided to Stani. They had been visiting the farm and his vegetables. Pandora had not joined them, diagnosing correctly that the two men would appreciate some time alone, to talk about her. The winter was almost over, the first stirrings of spring could be felt, but throughout the country there was a leaden feeling of let-down after the enormous output of energy during the years

171

of war.

'Things will never be the same,' said Lord Hawksmoor.

They were walking down a grassy woodland ride; blue smoke from a forester's cottage hung motionless above the first bright-green shoots of bracken. He had never spoken of his son before, and even now he did not mention him by name.

'Saw the accountant last week,' said Lord Hawksmoor. 'I had made everything over to my boy just before the war to avoid his paying death duties when I kick the bucket. But as matters turned out there'll now be two lots to pay: Hawksmoor will be wiped out, according to that accountant feller; every-thing will have to go, land, everything, nothing for Pandora I'm afraid. A few pictures if they'll let me give 'em to her, but that's about it.'

They walked on in silence.

'I love this place,' said the old man. 'Pity it won't be handed on.'

Another pause.

'This filmin' business. D'you think she'll be able to make a go of it?'

'She's certainly determined to give it a good try.'

'Don't know any theatre people,' said Lord Hawksmoor, 'but I understand that the moment the curtain comes down they're all up each other like knives.'

'She's asked me to go to America with her,' said Stani.

'Yes, she told me. I'm glad about that. Look after her, won't you? She's all I've got now. Are you going to marry her? She's a good girl. Can't boil an egg, though.'

'I've asked her often enough,' Stani said.

'Well,' said the Earl. 'Once she's got this film nonsense out of her system she'll probably be only too happy to settle down.'

They walked on in silence.

'Sad about this country,' said Lord Hawksmoor. 'It's ex-hausted, like an old boxer. The best of my generation were all wiped out in the last war and now it's happened again, only twenty years later! Wonder where the new leaders are going to come from. Second raters I suppose, that's all that's left. By the way, would you like me to put you up for Whites?' Lord Hawksmoor failed to notice Stani's mystified expression. 'Afraid there's a long waiting list at the Club – takes over

172

twenty years before you get elected. But you might enjoy it once you're in. Top class gulls' eggs in May.'

'Thanks very much, sir.'

'Watch out for the people who play backgammon and go racin' though – got any gold fillings in your teeth?'

'Just one, sir.'

'Well, after lunch don't fall asleep with your mouth open – they'll have it off you.'

As they skirted a pond a flight of mallard took off.

'Should be pairin' off soon,' mused Lord Hawksmoor. 'Wild duck love potato peel, I have potato peel put down near all the ponds. One good thing about Whites is the Bettin' Book. If you say to some fella 'I'll bet you a fiver or a "pony" or a "monkey" ' – any sum big or small – it has to be entered in the Bettin' Book, with witnesses. All wagers have to be settled. Years ago, round the time of Beau Brummell, some fella, Duke of Newcastle I think it was, laid a bet of a thousand pound that he'd walk from Hyde Park to Whites at high noon on a Sunday, stark naked. It's all in the Book.'

'Did he collect?'

'Yes, Pretty hot what the fella did – had the floor of his coach taken up, then took off his clothes, told his coachman to drive slowly, and walked inside the coach all the way to Whites. Not very straight really . . . Should have been kicked out of the Club.'

The lights were coming on in the cottage windows when they came to a narrow road.

'I'll be back shortly,' said Lord Hawksmoor. 'I like to drop in at the Church of an evenin', just to sit down for a while. It's nice there all alone.' He coughed a little self-consciously and set off at a good pace.

Before they left England, Pandora had said goodbye to legions of friends.

Stani picked up his new passport and sailing permit (courtesy of the ex-S.A.S. lawyer) and bade farewell to two friends of his own. First to Colonel Zamowski in a tiny two roomed flat above a tobacconist's shop in Richmond. He found him wearing corduroy slacks, a woollen cardigan and carpet slippers.

'Ah! my dear young friend!' he exclaimed. 'Today is the

173

twenty-fourth of the month, and every good Pole knows that has the power to bring miracles . . . until you arrived, nothing miraculous had happened!'

Vodka was poured and ceremoniously dispatched. The Colonel explained that he and the commander of a Polish Armoured Corps which had suffered dreadful casualties at Monte Cassino had pooled their resources and were now selling cigarettes, chocolates and newspapers to the honest burghers of Richmond.

'We don't have much to sell,' he laughed 'even the papers are still rationed to a few pages.'

Courteously Colonel Zamowski listened to Stani's plans for the immediate future.

'I'm sure you have picked a delightful girl – your father would be pleased' he said, but his face clouded when he listened to the difficulties of running 'Fort Glassballs'. He shook his head.

'The Allies are amateurs at dealing with the Soviets' he said. 'Last July an old friend of mine, General Bor-Komorowski, was hidden in Warsaw with a whole underground army waiting to rise up against the Germans when the Russians arrived. They did. Just across the Vistula. They radioed Bor and told him to start his attack. Bor and his men fought in the streets day and night for sixty-three days. Nearly all were slaughtered by the Germany army. The Russians stayed the other side of the river and never lifted a finger to help, they had never intended to, it was part of their original plan to destroy all possible opposition to their take-over of Poland after the War.'

He downed another vodka.

'Did you attend the Victory Parade the other day?'

'No . . . Pandora is just out of hospital . . . we were down in the country.'

'It was very moving . . . soldiers, sailors, airmen from all the Allied countries, thousands of them marching together and millions watching – the end of the war against Nazi Germany!' He paused, took out his monocle and polished it. 'We Poles were not invited' he said quietly.

Stani was outraged.

'Why, for God's sake? . . . hundreds of Poles *died* with the British!'

174

'Over *seventeen thousand*' corrected the Colonel.

'Then why, for God's sake?'

'Because Stalin requested that it should not happen and the British Government did not want to upset him.'

There was silence in the little room till the Colonel spoke again.

'One good thing though. The R.A.F. refused to fly over the Victory Parade unless the Poles flew with them and when hundreds of warplanes thundered over, there was one Flight of Hurricanes exactly in the middle, flown by Polish pilots who had fought in the Battle of Britain . . . it was not mentioned in the programme; but the Poles knew.'

As Stani was leaving, the Colonel, in his most courtly manner, wished him all good fortune. Stani asked a question.

'And you, Sir?'

'I will return to Poland. One day our unhappy country will be free again. Freedom is not *in* our blood, it *is* our blood . . . so I will go back to do what I can to avenge the Katyn Forest and Warsaw and to prepare the next step; most likely you will not see me again.'

They shook hands. Stani walked to the corner to catch a bus. When he looked back Colonel Zamowski was standing very straight in his carpet slippers outside his tobacconist shop.

Stani's other goodbye was to his landlady. He took Mrs. Quansett-Fowles to dinner at the Mirabelle. 'Shampoo' flowed.

'It makes me feel like a frigging grandmother when you stand up when I come back from the loo,' she giggled. 'Wish I'd known you when I worked in 'Auntie's' in Malta. We wouldn't half have had some laughs!'

She wore an outrageous dress of red ostrich feathers, and attracted a constant stream of friends who came to their table to be refreshed from the bottomless well of her good humour.

'Amy, you really are incredible,' Stani said. 'You give so much of yourself to *everyone*. It must be nice to be loved the way you are.'

'Oh balls!' said Mrs. Quansett-Fowles. Towards the end of the evening she became a little teary. 'I'm not going to say goodbye to you, Stani, I hate goodbyes and maybe I'll see you very soon, anyway.'

175

'Wonderful!, Where?'

'In New York. I don't think you ever met Ray Kamber in South Audley Street, he was with the O.S.S.? Well for some reason he and a few other American blokes think they ought to repay my hospitality. *My* hospitality!! Christ! They produced all that food and booze and it was lovely for me having them around. Anyway, they're taking an apartment for me at the Pierre Hotel, any time I like for two months! So when the aeroplanes start up again I've got a ticket and I'm not allowed to put my hand in my knickers all the time I'm there! Just as well, when you think all we're allowed to take out of this bloody country is twenty quid! But aren't they generous, those Yanks! Marvellous isn't it?! I'm going to meet all their wives and girl friends, I'm really looking forward to it.' She paused. 'Kiss Pandora for me – that's a wonderful girl you have there – don't let go of her . . . now good luck! God bless! And piss off before I cry.'

13

On a grey day in 1941 President Roosevelt had roared with laughter when he set eyes upon it. 'What a dreadful looking thing,' he said. Under a crash programme which he himself had initiated, sections of it had been built in different parts of the United States, then collected and welded together; he was about to break a bottle of champagne on the sharp end of the result and name it *Patrick Henry*. Of 7,000 gross tons, she was the first of three thousand 'Liberty Ships' that the awakening giant of American wartime production would spew forth; she had taken only 245 days to build. Later, her sister ships, complete with armament, were built rather more quickly. The record, from hammering home the first rivet to being handed over ready for action to Captain and crew of eighty, had been an incredible fifteen days.

After three years of continuous war service *Empire Strongbow* was indeed 'a *dreadful* looking thing'. Barnacles encrusted her bottom, grey paint was flaking off between great streaks of rust; high above she displayed her hastily doctored wounds – jagged shell holes ripped in her superstructure during the D-Day landings.

'I think she's *beautiful*!' Pandora said.

Captain Magnusson, a Norwegian like the rest of her crew, had left his country in 1940 when the traitorous Prime Minister Vidkun Quisling had turned Trojan Horse for the invading Germans. His King and Government had moved to Britain, taking with them the entire Merchant Navy and Captain Magnusson, skipper of a fishing trawler, had followed with twenty young patriots, sailing like the Vikings before them across the surging North Sea in an open boat. He met Stani and Pandora at the top of the gangway.

'Welcome aboard!' he said and extended a huge paw. He was a powerfully built man with the square-jawed facial construction of a paratrooper. 'Come up to the boat deck. I'll show you your cabin, Number 25. Not quite the standard of Cunard I'm afraid but the best we can do!'

The box-like compartment contained two bunks, a basin and, behind a curtain, a functional toilet and shower.

'It's spacious,' Pandora smiled. 'And we're so lucky to have it.'

The Norwegian blossomed instantly.

'Up until now the gunnery officers lived in here. The only other space we have is the Engineer Cadet's cabin . . . we're not carrying them any more. Professor and Frau Hochstetter are in there.' He lowered his voice. 'The Herr Professor is one of the top scientists from Peenemunde where the Krauts developed those rocket bombs they fired on London. Now he's going to work for the Americans.'

'When do we get to New York?' Stani asked.

The Captain laughed. 'We don't. And we only do fifteen knots downhill with the wind behind us so it'll be ten or eleven days, depending on where they want us to end up. Sometimes it's Baltimore, other times it's places like Jacksonville, Wilmington or Mobile, Alabama. I'll know in a few days. I hope you enjoy the voyage, we may have a little movement for a couple of days, after that the forecast is good.' He saluted and withdrew.

The 'movement' of *Empire Strongbow* may have registered as 'little' on the Magnusson scale, but it resulted in three days and nights of groaning seasickness for Pandora and Stani. On the fourth day the mountainous seas flattened into a heaving slate-grey panorama beneath a watery sun, and they settled into a pleasant routine of playing gin rummy and backgammon for what Pandora described as 'serious stakes'. By the time they were half-way across the ocean, Stani owed her over two million pounds, which she gallantly lost on a 'double or nothing'.

The German scientist and his wife surfaced on the sixth day, looking pale. They spoke little English but with Stani as interpreter they became most agreeable and interesting companions. Stani's linguistic achievements were also appreciated by the Norwegian crew who could understand his Swedish.

Exercise was essential as an antidote to the helpings of stodgy food from the galley, but deck space being restricted by a cargo of military hardware, Stani and Pandora conscientiously did half an hour of cabin calisthenics every morning.

'I've *got* to look my best,' Pandora grunted, doing sit-ups with her feet wedged under her bunk. It was not only her looks that she was concerned about; with every passing day she became increasingly apprehensive of the whole Hollywood venture.

Stani had gone to his favourite spot on the ship, a sheltered space between two lifeboats on the starboard rail of the boat deck. He blessed his R.A.F. flying jacket, turned up the collar and snuggled gratefully inside. Staring out over the watery waste watching two escorting sea birds flying low over the swells, he wondered if they roosted at night in the rigging and his mind became alive with sea memories. On just such an evening he had seen the gallant cruiser *Curacoa* turn directly into the path of the on-rushing *Queen Mary*. He winced and ducked his head to avoid hearing again the terrifying sounds of the warship's death agonies and the pitiful prayers of Jervis's father. Jervis! He cleared his head of the horror of his friend's death and forced himself to recall instead the fun they had enjoyed together – sailing lessons, lobster catching, organizing the escape of the trapped wild swan . . . the swan! He looked out over the leaden water; the sinking sun, frustrated in its efforts to produce a spectacular departure, had managed a few patches of orange and some brush-strokes of pink and duck-egg green above the horizon. On just such a North Atlantic evening, lying in his minute rubber dinghy in a mixture of water, blood and vomit, he had seen the swan for the last time. Or *had* he seen it? His rescuers had told him later that he had insisted that the swan had landed beside him, but had he *really* seen it? Even in his feverish imagination? The sea! What a backdrop it had been for his life – his mother had died at sea, and Captain Rainbird and Jervis and the men in the Fokker-Wolf! His last days with his father. . . .

'I know what you're doing . . . you're doing a Polish gloom!' He turned at her gentle voice. She looked adorable – a little woollen hat was doing a bad job of controlling her hair and from neck to feet she was submerged inside his other wartime relic, his sky-blue R.A.F. greatcoat. He kissed her cool, wind-whipped cheek.

'Even when I get to New York and can buy a proper coat I'm going to keep this,' she said. 'I love it. You looked so smashing in it!' She linked an arm through his.

'What were you thinking about? I watched you for a long time – you looked so *lost*.'

When Stani explained, she turned him towards her and looked into his eyes.

'My poor one, don't be sad! We're leaving behind all that unhappiness, all that sadness, and too many people who died. Now we have a whole new deal . . . 'a whole new ball game' as Chuck would say. We're together, we're young, the War's over and we've got everything to live for!'

'Hollywood scares me,' said Stani.

'Scares *you*!! What d'you think it's doing to *me*!!?'

'It scares me because of what it might do to *us*. I saw Hollywood at a distance when I was in school in California, and I think it's going to be quite a shock to our systems.'

Pandora looked pensive.

'It may be a shock for *my* system but I *have* to try it. I *have* to see if I can do it. It won't be forever, darling, and there's no need for Hollywood to do anything to *us*. We're not children anymore. We can take the bumps. And if any success does come my way that's not going to make any difference to *us*. I'm not going to get a swollen head or a big movie star complex – and if I show any signs of it you have my permission to take down my panties and warm my bottom!'

They embraced again, then Stani said, 'I don't think I'm worried about what will happen if you hit the jackpot. It's fifty-fifty, isn't it. I mean, you could. . . .'

'Be a flop? Yes, of course, I could and probably will! The odds are thousands to one against my being a success – none of the big stars made it right away. Gable was an "extra". Garbo and Dietrich did little bits and pieces in their own countries before being brought over to Hollywood. Cary Grant worked in a circus and Fred Astaire was touring with a vaudeville act when he was five. I've never pretended to have a great big talent, have I? But I have had the same great luck all those big people had . . . I've been brought over to Hollywood! Now, it's up to me. If it works, I have a hunch it'll work soon, while I'm

180

still a new face. But I have no intention of sitting around while the face gets older, looking over my shoulder at all those gorgeous girls of nineteen. I think you and I should give it a year – two at the most. If it doesn't happen by then we'll fly away.'

Stani remained silent, she stood on tiptoe to kiss him.

'And another thing, the most important thing. I have *you* to help me and stop me from being as frightened as I am right now!'

'I love you so much,' he said. 'I'll do everything I can to help, you know that. I just hope I'll be good at it, that's all. I mean, people sitting around with nothing to do can be an awful pain in the ass. There won't be many people in Beverly Hills with Spitfires for me to fly!'

Pandora suddenly looked rather forlorn in the enveloping greatcoat.

'No. It's not going to be easy, but let's look upon it as a great *adventure*, darling. Let's have some *fun*! And – another "Chuckery" – let's just see "how the cookie crumbles". It's getting cold, come on back to the rabbit hutch and you can owe me another million!'

At last the long voyage, after many changes of destination, was nearly over.

'This ship doesn't seem very popular with American harbour masters,' Stani remarked.

'We don't carry a very popular cargo,' Captain Magnusson replied.

'You mean us, or all those tanks you have on deck?'

'No. It's what we have *below* decks. The Americans didn't drop *all* their bombs, there were quite a few left over!'

Two days off the American coast Captain Magnusson announced their final change of course.

'It's definite this time. Portland, Maine!'

Charlie Reiner, a nervous bespectacled young man, banged on their cabin door as soon as *Empire Strongbow* docked and identified himself as a junior Publicity operative from the New York offices of Metropolis.

'Mr. Pesnick,' he said, 'sends his regards from California and says to tell you to throw me off the top of the Empire State if I don't look after you properly. He's a great guy,' he added.

Reiner organized the speedy passage of their baggage through a cursory Customs inspection and stowed it in a limousine at the foot of the gangway. A smart chauffeur was in attendance and when the car rolled away, the ship's company waved and cheered from above. Pandora was misty-eyed.

'I really loved them all, they'll be going back to Norway now – how they must long to get home!'

During the hundred mile drive to Boston airport they enjoyed the frosty New England scenery, stopped at a drive-in for hamburgers, each of which was the equivalent of three weeks' meat rations in the Old England they had just left. They dozed or listened to Charlie Reiner's assessments of who was doing what to whom in Hollywood. It sounded like a news bulletin from outer space to Stani but Pandora was goggle-eyed. At Boston airport a reporter and a photographer from the *Boston Globe* recorded Pandora's views on the Boston Tea Party, and catalogued her past theatrical achievements and future film aspirations while Charlie Reiner handled tickets, baggage and tips with great assurance.

The flight to New York was preceded by drinks in the V.I.P. lounge, and in New York a flower-filled suite awaited them in the St. Regis Hotel. When the last heavily subsidized bell man had departed and Reiner had satisfied himself that Dom Perignon, vodka and caviar were in the icebox, he looked at his watch.

'It's just after six,' he said. 'What would you folks like to do tonight? I can fix house seats for any show on Broadway and of course arrange a nice table at any restaurant or night club. If you'd like me to come along to take care of things it'll be my pleasure – or if you prefer to be alone, of course I understand. Everything is on Metropolis.'

The travellers looked at each other, then Stani spoke for them both.

'We can't thank you enough for making the last part of the trip so easy, but I think we'd really like to unpack a few things, take a bath and just enjoy a quiet evening right here. What happens tomorrow?'

Reiner clicked his fingers.

'Jees! I almost forgot . . . I'm supposed to call Mr. Pesnick as soon as you get settled in – he wants a word with you.'

With bewildering American swiftness Chuck Pesnick was on the line from California.

'Welcome to New York, kids! Can't wait to see you out here! Everything okay?'

When she talked, Pandora's voice was shrill with excitement, then Stani joined in, enquiring about plans for the next day.

'Take it easy, enjoy yourselves, do some shopping, show Pandora round New York. Buy her some clothes. Reiner'll be around to fix everything and the limmo will be with you all day. Just one thing, I'd like you to have lunch at "21" – Lennie Lyons is a very important columnist; he wants to stop by for coffee and a couple of words with Pandora . . . let me just tell that to her.'

Stani passed the phone and Chuck explained the lunch plan, adding, 'I'm not fixing up any big interviews or photo sessions in New York because we're aiming at nationwide coverage when you come off the train in Los Angeles.'

'The *train*?'

'That's right honey. Mr. Greenberg wants you to come out by train so you'll be good and rested by the time you get here. You'll be taking the 20th Century Limited tomorrow evening, leaves at six from Grand Central, great dining car, wonderful sleepers. We've set up guest shots on a couple of morning shows for you in Chicago when you get there, Irv Kupcinet, for one, very easy. Then lunch at the Pump Room with a guy from the *Chicago Tribune*, no problem. After that you climb aboard the Santa Fe Chief, beautiful trip, great service and a couple of days later you'll be here in Sunny California having seen the whole goddam United States! Give me Stani again will you, Honey? Stani Baby? I've been talking with Mr. Greenberg: he wants you to keep a real low profile.'

'What the hell's that?'

'Just keep in the background. When the Press are around Pandora, don't let on that you're with her.'

'We've just crossed the Atlantic in the same cabin – what do I say about that?'

'Change the subject. Just don't let on that you are "going" with her. Think of a cover. Mr. Greenberg feels you should use your mother being from California. Get the gist?'

'Chuck, Pandora and I *live* together, remember! People will soon find out, what's the point of lying about it?'

'Don't let it upset you, kiddo, it's just that Mr. Greenberg wants this big splash when Pandora gets off that train, kind of her introduction to the American public and Mr. Greenberg feels that the male population will be less interested in her if they're told she's already shacked up with some guy. Got it?'

Charlie Reiner's last instruction before he left them had been, 'Just sign everything . . . the tab's on Metropolis'. But they were new to the ways of movie companies so they confused the telephone operator by asking to be charged personally for a call to Lord Hawksmoor and drank the champagne from the icebox with the 'Minute Steaks Maître d'Hôtel' instead of ordering a bottle of pre-war Château Mouton Rothschild which the waiter urged them to do and which they would have infinitely preferred.

The next day they rose early and Charlie Reiner whisked them off on a lightning shopping and sightseeing tour of the City. They sampled breathtaking views from the top of the Empire State Building, the glories of Saks Fifth Avenue, the Metropolitan Museum and the Museum of Modern Art and pressed back with embarrassment into the cushions of the limousine when the driver insisted they see 'the other side of the coin' – the Bowery, and sections of Harlem.

'Time was,' he said, 'when folks took in a Broadway show, had supper, then came up here to the nightclubs around Lennox Avenue. You sure couldn't get insurance if you tried to go that route these days! You can't order people to fight for America, then treat them like second-class citizens when they come back from the War. There's bad trouble coming from these black folks.'

At '21', on West 52nd Street, all had been prepared. Reiner escorted them through the bullet-proof door of the one time 'speakeasy', introduced them to the owner and promised to call for them after lunch. Mac Kriendler, the tall host and part-owner of '21', showed them to a banquette in the back of the room and passed their order for their pre-luncheon drinks to a hovering captain. They barely had time to look around the place and note that it was low beamed with a well populated

184

bar, a high decibel of noise and filled with, mostly, very attractive people, before he was back.

'Didn't I meet you two at Amy Quansett-Fowles' place in London a while back?'

As an Army officer, he had passed through London and now had great praise for the hospitality dispensed towards Americans on South Audley Street.

'Friends of Amy's are friends of mine,' he boomed and with a clapping of hands and waving of menus Stani and Pandora found themselves winkled out of their quiet backwater and promoted to a much-prized corner table in the front room.

Heads turned and Pandora's very special beauty was accorded an additional buzz of interest. They ordered carefully and greatly enjoyed their lunch. Half-way through dessert a large teddy bear of a man detached himself from another table and surged over.

'Mac tells me we all belong to the same club – Amy's! My name's John McClain.' He declined their invitation to join them and issued one of his own.

'I'm with Ed Murrow, we're nearly through talking a little business, if you feel like a "stinger" when you've finished we'd love to buy you a basin full for old times' sake – Ed's a member too!'

As McClain ambled back, Pandora pronounced judgement. 'That man has more fun in his face than anyone I've ever seen – I wonder who he is.'

Kriendler filled them in.

'John McClain used to go out on the Pilot Cutters to meet the big ships, straight from El Morocco as often as not, to interview the big shot arrivals. He did a column for the *Sun*, called "Up the Gangplank". During the War he was with the Navy in Europe – O.S.S. After that he wrote for the movies in Hollywood, now he's the Broadway critic for *The Journal American* and a goddam good one too. Ed Murrow is the big noise at C.B.S., you probably heard of him over in England. He did those great broadcasts during the London Blitz. "I'm speaking to you from a city in flames"? Sure brought people down to earth over here. Of course that was before Pearl Harbor.'

McClain ordered the 'stingers' – a mixture Stani found lethal, of brandy and crême de menthe – then he and Murrow, a

185

handsome man with sad brown eyes, hearing of Pandora's contract with Metropolis, unleashed a spate of appraisals, hints and warnings about Hollywood and its inhabitants. Both had rubbed shoulders with it and neither had any wish to make it their permanent home.

'It's fascinating if you're lucky,' they said. 'And frightening if you're not. There's a glut of inferiority complexes out there because a lot of people with no talent talk their way up the ladder and find they have nothing but vertigo when they get there. So be tough with the bastards and use *them*, because as sure as hell they'll try to use *you*!'

'Who are we talking about?' inquired a wiry little man with a long nose. 'Hi John! Hi Ed! And this stunning creature must be England's gift to Hollywood!' Leonard Lyons settled himself at the table and produced a notepad.

'I'll be with you for five minutes,' he smiled. 'No more.'

The supreme professional, once he had pried loose a few details of Pandora's theatrical past, he tried to ferret out a 'personal' story.

'And you, young man? How do you fit into the scene?' Stani felt his face flush.

'Jesus, Lennie!' said McClain good humouredly. 'You've got enough for your damn column, why don't you let these poor people enjoy their stingers in peace. Charles Boyer's sitting over there, go talk to him!'

Suddenly there was a disturbance in the lobby. Kriendler and several waiters headed briskly for the scene of the altercation, then the host re-appeared and beckoned urgently to McClain.

With astonishing agility for a man so large McClain hurdled the columnist.

In a few minutes he was back.

'It was only Bogie,' he laughed. 'He said he might drop by after lunch but he's brought along a full-size toy panda and wants a table for two and orders of bamboo shoots. I've persuaded him to try the Stork Club.'

'So long, folks,' said Leonard Lyons. 'Looks like I'm gonna get a scoop for my damn column!'

Stani and Pandora were kept spellbound by their companions until a note from Charlie Reiner was presented. 'Sorry to

186

break it up, train leaves in an hour – I'm in the lobby.'

A red carpet lay on the platform along the entire length of the sleeping cars of the 20th Century Limited. At the end of each car stood a train official checking tickets and reservations. The man at Stani and Pandora's car looked like a Grant Wood painting; he beckoned the black sleeping car attendant to take their luggage aboard. The attendant, very smart in black uniform with grass buttons and high peaked cap, smiled broadly.

'Follow me, folks,' he said. While Reiner stood in the passage way, the attendant unlocked two cabins of polished mahogany with two spacious bunks in each, one above the other.

'You've got the best staterooms on the car,' he told them, 'right in the middle, no noise from the wheels.' He stowed their bags, then showed them how to lower their washbasins and flush the toilets.

'I'll be back as soon as we pull out – I'm still a few passengers short.' He paused. 'Would you like the communicating door unlocked? It makes for more space.'

'Yes *please*,' they said.

Charlie Reiner said his farewells and told them that Stan Ziff from the Chicago office would meet them the next morning.

'There'll be a nice apartment at your disposal at the Ambassador East but he'll explain all that. So, I guess that's about it! It's been a real pleasure and, Miss Bryce, I do wish you the very greatest success in Hollywood.'

They were telling each other how genuinely sorry they were to see the last of Charlie Reiner when he reappeared.

'I forgot. The best way to get good service is to slip your car porter something at the start and tell him you'll give him the same again when you get off. Remember that when you're on the Chief tomorrow. I've just greased your guy with a ten from Metropolis! Goodbye now!'

Their porter, wreathed in smiles and now wearing a white jacket, reappeared as soon as the great train pulled out.

'Can I bring your dinner here, folks, or make reservations for the Dining Car?'

They opted for the dining car, were served by solicitous black stewards and a white Maître d'Hotel. Then, with the swaying coach adding a new dimension, they made love in a lower berth and slept in each other's arms till a jolting stop, followed by a mixture of raised voices and heavy metallic blows awakened them. Pandora lowered the window and gasped as a blast of Polar air seared her lungs. Below, a man with a long-handled hammer over his shoulder was crunching past on the frozen snow, icicles hung from frost-encrusted flat cars standing near-by beneath cold white arc lights. Pandora grabbed a blanket.

'Where are we?' she asked.

'Buffalo, New York,' said the man without looking up. 'And you've got a hot box, lady.'

Cooling remedies must have been administered because on the dot of seven o'clock their porter awakened them with orange juice, rolls and coffee and one hour later the Twentieth Century Limited eased to a stop in Chicago: Stan Ziff was waiting below their window.

On close inspection he turned out to be a tall lugubrious young man with whisky breath and eyes like a dog's balls.

'Errol Flynn's been in town,' he explained. 'I put him on a plane a couple of hours ago.' He squinted at a sheet of paper. 'Miss Bryce. Your first appointment is at 9 o'clock for Don O'Neill's Breakfast Show. I guess we'd better go on over right away – there's coffee and stuff there.' He looked at Stani doubtfully and checked the document again. 'Er . . . would you like to be dropped off at the hotel on the way, Sir? Or. . . .'

'Come with me darling, please,' Pandora said quickly.

'Good thinking,' said Ziff. 'I'll fix it for him to be in the sponsor's box during the show. Now just leave everything here in your compartments, the whole coach gets shunted around the city and tacked on to the Chief, you'll find it again this afternoon over at the other depot.'

The Breakfast Show was produced daily in the presence of several hundred blue-rinsed ladies, who had been bussed in for the occasion from outlying suburbs. To the accompaniment of their 'oohs' and 'aahs', the rattling of their coffee cups, and musical interludes, the genial Don O'Neil introduced his spe-cial guests to the ladies and to the huge radio audience. His guests usually included eminent local personalities, visitors to the City, performers in local theatres or Hollywood travellers of note *en route* to or from California.

Ziff explained this format to Pandora as they glided through the early morning traffic. A freezing wind was gusting off the Lake, heavily bundled pedestrians scurried red-nosed towards their jobs. He ended by saying, 'You'll like the Chief, I believe it's called the Super Chief now. Anyway it's silver all over.'

Stani soon found himself in a small airless room redolent of stale cigar smoke. Through a glass wall he had the sponsor's view of the production. An attractive girl brought him coffee and a doughnut, otherwise he was undisturbed.

The first guest, a local Irish politician, made heavy-handed efforts to charm the audience. Next came an inarticulate member of a high-wire family from the visiting circus who had lately saved his daughter's life by breaking her thirty foot fall. Both his arms and one leg were in plaster. A girl followed who had won the $64,000 Question and was still in shock. Then came a few hints from a grey-faced expert at catching fish through holes in the ice.

Don O'Neil gave Pandora a tremendous build-up as the latest European discovery of Metropolis Pictures, 'a woman destined to fill the shoes of Garbo, Dietrich, Hedy Lamarr and Luise Rainer.'

Her interview lasted no more than ten minutes. It was sparkling. But Stani had the eerie feeling that he was watching a beautiful stranger, an unattainable someone who exuded confidence and vitality but with whom he could never imagine sharing face towel, bath robe or bed. Afterwards in the limousine Pandora was still excited by her success. The ladies had responded very warmly to her, her actor's antennae had picked up their signals and she had bloomed beneath the star treatment accorded by Don O'Neil and his staff.

By the time the show was over Stan Ziff's breath had taken a turn for the worse.

'I had me a couple of Bloody Mary's at a Swedish restaurant across the street. Gable stopped by there a month ago and wrote in their book, "Congratulations! Your food just *cannot* be touched". They're still trying to figure it out.'

There was an hour to kill before the next interview so Ziff suggested a warm bar *en route*. 'We wouldn't have time to make it to the Ambassador East and back, you might like to freshen up and I have to call the office.'

The bar was red plush; dirty glasses and ashtrays full of soggy butts littered the tables, pale faced waiters with brooms were stirring dust into the stale air. But the owner managed a friendly greeting, cleaned off a booth and took orders for coffee from Stani and Pandora and a double brandy for Ziff, who returned from the phone booth with a business-like tread.

'Change of schedule,' he announced. 'After the next interview we make a side trip to *The Sun*. The magazine section wants a photo session with you, they just heard you on the Breakfast Programme. It'll be a bit tight but the paper's arranging a police escort. It'll be a big break if they put you on the cover!'

The police escort consisted of two revolver-toting Irish cops mounted on Harley Davidson motor cycles. They wore breeches and leggings and black leather jackets. The officers saluted Pandora smartly and when she apologized for inconveniencing them they smiled and assured her it was a privilege and a welcome change of routine.

The next show was an ordeal for her because she was interviewed not as an actress, as she had expected, but as part of a panel of eminent scientists and churchmen who were discussing the two atom bombs lately dropped on Japan.

Irv Kupcinet, the host, was a kindly and highly intelligent man, much beloved in Chicago where his talk show was enjoyed every Saturday night for over twenty years.

Stani listened proudly as Kupcinet steered the conversation towards the bombing of London, giving Pandora an opportunity to speak movingly about the wounded, the destruction, and how fear and worry increased people's craving for God's help.

To compensate for the show's running several minutes over, the police escort happily opened wide their throttles and their sirens blasted holes through the lunch-time traffic. At the end of a full speed slalom between trucks and streetcars, through red lights, back alleys and prohibited areas, the two cops jacked up their machines outside the *Sun* building, pushed up their goggles and beamed upon Pandora.

'Guess we made it this far okay!'

Ziff looked at his watch.

'I'll get you settled in here with the photographic guys, we have to be on our way again in forty minutes, then I'll slip over to the hotel, check you in and call that *Tribune* character, he's a grouchy old son of a bitch and thinks he's God Almighty.' He turned to Stani. 'How about you, Sir?'

'He stays with me.' said Pandora firmly.

Stani was glad he stayed, and quickly became engrossed in the proceedings.

'How long are you giving me?' was the photographer's greeting to Pandora.

'Only forty minutes, I'm afraid.'

'More than enough – even *I* couldn't take a bad picture of *you*! Let's go!'

One assistant kept three cameras loaded while the other two alternated rolls of coloured paper for backgrounds and set lamps as ordered.

Stani was instantly absorbed by the photographer's work, his use of indirect light, softening bright beams by bouncing them on to Pandora's face off flat white surfaces; after half an hour of encouraging, flattering and amusing her, the portrait photographer had taken over sixty shots. 'That does it!' he said. 'Three more to finish the roll . . . lovely! . . . I've got all I need!'

He turned to Stani. 'You look very interested in all this! We still have ten minutes, go ahead, take a few shots of Pandora for yourself – just tell us where to put the lights!' Stani had the time of his life and, to cap it off, the expert told him he had a real photographer's eye.

'I'll send you copies of the photos we use in the magazine, and the best of the ones you took,' he promised.

'Come on folks!' Ziff's voice boomed from the doorway. 'This is your cruise director! Yellow arm-bands follow me! That barman in your hotel shakes a mean Martini,' he confided to Pandora as he bundled her into the limousine. 'Let's go kids!' he yelled to the cops and, with smoking tyres, off they roared on their last blaring dash through the congested Chicago streets.

The Pump Room of the Ambassador East provided a colourful oasis of calm, after the hectic morning's programme, a wondrous mixture of Pump and Pomp. Against walls of deep blue, spacious booths of white leather were positioned, lighting from crystal chandeliers and candlesticks flattered, and a paternal Maître d'Hôtel materialized instantly at their side.

'Booth Number One for *you*, of course, Miss Bryce!' he said.

191

Since the man from the *Tribune* had not yet arrived, Stan Ziff stayed to effect introductions; he ordered a bottle of champagne.

'Know why the Maître D said this booth is for you, *of course*?' He pointed to a plaque:

MISS GERTRUDE LAWRENCE

Booth 1 is her domain.

She ruled here for ninety unforgettable nights

when The Pump Room opened

October 1, 1938

'I thought it might be because of *this*,' Pandora giggled, lifting a serving plate upon which was emblazoned Sarah Siddons declaiming against a sunrise.

'Here he comes now,' Ziff whispered, and rose to introduce a dignified figure. 'I'll be back for you in exactly one hour and twelve minutes – don't blow it,' he said, and hurried away.

Pandora and Stani waited for the opening barrage from the 'grouchy old son of a bitch'.

'Why is it?' he enquired mildly, 'that eager young men in the field of Public Relations always give the impression of being anxious to give ulcers to those they are supposed to *protect* from stress and strain?'

They chose wisely from the Pump Room's Ye Olde Englishe Menu being mindful of their war-restricted stomachs; and while waiters, resplendent in white tie, hunting pink tails and black satin breeches, served their guest with:

Pheafant Difjointed Ambaffador
stuffed with Chefnuts and Raifins

Stani and Pandora settled for

Petites Hamburgers
Bruffles Sprouts
Crifp Lettuce with
Thoufand Ifland Dreffing

The man from the *Chicago Tribune* proved to be an enchanting companion and once he had learned of Stani's Polish blood, disclosed an impressive grasp of the historic misfortunes of that courageous country. He propounded his theory for combating

192

the growth of Russian Communism.

'We should do everything we can to encourage the Russian leaders to educate their people, because well organized brains sooner or later will inevitably come to the conclusion that Communism is nonsense and that the tyranny and repression now practised by the gangsters in the Kremlin are far worse than anything perpetrated by the Czars.'

Conversation remained general, lively and illuminating till he pushed aside the remains of his Cheefe Cake and a black coffee boy, caparisoned like a circus pony in emerald green tunic and white-plumed turban, served him an Expreffo.

'Well, beautiful lady,' he sighed, producing notebook and pencil, 'now you and I must earn our living!' Almost immediately a flushed Stan Ziff rushed in. 'Sorry folks,' he panted, 'afraid we have to leave *right now*! Chuck Pesnick just called from the Coast. Mr. Greenberg wants you to *fly* out there this afternoon instead of taking the train, seems something's come up. I have to get you over to the Chief pronto to collect your baggage, the office is working on your air tickets ... I've checked you out of here.' While Ziff swallowed a Brandy and Benedictine and distributed largesse in extravagant quantities, Stani and Pandora made their apologies to the quiet man from the *Chicago Tribune*.

'Don't give it a thought,' he laughed, pocketing his virgin pages. 'I wish you both bon voyage and all the luck in the world. But you do realize don't you, that you're flying off to the place where even the lunatics no longer run the Asylum?'

Stan Ziff's efficiency declined in direct proportion to his intake of bottled goods and throughout the afternoon in sprawling marshalling yards, he encountered increasing problems locating their sleeping compartment and their baggage coach. By the time he had found these he had lost contact with the limmo; once that was found again they raced to the distant airport, arriving just in time to see the lights of their plane winking off into the sunset.

After a series of telephone calls from various airport bars, Ziff triumphantly ushered them into the Ambassador Lounge for V.I.P. passengers. Then he handed them their tickets for sleeper-berths on the night flight.

'Now at least Stani will be able to join the "Mile High

193

Club",' he said with a bleary leer at Pandora. Asked to explain, he said, 'Any guy who gets to hump a stewardess in one of those bunks flying over the Rockies qualifies. But I guess they'd bend the rules.'

14

The plane dropped lower, the dazzling desert fell behind; they flew a few hundred feet above the spine of the San Gabriel mountains. Snow was still abundant upon Big Bear and Arrowhead and the lakes were frosted glass, glittering in dark pinewoods. Almost immediately, the trees disappeared, the cliff-like mountainside fell away and they flew out high above a sprawling green valley containing the townships of San Bernardino, Riverside and Pomona – the outer suburbs of Los Angeles. Swimming pools like sapphires and emeralds of various shapes were dotted about, relieving the monotonous military formations of white one-storey houses nestling on their plots within blocks and partitioned by maxi-squares of main roads.

Pandora squeezed Stani's hand as the populated areas thickened. 'The city is *huge*! The mountains go round it like a horseshoe! They look as if they sort of clamp it in place against the ocean.'

'That's all new,' said Stani. 'That brown haze down there hanging over everything. I suppose they've built up so much industry since I've been away. But *look*! It's *crawling* with automobiles – they're like ants everywhere! It never used to be like that!'

Chuck Pesnick was waiting for them on the tarmac. He was tanned, wore sunglasses and was dressed in a light beige suit. Behind him some twenty photographers were strategically deployed. Stani looked down nervously as he collected the hand-baggage, while Pandora made unhurried last minute adjustments with eyeliner and lipstick.

The other passengers were encouraged to disembark, then Chuck ran up the gangway. He kissed Pandora, shook Stani's

195

hand and said in one breath, 'Gee you both look *great*! Stani, go on out and grab a cab, here's the address. Don't let on you're with Pandora. Give me the baggage stubs, I'll take care of all that, so long, see ya!'

Stani followed the other passengers off the plane. Outside the building, the glare of the fierce morning sun hurt his eyes; he joined a line waiting for cabs. After five minutes, a breathless young man in shirt-sleeves hurried up. 'I'm glad I found you in time, Sir,' he panted. 'Mr. Pesnick says for you to come on back – there's been a foul-up.'

'What's happened?'

'Seems there's been a change of plan about Miss Bryce's arrival exposure.'

The photographers were still grouped around the gangway. Inside the plane, Pandora was sitting patiently in her seat. Next to her was a sweating and agitated Chuck. 'Thank Christ we caught you!' he said. 'Mr. Greenberg's changed his mind, he thinks we'll get more mileage out of it if she's shown arriving with a war hero fiancé. The war still being fresh in people's minds, and he wants to build up the Polish angle, they're a big ethnic group in the mid-west and the coal mining areas.' He clapped his hands together. 'All right now, let's go kids and make it real lovey-dovey down there or Greenberg'll have my ass!'

In the broiling sun, Pandora and Stani were posed and positioned by Chuck, asked by the photographers to kiss, to walk arm in arm, to point at the mountains and to sit on baggage carts. Stani's face ached from smiling but Pandora remained calm and beautiful throughout. A Cadillac limousine whisked them through miles of streets, composed, for the most part of vacant space, used car lots and forests of billboards.

'It's not very pretty, is it?' Pandora remarked. 'I wonder why they don't put all those cables and telephone lines underground.'

'It gets much better further on,' said Chuck. 'This is speculator country out here – following the gospel according to the Astor family – "always buy real estate on the outside edge of a growing city". Down by the ocean, Santa Monica and Pacific Palisades, they're real nice. Brentwood and Bel Air are beautiful too, but where Metropolis Pictures has got a place for you,

196

Boy! That's the best – Beverly Hills! Every street is planted with different trees, palms, oaks, eucalyptus, jacarandas, magnolias, firs, chestnuts, and here's something to make *you* proud, Pandora – you know who planned all that? A limey! Some little guy from Kew Gardens – they brought him out specially.'

'What's the house like?'

'Well,' said Chuck, 'pretty damn good considering how hard it is to find *anything* right now. Spanish-style, nice yard and pool out back. It's a little old-fashioned for my taste. Kitchen's real nice though and there's lots of closet space.'

Pandora felt for Stani's hand. 'I'm nervous,' she said. 'I'm a basket case after those bloody photographers.'

'We've found a nice couple for you,' Chuck put in. 'At least, they *sound* real good. Very refined people from Boston. Mr. Greenberg's own personal secretary came up with them.'

'I'm sure they'll be fine,' said Pandora, looking out of the window. A cluster of oil derricks on a beige-coloured mound had caught her eye.

'Signal Hill,' said Chuck. 'It's supposed to have changed hands over a cold hand of poker.'

'Before or after they struck oil?' asked Stani.

'I'll check,' said Chuck. 'It's probably owned by Louis B. Mayer right now – the M.G.M. Back Lot's just over there, hundreds of acres of it, there behind those big trees. They've got Indian villages, a French chateau, lakes, campuses, rail depots, a submarine, a whorehouse and God knows what all in there.'

'And Gable and Garbo and Judy Garland and Ava Gardner and Lana Turner as well,' sighed Pandora. 'Oh, darling, I am so frightened now I'm here.' Her grip tightened on Stani's hand. 'There's so much competition. I'm beginning to feel *very* small.'

'You're going to hit it big, Pandora,' Chuck said. 'Mr. Greenberg's going to build you up so you just can't miss. Metro would be a tough lot to start on – you're in much better shape with us. This is just the right moment for a new face and Mr. Greenberg's the man to sell one.'

'Do you always call him *Mr.* Greenberg?' asked Pandora.

'He likes it that way.'

When they got to the house, Pandora said, 'It looks like a Moorish prison!' It was on North Alpine Drive, a white stucco

197

monstrosity with a roof of red tiles, small barred windows and a gigantic iron-studded front door. Unfenced, it stood astride a corner lot surrounded by a lawn of yellowing crab grass. From behind it, the top of an ill-kept palm tree showed like a broken umbrella.

'It'll be better inside,' said Chuck. 'Anyway, the Orbistons will fix it up for you.'

'The Orbistons?' Pandora queried.

'Yea, you know, the couple I told you about.' He pulled an iron handle and in the far recesses of the house, a bell clanged. Stani and the driver unloaded the baggage and lugged it up the path. They rang the bell again – nothing happened.

'Maybe they're back in the yard,' said Chuck. 'I'll go take a look.'

Chuck disappeared and several more minutes elapsed. They pealed the bell once more. Finally, the 'flap-flap' of bare feet was heard and the sound of bolts being unfastened. The massive door swung open to reveal a small, bald Magoo-like man, wearing nothing but a pyjama top. He stared at Pandora and Stani, took in the limousine, the chauffeur and the pile of baggage.

'Well, waddaya know?' he said.

Chuck appeared from the back regions. 'You Mr. Orbiston?'

'Right on,' said the man.

'Well let's get some action here, for Chrissake. These folk have come a long way.'

'Mrs. Orbiston and I,' said the man with dignity, 'were informed that our employers would arrive here at nine o'clock. We were not instructed as to whether it would be nine o'clock tonight or nine o'clock this morning. Since it is now almost eleven o'clock this morning, we concluded that we could safely expect them tonight.'

'So you decided to do a little light housework in your nighties,' said Chuck. 'Come on, let's get going!'

The man departed, attempting to cover his flaccid buttocks with his hand. 'I will inform Mrs. Orbiston of your arrival,' he said over his shoulder.

Chuck shook his head. 'Jesus! Just wait till Mr. Greenberg hears about *this*! He'll hit high "C"!'

The interior of the house was a nightmare of heavy Spanish

furniture, red brocade, highbacked chairs and sofas of maximum discomfort, large jugs filled with pampas grass, tiled floors, wrought iron and tassels. On a monstrous table, beaten with chains to transform it into a genuine antique, was a flower arrangement of overpowering vulgarity. Pandora read the card. It was typewritten:

WELCOME TO HOLLYWOOD
FROM ALL AT THE STUDIO

'Well kids,' said Chuck, 'I'll leave you to it now. I have to get down to the studio real quick, locals and the wire services are all down there waiting to get the handout to go with the airport pictures. It'll be a real big spread – great coverage. I'll bring the results up to you this evening as soon as the mornings hit the street.'

After Chuck had left, Mr. Orbiston, now in white alpaca jacket and black tie, presented his wife, a distinguished, matronly figure, at least six inches taller than himself with a beautifully 'coiffed' head of white hair tinted powder blue, a charming smile and vivid blue eyes. She kissed Pandora warmly on both cheeks. 'My! Are you gorgeous!!' she exclaimed.

'We'll have to do a little shopping later,' Mrs. Orbiston told Pandora. 'We're new to this area and I'm not familiar with the stores around here. That secretary at the studio ordered a few things delivered from Jurgensen's so I'll be able to give you a tuna fish salad for lunch and some coffee.'

'How nice,' said Pandora. 'By the way, I took a look at the pool. There's a dead cat in it, the water is dark green and it's full of leaves. Do you think your husband could do something about it?'

Mrs. Orbiston looked pained.

'Mr. Orbiston,' she announced grandly, 'is not a pool man.'

Mrs. Orbiston's tuna fish salad was served in an erratic manner by Mr. Orbiston, in the gloom of the dining room with Stani and Pandora seated at either end of a refectory table designed for thirty Augustinian Hermit monks.

'What shall we do after lunch, darling?' Pandora asked.

'Go house-hunting,' said Stani.

Instead, they spent the afternoon in bed and descended, in time to greet Chuck, proudly bearing an armful of newspapers.

'*Great* coverage kids!' he beamed. 'Mr. Greenberg's real pleased.' He handed over the newspapers with the relevant articles and photographs bordered by thick red ink. Pandora studied them and a cold hand of anger clutched her intestines.

'I think I'm going to be sick,' she said.

Stani looked over her shoulder.

'What the hell do you think you're doing?' he asked Chuck angrily. 'You've no right to do this!'

'Mr. Greenberg said he thought Pandora might be a trifle upset about it to start with,' said Chuck, 'but the decision had to be made real quick or we'd have missed the deadlines and the people here said you were sleeping. It's *great coverage*! I've never seen anything to top it! Mr. Greenberg's *real* pleased,' he sounded increasingly defensive.

Stani threw the papers on the floor in disgust.

'Greenberg can't do this.'

'But he *can*, you know,' Chuck replied. 'There's a clause in all the standard contracts that gives him the right to do just that.'

Stani stirred the offending pages with his foot.

JAN RICARDO IS HERE!
– Los Angeles Times
HOLLYWOOD WELCOMES
EUROPEAN STAR – JAN RICARDO
– Los Angeles Examiner
JAN RICARDO FLIES IN WITH
POLISH WAR HERO PILOT
– Herald Express
JAN RICARDO ARRIVES WITH STYLE
– Citizen News

In all the photos, Pandora looked marvellous and there were articles by Louella Parsons, Hedda Hopper, Jimmy Starr and Harrison Carrol that were paeons of praise for her talent, beauty, clothes and devotion to her handsome fiancé. (There were many variations of the spelling of Stani's name and wild exaggerations of his war service.) Pandora dissolved in floods of tears.

Chuck moved towards her but she swept his protective arms aside. 'I'll kill that swine,' she sobbed. 'What a dirty little pot-bellied doublecrosser!'

When Pandora had calmed down sufficiently, she put in a call to Hank Greenberg's office. 'Who wants him?' the studio operator asked.

'Pandora Bryce,' she hissed.

After a long pause the operator came back on the line. 'Miss Ricardo?'

Pandora made a sound like water boiling.

'Mr. Greenberg's secretary has gone for the day. She said if you called to ask if everything is okay at the house?'

'Well, it's not,' said Pandora, 'and I don't intend to speak to his secretary. I want to speak to him. Kindly put me through.'

'You're out of luck,' came the disinterested voice. 'Mr. Greenberg's cleaned out his desk – he's on his way to Honolulu!'

Pandora slammed down the phone and turned like a tigress upon the luckless Pesnick, demanding an explanation. The publicity man spread his hands in a gesture of helplessness.

'Everything sure happened fast,' he said. 'But that's Hollywood for you! We all knew it was in the works, has been for weeks. It's an old Hollywood game called "musical chairs", they play it all the time. There's a bigger mortality rate among studio heads here than there was in the Battle of the Bulge. The guy responsible for spending the bank's money makes a few bum decisions, the product doesn't sell, so they pay him off with millions in golden handshakes, severance payments and bonuses and he moves over to another studio taking the best story properties in his brief case.'

Pandora hunched in Stani's arms. 'But what about *me*?'

'Look on the bright side, darling,' Chuck said. 'Let's face it, Greenberg was a prick, and nobody trusted him. The actors got his wavelength long ago. He had the microphones on the sound stages wired to his office so he had a built-in spy system – but did they let him have it once they found out! If this thing has really happened in the last coupla hours, the flags'll be out by now, believe you me. You'll be missing nothing by not working for that jerk. And, you've already had the benefit of his publicity genius.' Pandora snorted and Chuck made for the phone. 'I'll make a few calls and find out what's cooking. Is your contract with the studio or with Greenberg personally?'

'With the studio.'

201

'You're lucky. If it'd been with him, the bastard would have had you in his goddam briefcase too.'

Chuck returned from the phone in an advanced state of excitement.

'Oh! Boy!' he said. 'Do I have good news! Russ is taking over!'

'Russ who?'

'Russell Bancroft! Pandora, you'll *love* Russ. And he already loves you. I was there when they ran some footage on you and he really flipped.'

After Chuck had left for the studio to 'kinda get the feel of things', Stani arranged the rental of an Oldsmobile convertible and took Pandora on a calming tour of Beverly Hills, Westwood and Brentwood. He brought her home at sunset via Mulholland Drive, winding along the crest of the Hollywood Hills with the lights of the San Fernando Valley twinkling below like a million stars on one side and the whole of the Los Angeles Basin glowing in a purpling mist on the other. The orange and gold of the afterglow was reflected in the great crescent of the Pacific.

'What do you think of it, darling?' he asked. Pandora snuggled close.

'It's a bit *much*, isn't it! And I still *hate* my new name.'

On their return to the Moorish prison, Mrs. Orbiston delivered a message. 'Your studio called. Mr. Russell Bancroft would like to see you at twelve o'clock tomorrow. You too, young man. And you're getting hamburgers, potato salad and ice cream for dinner. Okay?'

'There's something odd about Mrs. Orbiston,' Pandora said. 'I'm beginning to wonder if she can cook at all.'

'There's *definitely* something odd about *him*,' said Stani. 'He keeps looking out of the windows and talking to himself. But I suppose we're lucky. Chuck says it's impossible to find anyone these days because they all want to work in aircraft factories and the Japanese gardeners are still locked up on Santa Anita Racecourse.'

When they presented themselves at the crowded Reception Room, Pandora looked ravishing in a white shark-skin suit and shocking pink shirt. Stani, too, was the recipient of many

202

appreciative glances.

'Can I help you?' asked a fat heavily armed man in the uniform of the studio police.

'We have an appointment with Mr. Russell Bancroft,' Stani said.

'Names?'

'Mine is Skolimowski,' said Stani, 'and the lady is Miss Bryce.' The policeman frowned. 'Alias Jan Ricardo,' Stani added.

The effect of this announcement on the fat man was instantaneous, and a ripple of interest stirred the waiting room.

'Why, of course!' he beamed, rising from behind his desk. 'I recognize you now! Sure thing, Mr. Bancroft's expecting you, you're to go right on through.'

He pressed a buzzer releasing the latch on a gate. 'I'll just call the office to say you've arrived, the secretary'll be right down to take you over . . . if you wouldn't mind waiting in the garden for a coupla minutes – it's real pretty right now.'

Rose bushes, flowering shrubs and a cluster of palm trees sprouted from a bright green lawn flanked by Executive bungalows. Beyond the garden, they saw the aircraft hangar profiles of twenty giant sound stages.

'This is it!' said Pandora, . . . 'and I'm gibbering!'

An attractive secretary led the way to the most imposing of the bungalows. Inside, two other girls, busy at their desks, looked up with smiles and ill-disguised curiosity. In the inner sanctum – a large, cool, flower-filled room – the brilliant sunshine was carefully screened out. From behind an uncluttered desk, Russell Bancroft III rose to greet them.

Above medium height, lean, bronzed and fit looking, no more than forty with a crew cut thatch of black hair, Bancroft advanced towards Pandora with both arms extended, a charming smile of welcome crinkling the corners of his intelligent brown eyes.

'I hear the butler my predecessor found met you in his pyjama top, so I put on my jacket to make a good impression!'

He flicked the intercom. 'Marcia, protect me. Push all the crises under the rug like a good girl. Now,' he said, 'let's sit down. I've all the time in the world.'

After a little general conversation about their trip and their accommodations, he broached the subject uppermost in Pandora's mind.

'I'm really sorry you were never consulted about the name change. As you know, it all happened during Greenberg's departure. But let me make it quite clear – I'm delighted he left you behind!'

Pandora spoke her mind. 'I was shocked. Pandora Bryce is my real name and I like it very much. What's wrong with it?'

Russell Bancroft lit a cigarette and smiled.

'Nothing at all. But you are not to be hurt if I point out that it is not the best name for a beautiful girl. I have to look at you and think of you as a commodity to be sold to the American public. "Bryce" is a rather masculine-sounding name. As for "Pandora". . . .'

'What's wrong with *that*?'

Russell Bancroft dragged on his cigarette. 'This is Hollywood, home of the crummy wisecrack. My predecessor thought that Pandora's Box would be too easy a target. But then Greenberg had a dirty mind.'

'But why JAN RICARDO?' Stani asked.

Bancroft rubbed his hand on his hair.

'First you must realize that many of the top stars do not use their real names. Joan Crawford, Cary Grant, Fred Astaire, Lana Turner, even Garbo, you name them, it didn't do them any harm, did it? Now I didn't have anything to do with picking "JAN RICARDO" but in my opinion on a marquee it'll look good – it's short and has rhythm. And theatre managers like short names – it cuts down their electricity bills! Why only last week, I saw the star names of a double bill outside a theatre in San Francisco –

C. Gable

S. Tracy

and

M. Mouse!'

Pandora still looked doubtful. Russell Bancroft sneaked a look at his watch.

'According to the contract you signed, the studio has the right to choose a professional name for you – "your agreement to which will not be *unreasonably withheld*".'

'I didn't notice that,' Pandora said sadly.

'And furthermore,' he countinued, 'the name JAN RICARDO, in the last few hours, has been registered by millions of American moviegoers. We plan to keep it that way.' He rose. 'Ricardo could be Italian or Spanish and we are definitely going to sell you as European, not underlining the English side of it. Very few English girls have caught on with the American public because the English accent is not easy for American ears. British films lay eggs for the same reason. So we'll work with you on a carefully orientated campaign to Europeanize you. I want you to start right away working with a voice coach. Then I want to shoot a great test of you to show our producers.'

Stani was appalled. 'You mean Pandora has to speak with an Italian accent?'

Bancroft laughed. 'No, of course not. She has a beautiful speaking voice. I just want it to be more – well mid-Atlantic, less broad As and clipped delivery – know what I mean.' He reflected for a moment. 'More like yours in fact. Where did you get it, incidentally?'

'My mother was from California.'

'They always say the best way to learn a language is to have a mistress or a lover who speaks nothing else. Which brings me to another point. You two are living together, right?'

'Correct,' said Pandora sweetly. 'Unless of course that's a dirty word?'

Bancroft smiled. 'You mean it's none of my business? Well you're right up to a point. But your business is our business and our business is to entertain millions of people every week without offending them. We sell one hell of a lot of tickets in the Bible Belt and although people cohabiting is no longer taboo in some parts of the country, they are still "living *in sin*" in others. I'm just asking you to be discreet and to remember that even today the Legion of Decency insists that an actor and actress playing husband and wife having breakfast in bed together may only do so provided they're wearing pyjamas and dressing gowns and the actor has one foot on the floor!'

'We'll be careful. At any rate we promise not to do it in the street and frighten the horses.'

While Bancroft was talking, Pandora noted with approval that he was not flashily dressed. He wore a well-cut suit of light-grey flannel, a pink button-down shirt and a dark blue tie with discreet red stripes. She told him she admired it.

'Oh that,' he said, offhandedly. 'Goes with everything! It's the Hacking Club in New York. I think I'm the only member who has any connection with the movies, they regard me with some suspicion. My father put my name down the day I was born!'

He sneaked another look at his watch.

'We've all the time in the world,' he said again. 'I thought the three of us might slip over to the Derby for lunch. We could go to the commissary here but there'd be too many people coming at me. A changeover at the top of a studio leaves an awful lot of folks feeling nervous about how they're going to work out with the new regime.'

'Are you sure you have all that much time for us?' Pandora asked.

'Look,' said Bancroft. 'It'll be my pleasure. We'll yak about plans for you, then I'll take off for the Springs.'

He spoke into the inter-com. 'Marcia, is Pesnick here with the photographers? Okay, send him in.'

Chuck entered at once. 'I've got the two best on the Lot, Mr. Bancroft.'

'Okay, get some good shots of Miss Ricardo with me. Not the usual crap cliché signing a contract – something original.'

Stani watched the photo session and although impressed by the natural manner in which Pandora fell into poses as requested, he also noticed the highly professional way Bancroft checked to see where the best light was coming from, and looked behind to ensure that a lampshade, a flower arrangement or a palm tree would not be sprouting out of the top of his head. He was able to switch on a smile or a pensive expression at exactly the right second.

When they swept up to the Beverly Hills Brown Derby in the silver Lincoln Continental, Stani, who had been sitting beside the chauffeur, found himself opening the rear door for Bancroft and Pandora. Bancroft forced a path through a hundred autograph hunters and as Stani hovered behind during their slow progress through the restaurant, he was afforded an uninterrupted view of the impact made by the new head of a Major Studio, accompanied by that Studio's latest female discovery.

The tables of the Brown Derby were set in semi-circular booths, the backs of which were low, affording the customers all-round visibility; pots of flowers and greenery were distributed upon the flat tops between the booths and as the clientele raised their heads and noticeably hushed, Stani was reminded of a colony of gophers disturbed in the middle of their feeding. For Russ Bancroft the procession to a far table was obviously a triumphant one; men and women rose from their booths, shook his hand, slapped his back or kissed him. For Pandora, it was her entry into Hollywood. Many of the faces now smiling at her and murmuring platitudes were known to millions the world over and she glowed with excitement. For Stani the sudden stops and starts, like a shunting freight train, were sheer Hell. He was not made part of the introductions.

Once settled in their booth, he looked around him. On the walls hung double likenesses of all 'Oscar' winners, as themselves and also as the character for which they had received the Academy Award. The waitresses and busboys, Bancroft confided, were would-be actors and actresses in various stages of hopefulness or disillusionment and the headwaiter, the recipient of years of generous hints as to the most profitable distribution of his status symbols, was one of the richest men in Hollywood. Strategically deployed about the room were a couple of hundred of 'Hollywood's finest' – producers, directors, writers, actors, actresses, agents, bankers, theatre owners and distributors. There were no outsiders. Tables for rubbernecks were unavailable till those they had come to goggle at had long since departed. A steady stream of visitors now came to their booth to congratulate and to fawn upon Bancroft. Heads were shaken wisely.

'Best thing that's happened to Hollywood. . . .' they chorused.

'. . . so you finally made it, old buddy.'

'Couldn't have happened to a nicer guy!'

When the big shots had paid their respects, the smaller fry – the agents and the 'resting' stars came with varying degrees of heavy-handed subtlety, each to make an individual pitch. If Bancroft was impressed by all this, he gave little sign.

'You never find out how many passengers there are,' he observed, 'until you wind up in the driver's seat.'

The only visitor Bancroft appeared genuinely glad to see was a dishevelled director who, he whispered, was renowned for his brilliance and love of the bottle. This evil-smelling individual eased himself unbidden into their booth and, after ogling Pandora, addressed their host.

'They've really scraped the bottom of the barrel *this* time! You might inject a little taste and integrity into the Metropolis cess pit, but I doubt it, you'll probably turn out to be an unprincipled jerk like the rest of 'em.'

Bancroft had a charming smile in his armoury. He unsheathed it.

'Get dried out, Jack, then come and see me. I've a great property for you.'

'I'll consider it,' said the director and rose with dignity, sending two glasses of ice water and a basketful of rolls cascading to the floor.

Half-way through their swordfish steaks, a note was handed to Bancroft. He half rose in his seat, waving and blowing kisses across the room at a dumpy elderly woman wearing a dreadful hat.

'She says you're beautiful and she wants to do a Sunday feature on you,' Bancroft told Pandora.

'Who is she?'

'Louella Parsons.'

When Pandora looked blank, Bancroft shook his head in disbelief.

'I heard the British Press were short of paper but I never thought they were *that* short! Louella Parsons and Hedda Hopper between them have columns read by millions of people every day. Over two hundred papers and radio stations carry their junk. They're powerful out of all proportion to their command of the language, but boy! Can they be dangerous! They can also be very helpful if they like you, especially when you're getting started.' He took a paper-thin notepad from his pocket. 'I'll tell Pesnick to follow up on this.'

Pandora stole a glance across the room. 'She looks rather sweet and vague-looking.'

'Louella Parsons is about as sweet and vague as General Motors. She knows everything that goes on in this town almost before it happens and her husband is a clap doctor, which makes a lot of people very nervous.'

'What's the other one like?' Stani asked.

'Hedda Hopper is about the same age as Louella, they're both knocking seventy. Hedda's smarter and tougher but not so well informed. But she's dangerous because she's a failed actress, she's bitter. Louella can be flattered out of feuds and attacks but Hedda never gives up once she has it in for someone and she likes to attack the big ones. Charlie Chaplin, Dory Shary, the Head of R.K.O., and Orson Welles are her favourite targets at the moment.'

Stani noticed Pandora's cat's eyes shining as she drank in every word, and wondered not for the first time how he would fit into her new world.

'Will Pandora really have to kiss these ladies' asses?' he asked.

'How charmingly you put things!' Bancroft said. 'The answer is yes! Chiefly because she'll find out that everyone else does, it's just not worth the hassle, getting on the wrong side of the columnists. Louella is happily married and very sentimental about love affairs but Hedda was the fifth wife of an actor thirty years older than herself who screwed everything in sight. She finally caught him in mid-hump when he was sixty-five. She's also a Quaker and something of a prude. She and Louella are complete opposites; the only thing they have in common is a loathing of each other!'

'How will they take it when they find out that Stani and I are living together?' Pandora asked.

Bancroft pursed his lips. 'Let's just play it by ear for a week or two, okay?'

15

New faces and 'hot properties' being the traditional re-chargers of Hollywood social batteries, Pandora and Stani quickly became the most sought after young couple in town. Chuck vetted their invitations and made sure that Jan Ricardo's photograph was seldom missing from the daily papers, nor her name from the columns of the *Hollywood Reporter* and *Daily Variety*. While Pandora worked hard with her voice coach, preparing for her special test, Stani looked up old friends from Alwyn High, took up surfing at Malibu, frequented a beach bar in Santa Monica called 'The Athlete's Foot', and pushed into the back of his mind the distant sound of warning bells.

Russell Bancroft came to regard Pandora as his very own discovery, and personally orchestrated the careful build-up of her 'image'.

'BANCROFT PREPS RICARDO'S FIRST
U.S. VEHICLE'

Hollywood Reporter

'BANCROFT MASTERMINDS RICARDO'S
FUTURE'

Variety

Mr. and Mrs. Orbiston continued to run the Moorish prison after their own fashion and what meals their employers were forced to consume at home had an aura of 'déjà vu' about them, steaks or chickens with warm attractive exteriors progressing from lukewarm to cold at the epicentre.

'She gets awfully upset when I criticize,' Pandora sighed. 'But she tosses her head, which I enjoy hugely.'

'I think we should give a dinner party,' said Stani. 'Maybe they don't have enough to do . . . it's time we paid a few people back anyway.'

210

Pandora slowly warmed to the idea and twenty of 'Hollywood's finest', including Russell Bancroft and his wife, accepted for the following Saturday. The Orbistons professed themselves delighted by this development.

As the day approached Pandora's Hawksmoor upbringing asserted itself and Stani drove her to the Brentwood Town and Country Market to order flowers, the necessary wine and spirits and other goodies.

'Just leave everything else to us, Honey,' Mrs. Orbiston said.

'Yes, but what are you giving us to eat?'

'Mr. Orbiston and I have given it a lot of thought. I'll do a nice Vichyssoise first, the folks hereabouts will expect roast beef, you being English, so that will follow with two nice vegetables and we'll finish up with crêpes Suzette or Baked Alaska, whichever you like best. So what's it to be? Crêpes Suzette or the Baked Alaska?'

'I think we'll have the Baked Alaska,' said Pandora, striving to keep apprehension from her voice.

On the morning of the party, when Pandora asked Stani to go into Beverly Hills for some flower vases, his car was missing from the garage.

'Mr. Orbiston borrowed it,' said Mrs. Orbiston. 'We needed a few extra things.' She seemed a trifle tense.

'What can we do to help?' Pandora asked.

'Well, it'd be real nice if you could arrange to be out for lunch so we can get the place all fixed up and looking pretty.'

Chuck was pressed into action, and the three of them set off for the beach. He raised no objections to strapping Stani's surf-board on top of his blue Pontiac, and on the way to Malibu made a detour through Brentwood and Bel Air pointing out the houses of Humphrey Bogart, Marlene Dietrich, Constance Bennett, Tyrone Power, Joan Crawford, Gregory Peck and others. They skirted several holes of the Bel Air Country Club and had the great good fortune to spy through some bushes Fred Astaire with infinite grace and good humour hook his drive out of bounds into some oleanders. He put down a second ball, lined himself up and, encouraged by his opponent, executed a few dance steps to correct his rhythm, and smacked it two hundred yards down the centre of the fairway.

211

'I still can't believe I'm here,' Pandora breathed. 'And I can't believe how *natural* they all are!'

'Not *all*,' Chuck corrected. 'The ones at the top maybe, because they've got talent and they feel secure; they've got nothing to prove. But there's an awful lot of smucks around and a lot of pushing and shoving goes on trying to get up there. Not only among the actors, mind you – producers, directors, writers . . . everyone. It's a hell of a business in many ways. Sometimes I hate it.'

Sunset Boulevard wound through the lovely foothills of the Santa Monica Mountains, past the Riviera Country Club, the Will Rogers Ranch, the Uplifters Polo Field, the little village of Pacific Palisades, then dropped down to the coast where they turned north on the 101 Highway towards Malibu. The Ocean seemed oily calm but Stani's practised eye immediately diagnosed it.

'Surf's up!!' he cried happily.

The foothills, yellow with wild flowers, fell to the very shoulder of the Highway and far out beyond the golden sandy beach to their left pelicans were dive bombing a school of fish.

'It's fabulous!' Pandora sighed. 'But how *could* they have allowed all those dreadful little shacks to be put up on stilts between the road and the ocean?'

'Greater Los Angeles,' Chuck said grimly, 'is not renowned for its planning. The City is spreading in all directions, everyone wants to live in California because of the climate. They arrive in Los Angeles at the rate of thousands every day, from North Dakota, Michigan or wherever, rubbing their goddam chilblains and putting up these crummy little houses.'

At Malibu there was little except a small, red brick Sheriff's Office and a fishing pier with a restaurant at the end. In the hills behind the Sheriff's office, set in a grove of eucalyptus, a white cross stood beside a Spanish-style monastery of cream coloured stucco. North of the pier the beach for several hundred yards curved outwards towards an outcrop of black rocks. In this half moon a dozen surfers were riding the big Pacific rollers. Chuck pointed toward the rocks:

'Behind them for maybe a mile to that next headland is the Malibu Colony, a bunch of artists live there and a few actors. It's a pretty relaxed life they have, lots of swimming, booze and

212

"poon tang" – it's gotten quite a reputation! But they have a load of trouble when the big storms come, the conformation of the sand changes and they either wind up with their living rooms full of the stuff or their steps down to it dangling in the air twenty feet above the beach.'

Stani unloaded his surf-board and trudged off along the beach towards a group of bronzed, tow-headed teenagers squatting around a driftwood fire.

'I'll grab something to eat later,' he said. 'This surf's too good to miss.'

Pandora and Chuck walked to the end of the pier. Half-way along, admirers were clustered round a retired housepainter and a 30 pound halibut which had badly misjudged things and swallowed a herring attached to his hook. Men with rods and tackle boxes were coming ashore from the half-day, live-bait boat; they carried sacks of barracuda, rock cod, skulpin and striped bass. In the restaurant a delicious red snapper and a Caesar's salad was long lingered over with the help of a dry white wine from the Napa Valley. Finally Stani, green-fingered and chattering with cold, rejoined them. Pandora had questioned Chuck closely about Russell Bancroft.

'There are two sorts of faces,' she said. 'Those you can see into and those that are closed. It's not that his eyes are crossed or shifty or that he doesn't look straight into mine, but I just can't . . . see into his face!'

Chuck was instantly defensive.

'Russ is a great guy,' he said. He's been very successful too, with the two most impressive things in Hollywood going for him.'

Pandora's chin was cupped in her hands.

'Tell me,' she said.

'He has a happy family life with his wife and two kids –'

'And . . .?'

'And . . . "F.I.M." . . .' said Chuck. 'Fuck It Money' . . . He's rich enough now so no one can scare him or bribe him.

When Stani had wolfed down a Club sandwich they drove slowly back, stopping beneath the palms atop the Santa Monica Palisades to watch the sun slide below the glassy copper-coloured horizon.

'I saw the green flame as it disappeared!' Pandora claimed.

213

'That's a detached retina you have there,' said Chuck.

As they approached Beverly Hills, both Pandora and Stani, like actors on an untroubled Wednesday morning, suddenly remembering their mid-week matinée, felt a fluttering in their stomachs.

'I dread tonight,' Stani said.

'What are you giving the folks to eat, Pandora?' asked Chuck.

'Oh the menu's all right,' Pandora said, 'it's the people who are dishing it up I'm worried about.'

When they opened the massive iron-studded front door, the gloom of the place seemed to have intensified.

'I don't think it looks too great with the drapes closed,' said Chuck.

'And there's no smell of cooking,' said Stani. 'How long does it take to roast a big hunk of beef?'

'It's too quiet,' said Pandora. 'They can't still be taking an afternoon nap, can they? And it doesn't look as though the downstairs had been touched at all.'

Stani disappeared towards the kitchen.

A few seconds later he was back, beckoning silently. Pandora and Chuck followed. Flat on her back in the middle of the kitchen floor, not a strand of her blue-white hair out of place, lay Mrs. Orbiston. She was in flimsy black underwear and snoring like a warthog, the traditional empty gin bottle lay alongside. Of her husband there was no trace. The doors of the empty garage creaked on their hinges. Chuck broke the silence.

'The sons of bitches.'

They left Mrs. Orbiston undisturbed and sat down to a council of war in the dreadful dining room. The phone rang.

'I'll get it,' said Chuck.

He listened, then clapped a hand over the mouthpiece.

'It's someone for Mrs. Gary Cooper – she wants to know if it's okay to bring a couple of houseguests from New York?'

'Oh yes . . . fine,' said Pandora weakly.

They settled down again, ignoring the nasal barrage from behind the kitchen door. The phone rang once more.

'Mrs. Samuel Goldwyn's butler says he's been calling all day, wants to know if it's black tie,' said Chuck.

'Is *he* invited?' asked Stani.

Pandora was on the verge of tears.

214

'Darling, don't be funny, please.'

The front door-bell tolled mournfully. Two tough-looking officers of the Los Angeles Police Department stood upon the threshold, a patrol car was behind them. The sergeant saluted.

'Miss Ricardo?'

'Yes.'

'Thought I recognized you, Miss Ricardo, I wonder if you can help us.' He rustled among the contents of a folder. 'Does the name O'Hare, O'Hara, Carrington or Gower mean anything to you?'

'No, I'm afraid not.'

'These photographs ring a bell?'

Pandora looked at numbered, full face and profile mug shots of a man and a woman. Stani and Chuck peered over her shoulder.

'Please come inside,' Pandora said.

The policemen followed her through the gloomy house and into the kitchen. Mrs. Orbiston had not moved.

'That's her, all right,' said the younger policeman, unclipping his handcuffs.

'Is the man around here someplace?'

'Mr. Orbiston?'

The sergeant laughed shortly but his hand had moved to his holster.

'That what they call themselves these days?'

'What are they wanted for, Officer?'

'Murder in Ohio, they knocked off a bank in Columbus . . . a cashier got shot, but there's a load of warrants out for them from all over, they're real bad news.'

Mrs. Orbiston's slumber was interrupted by the young policeman who marched her to the patrol car and locked her inside. The sergeant explained that 'Mr. Orbiston' had been spotted that afternoon outside San Diego, heading for the Mexican border, having presumably dumped his partner. He'd be picked up for sure, he said, but the house would be under surveillance just in case he came back. Chuck busied himself with the telephone, and with minutes to spare the redoubtable 'Prince' Mike Romanoff sent over from his restaurant a magnificent dinner, with waiters to serve it.

During dinner at the refectory table and faced with the

215

horror of the drawing room later, the guests unleashed such a barrage of good natured insults upon Russ Bancroft for allowing his new star to live in such squalor that he invited everyone over to his house to sit in luxury and be treated to an after-dinner showing of Rita Hayworth in *Gilda*.

His wife quickly came up with a modification of this plan. 'Sonja Heini has her big party tonight, why don't we all drop over there? I'll give her a call.'

It was quickly arranged and after dinner half the guests headed for Delfern Drive. Stani and Pandora went with Bancroft in his Lincoln Continental; his wife went home.

The Norwegian skating star, all smiles and dimples, made them welcome and indicated a striped circus tent in the garden. 'There's a buffet and an orchestra down there. Make yourselves at home, have a good time!'

It was a cool evening. Steam rose from the heated pool, and four long-haired blondes, hired from Central Casting to decorate the scene, had windbreakers draped over their naked torsos. They were seated on pedestals and from navel down were encased in mermaid tails. Glasses of hot toddy were in their hands.

'Ask someone to get us out of here, for Christ sake!' one called through chattering teeth.

Inside the tent were three or four hundred people, the men wearing dinner jackets, their companions outdoing each other with flashing jewels or plunging necklines. In the centre was a dance floor around which, on bright green nylon grass (lent for the occasion by Twentieth Century Fox), the guests were grazing at tables. Two buffets and two bars served them, a non-stop orchestra deafened them, and over their heads baskets dripping with thousands of camellias swung on chains.

Stani's movie-going had fallen off sharply during the War years but even he recognized one world-famous face after another. Pandora was as excited as a little girl at Christmas when Bancroft led the way to a table.

Stani avoided dancing whenever possible because of his foot, so with Bancroft monopolizing Pandora on the floor, he drifted about with a drink in his hand, taking soundings of his first big Hollywood party. It seemed curiously businesslike. A dozen photographers were ranging like bird dogs, looking for news-

216

worthy combinations. They too wore dinner jackets and were obviously company men, because before they used their flash bulbs, they meticulously moved bottles out of sight, straightened ties or helped bosoms return whence they had popped. At all costs the owners of Hollywood's famous faces must not be suspected by their public of drinking, nor above all of fornicating.

In addition to the relaxed groups round the well-known faces, some tables, Stani noticed, were populated only by men, portly, jowly, older ones with big cigars, unsmiling faces and engaged in heavy conversation. Nearby, twittering like starlings, sat their diamond-encrusted womenfolk. And everywhere, stunningly beautiful girls and muscular young men kept hopeful eyes on the cigar smokers, hoping to be noticed.

Stani was watching the dancers, some clearly uninhibited, when a round man introduced himself.

'Bud Werker, used to be with the Morris office, now with Triple A. Glad to know you.'

Stani shook the proffered hand.

'American Artists Agency,' added Werker. 'Who handles you?'

'I handle myself,' Stani said.

It sounded vaguely pornographic but Werker was not deterred.

'I've been watching you – half the broads in this tent have got the hots for you. Who are you with?'

'No one at the moment.'

'You gotta be kidding! You mean you don't have an *agent*?'

Stani shook his head.

Werker put a hand under Stani's elbow and led him to the bar.

'Fill us up!' he said to the barman. 'Know what they're doing over at Republic? They're making *The Musketeers Ride Again*. The other two parts are set but they're stuck for the young good-looking one. Can you ride?'

Stani nodded.

'Tell you what. Monday they're testing for the part. I play gin every Sunday with the head casting guy at Republic. What say we give it a shot?'

Stani shrugged.

217

'Give me your name and a number where I can reach you tomorrow around six. You'll have to sign papers with Triple A of course. Seven years okay?'

Stani wrote the number, spelled his name *Skolly Moski*, and they parted. He quite enjoyed the rest of the party, was invited to join several groups of young people, was groped by a red-head, propositioned by a waiter, and took great delight in the cool elegance of Pandora.

Pandora was well satisfied with the evening. She had been told by one and all how ravishingly beautiful she was and Russell Bancroft had been most attentive; Stani was negative.

'You do realize, don't you,' he said, as she was slapping night cream on her face, 'that everyone in this house tonight was successful? Next time we should invite people who are having a bad patch, or a tough time getting started, and I bet there weren't many "extras" at Sonja Heini's party.'

'Success,' said Pandora flatly, 'is what Hollywood is all about. I'm going to look at a house in Brentwood tomorrow. Russ is taking me. A producer is going to Rome to make two pictures, he wants to rent it for a year to someone he can trust. It's beautiful according to Russ, it's got a pool, a projection room and a couple who come by the day – wouldn't that be lovely?'

'Great,' said Stani. 'Any other news?' He felt rather mutinous.

'Yes,' said Pandora. '*Good* news, darling! Russ didn't want me to know till it was set, but he told me as we were leaving, the producer of *The Ruby Ring* is looking at my test tomorrow. If he likes it – I'm going to get the lead!!'

'Great!' said Stani again, but he wished he could sound more enthusiastic.

When Bud Werker phoned the following evening, at first Stani had only a hazy recollection of what the man was calling about. But having nothing else to do he agreed to meet the agent at seven o'clock in the morning outside the Garden of Allah. At least, he told himself, it would be fun pulling the flesh pedlar's leg. He said nothing to Pandora. He still for some reason felt rebellious.

At seven-thirty Bud Werker left him seated on a bench in the cold cheerless waiting room of Republic Studios casting office. Stani had declined to sign a seven year contract with Triple A until, as he said with a straight face, 'I have got the part.'

After an hour a spotty youth poked his head round the door.

'You Moski?'

'That's right.'

'Then get your ass over to make-up – room fourteen.'

Compared to Metropolis, Republic Studio was bedraggled. The early sun beat down upon the dusty concrete underfoot, and the glare hurt his eyes as he followed the youth's directions.

'Jesus,' said the make-up man. 'Not *another*!'

Pinned above the central mirror of his make-up table was a photo-reproduction of Frans Hals' 'Laughing Cavalier'.

'Get in that chair and don't talk.'

Stani settled himself, the make-up man studied him, then got busy squeezing tubes of make-up onto a palette and making a selection from piles of wigs, bristling moustaches and goatee beards. The spotty one reappeared to thrust a sheet of paper into Stani's hand.

'Here's the scene, learn it.'

What they're asking for is hot lead and cold steel and plenty of it, and we're the boys to give it to them, aren't we, men? . . . To arms then, Comrades!!!'

Stani read it once, and knew that under no circumstances could he ever forget such gibberish. Then the make-up man set about transforming him into a Laughing Cavalier. One hour and fifteen minutes later he was escorted by the spotty one to the Wardrobe Department, outfitted with cloak, wide-brimmed hat, doublet and hose, thigh boots, white shirt, leather jerkin, crossbelt and rapier, and pointed in the general direction of Stage 6. He tottered on high heels through 'Western' streets filled with cowboys, townsfolk, and a great deal of horse manure. Finally he pushed open the door of Stage 6. Its cavernous interior was dark except for one illuminated corner; like a moth to a flame he headed for the lights.

There he beheld a section of a French tavern of the d'Artagnan period, all the paraphernalia and personnel of a film unit, and a director in boots and breeches brandishing a fly whisk.

'We've been waiting for you, Goddamit,' said this individual. 'Stand in line with the others.' He pointed at a row of

219

eleven identical Laughing Cavaliers.

'You all know Miss Annette le Bon.' He flicked the whisk at a petulant unknown actress in ringlets and costume; half moons of sweat were beneath her armpits.

'Each of you in turn will kiss Miss le Bon then turn to camera and deliver the "hot lead" speech. First man!'

An assistant pushed forward a sweating actor and the hard-faced crew fell silent.

That of course would have been the logical moment for Stani to put an end to his schoolboy prank but he was fascinated to see what happened next. The film ran through the camera sprockets but the actor was so nervous that the awful speech came out in one big verbal blob. He was accorded no second chance, and was dismissed with ignomony.

In quick succession other Cavaliers in the most brutish fashion were given their marching orders by the director. One or two, more seasoned than the rest, enquired how he would like them to play the scene, but they too were contemptuously discarded. Stani was moved by the plight of the actors. All, he was sure, had pinned desperate hopes on the outcome of the morning but the cattle market ordeal they were being subjected to and the refinement of the torture of having to endure it before their peers – seemed like an abominable imposition.

When only two remained between him and having to face the ordeal himself, Stani waited till the camera was turning and all eyes were focused upon the current performer, then tiptoed silently away.

The make-up man had gone to lunch so he left the hairpieces on the table, hung up his wardrobe and left the studio. No one questioned his departure.

Pandora had left a note saying she had gone for her meeting with Maxwell Stern and telling him that Russell Bancroft had called and wanted to see him at three o'clock. 'Sounds exciting!' she had written. He was making himself a sandwich in the kitchen and reflecting on his little escapade when the phone rang. It was a very angry Bud Werker.

'What the fuck did you do that for, you stupid jerk? I break my ass to get you the job, use my contacts, put myself out on a limb and you have the goddam nerve to walk out without a goddam word! Let me tell you *this*, I'll see you never get work in this town *ever. You think you're an actor?'*

Stani waited till Werker had finished, then he answered quietly, 'No, I don't. But *you* did.'

He was not proud of himself and was increasingly worried for Pandora, after his glimpse of a darker side to her glamorous profession.

16

Maxwell Stern was a Broadway producer with a formidable string of successes behind him and a fearsome reputation for tricky dealings, and dreadful feuds. None who worked for him enjoyed the experience and although they welcomed being piloted to the safe harbour of success beneath his guiding hand, few except the destitute and the masochists returned for a second dose. Unfortunately, what counts with the backers of productions is the producer's 'track record', so Maxwell Stern was always in demand on Broadway. He had never before tried his hand at film production, looking upon it as a step into the unknown, an unnecessary risk. But the blandishments of a major studio and the flashing before his eyes of 'complete production control' – plus a financial offer of King Solomon's Mines proportions, persuaded him to sign a three picture deal and to rent a house in Holmby Hills.

Chuck had brought Pandora up to date on Stern's background as gently as he could but even so she found herself knocking upon a door marked 'STERN PRODS – THE RUBY RING' with noticeably diminished control of her limbs.

A secretary who looked like a prison wardress and who had worked for Stern for twenty-two years bade Pandora wait. This she did, for almost an hour, a none too enjoyable experience for someone on the verge of taking the red carpet treatment for granted. But finally the drawbridge was lowered and Pandora was instructed to enter the inner sanctum.

Blinds and curtains were almost completely closed against the California glare; it was so dark inside his office that at first Pandora did not even see Maxwell Stern. A movement behind a Mussolini-sized desk attracted her attention.

'Sit there in front of me so I can see you,' commanded an

expressionless voice. Stern made no effort to stand or shake her hand so Pandora sat down. A long silence ensued during which, as her eyes became accustomed to the gloom, first the outline, then the various features of her producer-to-be came into focus.

The first thing Pandora saw were large brass buttons on the front of a double-breasted blazer; smaller ones were on the cuffs. A white shirt with polka dot bow tie also came into view. And at last the face, or rather what had once been the face. An ill fated 'lift' had denuded it of all lines – and therefore of all expression. A mournful moustache seemed pinned beneath a nose of misguided design. The eyes were masked behind very dark glasses and the whole topped off by an unfortunate copper-coloured toupee worn at a rakish angle, like a yachting cap. Pandora was startled out of her appraisal when Stern smiled. Dentists do not normally 'go for Baroque' but Maxwell Stern's teeth resembled the keyboard of a harpsichord.

'I saw your test,' he said, 'you are very beautiful. What a pity you can't act.'

Pandora grew very still, stunned by such calculated rudeness. Bette Davis, Katharine Hepburn or Lauren Bacall, she thought, would surely have come up with a devastating response, but her mind went blank. 'When in doubt' she had been taught 'return bad manners with compliments'.

'How sweet of you,' she murmured.

The ivories snapped out of sight, Stern leaned forward and folded carefully manicured hands on his desk.

'I wanted Ava Gardner for *The Ruby Ring*.'

'Why didn't you get her?'

'Because Metro won't loan her out.'

'Perhaps she didn't like your script.'

'Do you?'

Pandora weighed her answer carefully.

'I've had very little experience with screenplays, as you of course know, but I naturally thought that if you and Mr. Bancroft and the director all wanted to do it, then it *must* be good.'

'Hmm,' said Stern.

There was a pause punctuated by an occasional 'zipp' from behind the shades as flies settled on specially baited electrical incinerators on the window-sills.

223

'Hmm,' Maxwell Stern said again. 'Russell Bancroft is only an executive, he doesn't know a goddam thing about scripts. Ted Gruskin is a bird brain, a phony intellectual.'

Pandora sensed an advantage.

'Why do you let him direct your film then?'

'I got him cheap. At least he has a fresh approach to canned entertainment. He did get some good things on live television in New York. He'll make an interesting change from the old movie has-beens, with their dreary long shot, medium shot and close-up techniques. He can make the show move. It's crap but I've gotten a new writer on it. I've got a great cameraman who'll make the best of your looks and your body, and one of the best film editors in the business. So, provided you stop shouting, between them they'll cover up your shortcomings as an actress. It's not a very demanding role anyway.'

'Shouting?'

'Yes. Stage actors always shout when they make movies, they feel they have to project so people at the back of the sound stage don't miss a syllable of their golden performances. They're so dumb they forget the microphone is right over their heads and that's where the furthest seat in the House is. So, all you really have to do is speak clearly, normally, and learn to work to the camera. *That's* the audience . . . make love to it.'

Pandora's fear of Stern was diminishing.

'Wouldn't you be much happier if you got somebody else instead of me?'

'Yes.'

'So, why don't you?'

'Bancroft is the boss.'

'And?'

'And. It's *you* he wants to fuck.'

The logical moment for Pandora to bring the interview to a classical conclusion by smacking Stern's face was lost when he stood up – his head remained at almost the same level as before; he was really too *small* to hit.

In the outer office the wardress was waiting with a mimeo-graphed schedule.

'It's all here, Miss Ricardo,' she said. 'Two weeks of pre-production – wardrobe fittings, make-up tests and script readings. Then off to location, in Mexico someplace – down near Santa Cruz. The set designer and construction gang are there already.' She smiled a grisly smile. 'They don't like it a lot. Snakes!'

'Mr. Stern didn't say anything about who else will be in the cast.'

'He will only take the best for the supporting roles, you can rely on that. And Judd Dugdale of course is opposite you.'

'What's he like?'

'Oh, typical Hollywood,' the wardress sniffed. 'White Cadillac, dark glasses, big smile. Supposed to be right up there with Van Johnson, Alan Ladd and Rock Hudson at the box office.' Her lip curled. 'The bobby-soxers go nuts over him.' She handed Pandora a typewritten memo. 'Here are some instructions for you.'

It read as follows:

Mr. Gruskin is at his place up at Arrowhead. You are to go up there this afternoon and bring your script. It's a long drive there and back so he suggests you take an overnight bag. Here's his address and phone number.

When Stani arrived at Metropolis Studios that afternoon, he too was given V.I.P. treatment at the reception desk.

'You know the way, Mr. Skolimowski,' smiled the fat Security Man. 'Mr. Bancroft's expecting you in his bungalow.'

Russell Bancroft rose from behind his desk, shook hands and settled an arm round Stani's shoulders.

'Stani,' he said. 'I asked you to come over as soon as I saw Hedda's column. I'm used to this kind of thing. But my wife still gets upset and I thought you and I should get together on it.'

Stani looked bewildered.

'Didn't you see the piece?'

'No, I don't read the columns. I don't know what they're talking about.'

Bancroft smiled. 'Unfortunately, I have to keep an eye on them. Take a look at this.' He handed over a clipping. '. . . yet another sighting has been reported, this time in an out of the way eatery in Sherman Oaks, of a happily married Studio Head (newly elected) and his bombshell British discovery. Observers said they were very engrossed. Maybe her upcoming American

225

debut was occupying their minds.'

Bancroft lit a cigarette.

'That story was probably planted by some jerk waiter for fifty bucks,' he said. 'I just want you to know, Stani, in all sincerity, that I respect you and Pandora and I think you respect me enough to know that I would never make a play for your girl under any circumstances, nor would I ever cheat on my own wife.'

Bancroft examined the end of his cigarette. Stani wondered why he was saying all this.

'Tell you what. And this is why I asked you over. I was planning to take a ride down to Mexico once *Ruby Ring* gets under way, to make sure the picture's going okay. But I have to get over to Europe for a few weeks to shake up our operations over there. The Italians are using up our frozen dollars too fast. So I'd like you to go along with Pandora, as part of the Company. It would make her happy and keep you out of mischief. Whaddaya say?'

'I'd love to go, of course,' said Stani. 'But what could I do?'

'I thought we might attach you to the Production Staff in a general capacity, the Assistant Director'll find a million things for you to do. We'll pay you a couple hundred a week from here so that Stern can't kick and, who knows, you might end up taking my job in a few years' time. Like the idea?'

'Very much,' Stani said. 'It's very kind of you. The only thing is, I really couldn't accept a sort of . . . hand-out to the boyfriend to keep the leading lady happy: and I wouldn't want your production staff making up jobs to keep *me* happy either. Unfortunately I'm not trained in anything in which I could pull my weight in a film company – I wish I were.'

Bancroft nodded. 'I appreciate the way you feel, Stani, you're obviously not the sort of guy anyone would accuse of taking a hand-out, of course . . .' He smoked in silence till Stani spoke again.

'While I was recovering from an operation, I took a course in photography. I'm very intrigued by it – I didn't get a diploma or anything – but is there anywhere I could fit in and be genuinely useful in that department?'

Bancroft snapped his fingers. 'Sold! You'd be a great help to Al, the still man on the picture. He's allowed an assistant on the

226

Budget – I'll fix it right away!'

'Of course, I'll do anything else to help out.'

'Don't worry!' Bancroft laughed. 'They'll work your ass off down there. You'll be asking for a raise after the first week!'

Bancroft removed a linen jacket from a hanger and carefully threaded his Hacking Club tie through his pink Brooks Brothers buttondown shirt.

'I have to get over to Twentieth Century to see Zanuck. Sorry to run out on you. I'll have Marcia start payments as of today.'

Back at the Moorish Prison, Pandora was in the bedroom throwing things into an overnight bag.

'What did Russ have to say?' she enquired over her shoulder. Stani told her and she burst out laughing.

'How lovely! We'll be together! He must have a guilty conscience, how funny! Several people called about Hedda's little number: poor thing, she has to sell papers I suppose. I can't remember, did I tell you we'd stopped off for a drink the night Russ dropped me home?'

'If you did, I didn't give it a thought anyway.'

'You don't have to, I love you.' She kissed him. 'And I'll miss you tonight. Now you be a good boy. Stay away from the 'Athlete's Foot' and all those randy little beach bunnies or I'll call Louella Parsons and ask for an appointment for you with her husband. By the way the house in Brentwood is a *dream*! You'll *love* it. We can have it next week. Lovely pool, beautiful garden, play house and projection-room. Everything!!'

'Everything for the built-in movie star?'

Pandora kissed him again.

'I didn't hear that,' she said.

Pandora drove her new Buick convertible carefully. Once out of the city she began to enjoy the drive. She was not yet used to being greeted and whistled at when held up by red lights and had been alarmed when carloads of young men cruised alongside on the open streets to get a better look, so she had closed her automatic top. Now, on the outskirts of Alhambra, she re-opened it and allowed the sun and wind to play upon her flowing hair and augment her golden sun tan.

227

She cruised through miles of citrus and walnut groves around Pomona and sprawling vineyards on either side of Colton, ahead the glorious range of the San Bernardino Mountains soared one mile high. After two hours rocky foothills were displaced by pine forests and the air became appreciably cooler. She climbed past the blackened remains of the once-famous spa hotel of Arrowhead Springs, a burnt out relic of pre-war Hollywood high jinks and expensive 'dryings out'. On top of the ridge, snow still lay in the hollows. She shivered and slipped a cardigan over her shoulders. Midway between Lake Arrowhead and Big Bear she turned right and drove slowly along a pot-holed track, wondering if her director could possibly be any worse than her producer.

Ruby Ring was certainly not a work by William Faulkner or Robert Sherwood but it was an exciting story of skullduggery in the shadowy world of fake gems. Pandora's part was without question a perfect show case for her, with, as Stern had said, no demands for great acting. But by the same token, should she fail to measure up, the whole project could be doomed; much would depend upon the director.

Perched on the very edge of the void was a rambling one storey house of mock alpine design, half chalet, half ye olde stockbroker Tudor, with a sloping roof of large slate slabs. Five thousand feet below lay the township of Redlands.

Ted Gruskin and an Irish wolfhound opened the door.

'Hullo!' he said. 'I was just going to take Parnell for a run . . . mission aborted! It's nice to meet you, Jan.'

When Stern had described Gruskin as one of the thrusting young Turks of Live Television, Pandora had imagined that he would be long, thin, vibrant and good-looking. But before her, in a red flannel shirt out of which sprouted a tuft of grey hair, stood a shortish, fattish, fiftyish man.

'Your pictures don't do you justice,' he said and took her bag. Inside the place was aggressively hunting lodge, with slices of varnished pine logs embedded in concrete walls, a long dining table of varnished pine and bearskin rugs dotted about a pine floor. There were comfortable chintzy sofas and chairs, a huge stone fireplace with the entire front section of an embalmed stag above it. And in one corner the lower part of a dead oak with a grey squirrel, a white owl and a couple of

228

possums wired to its branches. The firelight reflected in their glass eyes.

'It's beautiful!' said Pandora, trying not to let her eyes linger too long on a coffee table in the shape of a monstrous brown snail with an oval glass top resting upon its shell and two knobbed horns. 'Really beautiful.'

Gruskin bubbled with laughter. 'It's a hideous dump. But it's in a great spot, we just rent it.' The other half of the 'we' soon appeared, a towering blonde of Teutonic extraction with rather masculine, sun-kissed good looks, a voluptuous mouth and spectacular proportions.

'Hi!' she said. 'I'm Heidi. Ted, honey, why don't you show Jan her room?'

'Yes, dear,' said Gruskin.

In a functional bedroom with a double bed and a remarkable view Pandora removed her rumpled jeans and T-shirt, showered luxuriously, carefully re-did her make-up, paying special attention to the by now famous cat's eyes, and slipped into a pink shirt and slacks. Over her shoulders she draped a shawl of pink and apple green. Downstairs Gruskin and Heidi were waiting. The glass top of the snail table was freshly covered with a fallout of diagrams, notes, blow-ups of locations, shooting schedules and pages of script.

They settled round the snail, Heidi with shorthand notebook and pencil poised. Parnell crouched nearby munching something that looked like the kneecap of a camel.

'Well,' said the host, 'what do *you* think of *The Ruby Ring*? Because we both think it stinks.'

Pandora's heart sank. Did nobody have faith in the film?

'This is all very depressing,' she sighed. 'Obviously this picture means so much to me, but everyone connected with it seems to be against it!'

'Not everyone,' Heidi corrected. 'Russ Bancroft thinks it'll be a blockbuster.'

'That's true, dear,' said Gruskin. He leaned forward.

'Look, you're in a tough spot. Studio politics reek and the people playing them are creeps. Maxwell Stern happens to be a major stockholder and Head Office wants to involve him in Production, so they offered him any three pictures on their schedule.'

'Why did Mr. Stern choose this one?' Pandora asked.

'Because it's a safe bet . . . up to a point. The hot pictures right now are adventure, crime and sex. This story's corny as hell but it has all three ingredients and also, Judd Dugdale's big at the box office: there's no way he can last because he's queer as a goat, but the kids haven't caught on yet and they really go for him. Stern's encouraging this big publicity build-up Bancroft's giving you so if the picture flops he'll be able to say, "It's the girl's fault! You forced her on me and she's fucked up my film." You'll get all the blame – Russ won't be taking it, Studio Heads never do – they keep ahead of the sheriff – and Stern will come out smelling like a rose with two pictures to go.'

'How about you?' asked Pandora. 'Doesn't the Director get blamed if a picture's a flop?'

'The Director gets blamed if the direction is bad. It won't be,' said Gruskin. 'I can look after myself.'

'But why do you take it on if you don't like the story and have such a low opinion of the Producer?'

Again Gruskin and Heidi exchanged glances.

'You don't know much about American divorce settlements, do you? My wife has wiped me out, but good. I just take the next job that comes along so I can pay off and get free.'

Without much enthusiasm Pandora read through the pages, with Gruskin and Heidi handling the other parts.

'You'll be fine,' Gruskin said when they came to the end. 'I've marked down the passages that don't come easy to you. I'll get with the new writer and see if he can paper them over. The only problem is the story line . . . it's full of holes a mile wide; but who knows, Stern is no fool, maybe the sonofabitch will listen for once and do something about it. The problem is "Needle Ned", his physician, tops him up every day which means he's either on a high or in a trough and unless you can time it to catch him exactly in the middle, you can't get a decision out of him that makes any sense.'

Heidi laid down her notebook.

'Ted, honey, how about fixing us a drink?'

'Good thinking, dear.'

The drinks flowed, steaks were barbecued and the evening unrolled, relaxed, though Pandora's antennae early detected that Heidi was paying an increasing amount of attention to the

230

contents of her pink shirt and pants. Their dog Parnell too was in a peculiar condition, endlessly pumping up and down against her leg. The dog was easily shaken off but sterner refusals were necessary around midnight when Ted Gruskin, wrapped in a sheet, opened Pandora's lockless bedroom door, waved a joint of 'grass' in her face and announced that Heidi was awaiting them both in the sauna.

The next three weeks passed quickly for Pandora and Stani. They shook the dust of the Moorish Prison off their feet and moved into their beautiful new abode in Brentwood. Pandora spent most of her time at the studio working with her voice coach, doing wardrobe fittings, make-up tests and absorbing injections to protect herself against typhoid, tetanus, typhus, yellow fever, hepatitis, cholera and smallpox.

'What *is* El Triunfo like?' she asked Russell Bancroft.

'It's in Tabasco County,' he said, 'about a hundred miles past the isthmus of Tehuantepec on the way to Yucatan. And I can confidently describe it as the asshole of the world – Stern chose it, makes him feel at home!'

Stani's new duties on the payroll hardly interrupted his surfing, but on one occasion he was summoned to spend a day loading different cameras for an excitable photographer doing cheesecake layouts on two nubile starlets. On another he sat in on a Production Meeting conducted by a sardonic chain-smoking New Englander, Otis Champion, a veteran of twenty-five years' service with Cecil B. de Mille and Jack Warner. Champion was no animal lover, having been bitten by a camel during the production of *The Desert Song*, by a horse while filming *My Friend Flicka* and savaged by a huskie on *The Call of the Wild*. On the day of Stani's initiation into the mysteries of Production he was wrestling with the logistical problems of providing fully-trained donkeys, ospreys, alligators and apes for *The Ruby Ring*.

'Our main difficulty,' Champion was saying to his staff, 'is casting the part of "Jimbo" because this monkey has to react to a hot love scene between Judd Dugdale and Jan Ricardo without stealing it or jerking off.'

At that moment the door of Champion's office opened and through it whizzed an orangutang on roller skates. The animal circled the room several times at high speed, causing two screaming secretaries to take refuge on top of Champion's desk, and ended up in his lap with its long hairy arms entwined around his neck.

'Get this thing off me,' he yelled.

Stani unclasped pink scaly fingers from behind the Production Manager's head and with the animal's trusting paw in his hand, wheeled it out whence it had come. In the outer office a man reclaimed it, explaining that he was its agent and had pushed his client into the meeting hoping it would land the part of 'Jimbo'.

'Do you think that did the trick O.K.?' he asked.

Stani took the man's card and promised that Champion would let him know later.

Russell Bancroft involved himself in everything to do with Pandora's pre-production activities, checking on her make-up and costume tests, her publicity handouts and her portrait sessions, even attending occasionally her voice lessons. Maxwell Stern was not pleased about this but he was revelling in a fast building feud with Ted Gruskin, word of which had already leaked to the gossip columns. Harrison Carrol of the *Herald Express* sniffed it first.

'*The Ruby Ring Company will soon be leaving for a hot tamale of a Mexican location and Jan Ricardo's much publicized debut in American pictures, but the Metropolis Lot is buzzing with flies too. The scam there is that Producer Stern and Director Gruskin are not speaking and Russell Bancroft won't be on hand to knock their egos together because he takes off for Europe next week on a fact finding tour of Metropolis flicks.*'

The last days before departure were chaotic for Pandora. Pages of script changes, mimeoed on paper of a different colour for each date of issue, arrived every few hours by messenger. Gruskin, when asked for clarification, told her that Stern had written them himself.

'The little sonofabitch is a frustrated writer. I'm just paid to direct what he gives me. He fired the guy he hired to fix the script. Judd is all steamed up over it too, don't worry, it'll work out.'

Russell Bancroft called to say goodbye and wish her luck.

'You'll be a smash, darling,' he said. 'I'm leaving for Paris

232

tonight . . . back in four weeks . . . I'll miss you.'

Pandora felt deserted. The next morning Ted Gruskin telephoned.

'Jan? I just wanted to say hello and goodbye.'

'Aren't you coming on the same flight?'

'I'm not coming at all. Stern's fired me.'

'FIRED YOU! For *what?*'

'Have you seen the *Reporter* today?'

'It's here – I haven't opened it.'

'Take a look. Mike Connally's column. I'll hold on.'

Pandora found the piece.

'. . . sparks, it is rumoured, are flying yet again at Metropolis between dimunitive Producer Maxwell Stern and outspoken director Ted Gruskin, this time over the script re-writes on *Ruby Ring*. This reporter asked Gruskin for his views on the situation and Gruskin replied as follows: quote "Maxwell Stern may be a big man on Broadway but to me he's a pony's ass" unquote.'

Pandora's heart sank. She picked up the phone once more.

'But Ted,' she said. '*Can* he fire you just like that? I mean, it's not as though you've refused to start shooting or something.'

'Well he *has*,' said Gruskin. 'And Heidi and I are taking off for New York tonight. I'll sue the bastard of course. I may have insulted him, but you're right, I haven't broken my contract. I'm sorry as Hell for you, Jan. It's too bad Russ has gone to Europe because Stern has "full artistic control".'

'Help me, Ted, *please*,' Pandora begged. 'This is awful for you, but . . . what about *me*, what do I do now?'

'Just sit tight. Stern's looking for a new director, it's bound to take a few days because nobody worth a damn is going to take over on this short notice. Don't do a thing. Wait till the Studio calls you.'

Stani was enjoying a last day on the surf so when Gruskin hung up Pandora felt panic rising. The phone rang again.

'Jan?'

'Yes.'

'Judd here.'

'Judd! What's going on?'

'I'm being sued for five million dollars, *that's* what's going on.'

'By whom?'

'Stern! He's signed some little second unit director from Monogram and I told him I wasn't going to work with *that* jerk . . . I mean the guy's a *nothing*! Well! I don't have "director approval" so that miserable little *toad*, he's quite insane anyway, is slapping a lawsuit on me for the cost of the entire film . . . five million *bucks*!'

'What are you going to do?'

'I don't *have* five million bucks. Goddamit! As a matter of fact I don't think I have five *hundred* bucks, so I guess I'm just going to Mexico and make the picture with some cruddy little queen from Monogram. But Boy! do I hate that dwarf's guts.'

'I don't like to bother you in the middle of your problems, Judd,' said Pandora, 'but what about *me*?'

'Stay right where you are, Angel, don't move an inch. Just play it by ear. Goodbye now.'

Pandora made no move to contact Stern or even the Production Office and the supposed date of departure for Triunfo came and went. Speculation as to what was going on at the Metropolis Studios was widely debated and *The Ruby Ring* grabbed headlines from both Hedda Hopper and Louella Parsons, dramatically opposed opinions as usual but headlines nonetheless:

'DISGRACEFUL BEHAVIOUR OF DIRECTOR DEPLORED BY ENTIRE INDUSTRY!' bemoaned Louella.

'STERN FINALLY GETS HIS COMEUPPANCE!' screamed Hedda.

Chuck Pesnick gave Pandora his personal diagnosis of what was going on.

'It's a standoff,' he said. 'Gruskin should never have shot off his mouth but Stern was wrong to fire him. Russ Bancroft has hit the roof over in Paris because the costs down in Mexico are astronomical and going to arbitration takes too long.'

'What about me?' Pandora asked, in her usual refrain.

'Just sit back and enjoy yourself at the studio's expense,' he counselled. 'There's too much money involved, sets are built and contracts are signed, they'll *have* to go ahead sooner or later. They'll work it out.'

The next day Ted Gruskin 'phoned Pandora.

'How are things in New York?' she asked.

'I wouldn't know – I'm back in California – and back on the picture.'

'That's *wonderful*! What happened?'

'The Directors' Guild told Stern he couldn't fire me for calling him a pony's ass and that in future he would be unable to get directors here or on Broadway to work with him unless he reinstated me immediately.'

'Under what conditions?'

'Under *my* condition, that Stern never sets foot on my set while I'm shooting.'

When she repeated the conversation to Stani, he said. 'I remember small boys at school calling each other names and sticking out their tongues. But at least they did it with style!'

'Oh, God!' said Pandora. 'What have I got myself into?'

17

The film company waiting at Los Angeles airport for the first leg of the trip to Mexico City numbered sixty odd. All were in a relaxed and happy mood at the prospect of *The Ruby Ring* finally going before the cameras. Otis Champion was handing out the tickets. Stani was talking with Pandora, Ted Gruskin, Heidi, Judd Dugdale and a luscious, hard-looking actress named Rita Haas who would be playing 'the other woman'. Maxwell Stern was said to be already at El Triunfo. The production manager drew Stani aside.

'Don't take this the wrong way kiddo,' he said, 'but the director, his secretary, the leading actors and the cameraman get to ride first class, the rest of us go steerage.'

'Of course,' said Stani, flushing, 'I never expected anything else.' Otis Champion smiled kindly.

'I'm sure you didn't, pal, but sometimes the guys who're boffing the stars get their signals mixed.' He became heavily confidential. 'And while we're talking shop, you'll be checking into a hotel, if it can be called that, with the rest of the crew, but where you *sleep* is nobody's business, got it?'

'Fine, thanks,' Stani laughed.

It was afternoon when the big transport touched down in Mexico City and when the charter plane for the second leg of the journey flew past Popocatepetl the volcano's snowy helmet was pink in the setting sun but the jagged crater was so dark and ominous that the mountain looked like a huge tooth minus a filling.

The final landing was made on a bumpy grass runway near Villahermosa; it belonged to a group of American oil companies and the surrounding jungle was flare-lit by millions of cubic feet of gas being burnt off into the sky because, Stani learned, enough pipe had not yet been produced to deliver it to Mexico City. After a two hour ride along appalling roads in ramshackle buses the exhausted Company was finally disgorged. The heat and humidity were horrendous.

The Hotel Real in El Triunfo boasted one air-conditioned suite which, much to the chagrin of Rita Haas, was allotted to Pandora. The cooling apparatus consisted of a large brown box screwed to the wall; it thundered and wheezed and apparently extracted the air from the public lavatories, heated it and puffed it in the direction of the large and sagging bed. The feet of the bed stood in iron bowls filled with water – four individual moats to frustrate the cockroaches (beige-coloured and the size of mice); they scuttled for corners when lights were switched on, and lived in families in the folds of the curtains. A basin, a rusted shower and a stained toilet were concealed behind one of these curtains; a couple of armchairs, a divan and a table completed the amenities. The dusty concrete stairs leading up from the lobby were carpeted with the squashed remains of more cockroaches. Stani and Pandora, mindful of dire warnings of the gut-wrenching pains of 'Montezuma's Revenge', spurned the Room Service recommendations of 'Chili con Carne Hotel Real' or 'Shrimp salad Triunfo', and dined instead off hard boiled eggs and bananas, then fell into the sagging bed and a troubled sleep.

They were first awakened, as the oyster-coloured streaks of dawn filtered through the curtains, by the scrabbling noise of the cockroach families evacuating their sleeping quarters for darker accommodation in the toilet; then they heard an appalling commotion outside the window. Stani leaped out of bed. The jungle, he saw, was very close to the back of the hotel, the branches of a large tree actually touched it and from these several hundred large black birds were now de-roosting themselves, shrieking, pecking one another and flapping off upon their lawful occasions. He groaned, returned to bed and snuggled up once more against the satiny curves he knew so well and loved so much. He had much to be thankful for, he told himself.

The location work of *The Ruby Ring* was scheduled to be shot aboard a wooden-built river steamer of 1900 vintage. Sometimes the steamer would have to move through alligator-haunted jungle channels, or steam upon the shark-infested waters of the Golfo de Campeche. And for long and uncomfortable periods, it was to be wrecked and lying upon its side on a sandbar between the two.

By eight o'clock in the morning it was over a hundred in the shade and climbing steadily; the humidity remained constant at Turkish bath level. Make-up melted, wigs lifted at the forehead and unsuitably clad actors, sweating beneath the arc lights, became fractious, forgetful and finally dehydrated.

It was soon apparent that Ted Gruskin was a sadist who revelled in the discomfort around him. He seemed to choose the most awkward and most dangerous positions for his camera crew and artists to work, goading them through an amplified megaphone to the farthermost limit of their abilities and frequently using his 'goosing stick' on the unsuspecting.

This 'goosing stick', a weapon, specially constructed to his specifications, consisted of a ten foot bamboo pole at the end of which was the plaster cast of Gruskin's own hand, fist clenched and second finger rudely extended. The sight of an unsuspecting human posterior was irresistible to Gruskin who, winking at Heidi, would apply the finger. Most people took it good humouredly the first time and thereafter stayed out of range but a few jumped in the air when touched and let out weird cries. These unfortunates became marked by Gruskin for future sport and it was not uncommon to see him in a skimpy pair of swimming trunks beneath an outsize sombrero stalking his prey on decks, or along jungle trails.

Al, the 'still' photographer, one of Gruskin's prime targets, became a gibbering wreck, unable to focus his camera without looking apprehensively behind; but Stani, his assistant, was only once accosted. He smiled at Gruskin and said quietly: 'Do that to me again and you're with the alligators.'

For several days the work for Pandora was easy. At five a.m. the make-up artist knocked on their door, one hour later the hairdresser arrived and by seven-thirty, with her hair in a pink net, she embarked in a dugout canoe, grossly overpowered by a 50 h.p. outboard motor and driven by a silent Indian with a reputation for getting high every evening on mushrooms. An hour's ride through jungle waterways flanked by orchid-bearing mangroves passed quickly enough, thanks to a colourful performance by flocks of parrots, parakeets, macaws, toucans, grackles and chachalacas: on the return trip at dusk Pandora's goosepimples were raised by the sight of dangerous vampire bats, swooping against the sunset, and ominous nostrils or slimy armoured backs disappearing in sudden swirls near sandbanks.

Four days of action shots elapsed before she was due to utter her first words in *The Ruby Ring* and the night before she slept not a wink, turning over and over in her mind the pages she had long studied and knew perfectly.

On the great day, feeling drawn and edgy, she presented herself in the dining room of the old riverboat 'for read through of scene No. 38 and rehearsal'. Judd Dugdale was not 'on call' that day, scene No. 38 concerned only Pandora and Rita Haas.

Ted Gruskin and Heidi were already in the saloon when Pandora arrived; both looked odd and distraught.

Rita Haas was late. Pandora enquired if Maxwell Stern would be present.

'It's a matter of complete indifference to me whether the bastard is even in Triunfo,' said Gruskin.

Forty minutes later Rita Haas finally appeared; in her hand was a half-filled tumbler of yellowish fluid. She kissed Heidi lingeringly, Gruskin perfunctorily and stepped over Pandora without a word.

'I'm still stoned,' she announced. 'D'you think this tequila will do me any good?' She downed the remains of the glass and leaned towards the Director.

'Well, Ted,' she said, 'are *you* going to tell her or shall I?'

Pandora turned the pages of her script. Gruskin looked embarrassed.

'You go ahead, Honey, you tell her.'

Rita Haas, like a hen looking at an aeroplane, turned her head jerkily towards Pandora. Then she reached across and took the script off Pandora's lap.

'These pages are *out*,' she said, ripping away a chunk of scene No. 38, tearing it into little pieces and filtering it through her fingers.

Pandora stared at the confetti lying at her feet and looked at Gruskin.

'Jan,' he said, 'I'm real sorry to spring this on you but there's

239

been . . . er . . . a rewrite . . . you'll have a couple of hours to memorize new lines while they're lighting . . .' He passed across several typewritten pages. 'Here's what we're planning to shoot today . . . read it and see how you feel about it.'

While she was reading, Heidi and Gruskin sat staring at her, Rita Haas looked at the ceiling. As the words registered Pandora's heart started pounding; when she had finished she carefully folded the pages four times, then tore them up and added the fragments to the pile already at her feet.

'Who wrote that nonsense?'

Gruskin shifted uncomfortably. 'Well, the girls here worked on it together. It didn't play the way it was.'

'You do realize, don't you, that this . . .' Pandora stirred the debris with her foot . . . 'wrecks the entire construction and balance of the picture.'

Gruskin rose from his chair. 'Heidi honey,' he said, 'let me take a look at your copy.' He stepped forward, fell flat on his face and remained motionless.

'What's the matter with Ted?' Pandora gasped.

'Oh nothing much,' said Heidi. 'I forgot to give him his shot this morning . . . he's short on sugar.'

'*Sugar?*'

'That's what I told you, Honey. Sugar.'

Pandora went out on deck while Heidi ministered to the Director. When she returned he was back in his chair, and Heidi's copy of the scene was in his hand; it was as if his trip to the floor had been edited out in the cutting room.

'I can't entirely agree with your point of view, Jan,' he said, 'but we didn't like what Stern gave us, did we Heidi?'

'It was *awful*, just awful,' said the Valkyrie.

'It stank,' added Rita.

Pandora swallowed.

'I'd like to see Mr. Stern. I want him to tell me that he approves of these changes . . . he is the Producer, I mean it *is* his picture, isn't it?'

'Stern doesn't interfere,' said Gruskin, with a heavy wink at the girls. 'He's only interested in coming in on schedule and not going over budget. He won't object to us getting together and making the dialogue more playable – more natural – this is an "action" picture, the words come second . . .'

240

'I'd still like to talk to him . . .' said Pandora. 'I don't want to get in wrong with Mr. Bancroft . . .'

'I'll bet!' said Rita Haas.

Heidi rose majestically from her seat.

'Ted, Honey, I think I'd better take Jan to the "walkie-talkie", they'll be listening out for calls right now.'

Pandora followed Heidi's 'Gruppenführer' march to the crowded after-deck where the Assistant Director was coping with forty nonplussed Indian extras, an hysterical wardrobe lady with nowhere to hang anything and two dozen smelly monkeys.

'Are you in contact with Production?' Heidi demanded.

'Sure thing,' said the tall young man clad in baseball cap, swimming trunks and sneakers. 'Morning Miss Ricardo. Everything okay? Who d'you want to speak to?'

'Mr. Stern,' said Pandora firmly and knew that fifty pairs of ears were listening. When the Producer's voice crackled out of the instrument, the Assistant handed it to her.

'Try to find a quiet corner,' he smiled, 'one of the monkeys works for Louella Parsons!'

Behind a pile of deck cargo Pandora told Stern what had transpired. He was a long time answering.

'The first rule an actor or actress must learn,' he said, 'is to follow the directions of the Director.'

Pandora felt the sweat trickle down between her breasts. She tried to keep her voice calm. 'But Mr. Stern, surely the first rule a *Director* must learn is to follow the instructions of the *Producer*?'

'Correct,' Stern replied, 'that is why when the timing is right I shall sue Mr. Gruskin for every cent he has.' A click ended the conversation.

Back in the stuffy dining saloon Gruskin glanced up. 'Well?'

'He told me to follow your instructions to the letter,' said Pandora. Gruskin looked uneasy. 'Why, that's just *great*!' he said, 'now then, let's kick the scene around, shall we, and make sure everyone's comfortable.'

Film crews are like bird dogs, they sniff and snuffle around for a while but sooner or later they make up their minds unerringly about actors, directors and producers . . . they seldom get it wrong.

The crew of *The Ruby Ring* early had marked down Maxwell Stern as an efficient Producer but 'some sort of a nut'. Gruskin they admired for his craftsmanship and the speed of his decisions, but they cordially disliked his sadistic treatment of those least able to defend themselves, his subservience to Heidi and his loud public denunciations of Stern. Judd Dugdale they dismissed as 'a decent sort of fruit cake'. Rita Haas they were not too keen on, they looked askance at her drinking and her obvious moves to further her career at all costs . . . 'the only thing she ever turns down is a bed cover,' they said. Pandora was their favourite, the one they loved; they loved her for her genuine sweetness to them, for her beauty and because their instinct told them that she would soon be needing their protection.

When Pandora's Indian rammed his canoe alongside the dock, Stani in T-shirt and jeans, his tan a shade deeper in the evening light, was waiting for her. He looked so handsome and his smile so inviting that her frustrations and worries of the day melted away and she ran into his arms.

By daylight El Triunfo was bad enough, the gathering darkness did little to improve it; ramshackle stalls with roofs of palm fronds and lit by acetylene flares were crowded with peasant women, their babies curled up in blankets slung across their shoulders. Men in floppy sombreros and baggy white pyjama suits stood around in groups, staring at the women or nibbling sticky little cakes, most were barefoot. Carts on solid wooden wheels with sad-eyed oxen roped between their shafts, and weighed down by heavy yokes, stood untended everywhere; against the walls of the more prosperous buildings, the boarding houses, bars, shops, chili joints, brothels or offices, whole families were settling down for the night, some already stretched out beneath their blankets, others, adults and children, crouching round pitiful bowls of maize and beans. An acrid stench that rose into the humid air bore witness to the paucity of arrangements for ablutions but perched in nearby trees the local Sanitation Department was poised ready for action – obscenely ugly black zopilote buzzards, protected by law as necessary scavengers.

Pandora took in the poverty. '*My* troubles seemed so enormous a little while ago,' she said.

242

Stani suggested a bar called 'Casa Mario'. 'The construction crew were here for a month, they say it's the only place where you don't get poisoned and they've taught Mario to make daiquiris. Shall we give it a try . . .? It'll be a change from hard boiled eggs and bananas.' The bar, a converted barn, was not full, just two tables of gigantic Texans from the drilling rigs rectifying their dehydration with bottle after bottle of Santa Cruz beer laced with tequila and two foursomes of well-to-do locals with white shirts and flashing gold teeth playing cards. They ordered daiquiris, tortillas and grilled, freshly caught fish; after an initial shock they became accustomed to a two-way traffic of rats hurrying across a beam above their heads.

Stani listened with growing concern to Pandora's description of her first important day of shooting.

'What really miserable luck that Russ is in Europe. Why don't you put in a call to him – he'll sort it out.'

'I tried to get him last night when I got back just to say "Hello". It's *impossible*, forty-eight hours delay minimum and unless you're right by the phone when it comes through, you go back to the bottom of the list.'

'Send him a cable,' said Stani, 'tell him what's happening.'

'Oh! darling,' Pandora sighed. 'It all seemed to be going so beautifully didn't it? . . . now it's sort of out of control. I don't know how to cope with people like this . . . a producer being topped up by a doctor called Needle Ned, an actress on booze and a director on God knows what!' She giggled. 'I wonder what Judd gets up to, in his spare time, besides the obvious of course!'

'Let's ask him,' said Stani, nodding towards the door.

Judd Dugdale stood surveying the scene. Beside him was his stand-in and double, a good-looking young man of roughly the same dimensions as himself. Both wore white shirts and slacks and were decorated at neck and waist with chains and belts of silver and turquoise.

The Texans fell silent, then one of them gave a derisive wolf whistle. Pandora reacted swiftly.

'Judd! . . . Judd darling! Over here! . . .' Dugdale and his companion moved towards them. Stani pulled up chairs; the Texans started talking again.

'That was very sweet of you, Jan,' smiled Judd, 'very sweet

indeed.'

The daiquiris loosened tongues and Pandora repeated once more the saga of the re-written script. Judd was not surprised. 'That Heidi is bad news,' he said. 'I knew Gruskin back in New York and admired his work a lot, but since he's been shacking up with that policeman in drag he seems to have lost it. My guess is he hasn't been properly laid for years and now he's getting it from an expert, at his age he's losing a couple of million brain cells every time he has an orgasm.'

'What do you think Jan can do?' asked Stani. 'She's in an awful spot.'

'Not much,' Judd replied. 'The trouble is that when Stern was forced to take Ted back after kicking him out in the full glare of Hedda and Louella, Ted let that big Holstein heifer talk him into rubbing his nose in it. Ted's told everyone about barring him from the set, and that's a horse's ass thing to do for a start. But I heard today through the grapevine that he also had his contract re-written giving him the final cut instead of Stern.'

'You mean the final version of this movie will be the Director's and not the Producer's?' asked Stani.

'That's about the size of it,' said Judd.

'I'm going to have another daiquiri,' said Pandora. '. . . in other words we're making a picture for Heidi and Rita?'

Judd nodded.

'Looks that way, Jan . . . two "grazers" . . . and it's a lousy break for your first time out being caught in the middle.'

'What about you?' asked Pandora. 'It's bad for you too, isn't it?'

'There's not much they can do to my part,' said Judd, 'and anyway this is my last picture for Metropolis – Universal have bought up my contract.'

Judd's stand-in, who so far had remained silent, suddenly groaned loudly and clutched his stomach. His face had turned olive green and he glistened with sweat. 'Oh my *God*!' he muttered through clenched teeth. 'Montezuma's got me! – that chicken in today's lunchboxes was buzzard, I knew it.'

Judd was instantly solicitous.

'Jus*tin*! Can you make it back to the room?'

'I'll try,' said Justin bravely and bending forward like the

244

Hunchback of Notre Dame he scuttled for the exit. Judd followed clucking like an anxious hen.

The next day dawned cloudless, for a couple of hours it was cool but by the time Stani had walked to the landing stage his cotton shirt and pants were sticking to his body. He was glad to be clear of the dusty streets, still refuse-strewn despite the flapping early morning efforts of the Sanitation Department. He was becoming increasingly interested in learning all he could about photography and looked forward to his day's work with Al, the 'still' man. First to arrive at the jetty, he savoured the moments before the claustrophobia generated by a hundred people aboard the small river steamer. The landing stage stood at a junction of the Miskito River and a jungle waterway, cormorants evil and black were flying singly, headed for the open sea, snowy white egrets in formations skimmed purposefully in the opposite direction towards their hunting grounds in the mangrove swamps, and flocks of green parrots flashed by to all points of the compass.

The heavy launch arrived and the first arrivals, carpenters, painters, prop men and electricians, shouted cheery greetings to him as they clambered aboard. The location of the jetty was somehow symbolic to Stani; he pondered increasingly over his future. Soon he would have to make a decision but it would not be as easy as a cormorant heading East for fish or an egret going West in search of frogs. Life with Pandora before her Hollywood venture had been an uncomplicated one of great happiness, but now the ground rules were changing rapidly, all sorts of problems were looming up, not least the mundane one of their balance of payments. Stani knew one thing for certain, that life without Pandora was unthinkable, but it would be difficult to hold his own.

'Stani, old Buddy, take off your photographer hat and put on your "stand-in" one!' The Assistant Director was approaching, walkie-talkie and clipboard in hand.

'What's happened?'

'Justin is real sick. The poor guy is throwing up and he's been on the can all night . . . the doctor's with him now, looks like amoebic dysentery . . . what d'you say? Will you stand in for Judd? And take a couple of easy falls for him? We'll make a new deal for you of course. You'd really be helping me out, it'll take two days to bring someone down from Hollywood and we're way behind schedule as it is?'

'No problem with the standing in,' said Stani. 'We're about the same height but I'm not too athletic because of my leg.'

'Don't worry, the only fall we're stuck with today is into water, can you swim?'

'Yes.'

'Will you do it for me?'

'If it helps . . . yes, okay.'

'Thanks a million, you're a pal.'

The steamer was waiting a few hundred yards down river. Once everyone was aboard she headed out into the Golfo de Campeche, the air was cooler and a festive air prevailed among the personnel of *The Ruby Ring* reprieved from their penance of mosquitoes and muggy jungle heat.

For the scene to be shot that day Judd Dugdale had already been disguised as the ship's drunken captain complete with red beard and white uniform so Stani was similarly decorated with the utmost despatch. This turned out to be a most unpleasant experience because he had shaved only a short while before and the spirit gum, when applied to his skin, first stung then tickled abominably. The make-up artist held a handful of red hair in one hand (he told Stani that Roumanian nuns, like farmers, grew biennial crops of it for sale), in the other he wielded scissors: first he 'laid on' the hair in longish tufts all over the lower face and upper lip, firmly pressing it onto Stani's gummy skin with his thumb before tailoring it to the correct length with the scissors. The whole operation, with constant references to a blown-up photograph of Judd, took almost an hour. By the time it was completed the rising temperature caused Stani to perspire, the spirit gum entered his pores: and a million mini-ants seemed to be crawling over his face. When Stani was paraded for inspection before Ted Gruskin and the camera-man, neither knew it was he and a certain amount of merriment ensued when the assistant director appraised the crew of the identity of the new stand-in and double.

During the first hour Stani performed the duties of 'stand-in'. The scene was a relatively simple one, Judd impersonating the drunken captain would appear from a hatchway, whisky bottle in hand, totter across the deck, pause to speak with the quartermaster, continue to the rail, react to something in the far distance, look round the deck furtively, reach for his telescope and then start to climb the rigging. 'Only two rungs though; . . . I don't go higher than six feet,' announced the hero. 'It's in my contract.'

'Two rungs it is, Judd,' Gruskin agreed. 'Just start up.'

The cameraman watched while Judd wandered through the simple manoeuvres, chalk marks were put down for his two stops, and positions selected for the camera. The director then returned to his chair and the joys of his 'goosing stick' while Stani endured the wearisome business of walking the scene through countless times so the cameraman could place the lights to his satisfaction. Huge arcs were soon deployed, Stani squinted in the glare and stumbled about like a green-eyed Chinaman, but at last all was ready, with the 'American' sailors (recruited from among the tallest inhabitants of nearby villages and sprayed with 'fair skin' mixture) busy at their allotted tasks, coiling ropes, winding winches or spitting over the side.

'Where the hell is Judd?' Gruskin demanded. 'C'mon, let's go!'

The leading man surfaced and it quickly became evident that he was in a strange condition: he wandered erratically through the first 'take' wild-eyed and giggling uncontrollably, over-shooting his marks, answering the quartermaster's questions before they had been put to him and winding up at a darkened and hitherto unvisited part of the rail.

'Cut!' yelled the Director. 'What's the matter Judd? You okay?'

'SHROOMS!!' Judd giggled. 'Lovely ivory-coloured shrooms with pale green veins all *over* . . . WHEEE!!!'

'Save the lights. Get him a glass of water . . . what the hell are "shrooms"?'

'Mushrooms, sweetheart!' said Judd. 'Oops! The MAGIC MUSHROOMS!! SHSSH! . . . don't tell a *soul* . . . the jungle's *full* of them! . . . tonight I'm giving a "SHROOM" party!' He lifted both arms in the air and addressed the onlookers:

'SHROOMS tonight kids! – or cactus buttons, dry 'em, chew 'em and oh! Baby! Do they give you a high! *Great* for sex too . . . brings the nerves to the surface . . .'

247

'What the hell's going on here?' stormed Gruskin.

'A shroom, is a shroom, is a shroom!' Judd announced. 'A little chew goes a *long* way.' He burst into roars of laughter and pointed at Gruskin's irate face. 'Comes back in waves for hours; not just straight up and down like that junk Eva Braun shoots into *you* baby!'

Attempting a few steps of an Indian dance he then fell into a basket of white ducks and lay still. He was helped to his cabin. Gruskin made an announcement:

'Okay fellas, we have a change of plan here, we do the end of the scene first, opening on Judd's double when he moves to the rail and starts climbing.'

Stani was then instructed to move to the rail, pause on Judd's marks, reach for the telescope and start climbing the rigging.

'How high do you want me to go?' he asked.

'Till I tell you when to stop,' Gruskin replied nastily. 'Okay, let's shoot it.'

From the rail the rigging sloped inboard towards the cross trees which helped a little but even so, with a bottle of whisky in one hand and a brass telescope in the other, Stani found the climb no easy matter, handicapped already by his damaged foot and an advanced fear of heights. As he toiled upwards on the slack wires set almost three feet apart, he had, at most, the help of two fingers on each hand and the higher he went the more nervously did he press his chin, chest, stomach and knees to the rigging like a leopard stalking its prey.

At long last came a shout from Gruskin: 'Okay, that's far enough.'

Stani peered down through the rungs and beheld a sea of faces far below.

'Turn around for Chrissakes,' Gruskin yelled.

This was a ghastly manoeuvre but somehow Stani managed it and leaned back panting against the steel ropes.

'Cut and print,' Gruskin shouted. 'How does it look from up there?'

'Very high indeed,' Stani answered and received momentary encouragement from a smattering of laughter from below; this dissipated quickly when he realized that his twenty foot climb had been made from deck level but from there to water was at least another ten feet; viewed through his eyes, the

248

total drop was a stupefying thirty-five feet in all.

'D'you want to come back down while we set up?' the Assistant Director called solicitously. 'We'll be ready in a few minutes.'

'No,' mumbled Stani. 'I'll stay up here; what happens next?'

'We're setting up three cameras so if you do it right you'll only do it once,' came Gruskin's voice. 'When I say "ACTION" you see the enemy gunboat over there on the horizon. Hold it for a beat of five then take a look through the telescope for another beat of five, lower the telescope and take a pull at the whisky bottle, then a last look through the telescope and hold that till I yell "FALL".'

'Then what?' Stani asked.

'Then you drop like a fucking stone into the sea,' said Gruskin with relish. 'Any problems?'

'The main problem,' said Stani, and his voice seemed unnaturally high, 'is that as this rigging slopes away from the sea I shall drop like a fucking stone onto the deck.' Stani watched heads below bend in consultation, then Gruskin looked up.

'Come down a couple of rungs and see if you can clear the rail from there.'

Gratefully Stani complied.

'I think one more would be safer,' he called down.

'Goddammit, you're not going off the Golden Gate Bridge . . . stay where you are and push out.'

While the three cameras were being positioned, Stani was rehearsed by Gruskin in his movements; he also had arguments about the best way to hold a telescope to his eye with two hands when one of them was already employed holding a whisky bottle.

'Do what comes naturally,' was the final unhelpful advice.

At last all was ready and Stani was reminded of his feelings long ago in mid-Atlantic, waiting to be rocket propelled off a cargo ship. He didn't remember having been so frightened since. Two cameras were at deck level, one in a boat alongside.

'Camera One ready?' called the Assistant.

'Camera Two ready?'

'Camera Three ready?'

'Sound ready?'

The affirmatives floated up from below.

'Stani – you ready?'

Stani's legs felt like overcooked asparagus.

'Ready,' he croaked.

'Quiet! TURN 'EM OVER!'

Stani braced himself. There was an endless wait.

'HOLD IT! HOLD EVERYTHING!' Gruskin was shouting.

'Stani, how big is that cap you have on?'

Stani sagged back against the rigging.

'Fairly large.'

'Great! Heidi here has an idea. We want that cap to bob up to the surface after you disappear so when you go under, make sure it comes off, then swim down and away from the ship as far as you can. Okay?'

'Caps don't bob up,' said Stani, hoping to prolong his reprieve.

'Yours will,' said Gruskin. 'We're putting cork in it . . . throw it down here.'

Stani dropped his white-topped captain's headgear to the deck. Ten minutes later a wardrobe man clambered slowly aloft. A slab of cork had been fitted inside the crown.

'I sure don't envy you this drop! A stunt guy on my last picture went half this distance into water and ruptured his spleen . . . try to go in headfirst . . . Lots o' luck, kid.' The man slowly, with white knuckles and eyes staring straight ahead, inched his way whence he had come.

'Okay!' yelled Gruskin. 'Here we go! And make it good because Stern only paid for one uniform for the double.'

'Camera One? – Two? – Three? – Sound?' Again the voices floated up and once more Stani braced himself . . .

'TURN 'EM OVER!'

. . . another endless pause followed during which Stani realized that his mind had become blank and he no longer had any idea of what he was supposed to do with his cap, the bottle, the horizon or the telescope. He stared down miserably at the brown, jungle-stained sea. 'Heidi has another idea,' yelled Gruskin. 'The crew of this ship must think their captain has drowned when he falls overboard, so we're gonna rig a tube to pass compressed air so bubbles will come up near the cap.'

Half an hour dragged by while the bubbles tube, attached by wires between the ship and an anchored dinghy was positioned and tested. By the time everyone was satisfied Stani doubted if his leg muscles, now cramped by fear, would respond to any commands passed down by his brain. On the fourth lift-off attempt he himself halted the proceedings at the extreme end of the countdown.

'WAIT A MINUTE!' he yelled. 'WHAT ABOUT THE SHARKS?'

Gruskin flung his script to the deck.

'For Christ's sake!' he bellowed. 'THERE AREN'T ANY SHARKS *HERE*.'

'Yes there bloody well *ARE*,' Stani shouted back. 'It was in yesterday's Santa Cruz paper . . . they ate three priests.'

Gruskin's voice was icy and very loud:

'You're not scared of getting wet are you?'

'No,' said Stani, 'but I'm only doing this once – the next time . . . *you* do it.'

Gruskin made no comment.

'Let's go!' he shouted, 'and don't forget, get that cap off underwater, then swim away as deep and as far as you can.'

The last unnerving instruction that came his way was relayed by the Assistant . . . 'Be careful not to hit those wires holding the tube, Stani . . . they could cut you in half.'

As the camera and sound crews for the fifth time announced their readiness Stani again remembered that mid-Atlantic catapult; everything then had depended on the nose of the pitching vessel pointing up not down; his present ship was rolling gently and whatever else happened he was determined to time that roll to give himself the best chance of connecting with water instead of deck.

'ACTION!!' came the cry from below. Stani remained frozen.

'ACTION!! GODDAMMIT!!!' roared Gruskin.

Stani looked down, a hundred faces looked up, then his brain, long clouded by fear, suddenly purified by adrenalin and the urge for self-preservation, became as clear as crystal; he stared at the horizon, pressed himself against the rigging and made all the correct moves. He ignored a frenzied shout of

251

'FALL' from Gruskin, waiting instead for the outward extremity of the roll, then leaned away from his perch and projected himself into space. The drop seemed interminable, he knew he was cartwheeling and prudently jettisoned bottle and telescope. He forgot about the dangerous wires. By great good fortune he hit the water as recommended by the wardrobe man, head first. He had expected visibility below the surface to be poor but when he opened his eyes it was in total darkness; the captain's cap had become jammed over his ears; he struggled to release it. Free at last of all encumbrances he swam strongly in the opaque nether regions away, he hoped, from the ship, having small wish to come up beneath it. He swam as far as he could thinking at every stroke what perfect shark bait he presented in his white captain's uniform. With lungs near bursting and his mission accomplished he finally kicked upwards towards the sunlight. Silhouetted against the pale under-surface above him he saw a long dark shape; his heart rose to his throat but he had no alternative, he had to come up; as he struggled towards the fresh air, something hit him in the small of the back and held him under. Frantically he tried to push it away and futilely punched at it. His fist landed a surprisingly solid blow and with a last convulsive heave he freed himself from the underside of – a dinghy. A face peered over the side.

'Dandy fall you made there, kid,' said a man, 'there's a coupla wires down there someplace, watch out you don't get cut.'

Stani accepted a ride back to the steamer and clambered aboard. Back on the mother ship he received a hero's welcome from the entire company; even Gruskin was grudgingly complimentary.

'Couldn't have done better myself.' As the Director spoke there was a swirling commotion ten feet from the ship's side, a slimy, slate-grey back topped by a triangular dorsal fin turned lazily away at the flick of a mighty tail, there was no mistaking what it was, a dozen pointed and yelled . . .

SHARK!

Stani grabbed Gruskin by the shirt and turned him to get a good look.

'Look at *that*!' he hissed.

252

'DOLPHIN', said Gruskin firmly . . . 'and your beard's coming off.'

Judd was still operating on a different planet so when it became apparent that he would not be further extending himself that day on behalf of *The Ruby Ring* Gruskin sent him back to the hotel and called out the reserves. Pandora, who had been 'standing-by', in case she was needed, was delighted when the summons to work reached her. She arrived aboard the ship, with a smile for everyone, and Stani watched with pride. She instantly raised the tone and morale of the entire crew. He sneaked up, put an arm around her and gave a squeeze; she recoiled at first from the bearded stranger in a damp suit, but let out a yelp of pleasure when she heard his voice. In a quiet corner on the upper deck he filled her in on the developments of the day so far.

'Well,' she said, 'now at least we know what Judd's "on" . . . but mushrooms! . . . that's mescaline isn't it? Aldous Huxley came to stay at Hawksmoor once and said he'd tried them but gave it up when he discovered it was the same as strychnine!' She shook her head. 'What a group! . . . I'm even beginning to feel sorry for that awful Stern, he asked for trouble, but what Ted Gruskin's doing to him is unbelievable . . . it's so – bitchy! The poor little brute is pathetic, he wanders round the hotel trying to pick up little bits of news about what's going on out here.'

'But surely,' Stani said, 'he must be able to stop all the changes they're making to the script?'

Pandora shook her head. 'I don't begin to understand what's happening.

'Listen to what I'm supposed to say in this scene with Rita, if she ever condescends to show up that is. They gave it to me this morning . . . "Rubies can be made artificially by adding chromium sulphate to purified alum, then calcinating the result at one thousand degrees centigrade in a fused quartz dish yielding an intimate mixture of aluminium and chromium oxide!!" Phew! And *that's* supposed to make the original line more *playable*!!'

'What was the original?'

'. . . "Fake rubies are easy to make – if you know how." Now *that's* short, easy to say and understandable – this,' she slapped the pages . . . 'Oh darling, I really am getting desperate!'

Stani didn't know how to comfort her and Rita's appearance towards mid-afternoon in an advanced state of intoxication did little to help.

18

A movie company, far from home, working under difficult and
uncomfortable conditions, poorly lodged, badly fed and plagued
by illness, can still rise magnificently to the occasion provided it
is well led. But if it decides that it is ill-served by its leaders, it
will slowly disintegrate and the chances of it turning out a good
film will be minimal. After five weeks shooting in and around
Triunfo the crew of *The Ruby Ring* had reached a very low
point; they knew that the picture was way over schedule and
gloom enveloped them all.

One especially annoying cause of delay during shooting on
the inland waterways had been a fisherman who, day after day,
seated in a canoe, shielded beneath a mammoth sombrero, and
apparently stone deaf, had either anchored fifty yards from the
ship and directly in the line of the camera, or trolled slowly past
it with penetrating noise from his outboard engine. The crew
named him 'Andy the Aztec' and at least extracted some enjoyment from the tantrums his appearances engendered in Ted
Gruskin.

One evening, tired of the high risk meals provided by the
Hotel Real, Pandora organized some sandwiches and a bottle
of California wine; her canoe driver gladly accepted a little
'overtime' and when the rest of the company had headed back
for Triunfo, she and Stani settled down to a quiet picnic on the
bridge of the battered old river steamer. The sunset and afterglow coloured the sky, they filled their paper cups and were
content. When the light had all but faded, the jungle became an
eerie, rather sinister place, a full wild life orchestra tuned up
and a moon as yellow as a melon rose above the trees; feeding
fish and alligators splashed and swirled about the ship. Complete with each other, they sat in silence, loving the strangeness

255

of it all, and the chance to be alone.

Their boatman had promised to return at nine o'clock so they were a little surprised when, only half way through their picnic, they saw the black outline of a canoe approaching down the middle of the golden carpet of the moon's reflection.

'How pretty!' Pandora murmured dreamily.

The engine coughed into silence and the canoe glided silently alongside. Stani glanced down, then turned to Pandora, putting a finger to his lips.

'It's Andy the Aztec!' he whispered. 'What's he up to, I wonder!'

Pandora stood and watched the Mexican tie up and climb to the main deck. After a while she came to Stani's side.

'I can't see too well down there,' she reported, 'but he seems to be doing sinister things. Come and look.' Together they made out the shape of the man. No longer wearing his sombrero, he was busy as a bird dog, moving purposefully about the cluttered deck. Pandora grabbed Stani's arm and pointed below: their visitor had produced a flash light and wedged it into a pile of sacks; in its beam he bent to some task with great concentration. They could see only the top of his head but when he shifted his position to examine something, the light fell upon his profile and they both gasped. A drooping moustache did little to disguise the fact that 'Andy the Aztec' in his baggy white suit was, in fact – Maxwell Stern!

They backed away from their vantage point and held a council of war.

'Let's keep an eye on him,' Stani whispered, 'but he mustn't see us. When he's gone we'll find out what's been going on down there.' They did not have long to wait; whatever Stern's mission on the main deck had been, he concluded it quickly and they scuttled away when it became evident that he was heading in their direction.

'He's coming up here!' Stani hissed. 'Quick!' As noiselessly as possible they snatched up their picnic and scooted down the narrow deck, past the wheelhouse and the doors of three or four cabins. Over the after-deck they stopped and positioned themselves so they could look back and monitor the Producer's moves.

Stern never hesitated, he popped into the wheelhouse like a

homing pigeon returning to its loft. Less than five minutes later, flashlight pointing the way, he emerged and descended whence he had come. The sounds of a few abortive tugs on the outboard's starter cord were followed by the first burst of its power. They watched the boat swing away from the ship's side and head noisily downstream, raising screeches and hoots of disapproval from the birds and beasts of the jungle night.

They behaved like two schoolchildren hardly able to contain themselves at the good fortune that had befallen them. Anticipating a lengthy investigation they decided to husband the fuel of their one cigarette lighter, and to fashion small torches from odds and ends about the deck; then they went to work.

The wheelhouse was filthy, littered with rolled-up charts, signal flags, dirty tin mugs, rusty spanners, oily rags and other junk.

'Let's be methodical,' said Stani. 'Go very slowly, starting behind the door a yard at a time from top to bottom.'

'What are we looking for?' asked Pandora.

'God knows,' Stani laughed. 'He may have decided to collect insurance by blowing up the ship, so keep an eye open for gunpowder trails as we go along!'

'It can't be hard to find, whatever it is,' said Pandora, 'because he was so quick.' They worked their way round to the big wooden shelf in front of the steering wheel and Stani made urgent signs for silence. Pandora held the flickering torch while he indicated two shiny wires protruding from beneath a pile of rags and tattered 'girlie' magazines. He carefully shifted the pile and revealed a small flat rectangular box about five inches long. Without touching it he examined it carefully, then led Pandora out onto the deck, shutting the wheelhouse door behind him.

'That,' he said, 'is a directional dipole aerial, attached to an F.M. receiver!'

'What the hell is that?'

'Stern has got hold of a Seefeld recorder made by the Swiss.'

'How do you know all this?'

'Once I had a hospital bed next to a guy who lost half his face when he moved one that was booby-trapped.'

'What's Stern doing with it, do you suppose?'

257

'He's taking a record of something that's going on here. That little box contains a tape which can handle a long recording, triggered by a V.O.R.'

'Darling,' said Pandora, 'please give this to me in simple four letter words!'

'Voice Operated Relay means that the little recorder in the wheelhouse only records when a voice very close to its microphone triggers it off. The tape has to be changed every couple of days or so. I guess that's what Stern was doing, like a fisherman pulling up his net, or a farmer collecting eggs.'

'But where would the microphone be? And what would Stern want to listen to for days on end?'

'The aerials of that recorder are positioned to pick up the signals of the mike so we should be able to tell where it is . . . somewhere down there where we saw him fiddling about. But don't forget, whatever happens, we mustn't *talk* down there or he'll be recording *us!*'

Down on the main deck they lit torches and spent a fruitless half hour searching the pile of sacks in total silence.

'What does the thing look like?' Pandora asked when they had returned to the upper deck for consultation.

'The "mike" itself is tiny, half the size of your little finger nail. But its transmitter and aerial together would be about the size and shape of a small cigar.'

'If we could only guess what Stern would want to record,' said Pandora, 'that might help. . . .'

They looked at each other.

'GRUSKIN!' they chorused.

'And what does Gruskin have near him all the time, in which someone could hide a cigar?' asked Stani.

'His director's chair?' Pandora ventured. Again it came to them simultaneously . . .

'THE GOOSING STICK!'

They found the little device inside the bamboo pole just above the clenched plaster fist. Stani replaced Gruskin's instrument of torture where he had found it, and they moved to the rail.

'What a little rat!'

'It's really pathetic,' said Pandora. 'Can you imagine being

258

so insecure that you have to find out what everyone's saying about you?'

'No, it's more than that,' said Stani. 'It's definitely Gruskin he's after – what did he say to you? . . . "I'll sue him for every penny he's got" . . . remember?'

'I see what you mean. He's collecting evidence. Do you think I ought to warn Ted?'

'Hell no, they're both creeps. Don't get mixed up in it, don't say a word to anyone.' He put an arm round her. 'Let's finish the picnic.' They climbed to the upper deck, refilled the paper cups and sat silent for a while. Pandora sighed.

'I'm not going to let those two upset me and put me off Hollywood,' she said. 'Most people have been wonderful to us, haven't they, ever since we first arrived?' She sounded a little wistful. 'I mean, could we ever meet nicer people anywhere? So kind and helpful and everything; Stern and Gruskin would be dreadful wherever they were or whatever they did, if they were taxi drivers or plumbers or stockbrokers – they'd still be dreadful. Wouldn't they?'

'They're a part of Hollywood,' said Stani. 'Hollywood is a suburb of a huge city but somehow it doesn't seem to bear much relationship to the rest of the world. Also I think it should be more *fun*. After all, it's a fun factory – but the place reeks of fear. The people at the bottom are frightened they'll never get to the top and the ones at the top are frightened they won't be able to stay there.'

'It sounds to me as though you don't like it.'

'I just think it should be more *fun*, that's all.' Then he bent and kissed her. 'Anyway, you're off to a great start.'

Pandora studied Stani over the edge of a sandwich before she spoke.

'And what about *you*?'

If Stani's instinct was to push things under rugs, Pandora's was for well swept floors, so he thought carefully before he replied.

'For me it is going to be much more difficult,' he said. 'I love you. I love being with you. I love everything about you. I also respect you and most important of all I *like* you. With all my heart I want you to knock Hollywood over and have a huge success because that's what you've always told me you wanted.

259

But I also know that you could never *really* love anyone you didn't respect. Isn't that right?'

Pandora put her arms around him, but did not answer.

'So . . . once this picture's finished, my holiday is over. I'm not sure what the hell I can do, but my self respect's wearing thin. I'm beginning to feel like a pimp.' He smiled and kissed her hair. 'I'm almost a kept man, angel . . . I love every minute of it! But as you go up, which you will, it's going to be more and more complicated for us.'

'I'm not losing you, am I? I couldn't bear that.'

'You could always marry me,' said Stani, nuzzling her cheek. 'I've only asked you five thousand times.'

'I don't see what difference a marriage certificate would make,' Pandora murmured. 'We've been living together for ages.'

Stani held her at arm's length, her hair was back-lit by moonlight.

'I love you so much,' he said. 'But for an intelligent lady that is one of the dumbest statements I've ever heard!'

Stern had positioned his microphone most adroitly and during the following day's shooting Stani and Pandora heard the grunts and squeaks of the assaulted flow in a steady stream onto the Producer's tapes – augmented by Gruskin's self-incriminating remarks.

'What's the rush? . . . time is money and we're on Stern time now, Boys!'

Or: 'We'll shoot the scene Stern's way first to keep the sonofabitch happy, then we'll do it the way it'll be in the picture – *my* way.'

The spectacle of Gruskin hanging himself was not altogether unattractive but Stani and Pandora deplored the setting of the trap; during the lunch break they searched anew their consciences.

'We don't have to warn Ted *ourselves*,' Pandora said. 'We could "discover" the mike, or tell the sound people there's a buzzing noise near Ted's chair and let them track it down, something like that.'

'Do nothing,' Stani counselled. 'Just soldier on – it'll all be over soon.'

260

Back at the Hotel Real a note from Otis Champion awaited Stani.

'Mr. Stern would like a word with you as soon as you come in – Room 32.'

Otis Champion.

Maxwell Stern, nattily turned out in a beige linen suit, received Stani with a handshake and a harpsichord smile.

'Sit down,' he said, pointing to a threadbare settee. 'Tell me how you have liked being apprenticed to our *still* photographer?'

'Very much indeed, Al's been most helpful. He takes wonderful pictures, he's taught me a great deal.'

Stern pointed to a dozen colour enlargements of life in a nearby village lying scattered on a table. 'This is your work, he tells me?'

'Yes,' said Stani. 'He let me try out a new Swedish camera for him.'

Stern stirred the prints.

'They're very good. Now Al is real sick, he's got jaundice. I'm sending him back home before he gets worse, he leaves tonight.' Stern paused and stared at Stani. 'He has enough portraits of the Principals and we're getting near the end out here, so I want you to do the job till we finish. Just do action stuff around the set and shots with good production value. Think you can handle it?'

'I don't have any equipment.'

'I've fixed that with Al, he'll leave behind everything you'll need; go and see him now, he'll show you what he's got for you.' Stern paused. 'It's Al's idea – he suggested you.'

Stani was elated.

The Producer bared his keyboard once more.

'Keep your eyes open and your finger on the shutter, who knows, you might wind up with something on the cover of *Life* magazine.'

'That would be nice!'

'Nice for *me*,' said Stern. 'The negatives are mine.'

Al was packing; his skin was vintage Fu Manchu and his eyeballs were like tangerines. He gave Stani his Swedish camera, a Leica, lenses, meters and dozens of rolls of film.

'Use it all up, don't try to be artistic. Just check your meter

261

and shoot at high speed. We'll sort 'em out when you come back. Try to get a shot of Stern and Gruskin together. . . . I haven't been able to get one yet. Do some soft-light shots of your girl friend – she's so beautiful you can shoot her from any angle. Rub your finger against the side of your nostrils, there's always a little oil there, then spread it on the lens, it'll give beautiful diffusion.'

Just before the scheduled end of the shooting in Triunfo, Heidi and Rita Haas had a brainstorm. They persuaded a malleable director that a peacock would provide a stunning background for a close-up of Rita – provided its tail was fanned out in all its glory.

'Ted, honey, we've been to see that garden belonging to the mistress of the Governor of Topolobampo,' Heidi said. 'It's pretty shabby, hardly any flowers, God knows why Stern chose it. And that's an important scene with Judd that Rita has there, she's got to look her best.'

'Okay sweetheart,' Gruskin sighed. 'Get ahold of Champion and tell him to have a peacock on location tomorrow.'

Otis Champion was under no illusions about the picture finishing on schedule. 'To get everything done we need an extra ten days,' he told Stern, but the producer merely shrugged.

'That's Gruskin's problem,' he said.

'He needs a peacock. Do I let him have one?'

'Can I amortize a peacock?'

'Personally I like them barbecued.'

Stern was not amused. 'What's their daily rate down here?'

'First I have to *find* one. You'll probably have to buy it.'

'Can you eat peacock?'

'You mean put it in the lunch boxes? Nobody would notice the difference alongside the chicken they give us. Yes, I guess you could eat it.'

'Okay,' said Stern. 'Buy one peacock.'

In Coatzacoalos, a few miles away, Otis Champion bought a peacock and on the day of Rita Haas' love scene a large dusty grey bird stalked nervously about, emitting ear splitting squawks every time anyone called for 'Quiet'.

'I can't play the scene with that fucking bird screaming at me,' Judd complained.

262

'You can't play it anyway,' said Gruskin. 'But we'll just leave the peacock in the background. We need its tail sticking up, though.'

During the day, as the love scene progressed, Stani was able to get some interesting shots, in different surroundings, away, for once, from water and jungle.

Towards evening the peacock's big moment came. Stani readied his cameras. The Property Man was intructed to position the bird behind a fallen log upon which the stars were seated. With the ingenuity of his ilk he sprinkled maize on the grass, and the peacock circled about within a restricted area, pecking away with great concentration.

'Put the feed down so the peacock's facing camera, just behind Miss Haas,' Gruskin said.

The Prop Man repositioned the grain in one small pile nearer the log.

'Get ready to hold its feet,' Gruskin ordered. The Prop Man lay full length on the grass out of sight behind the log, ready to grab one peacock foot in each hand.

'Turn the camera,' said Gruskin quietly. 'Start speaking on my hand signal, Rita – just the last long speech. Now – get a hold of those feet, Props.'

'Quiet!' yelled the Sound Man.

This occasioned an answering shriek from the peacock, a great flapping of wings, followed by a volley of oaths from the Property Man who shot to his feet with blood streaming from the back of his hand.

'The sonofabitch has a beak like a buzz saw!'

'CUT!' shouted Gruskin. 'Wardrobe . . . leather gloves for the Prop Man.'

'Better put leather eye glasses on me too, while you're at it.'

'Okay,' said Gruskin. 'Let's try it again.'

Judd then spoke up.

'It's none of my business,' he said. 'I'm just sitting here for Rita to look at. But isn't the whole idea to get the peacock's tail to come up behind her head?'

'Correct,' said Gruskin.

'Well,' said Judd, 'a peacock's tail only comes up when it's horny; would *you* get a hard on just because some guy grabbed your feet?'

'Hold everything!' Gruskin ordered. 'What we need is a peahen, is that it?'

'Right,' Judd replied. 'Unless it's Queer, of course.'

The cameraman squinted at the sinking sun and checked a meter.

'Light's going!' he announced, '. . . only about five minutes left.'

'How come you know so much about peacocks, Judd?' Gruskin enquired.

'A friend of mine in Montecito has them in his garden.'

'Is there any way to get that tail up without the help of a peahen?'

Judd Dugdale's expression was choirboy beatific.

'You could stick your finger up its ass,' he suggested.

'Okay, Props, you heard him. Stand by to stick your finger up the peacock's ass.'

The Property Man rose, flushed of face.

'No,' he said.

Gruskin addressed the crew.

'Does anybody volunteer to stick a finger up the peacock's ass?'

Silence reigned.

'Light's going fast!' the cameraman said.

Judd smiled at Gruskin.

'Looks like it's you, baby.'

Gruskin studied the averted faces of his crew and frowned.

'What about the Goosing Stick?' suggested the Assistant Director.

Gruskin's grip tightened protectively on his prized possession.

'This,' he said, 'has been in contact with some of the most famous butts in show business. But up a peacock – NEVER.'

The cameraman was checking his meter again.

'Mr. Gruskin, I have a surgical glove in my Box,' said the Prop Man. 'And some petroleum jelly.'

Rita Haas sat silent on the log, biting her lip. Judd Dugdale smirked. And the peacock replenished its grain stocks. Heidi finally broke the silence.

'Ted honey, it'll only be for a second, and this is *such* an important shot . . . *please* . . . do it . . . for me.'

'O.K.' said Gruskin, 'give me that surgical glove.'

The glove went on. Like two book-ends with the peacock in the middle Gruskin and the Prop Man prostrated themselves behind the log. The camera turned.

'Quiet!' yelled the sound man. 'Squawk!' went the peacock.

'Jesus!' shouted the Prop Man. 'The bastard's got me by the ear.'

The peacock's tail never went up, nor did Gruskin's finger, as he jabbed vainly at a wildly fluctuating target. Stani shot off a flash bulb which panicked the peacock into a last flapping, honking convulsion, leaving Gruskin lying on his back with outstretched arm and surgical-gloved finger pointing skyward. The peacock took off for the trees.

'CUT!' said a loud voice.

All heads turned to see Maxwell Stern emerging from a thicket of oleanders.

'I enjoyed that very much,' he said.

'What the hell are you doing on my set?' Gruskin asked, rising to his knees.

'I came to inform you officially,' said Stern, 'that I expect you to finish shooting on schedule, four days from now.'

Gruskin stood and there was total silence as the two men faced each other in the gathering dusk.

'If you order me to, Mr. Stern, I shall finish on time,' said Gruskin with an icy smile. 'And I'll show you just how I'll do it.'

'Please do.'

Gruskin picked up his script, tore twenty pages out of it and handed them to the Producer.

'I still have enough work for four days. Those pages I have not yet shot, they are yours and here's what you can do with them. Go to the nearest village and buy a pineapple. Cut the top off it, scrape out the inside, roll those pages into a tight ball and place them inside the pineapple; then put the top back on again and . . . stuff it up your ass.'

Stern stood very still. Then he inclined his head.

'Thank you,' he said. 'You have made things very easy for

265

me!'

He turned and with bantam cock dignity retraced his steps. Only Stani guessed what Stern would retrieve from the oleander thicket.

19

Work on *The Ruby Ring* in Triunfo ground to a halt. Stern flew North, made his report, and early the next morning was in Russell Bancroft's office, laying the blame for the debacle on Ted Gruskin, who arrived back in Hollywood three days later, leading his dejected army through the gates of Fort Metropolis.

Russell Bancroft reacted swiftly. He closed down the picture, relieved both Stern and Gruskin of their commands, laid off all contract employees and fired everyone else.

'Now,' he said happily to Otis Champion, 'we have three weeks' shooting left to complete the picture. You leave for Florida tomorrow, pick locations in the Everglades that'll match up with what we've shot so far, and we'll start up again down there in two weeks. I'm signing a top Director today, he'll come with you. I was never happy with the scenes we still have to shoot, now I can have them re-written the way I want them.'

'What's all this going to do to our Budget, Mr. Bancroft?'

'Nothing,' Bancroft replied smoothly. 'Stern has already filed suit against Gruskin, Gruskin will be suing Stern and Metropolis is suing them both. The damages we're asking will more than cover additional costs of production; they both took big percentage deals and very little up front, so we indulge in a little sophisticated book-keeping. In short, no problem.'

Pandora, once she had met the replacement director – an old pro with a great reputation – welcomed the two week respite and utilized the enforced holiday to move into their new home in Brentwood. Stani hovered about getting in the way till she suggested he might be happier surfing, or making himself useful to Al. These turned out to be opportune suggestions because armed with a borrowed speed graphic camera, some underwater apparatus and a telephoto lens he spent ten days on the beaches of Malibu and Point Dume. He shot over four hundred pictures. On days of disappointing surf he made studies of surfers waiting expectantly like seagulls at the water's edge, roasting 'winies' round driftwood fires, or necking with their girls among the rocks.

When the surf was up (and he was lucky because for six days there were monster waves of ten, fifteen and occasionally twenty feet) he caught a girl with gleaming ash blonde hair going 'over the falls' – straight down the face of a big one. He shot boys doing angled take-offs just ahead of the curling lips of others; and blasé young experts distributing their weight by scampering back and forth along their boards, showing off outrageously, 'nose riding' with their toes gripping the front edges, 'hanging five' or 'hanging ten' as they called it. Against the orange backdrop of a Pacific sunset he photographed the most magical moment in surfing – the 'cut back', an angled take-off at the very top of a wave followed by a long flowing movement, so fast that a rooster's tail of spray is thrown up by the board as the surfer executes a full 180 degree turn down the precipitous face of the wave.

From his own board with his waterproof camera strapped to his wrist, he got a rare gem – a boy 'riding the tube' – emerging from the tunnel formed behind the curling lip of a big breaker. The boy was yelling with satisfaction at his achievement, the shining wall of water behind his golden body was a deep emerald green. Stani also focused his high speed camera on spectacular 'wipe-outs' – surfers parting company with their boards, plummetting head first down the cliff-like drop faced with tons of water crashing down on top of them, and whirling boards trying to decapitate them when they surfaced.

When Al developed the pictures he was ecstatic.

'You have a bonanza here, kid!' he cried. 'You're really good! Some of this is *great stuff*! You *really* have an eye! I'll bet you can sell them to an agency, one of those big outfits in New York that service *Life*, *Look*, *Post* and *Paris Match*. They'll go crazy over these, there's never been a lay-out on surfing, you'll make hundreds, maybe thousands of dollars.'

Pandora was equally enthusiastic. 'They're sensational! Wonderful!' she cried. 'I always knew I was living with a genius! Now come and see what Vergis and Lillie-May have done upstairs!' Two beaming black ladies, round and giggly, led the way, and proudly displayed a major redistribution of furniture in the master bedroom and the sparkling results of an overall spring cleaning.

'Ain't no good 'specting us to call you Mis Jan or Mis Ricardo,' Vergis announced. 'Your own name is real pretty, so we'll be calling you what Mr. Stani calls you – Mis Pandora.'

Chuck Pesnick dropped by to be given the two-dollar tour of the new establishment and approved mightily. The house, of white wooden shingles, was built on an incline with the front door on the same level as the bedrooms; crescent-shaped stairs descended to a large living room with dining alcove, French windows opened onto a shady patio, a lawn and flowerbeds sloped down to an elegant pool. Beside the pool was the annexe consisting of two dressing rooms and a comfortable 'movie-room' with a fire-proof compartment housing two projectors. It was the perfect setting, if not for a full scale movie queen, at least for a possible princess. Pandora blessed Russell Bancroft for finding it and purged from her memory the Moorish Prison and the Orbistons.

Chuck made himself an Old Fashioned and sat down to talk.

'I hope Hollywood won't mess you up,' he said. 'It's changed a lot while I've been away. Before the war the place was controlled by the six major studios and each of those was controlled by one boss – the guys who invented the business. Mayer at M.G.M., Cohn at Columbia, Jack Warner at Warner Brothers, Laemmle at Universal, Zukor at Paramount and Schenck and Zanuck at Twentieth Century Fox. Sam Goldwyn and David Selznick were the biggest Independents and nobody called the shots on any of those guys, that's for sure! Tough as they come, but great showmen, all of them.'

'Aren't most of them still around?'

'Yes, but they're getting older and richer and pictures are costing more and more to make. Why, Sam Goldwyn's great publicity pitch used to be "I only make million dollar pictures". Now, he can hardly get a "trailer" of one of his pictures made for a million bucks! The banks have gotten into the act in a big way.' He shook his head. 'When the old men go, the studios will be run by those banks, by attorneys and by computers; and finally by Television. Most of the old timers stuff their heads in the sand and hope Television will go away, but it won't and they will just make it stronger by selling off their old movies to it.'

'What about Metropolis?' Pandora asked.

'Russ Bancroft's not running away from it, he's already working on getting a slice of the Television action. He's the new kind of young and aggressive executive, Lew Wasserman's another and Buddy Adler, those guys'll be taking over studios one day soon. Maybe they'll stir things up, I sure hope so . . . there's too much uncertainty, too much fear around now. Hollywood used to be one big family, it was exciting then. And, it was fun!'

'How about our great big movie star here?' Stani asked. 'Is she going to make it?'

Chuck smiled, then he rapped a finger on his forehead. 'Pandora's got lots of stuff up here, but it's still not easy. And I'm one of the guys who make it difficult.'

'How?'

'I'm paid to get people's names in print. I spend my day kissing asses – Hedda, Louella, Sheilah Graham, Winchell. *Reporter*, *Variety*, the syndicated guys. They know what I'm doing and I know they know, it's a game. We all play it, they have their problems too – they have to fill columns so they're happy to print a lot of the stuff I pass on to them.' He laughed. 'Then the people who paid me to dream up that stuff – even Studio Heads – read it – and BELIEVE it!! But it's tough for actors and actresses to keep a perspective when they get thousands of letters a week telling them how wonderful they are. I'll bet you, Stani, that if you read a hundred times a week what an attractive twitch you have your right eye – in a coupla months you'd be twitching like a sonofabitch!'

'Do you hate your job, Chuck?' Pandora asked.

'No, I like it okay. Sometimes I hate myself, though. Anyway it's all I know and . . .' he shrugged, 'like all good Jewish boys, I have people to take care of.'

The final three weeks of shooting on *The Ruby Ring* provided Pandora and Stani with the perfect antidote to the misery and frustration of the weeks spent at Triunfo: this was Hollywood film-making at its best. Most of the original company were re-employed, the re-written scenes were well constructed and

270

fun to play. Rita Haas' role had shrunk like a Cashmere sweater in a washing machine, the new Director knew exactly what he wanted, could explain it clearly and concisely, was extremely efficient and at the same time kind and thoughtful. The crew flourished under his benevolent leadership, willingly scurrying about ministering to his slightest needs: relieved of the lurking presence of Stern and the menace of Gruskin's goosing stick, they bent to their tasks with a will. Otis Champion achieved wonders of re-deployment, a charter flight from Los Angeles delivered the company to Miami, comfortable transport whisked them through stands of pine, cypress and mangrove, across plains of sawgrass and along the banks of a network of canals, finally disgorging them before attractive motels in Belle Glade, Bean City and Pahokee, small townships upon the shores of Lake Okeechobee.

Pandora and Judd Dugdale were provided with luxurious trailers parked wherever the shooting took place. Judd failed in an early search for mushrooms among the nearby Seminole Indians, but eventually came back with some 'grass'.

One evening he and Justin invited Pandora and Stani to sample a few 'joints' at sunset. They watched herons fishing in the marsh ponds round their caravans, teal and widgeon were flighting in from the grasslands; they dragged the weed deep into their lungs, a strange peace came over them and it became difficult to remember that at any minute they could be marched off to prison.

Pandora, toiling long but happy hours, blossomed beneath the guiding hand of the new director, and Stani, now working daily with Al, profited immensely from his exposure to the craft of an expert. Al on occasion sent him far into the Everglades and was always constructive in his criticism or praise of his perceptive studies of the isolated inhabitants, the wildlife and the eerie beauty of that remarkable part of Florida.

'You've really got it, kid! We'll sneak a few of these in with those surfing pictures when your contract's up, then you'll really have something to show.'

Chuck Pesnick arrived for a few days to gather background material for further publicity. He brought a sheaf of clippings to show Pandora; there was no question she was generating a great deal of interest all over the country.

'There seems to be quite a change of policy,' she remarked

half jokingly. 'When we first arrived the studio always had me happily paired off with Stani, which I *am*, thank God! But now my "Polish-War-Hero-boyfriend" seems to have been replaced by my "steady-as-they-go-handsome-Producer-admirer". It all seems infinitely childish to me! *Is* that the way I am now to be presented . . . as the back door bit of crumpet of Mr. Bancroft? How does his wife sitting in Bel Air feel about all this?'

Chuck looked embarrassed.

'Bancroft wants it this way, Honey, it satisfies his ego I guess. I have to go along with it. But every now and then I try to slip in someone else who's crazy about you too . . . it kind of spreads the general admiration. But definitely Bancroft's decided that a permanent boyfriend like Stani is bad for your image. If Stani was a big name in the business, perhaps it would be O.K. Hollywood's very class conscious, you know! By the way, Parsons wants to do a big Sunday piece on you when you come back – with Stani. *She's* a romantic.'

'I'll try and talk Stani into it.'

'Hopper's given us a lot of breaks on you too . . . and she'd like to have you over to her place one day soon. Trouble is, when one of them does a piece the other one doesn't want to come second. It's like juggling a coupla goddam coconuts.'

'I rather liked both of them when I met them,' said Pandora. 'Which is the most difficult to be interviewed by?'

'Hard to know. Hedda pours double gins and tonics to get your tongue wagging but only puts tonic in *her* glass; and next day you read all sorts of things you probably never said. Louella pours singles for you, drinks triples herself and next day *she* prints quotes you probably never made. It's about fifty-fifty I guess!'

The happy 'Ruby Ring' Company returned to Metropolis Studios two days under schedule to find that the columnists had been enjoying a field day with stories of the war between Stern and Gruskin.

'GRUSKIN'S FINGER GOES TOO FAR!'
                                                    STERN CLAIMS.
. . . PEACOCK PROSTRATE.
'GRUSKIN NOMINATES STERN FOR RAT OF YEAR AWARD!
. . . MORE LAWSUITS PENDING'.
'STERN NOT FAR ENOUGH OUT OF GROUND

272

TO BE SANITARY' QUIPS GRUSKIN.
'HOLLYWOOD DESCRIBES FEUD AS "TASTELESS
TIFF OF TWO TADPOLES".'

All in all, *The Ruby Ring* was seldom out of the papers. To profit from this bonanza, Russell Bancroft ordered an immediate assembly of the footage shot, arranged for 'sneak previews' in San Francisco and San Diego, and brought forward the date for a Black Tie Première in Hollywood. Chuck kept Pandora on a treadmill of interviews, radio and television appearances, home layouts, cheesecake art sessions by her pool, fashion layouts at I. Magnin and girl-next-door poses in an A.&P. She spent days cooking, playing tennis, running on the beach, riding an old hired 'plug' in the hills, sailing somebody else's ketch off Balboa and playing with a borrowed Boxer which dribbled all over her. Other than the one interview at the home of Louella Parsons, Stani was happy to be excluded from all this activity and, when not with Al, he tied his surfboard to the roof of his car and answered the call of the 'Beach Bums' – SURF'S UP!

Russell Bancroft, running a big studio with a multitude of problems, still found time to drop in on many of Pandora's photo sessions.

A week before the Première of *The Ruby Ring* he asked Stani to come to his office. He met him smiling broadly, both arms outstretched.

'Good news and bad news!' he announced. 'Which shall I give you first?'

'Let's have the good news.'

Bancroft motioned him to a chair.

'Otis Champion says the reports on your photographs are just great, so I've been talking to New York. They've come up with something I think will interest you. Ever heard of Richard Avedon?'

'*Avedon?* Of course. I've seen lots of his stuff. I think it's wonderful.'

'So do I. The people who know say the only way to learn photography is by watching an expert at work. You've learnt a lot from Al, and now we want you to go a step further. The guys back East have arranged for you to work with Avedon for a month, as a kind of apprentice. How does *that* grab you?'

'I'd love it, of course. When do I start?'

'Well, that's the bad news. Avedon wants you to start one week from today. I'm afraid that means you'll have to miss Pandora's opening.'

Stani looked stricken.

'I know,' said Bancroft. 'You're thinking about how much help you could be to Pandora on her big night? Well, let me tell you something . . . I know Hollywood. I've been to a hundred of these things. Publicitywise and in every other way *she* must be the star of the evening, the jewel in the crown, it's *her* night . . . she *must* show up *alone*. Of course Chuck will be on hand to stage-manage everything, to steer her through the interviews and look after her. But she must be the focal point and the best you can do for her is to make sure she comes by herself.'

Stani nodded. All he wanted in the world was for Pandora to have a dazzling success. He was grateful to Bancroft for the advice.

'I'd probably be in the way,' he said, 'and make her even more nervous. It must be like having a baby, she'll be much better off with the experts'

'I reckoned you'd see it that way,' said Bancroft. 'After it's all over I'll try to fix it so she can join you in New York.'

He steered Stani towards the door. 'Take my tip though, don't let on I put you wise to all this, she's a very persuasive girl and she'll talk you into staying!'

As Stani was leaving, Bancroft, in high good humour, threw in a fifty dollar a week raise and told him that Otis Champion would arrange his travel, hotel and expenses.

Al was delighted when he heard of Stani's progress and told him to be sure to take his photographic samples with him.

But Pandora was shattered and had the greatest difficulty keeping the disappointment from her face, the terror of her first exposure to the eagle eyes of Hollywood had been increasing with every passing day, and she had been counting totally on Stani's love and understanding to get her through the ordeal. However, she addressed herself sternly. 'You're a big girl now, you've been through worse than this and things have not been all that easy for Stani. *His* ego needs a polish too. So remember what Daddy used to say. "A good man is like a good horse, should be ridden on a loose rein, or he'll bolt." '

. . . Brave directives these, but deep inside her she felt let down, defenceless, deserted and very much alone.

274

20

Plans for the première of *The Ruby Ring* were personally directed by Russell Bancroft.

'We'll use the Cathay Circle, and I want no slip-ups on this one,' he told Chuck. 'It's black-tie all the way and tell the Police Department there'll be bleachers for a couple of thousand across the street. We'll want permission for searchlights for sky illumination. And of course valet parking. Can you get Army Archerd to do the interviews of the celebrities as they leave their automobiles?'

'I'll talk to him, Mr. Bancroft,' said Chuck. 'He's certainly the best. What have you arranged with the networks?'

'NBC or CBS,' said Bancroft. 'Full coverage.'

'It's a long walk between where Archerd will be and the foyer where you'll be greeting the guests,' said Chuck. 'Twenty-five yards or more, covered over of course. In the foyer I'll have the photographers, almost a hundred I guess, but I'd sure as hell like to milk that long walk – everyone in Hollywood will be making it.'

'I'll tell you what you do,' said Bancroft. 'Have a red carpet put down and ropes on either side of it. Then, when, say Gable or Garland or Flynn get out of their limousines, the bleachers will spot them and raise hell, then Archerd grabs them on the sidewalk – and remember to have his podium pre-lit. Then, on that long walk, up that red carpet, on either side of those ropes you have reporters from big city dailies across the country, the women's magazines with their photographers, and local T.V. and radio guys getting interviews: lots of people will get trapped because the crowd will be moving up that carpet real slow – get it? You'll get saturation coverage. I'll meet Jan myself and hold back till most people are in their seats.'

'I'll get on it right away. Louella and Hedda'll be in your block of seats but well separated, I'll make sure they don't arrive at the same time.'

Bancroft stopped Chuck at the door. 'How do you plan to keep Gruskin and Stern out of sight? I don't want either of those bastards around.'

'Gruskin's no problem,' said Chuck. 'He's quite sick, he's in the Clinic right now, I spoke with Heidi today, it's a suspected heart condition . . . stress brought on by the way Stern's bearing down on him according to her.'

'What about Stern?'

'We sent him an invitation, and he came back with some crack about the picture being out of his hands and having no further interest in it.'

Bancroft smiled. 'Just so long as the little sonofabitch stays underground, that's all we need. You got the applause and laughter rigged okay?' Pesnick nodded. 'All set,' he said. 'I'll have a coupla hundred Studio people scattered all over, they know what to do.' He paused. 'Will Mrs. Bancroft be coming with you?'

'No, she'll be watching on Television.

It had been a simple matter for Maxwell Stern to gain the confidence of the doctor who was looking after Ted Gruskin; confidential calls expressing great concern for the director's condition had been made nightly to the physician's residence and promises extracted of instant reports of any changes in his progress, so it came as no surprise to Stern on the day of the Premiere when he received a call from the Clinic late in the afternoon.

While Stern was talking to Ted Gruskin's doctor, Pandora was receiving the attentions of an Egyptian masseur sent over by Russell Bancroft. Known by day as 'Fingertips Feisal', he had the lightest touch in the business; by night, wearing a white robe and a fez, he worked the restaurants of the Sunset Strip, conjuring baby chicks from aluminium cups.

'You are *very* tense,' Fingertips said.

'I am *very* frightened,' Pandora answered.

'Don't be, beautiful lady. It's only a movie you have made, you have not built a bridge between San Francisco and Oak-

276

land!' This well rehearsed advice, expounded while kneading a hundred nervous star-spangled bottoms, was received in silence. Pandora knew that in two hours' time, like an aristocrat in the French Revolution, she would be bundled into a tumbril *en route* to a possible guillotine. Chuck Pesnick would be escorting her, and Stani – Stani, now on his way to the airport, would be somewhere over Arizona when she needed him most. Certainly the whole evening represented the realization of her most extravagant dreams. But Pandora knew that, despite the cosmetic surgery performed by Bancroft, there were serious flaws in *The Ruby Ring* which the experienced guests now readying themselves would be quick to detect; and in addition all Hollywood was enjoying the prospect of viewing the result of the well-publicized mayhem in Mexico. So much for the picture. For herself, Pandora felt more alone than ever before in her life. She was a wobbly blancmange of nerves.

Her hairdresser from the Studio arrived at six sharp.

'Honey,' he lisped, 'you've just *got* to calm down. I've got some little white pills you can take, they're *fantastic!* A friend of mine, solo flautist with the Philharmonic, used to get so nervous before big concerts that he had trouble puckering his lips. He takes them, and now he looks forward to those performances, no nerves at all, he plays better than ever.'

'Thanks. You're sure nothing awful will happen? I mean, I take about three Aspirins a year.'

'Promise you, honey,' he said, through a mouthful of bobby pins. 'You take one an hour before you leave for the theatre and you'll be as cool as a cucumber for the next four hours. I'll give you a spare in case you need one later.'

'Any side effects?'

'Some people claim they rev up the sexual motors but that's not a bad thing either!'

Pandora's dress was laid out on the bed, the Head of Wardrobe at Metropolis was waiting to help her into it. She ordered up a bottle of champagne for them, and exactly one hour before her scheduled arrival at the Cathay Circle Theatre she placed a greyish white pill on her tongue and flushed it down with a glass of Moet et Chandon.

The dress chosen for the great occasion was stunning – a low-cut Schiaparelli original of black chiffon with a single

277

shoulder-strap of shocking pink satin crossing diagonally like a sash between her bosoms to join a cascade of 'shocking pink' chiffon falling from the opposite hip. Pink satin shoes and handbag completed the ensemble. When she pirouetted her helpers broke into spontaneous applause – she really was a vision.

A second glass of champagne, the hairdresser promised, would help the little pill work more quickly and by the time Chuck arrived, checked his watch and said 'This is it, Darling, let's go!' the fluttering spasms were melting from Pandora's body and she walked towards the waiting limousine feeling warmly confident and a good eighteen inches above the path.

As the Cadillac swung out of the gate the night-scented jasmine of the garden perfumed the air and she saw the distant beams of the arc lights weaving back and forth in the velvet sky above Hollywood. Fifteen minutes later Army Archerd on his podium spotted her and his excited introduction, 'And now the lovely Star of tonight's picture!!' provoked screams of delight from the bleachers. Pandora stepped into the glare of the floodlights and with Chuck at her elbow, sailed regally up the red carpet, her words and smiles being recorded by dozens of microphones and TV cameras. Russell Bancroft, resplendent in ruffled shirt and cuffs, was waiting in the foyer to escort her to her seat.

The flash bulbs of the massed media, still warm from popping in the faces of Rita Hayworth, Gary Cooper, James Cagney, Greer Garson, Robert Taylor, Claudette Colbert, Paul Muni and a hundred others, became a veritable firework display when Bancroft stepped forward and embraced his new star. Through it all Pandora felt pleasantly and happily detached.

Inside the theatre all heads turned and a buzz arose as the pair were shown to their seats. Heidi with Rita a few rows in front rose and blew kisses. Ten more minutes while the photographers worked from the aisles, and the lights dimmed. Russell Bancroft took Pandora's hand and raised it to his lips.

'Good luck, darling,' he said.

As the film unfolded Bancroft occasionally telephoned the projectionist to adjust focus or alter sound volume. But the audience were never restless and seemed to be enjoying them-

278

selves. Pandora, pleasantly surprised at the improvement wrought by a big screen and the addition of the musical score, nodded happily when Bancroft whispered in her ear, 'It's going great!' Or 'They love it!' But she continued to feel detached as though she were watching the performance of a total stranger. When the final crashing chords of the Metropolis Symphony Orchestra and massed choir signalled THE END, the lights in the Cathay Circle came up and the curtains slowly folded upon the screen. Sparked by the faithful 'claque' from the Studio, generous applause broke out and many people rose from their seats, clapping pointedly at Pandora. Bancroft kissed her hand again ostentatiously. 'Congratulations darling,' he said.

But as he spoke his eyes flicked over her head and he frowned. In the centre aisle the network television camera was being pointed towards the screen and photographers were readying their cameras. The lights dimmed again and a single spotlight illuminated the centre of the curtain. The audience preparing to depart subsided again into their seats.

'What the hell's going on?' Bancroft muttered.

The curtains twitched, then rolled back. The spotlight illuminated the meagre stage space before the screen. Into it, carried with difficulty by two immensely muscular young men wearing turbans and voluminous bloomers, came a sedan chair.

The spotlight followed this conveyance to the centre of the stage where it was deposited and out of it, dark glasses and copper coloured thatch gleaming, and wearing a white suit, stepped Maxwell Stern. There was a ripple of embarrassed laughter and a popping of flash bulbs.

He held up his hand for quiet.

'In the silent days when she was queen of Paramount, Gloria Swanson was carried in that chair from her dressing room to the stages, when it was raining.'

A glimmer of interest and more popping bulbs illuminated this odd announcement.

'Nowadays things are less comfortable' Stern continued. 'My film, which you have just so generously applauded, was made under the most difficult conditions. My dear friend Ted Gruskin was a tower of strength down there in Mexico, without his expertise and hard work it might never have been finished.

279

He never spared himself and was a highly respected and talented leader. Few among us did not feel the magic of his touch.'

(Sniggers arose from the graduates of the goosing stick.)

'My old friend drove himself to the very limit in my behalf and I shall forever be grateful to him. Unfortunately, he exhausted himself and has been seriously ill in hospital as a result.'

Stern fished a piece of paper out of his white suit.

'It was Ted's idea to show you this chair tonight and I went along with it for his sake but as I was getting into it I received this message.' He shook his head sadly and raised the paper.

'My poor old friend has just suffered a very serious relapse.' He looked round the Theatre, then spoke as though the idea had just hit him.

'Tell you what, let's all stand for one minute of silent prayer that Ted Gruskin may come safely through what has become his hour of trial, but should have been his hour of triumph.'

As the audience shuffled to their feet flashbulbs popped anew and Heidi ran past the turning television camera and the flashing light bulbs.

Russell Bancroft was tight-lipped as he helped Pandora into his Lincoln Continental, for several minutes he drove in silence.

'The little *sonofabitch*!' he said finally.

Pandora was mystified. 'Why did he want to do that? He *hated* Ted.'

'Sure he hated Ted, he hated his guts. But he had it all figured out . . . including that goddam sedan chair.'

'Poor Heidi,' said Pandora. 'Can you imagine getting the news like that?'

'The *sonofabitch*!' said Bancroft once more. 'So he's gotten several million bucksworth of publicity for the picture, which is why he did it. And maybe he's softened some poor reviews. But he's through at Metropolis, I'll see to *that*.'

Deep in thought Bancroft drove, aimlessly it seemed to Pandora, around Beverly Hills. Then he pointed the car up the winding curves of Tower Road, towards the crest of the hills.

'Where are we going?' Pandora asked.

'David Selznick has a few people for dinner, he's asked us to drop in. It's always very relaxed at David and Jennifer's, we can unwind and celebrate!'

The thought of 'dropping in' on the great David O. Selznick, maker of *Gone with the Wind* and other classics, gave Pandora's dormant nerves new life. She reached into her shocking pink handbag, located the reserve pill and without a moment's hesitation swallowed it.

'It's a fabulous house,' Bancroft continued, 'used to belong to John Gilbert, the great silent star. The talkies killed him off because he had a squeaky voice. Garbo was in love with him for years and stood by him but the poor bastard died of booze and a broken heart.' He turned the Lincoln into the private parking lot and they sat looking down upon the breathtaking crescent of Los Angeles.

'What a city!' Pandora murmured.

'You're lovely,' said Bancroft. 'And you were wonderful tonight. You've got a big hit. Look at me.' She did, and he kissed her full on the mouth.

As they climbed up the steps into David Selznick's hillside house, Pandora still felt oddly relaxed and detached. If either of them thought they would be 'making an entrance' of any sort they were mistaken; the twenty or thirty who had enjoyed a buffet supper were already engrossed in each other, as were half a dozen more who had joined the party after attending the Premiere.

David Selznick, large and smiling with curly brown hair and a broken nose upon which rested thick eyeglasses came over and shook Pandora's hand.

'I hear it went very well,' he said. 'I'm so glad. Now come and meet Jennifer and anyone you don't already know . . . make yourself at home.'

Jennifer Jones, marvellously like her glowing screen image, full of vitality, smiles, sweetness and heavily disguised shyness, introduced Pandora to Cary Grant, to Tyrone Power and Annabella, to Clark Gable and Sylvia Fairbanks, to Hitchcock, Charles Boyer, Jimmy Stewart and his wife Gloria, to Humphrey Bogart and Lauren Bacall, to Ronald Colman, Marlene Dietrich, to the writers Dorothy Parker, Ben Hecht and Harry J. Kurnitz, to Cole Porter and to many others.

Pandora took it all in her stride.

A few had attended the première, most had not, but all found time to be welcoming and encouraging before returning to their individual pursuits of happiness. If Pandora was jolted into remembering that every week in Hollywood there were two or three Major Studio Feature Previews, her state of euphoria cushioned the shock, and anyway, her beauty, lack of affectation and sense of fun combined with Hollywood's voracious appetite for newcomers made her the success of the evening. She was having the time of her life. And if Russell Bancroft, basking in her reflected glory showed signs of becoming possessive, it was a condition Pandora quickly diagnosed as amusing. In fact, the whole evening amused her. She drank happily of the champagne and gave herself up wholeheartedly to enjoying her big moment. She missed Stani, but she still felt he had deserted her in her hour of need, so she returned a fair proportion of the eye signals being flashed by her producer.

At about the time that Maxwell Stern was reaching the nadir of bad taste and publicity-seeking at the Cathay Circle, Stani, high above the Grand Canyon, stirred and glanced out of the window of the DC7. A change in the steady beat of its four engines had awakened him. He saw that the port side inboard propellor was motionless, with one blade, like an admonishing finger, pointing directly at the stars. Almost simultaneously the Captain's announcement came:

'Sorry folks, we have a little overheating problem here with one motor so we've shut it down. There's no danger but I'm afraid we have to return to Los Angeles. This flight to New York will continue as soon as we can make repairs or pick up another aircraft. Estimated time of arrival at Los Angeles is three a.m. I'm real sorry about the inconvenience.'

At four o'clock, the passengers, dozing fitfully in the airport, were roused, informed that their flight would now leave at 7.20 and that breakfast vouchers would be issued. Stani did not hesitate, he stowed his carry bag in a locker, grabbed a cab and headed for Brentwood. He decided not to frighten Pandora by slipping silently into bed, his original idea, but he promised himself his familiar berth alongside her if only for one hour and longed to hear about her big night. With no traffic abroad the yellow cab made the trip in record time.

To avoid waking Pandora, he bade the driver stop in the

282

street; he recognized Russell Bancroft's Lincoln Continental at once and hoped that he had arrived in time to join the celebrations. He also hoped that Chuck would be present. Finding no one downstairs he noticed a glimmer of light coming from the poolside projection room, and made his way through the French windows into the garden, delicious in the cool pre-dawn.

He walked silently on the dewy grass, anticipating Pandora's happiness when she saw him.

The curtains of the rectangular playroom were drawn so he slipped quietly into the projection room, to check on the number and identity of Pandora's guests before deciding on his most effective mode of reappearance. Between the two full size projection machines was an inspection panel through which, over the heads of the viewers, the projectionist could see the screen, check his focus and gauge the exact moment to change reels from one machine to the other.

The playroom was luxurious, two rows of deep chairs faced the screen, in the middle was a long sofa that could comfortably seat six.

Stani peered through the little square of glass. One table lamp illuminated the scene with a soft yellow light; at first he thought the playroom was empty. Then, as his eyes became accustomed to the light, he saw over the top of the sofa something white moving rhythmically up and down.

It was several seconds before he identified the buttocks of a suntanned man.

Frozen, he watched their steadily rise and fall. When the man's head momentarily showed Stani saw it was Russell Bancroft.

He placed his forehead on the ledge of the little window; his knees buckled, and his breath caught in his lungs. When he dared look up once more there was dreadful confirmation of his worst fears – a pink satin shoe on a leg he knew too well.

Numb with shock he staggered out into the fresh air, groped his way to a bank of azaleas and was sick.

Then a great surge of rage almost suffocated him – rage at Bancroft, not at Pandora; there was a cold well of loneliness where she had been.

He knew exactly what he would do. He went back into the

283

house, and obliterated all traces of his visit, then in the garage he picked up a clasp knife and a coil of rope used for securing his surfboard to the roof of the car. He glanced at the still dark purple sky and hoped he would not have long to wait; it would soon be daylight. He intended to kill Bancroft.

The Lincoln Continental, for reasons now apparent, was not parked where it would be visible from the road. It was well hidden by bushes on the driveway some twenty yards from the house. Stani climbed in the back and lay down on the floor to wait.

When his fingers felt the rough fibres of the rope he remembered the Cossack Colonel among the willows and the grotesque way his head had fallen forward on his chest. He was surprised to find that he still had no anger at Pandora, just a great aching sense of loss. He knew he would either hang Bancroft and leave him with popping eyes and lolling head, or he would stab him through the heart. Then again he might just force him at knife point to drive to Point Dume and push him over the cliff, to be found in late afternoon by surfers.

The longer he lay on the floor of the Lincoln, the more uncomfortable did he become. In the middle of the floor there was a hump housing the transmission shaft. Perhaps Pandora had been forced to submit to Bancroft? Perhaps she had got carried away by the excitement of her big night? He began to make excuses for her, to rationalize and he thought of Ulrike Bichlmaier. Perhaps Pandora had felt no guilt about wrapping her lovely legs around the thrusting Bancroft, after all he had felt nothing much when the Burgomaster of Feldbach had asked if his daughter might receive the daily list of requirements from the Commanding Officer of 'Fort Glassballs'. The beautiful pigtailed seventeen-year-old had given unsparing of herself in a barn beneath an order signed by General Eisenhower:

BE ON YOUR GUARD!
DON'T FRATERNIZE
WITH
GERMANS

Stani had not felt too badly about Ulrike Bichlmaier and had certainly never mentioned her to Pandora. So maybe, if the port inboard engine of his DC7 had not overheated he would never

284

have known about Pandora's fraternization and life would have gone on as before. He opened the clasp knife and tested the blade, then he shifted his position to ease his discomfort. He decided to review the sentence he had passed on Bancroft.

When he heard steps on the gravel; he looked at the luminous face of his watch, it was five-twenty.

Bancroft threw his jacket onto the back seat and eased in behind the wheel, then lit a cigar. Stani waited till Bancroft had been driving about five minutes along Sunset Boulevard before he raised himself up; the clasp knife was in his hand, he spoke softly:

'I gotta knife,' he said, disguising his voice. Bancroft gasped with shock. 'Feel it?' Stani pricked the skin through the fine linen of Bancroft's ruffled shirt, just below the collar.

'What do you want?' Bancroft's voice sounded shrill.

'Throw your cigar out the window and make a left up Stone Canyon till there's no more houses.'

Stani recognized the big wooded lot a real estate lady had shown Pandora. 'Turn in here . . . stop by those trees . . . Now, switch off, give me the key . . . and your shoes.'

Bancroft handed keys and footwear over his shoulder.

'Get out,' Stani ordered. 'And don't run away because I'll catch you and cut your balls off.'

Beneath the trees they faced each other, the glow of the distant city outlining the coil of rope in Stani's hand.

'My God!' Bancroft croaked. 'What are you going to do? . . . Who *are* you?' 'STANI!' Bancroft laughed wildly and advanced with outstretched arms. 'Jesus kid! You really had me fooled there! Boy! Am I glad to see you! How come you're not in New York?'

Stani waited till he could see the white caps of Bancroft's teeth before he brought his knee up hard. The producer fell to the ground groaning and retching. Stani stirred him with his foot.

'Get up you creep, and get your clothes off – all of them. I want them to find you naked.'

'Stani, for God's sake,' mumbled Bancroft, still writhing on the ground. 'Are you crazy or something? I just left your girl friend . . .'

'I know . . .' said Stani. 'I saw you. Now get off your ass and take your clothes off.'

Bancroft staggered to his feet; the first silvery streaks of dawn were etching the mountains to the East and he watched with horror as Stani threw the coiled rope over a stout branch and fashioned a loop at one end.

'Get *undressed*, goddammit,' said Stani, pointing the knife at Bancroft's Adam's apple. 'You've got twenty seconds.'

Bancroft fell apart. He blubbered and begged. 'I can explain everything,' he whimpered; but he made a major miscalculation when he added, 'she *asked* me to do it.'

Up came Stani's knee again, harder this time, and Bancroft went down once more. By the time the nausea had died down his clothes had been ripped or cut off him and he was bound hand and foot with short lengths from the rope.

'Stani' he sobbed, 'don't *do* this . . . I've a wife and two kids . . . I'll do anything you say . . . I've got two million dollars in Bonds you can have them all – every dime *please*!!!' He was on his knees weeping hysterically.

'Shut up' said Stani 'you bore me.' He ripped a sleeve off Bancroft's shirt and gagged him with it, took the looped end of the rope and passed it over his head, adjusting it carefully under his chin – then Bancroft fainted.

Stani dragged the naked head of Metropolis Pictures to his Lincoln Continental, dumped him on the floor behind the driver's seat, covered him with his clothing and started the motor. He headed back to Sunset Boulevard and Beverly Hills. A few blocks east of the pink Christmas cake edifice of the Beverly Hills Hotel he turned right on Maple Drive. He had visited the house quite lately, with Pandora. He hoped he would recognize it quickly because Beverly Hills with its hundreds of rich and famous citizens was renowned for a zealous Police Department which treated cruising vehicles with the deepest suspicion and his cargo, to say the least, was an interesting one. The house when he found it was ideally suited to his purpose, set well back from the road and shielded from it by a hedge of obisporum.

From the tour of the place which the proud owners had given Pandora and himself he knew that they kept no live-in 'help' and themselves slept late in bedrooms overlooking the garden at the back; but dawn comes up quickly in Southern California and Stani had little time to lose. He backed the Lincoln into the driveway and dragged his captive across a few yards of lawn; contact with the dewy grass revived Bancroft and he moaned with fear into his gag.

Utilizing the knot-tying dexterity that Jervis, his sailing master, had implanted so long ago, Stani bound Bancroft securely to the one palm tree that stood in the centre of the lawn. Then he started up the Lincoln and drove away. From a call box on Olympic Boulevard he dialled the Los Angeles *Times* and asked for the Night Editor.

'I have a big scoop for Hedda Hopper.'

'Shoot,' said the Editor.

'The naked body of the Head of Metropolis Pictures is tied to a tree in front of a house in Beverly Hills.'

The Editor whistled. 'You got the address?'

Stani gave it to him.

'Know who lives in that house?' the Editor asked.

'Yes,' said Stani. 'Louella Parsons.'

PART THREE

THE END

21

Few people who put a stick in a hornet's nest and stir it around know what move to make thereafter, except to distance themselves from the scene with the greatest rapidity. Stani, as the fog of war began to clear, decided it was imprudent to drive about in a stolen car.

The giant of all the studios, Metro-Goldwyn-Mayer, lay between him and the airport; so he drove the Lincoln Continental to Culver City and left it in the parking lot of the Irving Thalberg Executive Building. Actors and actresses heading for make-up or hairdressing sessions were already filing through the main gates. A few cars were on the Thalberg parking lot. Stani put the remains of Bancroft's clothing in the trunk of the Continental and locked it. He did not lock the car, he left the keys in the ignition, then found a phone and called a cab.

At the airport the impact of what he'd done hit him, and with legs of lead he wandered about, trying to decide what to do, where to go and how to cope with the awful prospect of life without Pandora. He couldn't believe what had happened and again and again squeezed his eyes tight shut to drive out his last glimpse of her. In the coffee shop a donut went uneaten.

When his flight to New York was called, more to provide a place in which to think than for any other reason, he retrieved his carrybag from the locker, made his way to Gate No. 9 and boarded the plane. A mountainous man wearing a ten-gallon hat, a necktie upon which was a naked woman, and shod with cowboy boots, squeezed and wheezed himself into the seat beside him.

'Howdy!' he said, extending a hand that looked like a bunch of bananas. 'Chester Pocock.'

For Stani the prospect of spending eight or nine hours

clamped to the side of a stranger had never held great appeal. He shook the proffered paw and then, tapping dramatically at his throat, managed the faintest whisper: 'Sorry.'

'Can't talk, eh?'

Stani nodded.

'Lost your voice, have you?'

Stani signalled a sad affirmative and pushed his seat into the reclining position; there he remained for several hours till painful appeals from his bladder forced him to clamber over the sleeping hulk beside him. During his horizontal solitude he had reviewed the events of the previous night and had come to several obvious conclusions.

His abducting at knife point of a top Hollywood executive, then stripping, assaulting and leaving him naked, gagged and tied to a tree, even if he had not taken the precaution of advertising it to the most widely read columnists in the world, could hardly have gone unremarked by the Beverly Hills Police Department.

He visualized the handcuffs and the crowd of reporters who would be awaiting him at La Guardia airport. He could imagine the headlines already enlivening the morning papers . . .

'Bared and beaten Movie Mogul fingers Polish Pilot.'

'Jan Ricardo in Love Triangle.'

He squirmed on his seat when he thought of the anguish and scandal he had inflicted upon Pandora. The world has changed a lot, he told himself; perhaps a husband's destruction of his wife's lover might still be winked at in remote corners of Texas or encouraged in Patagonia, but even in Italy, the country which had once legalized crimes of honour and applauded the repayment of sexual insults by bursts of machine-gun fire, had now outlawed them. But the memory of the cynical calculation with which he had been tricked into leaving the field open for Bancroft on Pandora's big night caused another surge of anger and frustration and prompted a nagging query. 'Why didn't you go in there and beat him up? Or beat her up? What are you afraid of?' Stani tossed and turned during the remaining hours of the flight, sometimes touching Pandora's disc, occasionally dozing off to awaken, relieved for a few seconds of the dreadful weight over his heart. But when the cold reality of his loss came smashing down once more he turned his face to the window so that Chester Pocock would not see his tears.

Somewhere over the Allegheny Mountains his companion nudged him.

'Want some dinner? You missed lunch.' Stani glanced at his watch. 'It's almost seven, New York time,' Chester Pocock smiled. 'Reckoned you might be gettin' a mite hungry.'

Stani realized he had eaten nothing since before he boarded the original flight, seemingly days before; just in time he remembered his lost voice.

He nodded silently, raised his seat and accepted a tray from the stewardess.

Chester Pocock decided to adopt Stani's tone. 'Throat any better?' he whispered.

Stani shook his head.

'Too bad,' said Pocock. 'Well, if you can't talk to me . . . is it okay for me to talk to you?'

Stani didn't have the nerve to signal ear trouble so he managed a wan smile, a nod, and adjusted his watch.

'Should be there an hour from now,' said Pocock. 'You missed a lot of turbulence back there, slept right through it, wings were flapping like a wild turkey. A few years from now and we'll be flying above all this bad weather.'

While Stani picked at his food, Chester Pocock prattled on in hushed tones and Stani realized that he was sitting next to a fascinating human being and one of the most intelligent people he'd ever met – a scientist from Cape Canaveral who was working on supersonic airtravel. 'I've been out with Boeing, Douglas and Lockheed,' Pocock whispered. 'There's no question but that they can all build big planes to fly twelve-fourteen miles high and twice the speed of sound. But we still have to lick the problem of getting them back down on the ground again!'

Stani became fascinated and the more he listened the more he wanted to join in the conversation; but after many hours of silence he had constructed his own re-entry problem so he spent the remainder of his trip nodding appreciatively or widening his eyes in disbelief. When his ears began to pop and the 'Fasten Seat Belt' sign came on he suppressed a great desire to break through his self-imposed sound barrier and say: 'Thank you,

293

Mr. Pocock for all your kindness, you will never know what a help you've been and please don't be embarrassed when the police come aboard and take me away.' While his companion and the rest of the passengers were gathering together their belongings and making their way to the exits, Stani remained in his window-seat, anticipating the arrival of 'New York's Finest' and wondering if the skin of his wrists would be pinched when they snapped on the handcuffs.

The plane emptied, tired stewardesses became impatient. 'Can we help you?' one of them enquired. Stani managed a wan little smile, extracted his carrybag and, like Sidney Carton, bravely faced the steps leading to his doom.

There are sharp ridges on the trunks of palm trees. Russell Bancroft, when he heard the Lincoln Continental drive away, struggled little; he was still shaking like an aspen. The dawn was coming up quickly now, one or two cars passed, probably driven by stockbrokers cursing the time change between California and Wall Street. From a few houses away he heard the rattle of bottles and the electric whirr of a milk delivery van; a passing yellow cat had also heard it and paused to inspect Bancroft's feet as it slunk by, hoping for a spill. He prayed that his sleeping hosts were patrons of the approaching products. The tires squealed slightly and he heard bottles and packages of eggs and butter being loaded into the holder, then footsteps passed behind him towards the kitchen door. He was completely hidden by the palm trunk and no amount of grunting and squeaking within the confines of his gag could attract attention. The reappearance of the ginger cat, however, brought the milkman, on his return with the empties, a few yards onto the lawn.

'Come here Red,' the milkman whispered to the cat. 'I've got one with a couple of inches for you.'

When he saw a naked body attached to the palm tree, he said 'Holy Toledo!' loudly and dropped the empties on the grass. He ran to the tree and made efforts to undo Stani's knots; as he fumbled he issued clucking noises and words of encouragement before announcing, 'I've got a knife in my truck,' and added, '. . . stay right where you are.'

Soon Bancroft was unfettered and the gag out of his mouth.

294

His deliverer wore a white-topped peaked cap, white trousers and a white shirt with red bow tie, also a wind-breaker with the ADOHR insignia over the pocket.

'Here, take this,' he said, taking off the windbreaker. 'It's as cold as a whore's heart this time o' day. I've got a pullover. What happened to you anyway?'

Bancroft had the framework of a story ready. 'A couple of guys jumped me at a light,' he said, 'took my car and tied me up. Can I bum a ride off you – I only live a few blocks from here.' Bancroft was rubbing his arms and legs to restore circulation. 'I'll call the cops as soon as I get home,' he added, 'no need to wake the folks here.'

'Sure thing, be glad to. Did you get a look at those guys?'

'It happened pretty fast,' Bancroft said. 'Could we get going? I'd like to get home.' As they were leaving the garden Bancroft remembered the rope and gag and ran back. 'Might be useful to track them down,' he explained.

The milkman drove his electric wagon standing up, the sides of the cabin open. When they pulled out onto Maple Drive Bancroft hid his naked lower half by bending double; a black sedan was turning into the driveway. He caught a glimpse of the regal profile of Hedda Hopper staring expectantly ahead through the windshield; her hair was in curlers.

During the five minute drive to Bancroft's house the milkman kept up a steady patter. 'Five miles an hour is my top speed. Adohr have a lot of trouble with these batteries but they get the job done.' He turned left on Sunset Boulevard, past the Beverly Hills Hotel. 'When I first came out here from Wisconsin back in the early thirties people used to ride horseback here, right down the centre of Sunset; there was a bridle path, with tan and everything. And over on Wilshire, from the Beverly Wilshire Hotel all the way to Westwood Village was nothing but poinsettia fields, and the Los Angeles Country Club . . . sure was pretty at Christmas time.' He shook his head, 'Now it's all big stores and apartment buildings down there on Wilshire, soon it'll be skyscrapers.'

Bancroft, still shivering, made himself as inconspicuous as possible in the exposed cabin, behind him the serried ranks of the milkbottles rattled and clanked. 'Know where the company got the name Adohr?' asked the milkman, pointing to the windbreaker. 'Fella who started the company owned all the land between the ocean and the mountains, from below Malibu to way up almost to Oxnard. Had a big fight with the State of California because they wanted to run the 101 Highway through there; lawsuits and all that for years. Well, this fella decided to start these milk farms and name them after his daughter Rhoda spelled backwards. Kinda screwy to my way of thinking. This your place?'

'Yes,' said Bancroft. The electric wagon whirred to a halt. 'I'm really grateful to you and I'd like to do something for you. How would five thousand bucks be?'

'Five *grand*?' breathed the milkman. 'Jeez! I didn't expect a *thing*! I mean, all I did was what anyone would've done!'

'Well,' Bancroft said, 'I want to thank you, I was in real trouble back there, you did me a big favour. Just don't say a word to anyone. I've a hunch I recognized one of those hoodlums, he's big time. We have to leave it all to the Police Department. The last thing they'll want right now is any publicity.'

The milkman looked mystified but nodded. 'Sure, sure,' he said, 'you can count on me.'

'Drop by Metropolis Studios this afternoon and ask for Bancroft.'

'Thought I recognized you from the Television, Mr. Bancroft. My wife and I were watching that Premiere at the Cathay Circle last night.'

'Yes,' said Bancroft. 'Come down there and I'll have that little cheque all ready for you. What's the name?'

'Charlie McNee. You don't know what that'll mean to me. Goodbye mortgage!!'

'Now, if you'd be good enough to drop me off just by those bushes in the driveway there, I'll go through to the pool and take a quick swim . . . I'll keep these pieces of rope for the cops! Thanks a million.' They shook hands, Bancroft handed back the windbreaker and disappeared.

Minutes later, clad in a terrycloth bathrobe he emerged from the pool-house ready to slip into the house when the 'help' unlocked the garden door.

Normally his chauffeur would have driven him to work in the Lincoln Continental, but he left a note for his wife, a late

296

sleeper, telling her the car had been stolen and at eight o'clock departed in her Packard Town and Country.

At the Studio Marcia was already at work, the mail was sorted and reviews of *The Ruby Ring* from the morning papers, the *Reporter* and *Variety*, all laid out upon his desk. He winced when he read them, they ranged from dismissive to poor but Stern's sedan chair and one minute silence hit every front page; he flicked the intercom.

'Marcia, we got great coverage. See if there's anyone in the Legal Department yet, I want to see Mr. Hassloe as soon as he comes in.'

The Chief Attorney of Metropolis Pictures was a broad-chested, grey-suited gentleman with rimless eyeglasses. He smiled constantly with his mouth, never with his eyes.

'Morning, Russ,' Lyle Hassloe said. 'What can I do for you?'

'Last night,' said Bancroft, 'I got myself in kind of a jam with a broad.'

'Not again!' laughed Hassloe, 'tell me more.'

Bancroft motioned him to a chair and related in detail what had taken place the night before. Hassloe listened intently.

'Boy! You really do pick 'em,' he said. 'What d'you want me to do?'

'Cover for me, Lyle, be the beard.'

'First of all,' said the lawyer, 'tell Marcia to send this McNee character to me when he shows up for his cheque, don't see him again yourself – *ever*. He could get you into real trouble.' He eased himself out of his chair and stood in front of Bancroft. 'How exactly do you want me to cover for you?'

'Very simple,' said Bancroft. 'When I dropped Ricardo at her place after Selznick's party I came over to you to discuss various things. When I left you at around four-thirty my Continental had been stolen from outside your place. You drove me home and dropped me off by the garden entrance. That's all. Okay?'

Hassloe walked slowly round the desk and stood beside Bancroft, then he leant forward.

'Okay, now that I've taken something out of your little tape recorder – that wasn't very smart of you, Russ. I had it installed for you, remember?'

Bancroft looked out of the window. 'Are you going to cover

297

for me or not?'.

Hassloe considered his reply. 'Okay,' he said, 'I'll take care of everything. The only trouble is I'll have to take on some outside help to handle the problem of the deferments on last year's pictures. The actors are finally getting smart, they've hired some good law firms and they want to take a look at our books. It's very time consuming.'

'How much?' asked Bancroft.

'Special rates for old pals,' Hassloe smiled. 'One hundred thousand dollars to you.'

'You son of a bitch,' Bancroft said.

'Cheaper than a California divorce settlement,' said Hassloe.

When the lawyer had departed, Marcia told Bancroft that Chuck Pesnick was waiting on the line. 'Something about your automobile,' she added.

'Put him on,' said Bancroft.

'One of the Publicity guys over at M.G.M. just called me,' said Chuck. 'When he went to work this morning he noticed your Continental in the Thalberg Parking Lot, with all the windows down and the keys in the ignition. He took the keys to Reception but they had no record of your being on the lot.'

'The car was stolen last night outside Lyle Hassloe's. Great news it's been found!'

'I have to go over to M.G.M. today,' said Chuck, 'want me to collect it for you?'

It was late afternoon before Pesnick kept his appointment at M.G.M. When he returned with Bancroft's Continental he was thoughtful.

He delivered the keys to Marcia but when he reported the car undamaged he omitted to mention that he had checked in the trunk to see if the spare tire had been removed and had found the ripped and disordered remains of Bancroft's smart Premiere suit and ruffled shirt.

Pesnick had not been back in his office long before Pandora called; he had talked with her in the morning, to read her reviews of *The Ruby Ring* and discuss the local reactions to her performance. Being a realist, Pandora had expected disaster and had dreaded hearing the results, but the consensus was that the film, though uneven, would probably be a commercial success and that Jan Ricardo had come through as a promising

298

beginner with highly saleable physical assets. Chuck had pointed out that thanks in part to Maxwell Stern's ghoulish behaviour, *The Ruby Ring* had got so much publicity that it had registered with every American with the price of a newspaper, radio or television set. Also, the mixed reviews would be quickly forgotten in the general euphoria at the prospect of three other major previews scheduled for the near future – Fred Astaire and Judy Garland in *Easter Parade*, Humphrey Bogart in *The Treasure of the Sierra Madre*, and Clark Gable, Ava Gardner and Deborah Kerr in *The Hucksters*.

'I see what you mean,' Pandora had said. But she still seemed upset.

'Chuck darling, can you come over for a few minutes when you finish work? I need to talk to you.'

'Of course, Honey. Get ready with a tooth-pick, a cherry, a slice of orange, a twist of lemon, a couple of measures of Bourbon and I'll meet you at Old Fashioned time.'

'You look like you've been crying,' said Pesnick when Pandora opened the door.

She did not answer, but led him out to the patio. 'Here's the stuff for the drink. I hope I got it right.'

'I told you not to worry about those reviews,' said Pesnick. 'Honestly, I expected much worse, we could have been murdered!'

'It's not that,' said Pandora, looking away. 'I haven't heard from Stani. He promised to call as soon as he got to New York. The Studio booked him into the Warwick but he hasn't checked in and I know the plane arrived, I called the airport.'

'Did it arrive on time?' Pesnick asked.

'I don't know,' said Pandora. 'They just said it had landed.'

'What was he flying – T.W.A.?'

'No, American Airlines.'

'I'll call Russ Saunders at the airport,' said Pesnick. 'He knows more about what goes on with American than their own Board of Directors.'

While Pesnick was telephoning, Pandora for the hundredth time and with the utmost distaste turned over in her mind the events of the preceding night.

After Bancroft had dressed and left the playhouse, she had been swamped by remorse. As soon as she heard his car start up she had dived into her cold pool to wash away the lingering effects of the tranquilizers, the sour taste of champagne, and to disinfect her memory. 'What on earth could have made me do this?' she asked herself. 'What have I *done*? A pushover for a Hollywood stud! I must have been out of my mind.'

Lilly-Mae came out with a small white box.

'The flower shop said they're real sorry they couldn't deliver this before you went to the Theatre last night.'

Under the tissue paper, on a pillow of forget-me-nots, Pandora found a single perfect pink camellia and a card:

'*ALL* my love *always* — S'

She burst into tears.

Pesnick came slowly back onto the patio and took a hefty pull at his Old Fashioned. 'Stani's flight turned back because of engine trouble about three hours out of Los Angeles,' he said. 'Russ Saunders says they changed planes and took off again this morning, same Flight Number; they've arrived safely in New York.'

'Poor darling Stani,' said Pandora, 'what a bore for him. How long did they have to wait around?'

'Saunders said they came back at three o'clock and took off again around seven-thirty.'

Pandora went cold.

Chuck went on. 'Russ Saunders said he had to take care of several studio people on that flight. Stani was booked by Metropolis so he looked for him too, someone said he'd left in a cab as soon as he landed; but he definitely caught the flight this morning.'

Pandora had an empty feeling in her stomach and a lightness behind her knees when she stood up.

'I'm going to call the Warwick again, he must be there by now.'

'While you're doing that,' said Pesnick, 'I'll drop over to Brentwood, the morning papers should be out. We can take a look at Hedda and Louella and see what they have to say about the Premiere.'

Ten minutes later he was back. 'You've been crying again,' he said.

Pandora's voice was low. 'Stani called the Warwick. He's cancelled his reservation and left no address.'

Chuck tried to be reassuring. 'Maybe he met someone on the flight and got talked into going to another hotel, the Warwick's quite noisy. He'll call when he gets settled, he's only just arrived.' He handed Pandora the papers.

She glanced listlessly at the headline of Louella Parsons' column in the Examiner and read no further.

'TASTELESS PERFORMANCE BY PRODUCER MARS *RUBY RING* PREEM.'

In the Los Angeles Times Hedda Hopper was at her viperish best . . .

'MAXWELL STERN RUINS HIS FIRST HOLLY-WOOD CANTER BY RUNNING TRUE TO HIS BROAD-WAY FORM'

She continued with a full scale personal attack on Stern's phoney concern for Gruskin and ended thus:

'*At six o'clock this morning this reporter was roused from her beauty sleep to investigate a report that the body of a prominent Hollywood figure could be seen naked and tied to a tree in the front garden of a fast-fading newspaper columnist. I hurried to the given address; if there had been any justice I would have found Maxwell Stern. Nothing, however, was on view except a mangy ginger cat, which I found a great deal more attractive.*'

They put down their papers and silence reigned. Hanging overhead from an olive tree were little hibiscus-shaped glass receptacles which Pandora kept topped up with sugar and water; minute humming birds with whirring wings and gaudy little waistcoats of vermilion, green or peacock blue were zooming in, and helping themselves to nips of nectar. On the lawn a family of quail hurried by in strict formation, Dad in front, with an elegant little antenna arrangement on his head, proud Mum bringing up the rear, and in between, in line ahead, eight scuttling little babies.

The wildlife went unnoticed. Pandora was deeply concerned about Stani's whereabouts during his enforced grounding; and Pesnick was trying to imagine the circumstances under which Russell Bancroft would have removed his evening clothes, mangled them up and placed them in the trunk of his Lincoln Continental.

They sat trying to find the missing pieces of their respective puzzles. Chuck wondered, had his boss gotten himself into some kind of a hassle, a gang bang maybe? And at some point had his clothes ripped off? Was there any connection between his naked boss and the nude 'prominent Hollywood figure' Hedda Hopper had failed to find in a garden at dawn? He savoured a picture of the impeccable Bancroft being attached to a flowering eucalyptus by two sexpot starlets. He sipped his Old Fashioned. Sooner or later if Bancroft was in trouble he would order him to put up a smokescreen; through the years a powerful liaison had been forged between the local Police Departments and the publicity heads of the major studios. Stars or executives involved in brawls, orgies, drunk driving or attempted rapes had on many occasions breathed sighs of relief at the firmness of these links. If publicity heads could cook up good news they had also perfected ways of putting bad news in the freezer. Pesnick smiled to himself, all he had to do was keep his mouth shut and play it by ear.

When he noticed that Pandora was crying, he went over to her.

'What is it, Honey? He'll call when he gets settled in.'

'No, he won't,' Pandora said. He won't call, ever again.'

'What's happened?'

Pandora shook her head; she longed to talk to someone, to unload her dreadful nagging fear. Her insides felt weak at the thought of Stani; she loved him and needed him; was it possible that in one night of lunacy . . . Oh! God! *I didn't mean it*!

'Why don't you get it off your chest, whatever it is.'

Again Pandora shook her head. If only she had a girl friend to confide in, to share the burden with . . . but she had no one. Dozens of acquaintances, yes, lots of well-meaning people who would recommend a hairdresser or a gynaecologist, but she had no real friend, except . . . She looked up at Chuck.

'I know what you're thinking,' he smiled. 'I can't trust him . . . a publicity man . . . the most dangerous guy in the world to unload a secret on! I'm right aren't I?' Pandora remained silent. 'I don't blame you, on paper I'm a bad risk, the worst around. But you've known me longer than anyone else out here. On my mother's life, I would never fail you or Stani.'

Pandora rose from her chair and stood facing down the lawn; behind the pool she could see in the distance the great sweep of the Santa Monica Bay and the promontory of Palos Verdes; Catalina Island, misty and blue, looked romantic on the horizon. Slowly she walked down to the poolhouse and Pesnick watched her thoughtfully close the open door to the projectionist's compartment, and walk back. He stood to meet her.

'Last night,' she said, 'I made the biggest mistake of my life. I took pills, and drank too much.'

'That's not *so* awful,' Chuck laughed. 'Lots of people out here do that! You were under one hell of a lot of pressure.'

'Well,' said Pandora, 'I did and . . . I wound up . . . with Russell Bancroft. When I think about it I want to throw up.' She held him at arm's length and searched Chuck's face. 'Now you swore, Chuck, you swore on your mother's life didn't you?'

Pesnick raised his right hand. 'I swore.'

Pandora came into his arms. 'Oh, God, what have I done? What have I *done*?'

'Look, it's no big deal, so you got crocked and got carried away, it happens; Russ is a very persuasive guy and he really has been after you.'

'Ugh! I saw him coming a mile away. I just don't understand myself. All I had to do was say 'no'!'

Pesnick kissed her forehead. 'It's over, forget it, it was a slip up, a combination of circumstances. You're really upset about Stani, that's what it is, isn't it?' Pandora nodded and her eyes filled again. 'Well, we men have a way of talking ourselves out of that one. If it's only below the waist it doesn't necessarily count . . . it's when it's up here –' he tapped his forehead, 'that's when we have to worry.'

'I have an awful feeling that somehow Stani knows,' Pandora whispered. 'That's why he's disappeared. Do you think he could have come here, seen Russ's car and, you know, sort of put two and two together?'

'Were you upstairs?'

'No. In the playhouse.'

'What time did Russ leave?'

'About five, I think, it was still dark but only just.'

Pesnick thought for a moment.

'Russ told me he left here early and then went over to Lyle Hassloe's place. He said that while he was there his car was stolen. It turned up early this morning outside M.G.M. I picked it up for him. When I checked it out I found his evening clothes in the trunk, shoes, everything, the shirt was all ripped up and the jacket and pants were in pretty bad shape too.'

'What does it all mean?'

'It means that somewhere along the line he got himself naked,' laughed Pesnick. 'He didn't leave here like that by any chance?'

'No, he had everything on!'

'Mind if I freshen up the Bourbon?'

Pandora nodded absently. 'What could have happened after he left here, d'you think?'

'Early this morning,' said Pesnick, 'Hedda Hopper was tipped off that some well-known Hollywood mogul was tied naked to a tree in Beverly Hills. Russ fits the description okay and as sure as hell he was naked. But why would anyone want to tie him up?'

The 'flip-flop' of slippers broke the silence.

'Mis' Pandora, Honey,' said Lilly-Mae, 'Vergis and I are needin' a new clothes line out back. Mr. Stani forgot to get one before he left so he told us to use that cord that he ties that surfing plank on with. But I can't find it.'

'It was in the garage on the top of his car the last time I saw it,' Pandora said.

'And that's where it was last night when *I* saw it,' laughed Lilly-Mae. 'But it sure wasn't there this mornin'! I thought maybe you'd moved it.'

'No,' said Pandora in a small voice. 'No, I haven't been in there, Lilly-Mae.'

22

Russell Bancroft was preparing to leave his office. From the window he could see, high upon the Hollywood hills, house lights winking on. He was nervous. He called Lyle Hassloe and asked him to come over right away.

'What's on your mind?' the lawyer enquired.

'Have you located the Pole yet?'

Hassloe crossed, uninvited, to the wall cabinet and helped himself to a Scotch and soda.

'No. He arrived in New York but never checked into his hotel, someone called and cancelled his reservation, and someone, a woman, called Avedon's studio and said he wouldn't be going there either. She said she thought he was on his way back out here. Family problems.'

Bancroft's voice rose with alarm.

'That guy's crazy! He's dangerous! I want twenty-four hour surveillance. He could have killed me last night.'

'Bodyguards, you mean?'

'You're damn right, bodyguards – round the clock.'

Hassloe nodded.

'Okay, I'll set it up. But they don't come cheap, six hour shifts, that means four operatives, non-deductible. What are you doing about the girl, by the way? You'd better get her out of town.'

'I'm working on that,' said Bancroft. 'You know how I feel about Television. Well, we have a deal cooking with the Steel Industry. They want us to produce a "special", two hours of prime time on all three networks. America will have nothing else to look at that night! It'll be total coverage . . . the first time in history. It'll be a revolution in communications.'

'When's it scheduled for?'

'If we close the deal – which we will – work would start right away.'

'How does Ricardo fit?'

'The format will be a mixture of Hollywood, Broadway and Television – but strictly top line. Astaire if we can get him, Sinatra or Garland, and Hope and Benny are about ready to switch from Radio. Great Hollywood production numbers, some ballet with Fonteyn. A high wire act from the Russian circus. You name it! All that'll be on film. But there'll also be two dramatic sketches, "live". One will have a couple of top Broadway names – Helen Hayes and Olivier if possible, or the Lunts. The other will feature a couple of young Hollywood hopefuls.'

'And Jan Ricardo is earmarked for the Hollywood hopefuls "live", right?'

'Right. I'm trying to get Universal to lend me Judd Dugdale to team up with her again, that way we'd be selling *Ruby Ring* at the same time.

'Very smart, Russ. And if she does the show, it'll mean she'll be out of town real soon.'

'Yes. The "live" segments will be rehearsed in New York. She'll go East as soon as we finalize the deal.'

'Do you plan to see her again?'

'Are you *crazy*?'

With his carry bag over his shoulder, Stani had wandered about La Guardia airport, expecting any moment to be arrested. Nobody seemed anxious to oblige, least of all a cop twirling his night stick at the main entrance. So he sought to expedite the matter and asked the correct time. The cop indicated a large clock: 'Right over your head, Buddy,' he said, and turned away. Stani had plenty of time to kill, in fact he was beginning to realize that he had the whole of his future to fill in somehow. The morning papers were not yet on sale so he bought the *Journal-American* and took it to a coffee shop; newsprint blackened his fingers turning the pages, but he found no mention of dirty deeds in Beverly Hills.

The possessor of a tidy orderly mind and having nothing to do, he entered a phone booth, cancelled his room at the Warwick Hotel; he found the number riffling through the Yellow

Pages. He was half-way back to his table before the name of another hotel which his searching eyes had subconsciously photographed, flashed upon his mental screen. He immediately called the Hotel Pierre.

'Do you by any chance have a Mrs. Quansett-Fowles registered?'

'Ten fourteen and fifteen,' came the reply. 'Trying to connect you.'

There was a long pause during which Stani closed his eyes and willed the earpiece to deliver what he desperately wanted to hear. It did, but the voice sounded oddly muted.

'Hello.'

'Amy? Is that you?'

'Yes, who is it?'

'It's Stani.'

'STANI! You *would* call just when my face is full of fortune-telling cookies! Where are you, in California?'

'No, no, I'm in New York. At the airport.'

'Are you coming or going?'

'I'm not sure. Amy, I'm in trouble.'

'Then get in a cab and come here as fast as you can. I've got three inches of cream on my face, my hair's in curlers, I'm taking a night off with Chinese food after an absolute "Blitz" of hospitality. Hurry! I can't wait to see you!'

Amy Quansett-Fowles had removed her face-cream, covered her curlers with a scarf and donned satin pyjamas. Weaned from wartime rations, she had filled out a little since Stani had last seen her, and it suited her. She enveloped him in a long hug of welcome, poured him a tumbler of 'shampoo', inspected him anxiously and pronounced that he looked 'bloody awful'. 'What's happened?' she asked.

Stani had intended to unload an unabridged version of his unhappiness upon his friend. He filled her sympathetic ear with the sad news of Pandora's defection but omitted the details; he found it too painful to describe the scene in the playhouse.

'Falling for her Producer!' Mrs. Quansett-Fowles sniffed. 'Sounds like an old-fashioned Hollywood movie to me. Is she *in love* with the man?'

'I don't know,' said Stani, with misery in every syllable.

307

'Have you asked her?'

'No.'

'Have you spoken to him?'

'Yes.'

'Well?'

'He didn't say much. He thought I was going to kill him.'

'Did you beat him up?'

'No. I tied him to a tree.'

'You *what?*'

Stani still skated around the last scene in the projection room but recounted almost with relief the rest of the story.

'What a bastard!' said Mrs. Quansett-Fowles. 'But you really *are* up shit creek without a paddle, aren't you?' She filled his glass and became very efficient.

'First of all – no decisions of any sort tonight. Do you have a place to sleep? No? Well look at this bloody great apartment those wonderful crazy Yanks have given me! There's an extra bedroom in there and it's all yours.'

She fussed over Stani like a mother hen, forcing him to swallow a club sandwich, some soup and a sleeping pill, then she issued further orders.

'With three hours difference between here and California and that pill, I don't want to hear a peep out of you before nine o'clock tomorrow morning. I'll call Avedon's studio first thing and say you can't come . . . "urgent family problems". Tomorrow things'll look better. Then you can make plans.'

Amy's confidence was premature. By six o'clock Stani was wide awake, and the dreadful reality of his loss came smashing down upon him once more. He lay poking about among the dead leaves of the past weeks trying to find the first signs of Pandora's infatuation with Russell Bancroft, but they remained hidden. The body-blows of what must have been going on, behind his back, rained down upon him, and he felt physically weak, 'gutless'. Not for the first time in his life he pondered upon King Henry V's majestic description of his condition: '. . . he, which hath no stomach to this fight . . .'

He dressed and left the hotel by the Fifth Avenue entrance. The sun had risen on a cool, lovely September morning. He walked aimlessly downtown, past famous jewellers and great department stores where young people in the windows were

308

arranging new displays. The sidewalks were already astir with girls bound for coffee and doughnuts before long days in offices or stores, night cops were going off duty, sanitation crews and garbage collectors were still at work; but of all this activity he saw nothing. On 52nd Street he turned west, then down Broadway for a few blocks. finally west once more into the mean littered streets leading to the docks, with drunks lying in doorways and hopeless bedraggled whores leaving sleazy flop houses.

His feet and heart leaden with unhappiness, he trudged down towards the river. The mean streets became even more sordid and the grey refuse took on an air of permanence: from time to time his deep depression escaped in great heaving sighs. When he caught himself he remembered his mother warning him as a child that each sigh would shorten his life by five minutes. He wished he could sigh enough now to get it over with and avoid the agony of his loss.

He tried not to, but he still sought contact with Pandora and for the thousandth time his fingers felt for her golden disc against his skin.

'Go slowly, come back quickly' . . . how much that once had meant to them both.

From a few blocks away the officious 'toots' of tug boats on the river brought him to a stop. He worked the gold chain over his head and held it in his clenched fist. Maybe he would sign on some rusting freighter and leave forever the country of his disillusionment and defeat? At the very least he would throw her once loving message into the fuel-oil, scum and muck of the Hudson River and, who knows, he might even go with it.

At the end of 49th Street all was hustle and bustle, a double line of trucks, taxis and private cars was passing through the dock gates, inside a crowd of several hundred was assembling: Stani found himself borne along by the excited throng, happy expectant faces and voices were all around him. In the cavernous Customs shed he beheld massed ranks of long-shoremen beneath suspended letters of the alphabet, manning gang-planks or waiting to collect baggage. Giant cranes on rollers were moving into position. He pushed his way to the very end of the dock where for many hours the river flowed by on its way to the sea but now lay slack and mottled with flotsam at the height

309

of the tide. He looked out across the river towards New Jersey and there she was! Six tugs were coaxing her round, turning her great slicing bow into the dock. Her black paint gleamed in the early morning sun, her superstructure and lifeboats sparkled white and newly painted, and towering above them were her three great smokestacks of the brightest red topped by a band of black. Twenty minutes later she tied up alongside her berth and the familiar deep rumbling blasts of her foghorn announced to the City that *Queen Mary* had completed her first voyage with civilian passengers since 1939.

As Stani had watched her cliff-like sides easing alongside the dock he heard anew the screaming death of *Curacoa* and saw once more the anguish of Jervis's father. And when he looked up at the hundreds of waving men and women on the decks above, he remembered the fifteen thousand young Americans who had sailed with him so full of life and adventure.

How many, he wondered, were now asleep beneath the sands of Anzio, the lush grasses of Normandy and the sighing pines of the Forest of the Ardennes, and how many families were still disembowelled by their loss. Thoughtfully he replaced Pandora's chain around his neck and headed back to the hotel.

Mrs. Quansett-Fowles, wearing a pink dressing gown with marabou trimmings, looking like something for Easter, was anxious.

'Where the hell have you been? I thought you'd jumped out the window!'

'I took a long walk' said Stani. 'Pandora's gone. I've got to get used to it and get on with life ... worse things have happened.'

'That's better,' said Mrs. Quansett-Fowles. 'You certainly can't sit around all day looking at the empty chair. You've got to get busy on something to take your mind off it. It's impossible to think of two things at once.' She looked at Stani carefully as she spoke. 'But I still don't see why you don't call her and ask what the hell she thought she was doing – it sounds so unlike her, the little I saw of her – she's no cheap pushover.'

'That's exactly it,' he said. 'She'd never in a million years go for a one-night stand so it must have been going on for a long time. That's why I don't want to call ... I don't want to hear her say it ... I'll get over it.'

310

'H'mm' said Mrs. Quansett-Fowles. 'However bad the news
. . . you'll never rest till you've heard it from her.'

Over breakfast Stani displayed his photographs. Mrs. Quansett-Fowles emitted little gasps and squeaks as she leafed
through his surfing pictures and Al's generous selection of his
other efforts.

'Stani darling!' she cried. 'Honestly I think you're *good! Really*
good!'

With Mrs. Quansett-Fowles in charge Stani was allowed less
time to be miserable, but he had learned the true meaning of a
heavy heart, a different kind of pain from that which had struck
him down on being told of the deaths of his parents. That had
been terrible, unbearable, but final and unchangeable. The loss
of Pandora was a lingering distress, a wound re-opened by
every chance reference – a photograph in a newspaper, even a
poster advocating a holiday in Mexico, or a visit to California.

Mrs. Quansett-Fowles' suite in the Hotel Pierre was not just
a replay of her 'salon' on South Audley Street; many indeed
appeared who had blessed that wartime oasis of fun and forget-
fulness. They brought with them others of every age and Stani,
prodded by his hostess, was soon caught up on a wave of
hospitality. Mrs. Quansett-Fowles displayed his photographs
on every occasion and in less than a week she awakened in him
a state of some excitement.

'Last night while you were out making a beast of yourself,
Jean Roy – Free French, remember? – and Bob Capa dropped
in.'

'*The* Bob Capa? The one who took those incredible pictures
of the D-Day landing on Omaha Beach?!'

'That's him. I don't think you were around when he was in
London.'

'I would have loved to have met him – is he coming
back?'

'No, he's leaving tonight for Korea – he says there's a shambles out there. The Russians agreed to pull out but they're
building up an Army instead. I didn't understand what the
Hell he was talking about but he's off because he's sure there's
going to be trouble. Anyway, he took your pictures with him.'

'To Korea?'

'No, you twit! To a big agency, because he thinks they're

311

great and he's sure they'll want to buy them.'

Stani was flabbergasted.

'Bob *Capa*! He's the *greatest*! Which agency?'

'I don't know, darling. Magnum? Magnus? Acne? Acme? He wasn't quite sure himself which one he'd take them to but whoever they are will be calling you today – that he promised.'

Stani's hero worship of Capa notwithstanding, when by lunchtime no agency of any sort had even acknowledged possession of his precious photographs, he became anxious. Mrs. Quansett-Fowles left to join some friends so he attempted to calm his nerves by a visit to the Museum of Modern Art. Two hours later, stunned by the vitality of Francis, Hartung, Pollock and de Kooning, he returned to find a sheaf of messages enjoining him to call a Jack Mulligan as soon as possible.

Mr. Mulligan, who turned out to be the senior partner of Mulligan and Ryan, was not a man who wasted time.

'We all think your stuff is wonderful,' he said. 'How soon can you leave for British Columbia?'

'*British Columbia*? What do I do when I get there?' Stani asked.

'A photographic report of the Doukobors,' said Mr. Mulligan.

'Er . . . I think I'd better come and see you.'

'113 East 55 Street. I'm ready when you are.'

Jack Mulligan, red-haired and moustached, was about five years older than Stani; like Bob Capa he had been a combat photographer during the War. Stani's pictures covered a table in his spacious, well-decorated office.

'I've a big offer for this lot from *Look*,' he said. 'They're crazy about them. *Life* wants them too but they'd like to tie you down to a contract.' He laughed. 'By the way, do you want us to represent you or would you rather look around first?'

The business was soon concluded. Stani was offered the choice of a contract whereby Mulligan and Ryan would act as selling agents for anything he chose to produce, or an arrangement under which he would accept special assignments selected by them and be paid a handsome weekly retainer against a fifty-fifty split of what they obtained from the results. With little of his Metropolis money left, Stani did not hesitate and by the time he left the office he had a cheque for four weeks salary in advance, expense money, a round trip airline ticket to Calgary, Alberta, a written agreement covering the hefty sale of his surfing pictures, the camera of his choice with necessary accessories, a map of Western Canada and a very sketchy idea indeed of what to expect of the Doukobors.

'Use up a lot of film,' said Mr. Mulligan, 'and don't rush it. A week there should do it easy. Keep in touch with us . . . we may have something even bigger for you on the way back.'

They shook hands and like a little boy with a good report card from school, Stani rushed back to the Pierre Hotel to show Mrs. Quansett-Fowles the latest fruits of her warm heart.

23

In New York the firm of Mulligan and Ryan had seemed the very peak of American efficiency; by the time Stani had reached Calgary he had downgraded this opinion.

He had been dispatched on overbooked planes via Chicago, Winnipeg and Saskatoon and for forty-seven hours had chafed, cajoled and languished in overheated and overpopulated waiting rooms. Trying to keep his thoughts from flying like homing pigeons to Pandora, he had waded through mounds of magazines and expended several rolls of film, preserving for posterity the misery of air travel when it goes wrong. He also learned by heart the meagre summary Mulligan and Ryan had provided on the subject of the Doukhobors:

The word meaning 'Fighters against the Spirit' was given by Russian Orthodox Church in 1880's to group of peasants who, church decided, were fighting against the Spirit of God. Group therefore renounced Church preferring own prayer sessions and weird chants. Also considered men and animals equal, including government officials whose laws they disregarded notably military service.

Persecuted by following Czars; –

Nicholas I

Alexander III

Nicholas II

Banished to Caucasus 1890 where thousands died. Saved 1900 by Tolstoy and 'Society of Friends in England' who raised funds to ship them to Saskatchewan, worked building Canadian Pacific Railway till outbreak World War I 1914. Refused military service even to become conscientious objectors. Outbreak WORLD WAR II 1939 same reaction. Refused arms and bombed Canadian Pacific Railway for transporting guns many jailed. Now settled Kootenay Hills British Columbia hard core group again raising hell today.

314

In Calgary Stani rented a Ford Convertible and headed West to the foothills of the Rockies. He had intended to cross the mountains at Kicking Horse Pass and spend the night beside the Columbia River, but after a hundred miles he decided to stop amid the beauties of Banff, where Queen Victoria had ordered a large area reserved for future generations to bathe themselves in the hot mineral springs that gush from the mountains. The hotel, a huge baronial edifice that would not have been out of place in Bavaria, was echoing with out of season emptiness but his room was warm and comfortable with a magnificent view of cataracts at the bend of the river below and the summit of Cascade Mountain pink-sugared where the setting sun kissed the first dusting of snow. Stani bathed, then wandered downstairs in search of a pre-dinner drink.

After passing through vast halls and an empty lounge in which three men in kilts were singing lustily to guitars, he came to rest before a red-coated barman in a panelled room with an open fireplace. He ordered a Scotch on the rocks.

The barman placed the drink before him and nodded at his sparsely populated domain.

'When the snow comes you won't know this place,' he said. 'They're just getting around to developing the skiing around here. We'll soon have miles and miles of it, great powder too – real dry. You a skier?'

'I did a bit as a kid in Europe.'

'Come back later,' said the barman. 'I was born and raised here, there's a guy I know has a helicopter, we could go up to the Bugaboos, a bunch of Austrians here last Spring said it's the best they'd ever struck anywhere in the world, not for beginners though – damn near perpendicular some of it!'

'I think I'll pass.'

Above the barman's head was a long mirror. Stani happened to look up from stirring his Scotch and for a split second his heart missed a beat. A tall girl crossing behind him held her head the same way and walked with the same sensuous, graceful assurance as Pandora. Even as he caught that first reflection, he knew there could be no further resemblances, but he continued to watch her with a sad fascination.

She was dressed in an expensively tailored, grey-green jacket, and slacks to match, with turtleneck sweater of slightly

315

lighter shade. Her hair was auburn and shining as though polished. A balding man of comfortable girth rose from a corner booth at her approach. When the girl had settled herself the man lit her cigarette and she glanced casually around the room; her gaze fell upon Stani. It was too late for him to turn away and for a long beat their eyes held. Stani broke the contact, ordered a refill and engaged the barman in further conversation. From time to time, however, he checked in the mirror, seeking, in his loneliness to extract a pinch of pleasure from witnessing Pandora's movements if only by proxy. On several occasions their eyes met again and once in the distortion of the mirror he thought she smiled. The barman droned on about the changes that had been made in the hotel and how the clientele had gone down since before the War.

'There's a lot of money around, I grant you,' he said mournfully, 'but it's changed hands, the wrong people have it now.' Stani expressed the opinion that the couple in the corner booth seemed to uphold the standard. The barman shrugged.

'Just came in today. American East Coast from the sound of 'em, never seen 'em before.'

Stani sipped his drink.

'Pardon me,' came a voice at his elbow. 'Mrs. Podlubny and I were wondering if you're alone, and if you might care to join us for a drink?'

'That's very kind of you,' said Stani.

When the girl shook hands he noticed the set of her eyes, her uptilted nose, the length of her fingers and of her highly-lacquered nails.

'We thought you looked a little forlorn sitting there.' She smiled (the teeth looked American-perfect). 'Big hotels out of season are like Grand Central at four in the morning.'

After the points she had so far notched up, Mrs. Podlubny's voice was something of a disappointment, high-pitched as though she had been speaking too much in crowded restaurants.

The tubby man introduced himself as Jerry Gonzler and announced, 'Loretta here is celebrating!'

The reason for the celebration was explained. Mr. Gonzler and Mrs. Podlubny had lately been in Reno where he had cleverly negotiated a more than satisfactory settlement for his

316

client in exchange for which Mr. Horace K. Podlubny had obtained his freedom to marry the lady of his second choice.

'And what brought you up to Lake Louise?' Stani enquired.

'Horrie had an investment here in Alberta . . .' Mrs. Podlubny began.

'. . . and now Loretta has it!' the lawyer interrupted. 'Five hundred prime acres up around Leduc. Last week, just after Loretta's settlement was signed, a big well blew in for Atlantic about a hundred yards from the corner of her piece. I've scheduled a meeting with some big hitters from Edmonton over dinner tonight – they want to talk with us about it.'

'Mr. Gonzler does my talking for me,' said Mrs. Podlubny. 'Do you like sparkling Burgundy?'

Among French offerings Stani rated sparkling Burgundy down among the frog legs, the blood sausage and the tripe, but some male urge to please made him claim to love it. Mrs. Podlubny was delighted.

'Let's have a bottle!' she cried happily. 'Horrie just *loved* sparkling Burgundy.'

Mrs. Podlubny permitted no back tracking. Before and after the departure of her lawyer to keep his appointment, she directed a steady stream of sparkling Burgundy into both Stani and herself. She was a guileless creature, he decided, and curiously vulnerable considering the background she unfolded. Her election at the age of seventeen as Miss Whole Wheat of Spartanburg, Iowa had led to modelling jobs in Chicago and Detroit, graduation to becoming a sought-after Powers Model in New York, with comfortable accommodation in the girls' hotel the Barbizon Plaza, and a constantly ringing telephone. Among her most persistent callers had been Horace K. Podlubny, twenty years her senior, a man, according to her, of flashing good looks, dark curly hair, a persuasive turn of phrase and a fetching line of footware pouring from his factories in New Jersey. To start with, she told Stani, she had enjoyed 'Horrie's' company and the bulwark a steady boyfriend provided against 'all those young guys who liked to be seen with a good-looking doll and hoped for some action at the end of the evening'. Loretta Podlubny related in detail her late husband's maneuvres to persuade her to leave the Barbizon Plaza, where men were allowed to penetrate no further than the lobby, and the

317

problems of finding a flat in a nice part of town where she could receive a gentleman caller.

Hungry and flushed with the despised sparkling Burgundy, Stani sought to stem the tide of minutiae which lapped around her descriptions of refurbishing her final nesting place, and suggested some blotting paper in the form of dinner.

A maitre d'hotel bowed them to a distant corner of the largely empty dining room; during the long approach march Stani put a supporting hand beneath Mrs. Podlubny's elbow. No sooner were they seated and peering at each other over the tops of immense menus than Mrs. Podlubny announced: 'I need to go to the little girls' room.'

During her long absence Stani toyed with the idea of deserting the field and leaving the lady alone with her awful wine, but hunger and loneliness kept him anchored to the booth, staring owl-like at the 'Chef's selections'. He decided that he must eliminate all comparisons with Pandora, concentrate on his companion's very beautiful face and other attributes, and display some interest in the catalogue of 'Horrie's' virtues which would surely be continuing.

During the meal Mrs. Podlubny gradually moved closer to Stani. The pressure of her knee, followed by the warmth of her thigh against his, was not unpleasant and on the few occasions when she asked him about himself he had little hesitation in presenting a picture of a travelling bachelor of no fixed affiliation. The sparkling Burgundy was tasting better too. If he had been asked later to testify under oath as to who had made the decisive move, he would have been hard put to comply: probably it had been a joint effort because a possible outcome of the evening had long been on both their minds. In any event, outside Mrs. Podlubny's door they kissed; gently, almost shyly at first, then desperately with thrusting loins and groping hands.

Mrs. Podlubny broke off the long encounter. Holding him at arm's length, she smiled up into his eyes. 'Are you going to tuck me up in bed?' she asked.

Even as Stani nodded he wished he'd had the nerve to shake his head. During the long minutes when the warm body had been undulating suggestively against his, he had once more been thinking of Pandora, and had most unfairly become dis-

318

turbed by the discovery that the 'American Perfect' teeth of his companion were encased in caps. Loretta Podlubny handed him her key.

The heavily overfurnished room was dominated by a large mahogany bed. Prominent on a side table were two bottles of sparkling Burgundy.

'I thought it might be a good idea,' she giggled. 'I asked for them to be sent up when I went to the can!' There was a strange, metallic hardware-store odour about the room which she quickly explained. 'They've been cleaning the carpets on this floor since it's out of season, but the view's so gorgeous from these rooms I asked to be put up here anyway.'

As far as Mrs. Podlubny was concerned, the preliminaries were at an end and the main bout due to start. She filled two glasses, removed her jacket and slipped the turtleneck sweater over her head, then she put her arms round Stani and pressed against him.

'You have to be the best-looking thing on two legs,' she breathed. 'Unhook me.'

She turned her back and as he fumbled with the catch of her bra the first contact between his fingers and the gleaming skin of her beautiful back signalled a slight coarseness of texture which came as a jolting contrast to the satiny softness and exquisite patina of the one he missed so much. Lacking the nerve to extricate himself at this late date from the game-plan to which he was now committed, he bent and kissed the nape of her neck. She wiggled her behind against him and led him towards the battlefield of the bed, there she sat, smiled very sweetly and extended her long legs in his direction.

'Shoes,' she said. 'One at a time please.'

Stani obliged by slipping them off her feet and dropping them on the floor. She undid a zipper and helpfully arched her bottom off the bed.

'Next please!'

Off came her slacks with a conjuror's flourish. She ran her tongue across her lips.

'If you think you're going to rape me you'd better get undressed yourself!'

Stani, beset with guilt that he felt so little enthusiasm for the scenario, hoped he might at least succeed in moving Pandora further back in the stalls if he entered more wholeheartedly into the spirit of the evening, so, after a flurry of unlacing, unbuttoning, unzipping and copious swigs of wine he advanced upon the expectant Mrs. Podlubny clad only in his underpants.

'Ooh!' she squealed and disappeared beneath the bed. He bumped his head as he followed, but gamely flushed her out on the far side, grabbing her by the ankle and ripping at her panties.

'Oh! You *beast*,' she cried happily. 'You *are* raping me!'

In the act of sexual fulfilment Stani was far from selfish. He enjoyed giving pleasure, and within reason believed in diversification as part of that service. One lady long ago had confided that she liked nothing better than to sit in chocolate cakes and he had gone along with the game. So now he played cat and mouse all over the rough, evil-smelling carpet, cornering the lovely Mrs. Podlubny behind chairs and pouncing upon her in the open spaces. Pandora's disc and chain swung into the scene at the most inopportune moments, but he gamely stalked her, captured her, kissed her, played with her and slapped her bottom when she presented it for that purpose, until at last she begged him to take her.

This was the moment he had been dreading. Every instinct told him that this was no trollop, no cheap little bar pick-up . . . this was a nice and very unhappy girl, paying him the supreme compliment.

He summoned all sorts of erotic fantasies to his aid and pumped up and down desperately while the compliant creature beneath him did her best to bring matters to a successful conclusion. But Pandora was in his brain, heart and body and there was nothing he could do to alleviate the frustration of the beautiful girl in his arms.

'I'm sorry,' he panted at last. 'I'm just *terribly, terribly* sorry.'

The girl became very still. 'I've turned you off,' she said in a small voice. 'It's all my fault.'

Then with great wracking sobs she started to cry. 'OH! Horrie! . . . Oh! Horrie!'

Stani moved beside her and to comfort her hesitantly put an arm across her body. She did not flinch nor seek to repulse him; he could feel her misery. After a while her sobs turned to shivers so he carried her to the bed as defenceless and unresisting as a

320

child. He turned off the light, slipped beneath the sheets and lay with her in his arms till she was calm, then very gently and using another name he told her of the existence of Pandora.

The dawn light was filtering through the curtains when he gathered his scattered clothing and dressed. Before he left he crossed to the bed and looked down at the dark silhouette of the girl's head against the whiteness. She stirred and he could see the outline of her smile. She held up her arms.

'Please come here.'

Stani lowered his head, her hands framed his face, then she kissed him innocently on the lips.

'Good luck.'

'You too,' said Stani.

In the early light the pines were inky black against the grey sky, a sure sign of rain, and indeed before he reached the summit of Vermilion Pass the downpour was considerable. On the Columbia River side of the mountains, however, the sky cleared and to the West he was able to enjoy the soaring views of the Purcell Range. Down in the valley the great freight trains of the Canadian Pacific were huffing and puffing along the banks of the River, smoke was spiralling from the Indian dwellings of the Reservations. Among the pine trees he noticed so many Scottish names upon the roadside mailboxes that his mind wandered back to Spitfire training in Scotland, to his days as Mrs. Quansett-Fowles's lodger and from there, of course, to Pandora. Would he ever be whole again? Would it ever heal over? He wished desperately that she was beside him now, hair flowing as she enjoyed this adventure in a different country.

It was evening when he pulled in to a motel beside Lake Windermere. He booked a room and made his first inquiries about the Doukhobors.

'They're crazy!' said Mr. Farquharson, the owner. 'Just plum crazy! You'll find their settlements up them little valleys around Mount Farnham, Horsethief Creek, Dutch Creek, Toby Creek and there's others on down at Skookcumchuck. I don't meddle with them myself . . . they're crazy I tell you!'

Once he had tracked them down Stani spent three days among the Doukhobors, surrounded by grim foothills, in a flat area in the pine forests called Redknife. Grey granite boulders

the size of haystacks dictated the shape of the cultivated patches, clusters of small stone and wood dwellings were visible
among the trees. When he arrived, one of these was on fire and
a group of around a hundred men, women and children stood
watching the blaze with apparent satisfaction. They had the
build of Russian peasants. Stani recognized the design at once.
When his father had been with the Embassy in Sweden and he
had been taken on trips to Leningrad, the sunlit fields *en route*
had been full of these sturdy square shapes wielding scythes
and pitchforks; and on May Day and other ominous occasions,
photographs of the top of Lenin's Tomb in Moscow's Red
Square had displayed a human frieze of these squat forms,
blurred by box-like overcoats and eccentric headgear.

There was certainly no mistaking the peasant outlines of the
group now standing quietly around the burning building,
because most of them were stark naked. Stani clicked a long
lens to his camera and went to work from a discreet distance.
Four policemen arrived in a jeep followed by a truck and he
duly recorded the arrest of three naked men and one naked
woman. As soon as they had been herded unprotesting into the
truck, four fully-clothed onlookers stripped down to the buff
and with no change of expression fed their clothing into the
flames. This routine was repeated till the truck drove away
filled with naked Doukhobors. Stani approached the police
sergeant, explained that he was a press photographer and
enquired about the burning building. The sergeant was chew-
ing gum.

'It's the School House,' he said.

'And what were those people being arrested for?'

'Arson and indecent exposure. They've been setting fire to
their schools up and down these valleys for a month or more.'

'What's the idea?'

The sergeant spat in the dirt and shook his head.

'They're crazy as loons. They're demonstrating against the
start of World War *Three*, for God's sake!'

'How many are locked up?'

The sergeant shrugged. 'The jails at Kimberly and Cran-
brook are filled up right now, about all we can do after today is
take their names. Most times they're real peaceful folk but
every now and then they burn down their homes and bomb the

322

railway!'

The Doukhobors of Redknife displayed a certain awareness of their nudity by turning their backs on Stani's camera so he soon tired of photographing white cubical rear ends, even though the weatherbeaten necks and forearms helped his compositions. He found other settlements in the foothills and witnessed several privately owned dwellings being put to the torch. The Doukhobors, despite their antipathy to his camera, were never hostile to him. Towards the end of his visit several posed willingly for portraits and he amassed quite a gallery of earthy square-jawed faces, all, including those of the children, remarkable for their clear and strangely calm eyes.

'We don't want schools or churches,' they told him. 'The spirit of God is inside each of us and tells us every day what to do; we go to church when we talk to each other, we don't need meeting places to say our prayers, we pray inside all the time.'

'But why do you burn your own houses?' Stani asked.

They looked at each other, smiled and spoke as though they were teaching a child.

'Worldly goods mean nothing to us,' they explained. 'We remind ourselves of that now and then.'

'And the schools?'

'We pass on our knowledge to our children,' they said. 'We don't need books. God tells us what to say.'

An old man spoke up. 'You see, young man, Love is all for us. When one of us is ill or hungry or needs shelter we have a chance to show that love. That's why we never fight or drink or carry weapons of any sort because killing and violence, even towards animals, is the opposite of what God has taught us and what we have taught our children.'

'A policeman told me about bombing the railway.'

The old man smiled indulgently. 'Only when nobody's about,' he said. 'We want people down below these mountains to remember that God will never forgive another war and those big bombs they're planning. He'll know then that his message of love has not gotten through to this earth and he will surely destroy it. They can lock us up, do anything they please with us, but when they ask us to take an oath 'to tell the truth, the whole truth and nothing but the truth, so help me God', we ask them one question – Whose God? Yours or ours?'

323

Before he left those mysterious valleys Stani decided that he would destroy any pictures he had taken that might have the remotest chance of holding up the Doukhobors to ridicule.

24

The return trip to Calgary was beautiful but like watching the same movie twice in one week – there were no surprises; Stani's attention wandered. He was anything but proud of himself when he reviewed his treatment of Loretta Podlubny; in trying to forget his own problems he had probably compounded hers. But during the course of that odd evening she had made an observation which returned to haunt him.

'I've learned one thing about close relationships, and that is that both parties have to give much more than they think they're giving if it's ever going to work out. If you both honestly and truly *think* you're giving fifty per cent, you might in fact only be giving thirty per cent. I'm a high school drop-out but I can figure out that leaves forty per cent unaccounted for and *that's* where it gets all fouled up. Next time around I'm giving a hundred and fifty per cent, just to be sure.'

All the way to Calgary he checked and cross-checked his memory for warning signals he might have failed to pick up that Russell Bancroft had had his foot in the door with Pandora. He tortured himself, too, with questions: Had there been others? Was it his fault? Where had he gone wrong? Should he have been on hand day and night in case she needed him?

He thought she had wanted him not to feel tied down. She had seemed worried about *his* happiness. But had he worried enough about *hers*? Had he taken her too much for granted? By the time he reached the outskirts of the city, of one thing he was sure: he would stop running, he would face the problem.

In the centre of town he found what he needed: a quiet room in a quiet hotel. He checked in, soaked in a hot bath to relax, compose his thoughts and pluck up his courage; then he placed a person to person call to Pandora.

For days and nights he had longed for the sound of her voice, but now he found himself afraid of what he might hear. Tones of cold distaste and dismissal? Tethering Bancroft to Louella Parsons' palm tree had been an act of pure schoolboy lunacy, which could easily have ruined the career of the woman he loved. And then, why had he failed to give her an explanation, at least, of his disappearance? And at least a chance to explain the tableau he had seen in the projection room? Perhaps she would refuse to take his call. Perhaps he would hear the oily voice of Bancroft himself!

'Miss Ricardo's residence.'

(It was the voice of Lilly Mae.)

'This is Calgary, Canada, calling for Miss Ricardo.'

'Well, she's not home right now.'

'Can you tell me when she will be available?'

'She's out of town, won't be back for a while.'

Stani was sure she must be somewhere with Bancroft. So when the Calgary operator asked if he wanted to keep the call in, but he mumbled 'No – it's okay.'

He placed a call to Chuck Pesnick. He liked Chuck, it would be good to talk to him: but he was such a 'company man' he might not want to become involved if Bancroft was calling the shots. Stani was sitting on the edge of the bed with a towel round his waist, another over his shoulders. He shivered; he had not dried himself properly.

'Mr. Pesnick is on his way to New York, he can be reached at the Metropolis Offices there, Murray Hill 8 3672.'

When that number did not answer Stani realized it was ten o'clock at night in New York. He decided to try Mulligan at his home, and found him, bubbling over. Sales of the surfing shots were booming, he reported, picture magazines and periodicals all over the world were falling over themselves to get them. When might he expect Stani's Doukobor stuff?

'Hey! We've a chance to get lucky. Old Henry Ford has said he might go for a home layout. If we can get it – that's a sure winner. Can you drop off in Detroit on your way back? It'll mean hanging in there for a few days while he makes up his mind. But if you keep your eyes open while you're waiting you might pick up something real good in that place. Motown is really jumping right now.'

326

Stani agreed to go to Detroit for a few days on spec; he told himself he would talk to Chuck when he got there. He dressed and went down to the coffee shop for a meal. With one hand he picked unhappily at a tuna fish salad, with the other he turned the pages of the *Calgary Clarion*. Unable as usual to bear the pain any mention of Pandora brought him, he shunned the Entertainment Section, so he missed Louella Parsons's Column which carried that day a breathless description of 'Metropolis Pictures Big Upcoming 3-Network Television Show'.

After Lilly Mae's illuminating request for a new clothes line Chuck Pesnick had spent several days dissuading Pandora from making any far-reaching decisions. She had considered everything from returning forever to Hawksmoor to diving headfirst into monasticism.

'Why doesn't he call? I *hate* this house now,' she moaned. 'I've wrecked everything, we were *so* happy together, I can't bear it that I've made him so miserable. You *must* find him for me, Chuck. *PLEASE.*'

Pesnick had done his best to cheer her up but his own heart was leaden. Stani was a proud young man and he had serious doubts that Pandora would be seeing him again.

Russell Bancroft called Pesnick to his office and ordered him to milk the story of Metropolis' 'Three Network entry into Television'.

'You can really lay into this one!' he crowed. 'The other Studios say we're going over to the enemy, but they're just pissed off because we're way out ahead of them!'

Together they mapped out a campaign for announcing every feature of the forthcoming programme, acclaiming the signing of each well-known performer and rubbing in the the fact that ninety per cent of the whole would be on film.

'Canned Entertainment will always be on top,' said Bancroft, biting the end off a cigar. 'Television will drown without it, except for sports, news and talk shows. What's the point in all that effort and talent being wasted, seen just once then flushed down the toilet? "Live" shows are for the birds! The Networks insist we give them one dramatic segment "live" – so we'll keep in the one with Jan Ricardo and Judd Dugdale. That way, we get to plug *Ruby Ring*. Except for that segment, and the Master of Ceremonies, the whole show will be on film.'

'That's one hell of a break for her – million dollar exposure! Have you told her yet?'

Bancroft rolled his cigar between his fingers and leaned back in his chair.

'No need. She's under contract. She does what she's told. Go ahead and announce it. Casting will contact her.'

Pesnick did not look up from the notes he was making.

'I just thought that since you had been moulding her career personally – you might prefer to give her the good news yourself.'

Bancroft exhaled blue fumes and smiled.

'Confidentially, just between you and me, I've had to back off a little in that area. She was beginning to think she had a Favoured Nations clause in her contract – you know how it is with all these chicks, sooner or later they wind up with one eye on that casting couch.'

He rose from his desk to signal the close of the meeting.

'That tame Pole of hers turned out to be a real ungrateful son-of-a-bitch. After all I did for him, the bastard never even showed up for the job I got him with Avedon.'

'Where is he now?'

'We're looking for him.'

'I'll have a word with my contacts at the Police Department if you like – they have an inter-city Missing Persons set-up.'

'Yea, do that, will you – be sure to let me know.

'Will do,' Pesnick said. 'Incidentally, the air date for the show's awful tight, isn't it?'

'You said it! The Network contracts took a lot of ironing out. But we still can make it. I plan two crews to film the acts being gotten together out here and two more for the stuff back East. Each segment will have its own director and I'll hire one overall Super Producer to integrate the whole show.'

'Who d'you plan for that?'

'I can't stand the son-of-a-bitch, but he's well organized. Also, by giving him the job I can pay off his contract and avoid a long lawsuit. Maxwell Stern.'

As soon as he could, Chuck Pesnick hot-footed it out to Brentwood, but the electrifying news about the TV show –

328

news that any young Hollywood actress would have given her soul to hear – passed almost unnoticed by Pandora.

'I'm delighted Russell has decided to avoid me,' she said. 'What a dreary, pretentious little man he's turned out to be. But where is Stani? That's all I care about. I *have* to talk to him.'

Chuck tried hard to console her.

'It's this place,' she wailed. 'It's evil. I wish I'd never set foot in Hollywood.'

'Don't give up so easily, Honey, there's a lot of good in Hollywood. You've been unlucky with the people not the place. Don't forget, for every Sam Goldwyn, David Selznick or De Mille there's scores of Russell Bancrofts and Maxwell Sterns. For every director as great as Ford, Wyler, Huston or Zinnemann there are hundreds of Ted Gruskins. And for every Gable, Garbo, Bogart or Astaire there are thousands like Judd Dugdale and Rita Haas. Think of Hollywood as a lily pond – colourful as hell on the surface but underneath it's a tangle of rotten weeds, full of frogs and water rats.'

Pandora hugged him.

'You're a sweet man, Chuck, and you sound like a drunken landscape gardener! You know what I really mean. I'm disgusted with *myself*!'

The Studio dispatched Pandora to New York ten days before the Big Show. Not able to face the memories of the St. Regis she booked a small suite in the unobtrusive Blackstone Hotel. In his hotel in Detroit Stani missed Louella Parsons' next titillating reference, as follows:

'Judd Dugdale wings to New York today to join his co-star in the only "live" part of the Great Hollywood Orientated Super Spectacular! Dazzling Jan Ricardo is eagerly awaiting his arrival . . . is this an ongoing, meaningful romance?'

Stani was still awaiting word that he would be granted a couple of hours of Henry Ford's time. In the end, Ford suddenly fell dangerously ill and Stani booked himself on the evening flight to New York.

To fill in time he indulged in an afternoon of practice photography along the banks of the Allegheny River. While lining up a routine shot of water cascading over a thirty foot weir he noticed in the top corner of his frame a large cabin cruiser. Cries of alarm floated downstream and he raised his head. Eight people were aboard the boat. She was gyrating slowly in the deceptively lazy current; there was no sound of an engine. Before his horrified eyes a man and a woman jumped overboard and attempted to swim ashore. They were swept ahead of the boat and at increasing speed over the fall; thousands of tons of water fell on them – they never surfaced.

People ran shouting and gesticulating to the bank; but by the time the cruiser was twenty yards from the brink a horrified silence had fallen and in slow motion the tragedy unfolded. The cruiser seemed to slide serenely down the face of the waterfall, maintaining an almost upright position; screams were heard above the roar of the water until with a noise like thunder it cascaded upon the deck, washing three people overboard and slamming the rest against the rail or parts of the superstructure. The cruiser did not drift away from the fall because the undertow against her keel kept her stationary, pinned beneath the killer cascade. The watchers on the river bank wept or cursed helplessly as one after another the yachting party were prised loose from their handholds, sluiced down the deck and over the side. Stani helped retrieve their bodies from sandbanks half a mile downstream.

In New York Mr. Mulligan listened spellbound as Stani described the scene.

'Come on back,' he said. 'You've got another scoop there fella!'

'I didn't take any pictures,' Stani said.

25

The night before the first rehearsal Pandora did not sleep. She worked on her script; she loved the role and felt confident about it – it fitted her like a glove. She tried to learn some of the longer speeches but it was difficult to concentrate. She was worried.

She worried above all about Stani. *Why* had she heard nothing from him? It was so unlike him to leave things unfinished. He *must* give her a chance to try to explain! Or, to let her love explain for her. Had he been in an accident? Where was he?

Then, too, she worried about the unknown of the huge Television show and her first effort 'live'. Her heart thumped when she thought what 'live' meant. The actor's nightmare, recorded through the centuries, was to be on stage and suddenly not able to remember a word. On stage, salvation was always at hand in the shape of a prompter with an eye on 'the book'; making movies, it was ever present . . . you just started over again till you got it right or had the elusive line written on a board, a piece of scenery, or another actor's shirt-front. But 'live' on television – there was no way out, no one could help you, and if they tried, millions would hear.

She worried about the television actors. Would they like her? Most of them would be from the New York stage and she had heard they looked upon film actors as second-class citizens. She worried about Mr. Harbottle, the Director. Oh, how she hoped he would be *kind*, especially on her first day. She worried about what to wear, about her hair, about the change of time making sleep so difficult, about the alarm not working and the night porter forgetting to wake her, about the car which Metropolis had promised to send not showing up. She worried and worried, she cried a little too and dozed, but she did not sleep. At six o'clock the alarm went off.

In the bathroom her sun-kissed skin looked yellow, dark smudges under the eyes required camouflage. Coffee made her nerves feel exposed. She was dressed and downstairs waiting for the studio car twenty minutes before it was due; forty minutes later it had still not arrived and she was standing panicky in the street waving at cabs full of people. The rehearsal had been called for 8.30; at 8.45 Pandora pushed open the heavy door of a disused Drill Hall off First Avenue.

Inside it was cold, damp and sinister, its last occupants had been the American Bund. In the middle of a splintered floor was a row of thirty wooden chairs upon which sat actors and actresses of every age, shape and size dressed in wind breakers, sweaters, corduroys and overcoats. When a badly frightened Pandora burst in, they gazed upon her with little change of expression, but managed to convey an impression of hostility.

Facing the actors, seated at a table flanked by two assistants, a script girl, a coffee urn and cartons of paper cups was the Director, a dark, pale-faced man of thirty with horn rimmed glasses and a receding hairline. He glanced at his watch.

'You're late.'

'I'm *terribly* sorry,' Pandora panted. 'The Studio promised to send a car. It never arrived.'

'No excuse. Where is your friend Dugdale?'

'I'm afraid I don't know,' said Pandora, and then trying to be helpful added, 'the last time I saw him he was sitting beside Lake Okeechobee.'

One or two of the younger actors tittered and Mr. Harbottle frowned. He turned to an assistant.

'Give Miss Ricardo a script.'

'Oh, I have mine with me,' said Pandora brightly, grateful that she had done something right.

'What's it called?'

'*The Girls in their Summer Dresses*, by Irwin Shaw.'

'We're not doing that, we're doing *The Dogwood Tree* by Henri de Gâcher. Take a seat.'

Pandora settled herself at the end of the line next to a dignified looking actor with a senatorial shock of white hair. He rose and bowed. 'I'm Budleigh Salterton. I play your grandfather.'

The Director called for silence.

332

'While we are waiting for our other *Hollywood* star, study your scripts carefully. Most of you are from the Group Theatre and have experience in Live Television, so I don't anticipate any problems. Mr. de Gâcher, the author of this piece, will be here at ten o'clock for the read-through. Small changes could be made with his consent at that time, none thereafter. Three days from now everyone must be word perfect, scripts will be discarded. Air date in eight days.'

Pandora had loved Irwin Shaw's touching and beautifully structured short story; with the turn of each page of *The Dogwood Tree* her heart sank and her panic rose. She was to play a Southern Belle in crinoline and sash saying 'Hush-up' and 'Fiddle-dee-dee' behind a fan! And what about the Southern accent, in front of countless millions of Americans too?

'Sorry folks! Somebody goofed – no limmo! Christ, it's cold in here!' Judd Dugdale in ten gallon hat and belted ankle-length camel-hair overcoat stamped into the Drill Hall followed by a photographer, his agent and Justin. He spotted Pandora, rushed over and pulled her to him.

'Hi Doll! Sorry I'm late. You look *GREAT*!' The photographer took pictures.

At this point the Director decided to exert his authority.

'May I have your name please?'

Judd kissed Pandora again and spoke over his shoulder.

'Give me yours first, Buddy-Boy. My mother told me never to speak to strangers.'

Like occupants of the Royal Box at Wimbledon, the eyes of the onlookers swivelled back and forth; they were a partisan crowd, the lines were clearly drawn. The Hollywood 'stars', over-dressed, overpaid and over-publicized, were about to get their come-uppance. But they underestimated the street fighter cunning of a graduate from the extra ranks of the Hollywood Jungle. Judd Dugdale walked over to the Director, kissed him on both cheeks and said:

'You're *beautiful*! Now, can I meet all these lovely people – we're gonna have a lotta fun together.'

Introductions over, Judd dismissed his entourage and sat down next to Pandora. Together they studied their scripts.

'This is crap!' he whispered. Pandora nodded.

At ten o'clock the assembled company was presented to

333

Henri de Gâcher, a haunted-looking individual with the blackened eyes of an insomniac and the orange fingers of a chain smoker. The script girl started a stop watch and the Director described the setting of the first scene.

'A plantation in the Deep South, wicker chairs grouped beneath the tall columns of a high veranda. Elegant ladies and gentlemen are being served tea and mint juleps. Your cue Mr. Dugdale.'

'Just a minute,' Judd said. 'We're not supposed to be any good at this stage of the game, are we?'

'Yes,' answered the Director, 'you are. That's what you're paid for.'

'Jesus!' said Judd. 'Well, here goes.' He read his lines to Pandora.

'Mary-Lee honey, why don't you go fix your old Grandpa a drink?'

'Sho nuff,' read Pandora. 'Ah have buckwheat cakes fer you too, Grandpa.' Despite the cold in the Drill Hall, Pandora was perspiring.

The distinguished actor on the other side of Pandora gave his opening line the full benefit of his pear-shaped tones.

'God's nightgown! Child,' he boomed, 'don't give me no buckwheat cakes, give me *chitterlings*! An I'll show 'em one Southerner can lick a hundred Yankees!'

There was a pause.

'Who's playing Dan the butler?' the Director asked.

A well-dressed black actor with white hair spoke up.

'Sorry Mister Harbottle, my cue.'

'You enter left,' said the Director, 'carrying a silver tray piled high with bloodstained bandages. In the distance there is the sound of banjos and knucklebones. You speak.'

The actor cleared his throat.

'Ah done ast dem ter come on in de house cos seben darkies done died.'

'God's nightgown!' roared Budleigh Salterton again.

'Jesus!' whispered Judd.

After the harrowing experience of the read-through, the actors waited expectantly. Mr. Harbottle asked if anyone had any questions.

'Yes,' said Judd. 'Why aren't we doing *The Girls in their*

Summer Dresses?'

Harbottle swallowed.

'This Three Network Special is sponsored by the Steel Companies and it seems that the vice president of Jones and Laughlin, who's coordinating it, has a wife who comes from Atlanta.'

'So does most of this script,' muttered Judd. 'It's straight out of *Gone with the Wind.'*

'I think,' said Harbottle, 'that you owe Mr. de Gâcher an apology.'

'That's nothing to what Mr. de Gâcher owes Margaret Mitchell. "God's nightgown", for Chrissakes! Why, some old fart at the barbecue was saying that every other minute in the book!' Judd leaned forward and spoke across Pandora. 'Isn't that right, sir?'

Budleigh Salterton looked pained.

Henri de Gâcher rose from the table.

'If I am to be accused of plagiarism, I shall leave instantly. In fact I have never read *Gone with the Wind.'*

'Well I have,' said Judd, 'twice, and I'm telling you some old fart in it says "God's nightgown!" about fifty times.'

'I'm perfectly willing to change that line to "God's nightcap" if it makes you happy.'

'How about "God's underpants"? At least we'd get a laugh.'

After further arguments, including one concerning the improbability of southern gentlemen eating 'chitterlings' which Judd claimed were hog entrails, the staple diet of slaves not masters, the author of *The Dogwood Tree* departed 'to keep a prior engagement with my publishers'.

Coffee and doughnuts were available during a short break while the two assistants with plans of the Southern Mansion drew chalk marks upon the floor of the Drill Hall. Then rehearsal of the opening scene started in earnest.

As he would a hundred times during the next seven days, Judd Dugdale opened the proceedings.

'Mary-Lee, honey, why don't you go fix your old Grandpa a drink?'

Rehearsal ended at six-thirty.

'It's early, go home and learn your lines,' ordered Mr. Harbottle. 'Miss Ricardo, stay behind please.'

'I'll wait in the car,' said Judd. 'We'll have a belt or two on

335

the way home.'

Harbottle was not the type who helped old ladies at street crossings; young ladies, too, he had little time for.

'It's not your fault that you're British,' he said, 'nor is it my fault that you've been told to play a girl with a Southern accent. You must change your voice and your mannerisms completely. I've been in touch with Mr. Stern and he's located a lady who worked with Vivien Leigh before she made *Gone with the Wind*, that endless presentation which your friend Dugdale seems to admire so much. A Miss Huxtable is her name. She'll be calling you at eight o'clock tonight.'

Judd bade his driver stop at a 'gay' bar on 55th Street; at a corner table Justin was waiting.

'Any luck?' Judd asked.

'I've gotten hold of a lid of Sin Semilla, and some Kabul Black, goddawful prices though, double what they are on the Coast.'

'I'm drinking right now,' said Judd, 'I need to. How about you, Doll?'

Pandora ordered a gin and tonic, Judd settled for Bourbon, a large Old Grand Dad on the rocks. For an hour they fulminated about the horrors of *The Dogwood Tree*.

'Those goddam Method actors are a real pain in the ass,' said Judd. 'There's not one can get a word out without belching or scratching his crotch.'

'It's the females who scare me to death,' said Pandora.

'Forget 'em, they'd all give their left tit to be in Hollywood. So would that creepy Director. We'll just get through this thing the best way we can, darling. Roll us a few joints and the hell with it – it's only Television, nobody's going to remember it! Justin, let's take a look at that Sin Semilla.'

Justin handed over a small muslin bag. Judd tipped some of the contents onto his palm and poked at it with a finger.

'Great grass, this,' he said to Pandora. 'Look! Not a seed in it! Roll yourself one, Justin, while I climb outside another Old Grand Dad.'

When Pandora opened her door in the Blackstone Hotel, the phone was ringing. She found Miss Huxtable hard to understand but the necessary arrangements were quickly made and

336

she rushed to look at her telephone messages, hoping against hope to find one from Stani; she then made some soup, set her alarm for six o'clock and fell into a troubled sleep.

The next three days were hectic. Rehearsals in the Drill Hall were interrupted by cross-town dashes for fittings at a vast theatrical costumiers on the West Side. Pandora had a horror of wearing other people's clothes, but she hid her repulsion while trying on dozens of stained crinolines which proclaimed to the skies that they had already housed generations of performers. She longed for the pampered ways of Hollywood, first being shown designs and materials and later enjoying unhurried fittings with the Studio dressmakers. Here, it was pure production line, hundreds of actors and actresses from Broadway shows, touring companies, television, charity performances, night-clubs, ice extravaganzas, all milling around grabbing costumes off racks, struggling into them in the aisles and waiting in line for a look in a mirror.

Obtaining the right wig was no easier. One she fancied was ripped off her head by a six foot drummer from a drag orchestra.

Lunch was a sandwich and a cup of coffee and the interrupted rehearsals a continuing nightmare. Scenes from the pen of Henri de Gâcher were so badly constructed as to be almost impossible to learn and the meticulous inflections required by Mr. Harbottle were usually diametrically opposed to those insisted upon by Miss Huxtable. As the common enemy of the air-date loomed nearer, the New York actors became marginally less hostile but remained resolutely patronizing. Judd was a tower of strength, though the aroma of Old Grand Dad was noticeable earlier each day. He happily infuriated everyone except Pandora by enjoining them 'not to worry – it's only Television!' And whenever Mr. Harbottle lost his temper he would call out: 'As your medical adviser, Buddy Boy, it's my duty to warn you that you've gone a most peculiar colour.'

Each evening Judd and Justin took Pandora to their chosen bar where she tried hard to relax over a gin and tonic and they visibly succeeded with the aid of Sin Semilla marihuana, Kabul Black hashish or Peruvian Flake cocaine, the last being snorted up the nostril from a tiny golden spoon.

'Stick around long enough, Honey, and you'll be throwing

337

snowballs with the best.'

'Not me,' Pandora said. 'I have a question. A friend of mine had a one night affair she never intended to have, she took a couple of pills that night because she was very tensed up and somehow it just . . . happened. Are there such things as . . . seduction pills?'

'There sure are,' said Judd. 'Any idea what hers looked like?'

'She said they were about the size of Aspirin, a sort of chalky-grey colour.'

'Did she take any booze too?'

'I believe she drank quite a bit of champagne.'

'They're muscle relaxers, darling, only been on the market about a year. Mixed with liquor they can do for girls what ground-up rhinoceros horn's supposed to do for old Chinese studs. Tell her to skip 'em, nobody knows much about 'em.'

Justin watched Pandora's departure from the bar, fitted the dying inches of a joint into a pincer-shaped 'Roach Holder' and inhaled deeply.

'Well,' he said, 'I wonder who'd pull such a lousy trick on a nice girl like that?'

Alone in her hotel, Pandora felt desperately tired but for an hour she tried hard to memorize the ghastly output of Henri de Gâcher's pen. She tried to meld it with the cadences demanded by Miss Huxtable. Several times with full voice she tried the climax of her big speech in a blazing row with Judd.

'You're lyin' Jason Ballantyne! You're thinkin' of workin' fer the Dam Yankees. Better you learn to chop cotton like a darky field hand! Why Jason Ballantyne, you're no better than a Carpetbagger or a Scallawag or a trashy free issue nigger. Jason Ballantyne, you STINK!'

The phone rang.

'Miss Ricardo, this is the Assistant Manager. The occupants of No. 16 are complaining about the shouting again. Thank you!'

The thought of the next day filled her with a choking sense of dread. Maxwell Stern was coming to watch a full rehearsal. Everyone had to be word perfect, her Southern accent had to be perfect, her playing of the idiotic scenes had to be perfect, and all she felt was unwanted, incompetent, silly and very scared.

Ominous cracks were appearing in Judd's facade and she

was beginning to wonder how reliable he would turn out to be, a few nights hence, in front of every television viewer in the United States. How much would he rely on Old Grand Dad and a variety of other crutches to help him cope with a fear she now suspected was every bit as large as her own? She ordered a lonely, lack-lustre meal from Room Service and in deep depression ran her bath. No sooner had the warm scented water closed over her body than the phone rang again. For three rings she hesitated, dreading a cold clammy dash into the sitting room. But, what if it were Stani!

When she heard the voice at the other end she jigged with excitement and her hastily wrapped towel fell to the floor.

'Pandora? It's Chuck! Honey, I got back in last night, tried to get you all day but they won't take calls at that rehearsal place. When can I see you?'

'Now!!' Pandora shrieked. 'COME AT ONCE!!'

Chuck Pesnick was only half way out of his overcoat and still being hugged and kissed when she fired the first question.

'Have you found him?'

'Calm down,' he laughed, 'order me an Old Fashioned and I'll give you the news.'

After the call to Room Service he continued.

'Coming out on the plane I saw a four page spread in the new *Look* Magazine, great shots of kids surfing in California. When I spotted the credit I nearly fell out the goddam window – photographs by Stanislaw Skolimowski!! As soon as I got to the office this morning I called *Look* for the name of the agency and talked to the boss man there. Stani has been working for them in British Columbia.'

'British *Columbia*?'

Chuck held up a hand.

'From there he went to Detroit to see Henry Ford.'

'*Henry Ford*?'

'Now you don't have to repeat *everything* I say! Anyway, he didn't see Henry Ford.'

'Oh Chuck! You're a tease and a *stinker*! Where is he NOW?!!'

'He called me from Detroit, he'd tried to get me before from Calgary.'

'What did he SAY?'

The door buzzer sounded.

'That could be my Old Fashioned,' said Chuck.

'You're a *sadist*! I'm going to throw it out the window unless you tell me . . . *PLEASE*!!'

Chuck opened the door revealing the night maid with clean towels. He spoke over his shoulder.

'The line was very bad, you know, lots of static. But I *think* he said something about his plane arriving at La Guardia at one a.m. tomorrow morning!'

Pandora jumped up and down clapping her hands like a child in front of her birthday presents. Then she subsided into a chair.

'Chuck,' she asked in a small voice, 'does he want to see me?'

Chuck crossed to her, sat on the arm of her chair and took her hand.

'Darling, he talked of nothing else. He feels a little guilty, I guess.'

'*He* feels guilty!!'

'Anyway I'm sure between you, you two can work it out.'

Chuck ate dinner with her and departed around ten, making 'Company Man' noises.

'Get a good night's rest now, Honey, you have to be fresh for Stern tomorrow morning. This show will be one helluva thing for you.'

When he had gone Pandora put her hair in curlers, removed her make-up, creamed her face and set her alarm for six o'clock; for an hour she lay staring with distaste at the pages of *The Dogwood Tree*. Then she threw them aside, got out of bed, cleaned off the face cream, re-did her make-up, removed her curlers, dressed warmly and took a cab to La Guardia airport.

Few people were meeting the flight from Detroit, and the passengers, mostly business men travelling light, headed directly for cabs and limousines. Stani looked rather lost when he came through the gate and Pandora from her vantage point beside a closed Information Desk watched with pumping heart his uncertain progress towards the baggage racks. He was incredibly handsome. She followed him and took up station so close beside him as to be touching his elbow. Stani inched away, his eyes fixed on the arriving baggage carts, three times with increasing pressure, she snuggled up; and three times with mounting embarrassment he disengaged; at last he looked down.

She heard his quick intake of breath; instinctively his arms opened to her but slowly they fell back to his sides and she watched the wonderment, joy and relief on his face change to infinite sadness. She longed to touch him, to hold him but made no move and for a long, long moment they stood silent, both thinking they saw the love in the other's eyes but neither daring to take it for granted. Hesitantly Pandora put a hand on his arm.

'Are you surprised to see me?'

Stani nodded slowly as though he was not really listening.

'Thank you for coming to meet me,' he paused. 'When I've got my bag I'd like to go some place where we can talk.'

Pandora's legs felt empty; the muscles unresponsive.

'Of course,' she said in a small voice. 'I'm at the Blackstone – we could go there . . . if you like?'

Stani nodded. Without speaking they collected his bag and found a cab; inside, the silence became unbearable. Quietly, in her corner, Pandora began to cry, after a few moments Stani moved over and put an arm around her. After she had quietened she spoke with difficulty.

'When your plane lost an engine and you came back to the house, you . . . saw me with Russ, didn't you? . . . I mean you saw everything?'

In the dimly lit cab she saw him nod and turn his face away. She took a deep breath.

'When he left, and he was only there about an hour after the Selznick party, I was so *disgusted* with myself that I swam for a long time trying to wash him off my skin and out of my brain . . . I felt physically sick. Incidentally, I got no pleasure out of it . . . it meant absolutely nothing . . . I could have dreamed it . . . but that's beside the point. I just made the awful mistake of letting it happen when I could so easily have stopped it . . . I still feel sick when I think about it.

'I do have the tiny excuse that I drank too much on top of a couple of pills I knew nothing about . . . but that's all', she paused and looked up. 'I suppose I just went mad for one awful moment, I *can't* think what made me do anything so . . . so cheap.

341

'After my swim I went upstairs and cried my eyes out, then I scrubbed myself under the shower till my skin nearly came off so that at least I felt clean enough to call you in New York *and tell you what happened*. I nearly died when I couldn't find you.'

Stani stroked the top of her head and spoke gently into her hair.

'When we first came together and you spent the end of my leave with me in my flat and you gave me this' – he tapped the disc beneath his shirt – 'you warned me not to fall in love with you because you said you were too fond of sex . . . remember?'

Pandora nodded. 'I was trying to say that a couple of times in my life I'd mistaken sex for love and very nearly made bad mistakes – this time I wanted to be sure I'd got it right.' She turned towards the window. 'But Russell was different . . . it was just a horrible *mistake* – something I can't explain . . . something I'd give my soul to forget.'

She looked up at him and passing headlights made little stars of the tears on her cheeks.

'All I can tell you is that I *do* love *you* with all my heart and I just pray that you can understand.'

When Stani put his other arm around her and whispered: 'And I love *you* with all *my* heart . . . I never stopped for a minute', she buried her face on his chest and stayed there like a contented kitten till they reached the hotel.

Drained by emotion but with 'all evil shed away' they went straight to bed and slept unmoving in each other's arms till morning.

Pablo Picasso, walking at low tide on a French beach, was asked by a tourist if he would do him a drawing as a souvenir.

'Of course,' Picasso smiled. Then he led the man to the water's edge, picked up a stick and drew a girl's head in the sand.

No one knows what beauty was washed away that day, but when Pandora's alarm awakened them at six o' clock, both she and Stani knew that the flood tide of their love had removed forever any uglinesss from the background of their happiness.

The rehearsal in front of Maxwell Stern was no longer a major hurdle for Pandora; she arrived with little sleep but so radiant with happiness that she was inoculated against his bile. Judd, approaching with Budleigh Salterton, opened the proceedings.

'Mary-Lee, honey, why don't you go fix your old Grandpa a drink?'

Pandora replied.

'Sho nuff. Ah have buckwheat cakes fer you too, Grandpa.'

'Hold it!' said Maxwell Stern. 'Miss Ricardo, why are you playing the part with a Cockney accent?'

Pandora said very sweetly, 'Because in spite of all the help I've had from Miss Huxtable and everyone else, I haven't been able to master a Southern one in four days.'

Judd gallantly leapt into the ensuing silence.

'I have trouble with the accent too, Mr. Stern. I feel real awkward in the next speech when I have to say "Gee Willikins".'

'What do you find awkward about *that*?'

'Well, all the Southern boys *I* know say "Oh! SHEEAT!"'

Stern's reputation as a bully was well known and the other performers quickly united behind the small West Coast contingent with a hearty laugh.

Like all bullies Stern collapsed when outnumbered.

'Continue with the scene please.'

For twenty minutes the old Bund rallying point resounded with 'Gawdalmighty's!' 'Ah declare!' 'White Trash . . . that's all Mr. Lincoln is!' Giggles, squeals, 'Yas'm, Ah shore could do with some vittles if it don't deprive you none' and, of course, 'God's nightgown!' It was difficult for Pandora and Judd to visualize it from chalk marks but they tried to simulate their final exit in a horse drawn buggy.

'Tomorrow is another day,' Pandora sighed, looking lovingly into his face.

'I just got it,' whispered Judd. 'That sonofabitch writer even stole *that*. It's the last line from *Gone with the Wind*.'

Maxwell Stern left after a long discussion with Mr. Harbottle.

'The Producer has given me some notes,' the Director reported, 'which I will pass on to you. He is not too displeased with what he saw here and says the overall show looks spectacular. For the rest of today we will polish individual scenes, tomorrow we will rehearse in costumes and wigs. The following

343

day will be a long one. At seven a.m. at the Television Studio we'll start blocking scenes with all four cameras and the entire crew.

'Then, in the afternoon, we will have two final Dress Rehearsals, then . . .' he added with a grisly smile, 'at six o'clock you will be on your own. The horse will have left the barn.'

The last day in the Drill Hall was spent getting used to manipulating fans, breathing beneath tight corsets and sitting in ill-fitting Confederate uniforms while avoiding a painful encounter with one's own sword. All previous coolness towards Pandora and Judd had evaporated before the prospect of the coming ordeal. Judd, among his military equipment, found a water bottle which he filled with Old Grand Dad. Pandora was lovely in a white, starched lace crinoline and sash of her favourite apple green and pink. Later, against the background of war, her costumes became shabbier and her wigs more dishevelled, but everyone agreed she still looked adorable.

During the day Stani made himself scarce. Mr. Mulligan arranged for him to spend the time watching the great Gjon Mili at work in his studio and in forty-eight hours the maestro generously taught him more about composition, choice of lens and above all instant reaction to grab the frozen moment, than most photographers learn in ten years.

Mulligan also offered him a two-week assignment to photograph 'an Island Paradise a hundred years behind the times with pink beaches, alligators, voodoo and an eighty-year-old female dictator – take a girl and enjoy yourself!'

'I'll let you know in a week,' Stani said and dedicated his evenings to calming Pandora's twittering nerves. On the night before The Big Show, Chuck Pesnick came to the Blackstone and reported that the filmed segments were indeed sensational. 'Astaire of course is fantastic, he does a *great* number. The Russian Circus has a 600 pound bear riding a motor cycle and everything else looks *fabulous*. Now it's all yours, Honey!'

'Thanks,' said Pandora. 'I wish I were dead!'

'How's Judd bearing up?' Chuck asked.

Pandora shrugged. 'All right, I suppose, but he's been lapping down Bourbon all the time. Now he says he's discovered something that really helps him relax.'

'What's that?'

344

'Burning a pinch of hash on the head of a pin and letting the little stream of smoke go straight up each nostril. He says it works wonders.'

'It's too bad,' said Chuck. 'The word's not out yet in Hollywood but once it gets around he'd better watch out. By the way, Stani, I've fixed it for you to see the show from the Sponsor's box, there'll be one or two Agency guys in there. All the big wheels'll be catching it at their homes.'

Allowing an hour and a half for hair and make-up and another forty-five minutes for travel and emergencies Pandora set her alarm for four-thirty and at nine sharp they turned out the light.

The next morning Stani had the grace to make coffee but when Pandora left for the Television Studio he snuggled down in the still warm bed, totally happy and content.

There was little happiness or contentment in the make-up rooms and hairdressing departments. By a quarter to seven the actors were assembled. Mr. Harbottle's two assistants were rigged up in headsets and microphones through which they could maintain contact with him high up in a glass-walled booth; where he would be playing God before a bank of monitor screens and in sole control of four mobile cameras, as many pieces of sound equipment, thirty actors, a crew of sixty or seventy and an audience estimated at between sixty-five and eighty-two million.

Pandora had never before been inside a television studio. The floor was highly polished and upon its surface trolleys bearing the four huge cameras and their operators were being pushed and pulled by powerfully built young men wearing squeak-proof sneakers. All operators were in contact with the Director via their headsets and each camera trailed behind it a comet-tail of power, picture, and telephone cables.

Soon after seven o'clock Judd and Budleigh Salterton approached a group of ladies in crinolines and gentlemen in broadcloth jackets, grey, white or ochre trousers, frilled shirts and black cravats; Panama hats and fans were moving rhythmically.

'Mary-Lee, Honey,' Judd began. 'Why don't you go fix your old Grandpa . . .'

345

'Hold it!' came a disembodied voice from high above their heads. 'Mark those positions.'

Assistants drew chalk outlines round the actors' feet. Mr. Harbottle spoke again.

'I want a close-up on Camera 3 while Mr. Dugdale finishes that speech about the drink. Camera 1 hold on Miss Ricardo reacting to his arrival. Make sure I get that backdrop of rows of cotton. Hold it a minute.' He clicked off. 'Okay,' he continued, 'we don't have enough depth before that backdrop; get me a couple of midgets dressed as gardeners to give it some perspective.'

Positioning four cameras was fraught with technical difficulties, since it was of prime importance that one should under no circumstance photograph another.

From seven o'clock till midday the actors were grouped, shuffled and shunted, speaking only a few lines of dialogue at a time before being stopped to have their positions marked and the cameras realigned. It was a fatiguing, frustrating, cold-blooded business and with half the day already gone it seemed impossible that cohesion of any sort could be achieved before 'air time' at six o'clock. During a half hour break for sandwiches and coffee Pandora noticed that Judd Dugdale was never far from his waterbottle.

'We're not actors,' he snorted, 'we're patients going in for major surgery. Right now we're being wheeled along to the operating theatre with tubes sticking out of everywhere, in the hands of so-called specialists. I just hope they know what the fuck they're doing.'

From two till four, to save time, scenes were rehearsed out of order – all veranda scenes, then all scenes by the dogwood tree and so on, after which two dress rehearsals were scheduled – the whole twenty-three minutes straight through without interruption of any sort.

Just before the first dress rehearsal, the arrival of Maxwell Stern sowed instant alarm; his dark glasses and piano teeth were set in a gargoyle smile.

'Hold everything,' he said. 'The scene in the barn with the two soldiers in coonskin caps sharpening their bayonets on the grindstone; that's Out.'

'Out! Mr. Stern?' came a horrified voice from above.

346

'That's right, Harbottle, get rid of it. I've just had a call from the sponsor's Advertising Agency.'

'What don't they like?'

'They don't like the line, "nobody fancies cold steel".'

'*Why*?'

'Because they're paid several million dollars a year to get people to buy the Goddam stuff – that's why.'

'Take ten,' said the Director. 'I'll be right down, Mr. Stern.'

The actors smoked and pretended not to listen while Stern and Harbottle cobbled together a new scene for the two soldiers. A pot of hominy and a wood fire were substituted for bayonets and grindstone and the offending words removed. At least twenty minutes were then lost laying a gas line beneath fire-proof logs before the Studio Fire Chief gave his approval and the dress rehearsal got under way.

'Mary-Lee Honey, why don't you fix your old Grandpa a drink? . . .' It proceeded jerkily till Judd and Pandora were alone beneath the dogwood tree.

Before arriving at the last scene with Pandora buggy-borne and gazing dreamily into the eyes of Judd Dugdale ('Tomorrow is another day') a major snag was encountered.

To show the passage of time from Spring to Fall they embraced twice before the trunk of the dogwood tree: in the branches above their heads were two stage hands, one with a sack of petals, the other clutching bags of dead leaves.

During the first embrace, blossoms filtered down upon them; during the second they got the leaves. But in the interim, in less than sixty seconds, they had to change clothes and make-up, he from Confederate uniform to shabby suit, she from crinoline to a dowdy garment of fustian. Both had to be dirty and dishevelled which entailed a change of wig for Pandora, while Judd was required to have sprouted a heavy black moustache.

Like two boxers they had their separate corners on either side of the close-up camera and there the nimble fingers of their 'seconds' (wardrobe ladies and make-up men) flew from zippers to glue pot and from spray gun to shoe horn. The last item to go in place was Judd's black moustache. In order for him to be back in position before the red light flashed on the camera, informing the actors that they were once again in full view of millions, precious moments were saved by one make-up man

347

passing the glue brush across Judd's upper lip while a second held the moustache like a bull fighter's cape in exactly the right position so that he could walk into it *en route* to his place.

Maxwell Stern looked at the script girl's stopwatch.

'Hold it!' he said. 'You have to cut fifteen seconds off that routine and when you get together for the second clinch, change sides, otherwise it looks phoney.' They tried it but they could only arrive at the new positions within the time limit if Judd arrived first and Pandora joined him later, having crawled past him on all fours below the camera.

'Okay, do it like that,' Stern ordered.

On completion of that scene Judd and Pandora walked to the waiting buggy and Judd hauled her up beside him for the final words.

'Hold it!' said Maxwell Stern. 'What d'you plan after the pay-off line, Harbottle?'

'A slow fade out, Mr. Stern, with a superimposed field of daffodils to give a note of hope, then the words "The End".'

'Too corny. I want music. Get Research on it right away, find a recording, something real Confederate. Then, as the music swells to a climax, the mule pulls the buggy past camera which holds on the dogwood tree till fade out.'

'We don't have a mule, Mr. Stern.'

'Okay, get a rope and a couple of stagehands.'

By the time Maxwell Stern had further confused everyone it was well past five o'clock and the second dress rehearsal was cancelled. The actors were dismissed for half an hour to check make-up and wardrobe and try to relax while stagehands darted about hammering, spraying, repositioning the dogwood tree and preparing for the smooth departure of the buggy.

Adjoining the sound stage was a line of cell-like dressing rooms; with all the charm and gaiety of Death Row. Judd in shirt sleeves looked up as Pandora passed.

'One hour from now, Honey, and it'll be almost over! Then the goddam Dogwood Tree'll be flushed down the can along with the five o'clock news and last year's Rose Bowl Game!'

He didn't sound very convincing. A bottle of Old Grand Dad stood at his elbow.

Pandora sat at her bleak dressing table staring at herself in the mirror; her dresser, an old hand, moved silently about. She knew this was no moment for wisecracks and repartee. When Stani and Chuck came to see her; they knew too and stayed only a couple of minutes. In silence Stani held her close before he followed Chuck to the sponsor's booth. He could feel the tension in her body, as stiff as a frightened puppy.

Maxwell Stern's drugstore Indian smile appeared at her door. 'In case you "dry", just pray, because no one down here can help you.'

The minutes dragged by and Pandora, needing company desperately, went next door to see Judd. His feet were up on his dressing table, a glass was in his hand and he was smoking a carrot.

'A guy down in the Village invented this. It's a dandy idea. You bore a hole in the carrot, put a pinch of hash on the end, light up and pull the air through it; at the same time you take the smoke up your nose, you can nibble on the carrot too if you like. Helps you to see in the dark!'

'God! I'm terrified,' Pandora said.

'*I'm* not,' said Judd, 'not any more. In fact I'm going out there just before Air Time to show those bastards there's nothing to be scared about. Maybe I'll be able to calm 'em down. Look at old 'Grandpa', he's in shock, they all are!'

He took a long pull at the carrot.

'They're professional actors, overdressed and under-rehearsed it's true, but they're walking around out there with staring eyeballs like a bunch of runaway rocking horses.'

'Fifteen minutes!' a young assistant director was banging on the dressing room doors.

Pandora kissed Judd as she left. '*Please* be careful,' she begged.

After last-minute primping she was ready, part of the frightened herd.

'First Positions please!' an Assistant called, and the smartly dressed ladies and gentlemen shuffled towards the veranda like condemned prisoners.

'Ten minutes!'

The four cameras wheeled into position.

'Where's Mr. Dugdale?'

'Right here,' said Judd, wandering on stage.

The assistant looked worried.

'*Please* get dressed, Mr. Dugdale, everyone's in position.'

Judd spoke slowly. 'We still have eight minutes before we have to perform this crappy little playlet in front of seventy million people, right?'

'Yes, Mr. Dugdale, but the Confederate uniform and the . . .'

'I know, the equipment. Just give me five minutes' warning, kiddo, that's all I need and I'll be ready. Bright eyed and bushy tailed.'

'*Please* Mr. Dugdale! You're going to cost me my job.'

'In that case,' said Judd, 'I shall immediately go back to my crappy little dressing room, get inside my uniform which smells of armpits, then I shall return to join my equally smelly Southern friends upon the porch with the wobbling pillars.'

So far Judd's effort to calm his fellow actors had not been a conspicuous success, they had listened to his conversation with mounting alarm. Now, as they followed his snail-pace departure towards his dressing room, they buzzed like disturbed hornets.

'Quiet please! Five minutes to air time! Somebody go fetch Mr. Dugdale. Quick!'

There was no need. Judd reappeared as though propelled from a cannon, gone was the languid pose of self-assurance and steadiness under fire, his eyes were wild, his voice pitched high with hysteria.

'Help!' he yelled. 'I've locked myself out!! Someone break down the fucking door!!'

'Three minutes to AIR TIME!'

At least twenty people including two firemen with axes streamed towards the dressing rooms.

'Two minutes to AIR TIME!'

The unnerved actors heard shouts, oaths and the smashing of panels as they braced themselves for the final warning from the Assistant.

'SIXTY SECONDS!'

Pandora experienced a wave of nausea, her hands were wet and fluttering, her knees felt empty.

'TWENTY! . . . FIFTEEN! . . . TEN! . . . When the red lights show start to ad-lib! . . . FIVE! . . .'

Little red spots appeared simultaneously on all four cameras and from the actors a murmur of conversation and forced laughter arose; almost immediately Judd and Budleigh Salterton shot through the big door.

Judd was panting like a dog, the old man looked dazed as though he had lately witnessed a terrible street accident.

'Mary-Lee Honey!' Judd started, then he paused and took a deep breath, '. . . why don't you go fix your old Grand Dad . . . an Old Grand Dad?'

Pandora was stunned into silence. Judd tried to recover the situation. He slapped Budleigh Salterton on the back.

'Or give the old smuggler some Old Smuggler . . . Ha! Ha! Ha!'

As Pandora continued to gape at him Judd went further.

'Tell you what Honey . . . give the old turkey a shot of Wild Turkey . . . Ha! Ha! Ha! HA!'

The more experienced actors took up the laughter. Pandora gratefully scurried off, jabbering about corn pone as she went; behind her Budleigh Salterton got the show back on the track by loudly demanding chitterlings and for the next five minutes things seemed to be settling down.

It didn't last long. One of the two midgets dressed as gardeners stood in the wrong place and his giant nose-picking shadow loomed across the distant cotton fields. Then Judd, in a scene with Pandora and the butler, suddenly went blank, in mid sentence. He stopped ranting about Mr. Lincoln and States' Rights and stared at them slack-jawed with the eyes of a trapped hare facing two ferrets. The butler tried to help by outlining the next line for him.

'I think you wus goin' to tell Mis' Mary-Lee about dat cape jassamine bush down by de stables Suh?'

Judd shook his head like a prize fighter, some light filtered back into his eyes and he started an animated silent monologue with expansive gestures, smiles and much movement of his lips; all over America people must have been reaching for their telephones to call repairmen. Even in the control booth the ruse worked and Mr. Harbottle leaned forward to turn up the sound. Once again the show steadied itself and enjoyed a brief period of comparative calm. The actors began to relax, Judd regained control of himself and Pandora felt panic receding: even the cobbled-together scene between the two soldiers went

351

according to plan – until one of them caught fire.

The barn was full of dead and wounded lying on straw. In the background Pandora and other ladies were ministering to them while the camera in the foreground recorded the efforts of the two men in their coon skin caps before the pot of hominy.

One of the soldiers leant down to stir the contents of the pot and the tail of his coon skin fell forward. Smoke poured from his hat, in a second it was on fire. He ripped off his flaming headgear and flung it from him, it landed in the straw among the dead. Uttering cries of alarm, the corpses quickly evacuated their corner of the barn and two firemen moved in with extinguishers. High above the floor Mr. Harbottle froze at the controls allowing cameras No. 3 and 4 to record the firemen's efforts. The blaze was short-lived and the corpses settled down again but in the absence of orders from on high, camera crews had made their own arrangements to leave the danger zone and a crunching collision between retreating cameras No. 3 and No. 4 occurred in full view of Nos. 1 and 2. With the trailing cables of Nos. 3 and 4 horribly intertwined, they became stuck together back to back like oversexed dachshunds in Central Park. Their crews unplugged the lines and worked valiantly to sort them out, but in the general shambles they were reconnected incorrectly and Mr. Harbottle's urgent instructions to Camera No. 3 were received by Camera No. 4 which added considerably to the confusion. With the cameras now aiming in every direction the show lurched towards the final words of confrontation between Pandora and Judd in Pandora's bedroom.

'I can't stay heah,' Judd said. 'If the Yankees find me it'll be the end for both of us.'

Pandora clung to her hero.

'No one's left in the house, the servants have all run away. I'll hide you.'

'Where?'

'Under my bed. Here there are no prying eyes.'

She turned to the four-poster, lifted the material off the floor; and came face to face with a stage hand, in a bright red shirt, who found himself staring straight into the camera he was trying to avoid. He wriggled away across the floor.

'Who was that?' Judd asked.

'I thought he'd gone with the others,' Pandora ad-libbed, suppressing the first hysterical stirrings of laughter in the back of her throat.

After what had gone before, the spring blossom half of the scene before the Dogwood Tree went off better than Pandora had expected, except that Judd had also arrived upon the threshold of disintegration and to avoid looking into each other's eyes they played the whole thing staring at the tops of each other's heads.

When the red light went off they dashed to their corners and the frenzied fingers of their handlers went to work. Judd was finished first, and returned confidently towards his waiting black moustache. At the very instant of its placement upon his upper lip the zipper of Pandora's drab gown bit into the flesh at the top of her buttocks, she squeaked loudly with pain. An involuntary glance in her direction deflected the make-up man's aim and the black moustache ended up with its centre a good two inches to the right of Judd's nose. The red light winked on. Judd stared straight ahead thinking of his loved one, and warping his mouth to centre the moustache when over the top of it he saw Pandora crawling past his feet. Her zipper had not only bitten into her flesh, it had also fastened onto the seat of her panties and come to a dead stop with them and the hem of her gown gathered in a monstrous bustle near the small of her back.

When she joined him among the falling Autumn leaves, which dropped in heavy clumps, Judd was already shaking with silent laughter. They both knew that when they had finished their dialogue they must turn their backs to the camera and walk towards the buggy. If Mr. Harbottle was slow in the uptake, this would guarantee the entire television population of the United States a clear view of Pandora's bottom. Suppressed laughter is very painful, and by the time they turned away for their moment of truth, tears were spurting from their eyes.

Judd's next gesture perhaps owed more to Californian innovation than to Southern charm, but on the turn he slipped his arm around Pandora's waist, then allowed his hand to fall and cover the centre of the Great Divide. Out of range of the microphone he whispered.

'It's an old gag, but I *do* feel a perfect ass!'

353

Pandora folded her lips into her mouth and pressed them hard together hoping that her tears would be taken for grief and grabbed a dirty sack off the floor of the conveyance before climbing into the buggy. Judd pulled her close. Not trusting herself to look at him she kept her eyes shut and nestled into his shoulder.

'Tomorrow,' she sighed, 'is another day!'

The nightmare over, Judd slapped the reins on the imaginary mule flanks and made clucking noises. Nothing happened.

'Giddyapp!' he commanded.

No result. Through half closed lids Pandora could see four stage hands including her bedroom lodger in the red shirt hauling on a rope. The buggy refused to budge. Two more stage hands joined the straining team, they signalled frantically to Judd. He flourished the whip.

'Git goin' you critters,' he yelled at them. '. . . The dam Yankees are acomin'!'

Only then did he think of releasing the brake and the buggy, proud remnant of *The Dogwood Tree*, to the accompaniment of pent-up hoots of laughter from its occupants shot like a rocket from the Television screens of the Great American Public.

With all red lights finally extinguished, relief flooded over the actors and the whole spectrum of the Television crew; like soldiers returned from a dangerous patrol, past animosities were forgotten, irregularities or eccentricities forgiven and mutual congratulations became the order of the day. Bottles and glasses appeared as if by magic.

Stani and Chuck were happy to leave the confines of the sponsor's booth; the two executives of the Steel Companies' advertising agency had proved oppressive companions, being unable to make up their minds before hearing the reactions of their employers as to whether or not the laughter which *The Dogwood Tree* had provoked had been intentional. Stani and Chuck had no such difficulty; they knew in U.S. Service parlance that there had been a fair-sized 'SNAFU' (Situation Normal, All Fucked Up). Stani was worried.

'Will it hurt Pandora?' he asked.

Chuck avoided his eyes.

'I hope not . . . She looked *sensational* and handled the accent and the things that came out of left field better than anyone.

Anyway, it's all forgotten already, the people are looking at a Russian bear now, on a goddam motorcycle!'

On the sound stage Stani found Pandora the centre of attention. Budleigh Salterton and the whole New York cast were gathered round her, compliments were flying thick and fast, phone numbers and promises of eternal devotion were being exchanged, she had come through like a 'pro' and the 'pros' were opening their arms to her. A photographer from Metropolis Studios was recording the scene.

'Where is Mr. Dugdale?'

The hubbub died down and the company turned to find Maxwell Stern in shirtsleeves standing in the buggy.

'He had to rush to catch a plane back to California,' Pandora volunteered.

Stern looked down at her and spoke very distinctly.

'He should never have left there in the first place, nor should you Miss Ricardo. Between you, you have wrecked my show.'

A few gasps were heard but discipline in the theatre is deeply ingrained and a producer's appreciation of a performance is listened to in silence.

'You are a hopeless amateur, Miss Ricardo. Follow Mr. Dugdale, I beg you. Go back to Hollywood where you belong, where your ego can thrive on publicity and your so-called talent can survive because you only have to sustain scenes of a few seconds' duration.'

The blood rushed to Pandora's face and tears came to her eyes.

'Go back to the glove salesmen and pork butchers who call themselves producers, and the mid-European failures masquerading as directors, go quickly Miss Ricardo because you have no talent, your beauty will fade and you will no longer be able to climb the ladder of phoney stardom just by opening your legs. . . .'

Maxwell Stern got no further. Stani pushed through the crowd, reached up, lifted him from the buggy and tucked him under his arm like a toy poodle. The crowd, stunned into silence, parted to let them through. Stani ingored Stern's kicking legs, flailing arms and his cries for help. He left the sound stage with his wriggling cargo and headed for the dressing room passage.

'I'll sue you!' Stern yelled. 'I know who you are! . . . I'll sue you for every cent you have! For assault!'

'You'll be lucky if you don't have to sue me for murder,' Stani grunted and kicked open the door to the Men's Room. He had no plan for the disposal of his loathsome charge – wash his mouth out with soap? Leave him head down in one of the porcelain receptacles perhaps? His eye caught a control faucet on the wall. He tested Stern's belt, lifted him, hooked the back of it over the handle and departed leaving the most unpopular man on Broadway suspended above the flushing urinals.

At the Television Studio Pandora had been stoic, and the actors and crew had rallied to her side *en bloc* but when he turned the key of their Blackstone apartment Stani had the other arm round a deeply unhappy girl. Once inside she fled to the bedroom and gave way to her disappointment. After efforts to comfort her he left her to cry herself out.

Chuck arrived with the latest news.

'You're the hero of Broadway kiddo! You don't know the half of what that little bastard's done to people in the theatre . . . the word was round that building in two seconds flat! . . . They came in from all over the theatre district to look at the son of a bitch . . . some even brought cameras! . . . he wasn't hurting so nobody offered to unhook him . . . when I left they were lined up right down the passage and out into the street . . . like Lenin's Tomb!'

'What about Pandora?'

Chuck was evasive. 'The overall show was just *great*! . . . *The Dogwood Tree* was a lot of fun . . . people soon forget.' He did not stay long, publicity men become nervous in the presence of failure.

Pandora emerged red-eyed but calmer. 'What do I do now? Go back to Hollywood with a stiff upper lip?'

Stani led her to the sofa and held her hand.

'Look. You told me that Judd always said . . . "it's only Television." He's not so far wrong! You haven't made a shambles of Lady Macbeth on Broadway, you haven't wrecked Scarlett O'Hara on the screen, you've been in a small part of a one night television show . . . that part went off the rails but lots of people probably never even realized it and no one could

356

possibly blame *you*! They didn't pay sixty dollars a seat to see it anyway – they got it free and they're not going to cancel their new Chevrolet convertible because your zipper got caught in a show paid for by the Steel Companies!'

Pandora managed a wan smile.

'I still don't know what to do. I'm supposed to go back, right away . . . I'm under contract. But I'm not sure I want to go back . . . ever. I'm muddled about Hollywood and Russ Bancroft and Stern and everything. *Do* help me, darling, *please!*'

Stani stood up.

'I haven't helped you much up to now – tying your producers to trees and hanging them on walls! But if you do decide to go back I'll try to improve . . . meanwhile I'm taking charge. I'm calling Mulligan and tomorrow I'm taking you somewhere where you can forget *The Dogwood Tree*, Bancroft, Stern and anybody else and decide what *you* want to do.'

'But won't I get into lawsuits and breach of contract things?'

'Who's going to sue you – Bancroft? I'll go and have another little chat with him if you like!'

'Oh God, darling' Pandora giggled, '*please* don't do that!'

'Then let that little agent of yours earn his ten per cent; let him stick his neck out for once. Tell him to dream up some excuse, he's done it before – you're tired out . . . you need a rest . . . he knows what to say.'

'Another thing Judd came up with – "it's the squeaking wheel that gets the grease", so squeak a little for once! They respect you for it: if you don't they'll walk all over you.'

He smiled down at her.

'I know . . . you find it hard to put on an act and I love you for it, but for six years we both suffered from an overdose of reality. Now, for the past six months, we've been receiving massive injections of cloud cuckooland, so what we badly need is time: time to take a deep breath and get a few things back in perspective. You can decide later what to do with your life. That's why I'm taking you off to a place where there's nothing to do and plenty of time.'

The next evening after a DC6 of Avianca had dropped them off in Barbados a magnificently-bearded black pilot in a twin-engined Avro of Spice Island Airways delivered them to St.

357

Asaph. Apart from a jolly lady with a yellow headscarf, overly generous bosoms and a basketful of live chickens they were his only passengers; the Avro was the entire fleet of S.I.A.

'Know why the Island's called St. Asaph?' he asked over the roar of the motors.

'After a saint!' Stani yelled.

'No, after a village in Wales! Henry Morgan was kidnapped there when he was a little boy and brought to Barbados as a servant.' He pointed ahead across the sapphire sea. 'This was his favourite island. When he became governor of Jamaica he ran his pirate business from here!'

When the pitch of the motors changed and their ears popped Stani and Pandora had their first view of St. Asaph. Shaped like a question mark with a smaller island at its base, it was entirely encircled by coral reefs with deep blue water outside, emerald green in the lagoon. A mountainous backbone of rain forest and deep valleys ran along its entire length. In the most sheltered bend of the question mark was a small port filled with fishing boats and trading schooners; one medium-sized coaster lay a few hundred yards off shore.

The beaches were pink, the sky Prussian blue and decorated with fluffy white cumulus. The Avro banked steeply and they skimmed round the crater of an extinct volcano, the tops of giant mahogany trees and lush tropical forest swept below them.

Pandora grabbed Stani's arm.

'Look! Orchids are growing in the branches!'

They dived towards a minute grass landing strip near the sea, goats scattered and brown children ran out of wooden dwellings to stand waving in sugar cane and banana plantations. As an ex-pilot Stani classified their arrival as a 'white knuckle landing'. He closed his eyes as they hit the turf and bounced like a beach ball to within a few yards of the sand.

'Take off's a piece of cake' laughed the pilot.

The Poinciana Inn had sent its elderly taxi to meet them and they set off on a Kamikaze type drive along the mountainous spine of the island.

The driver, an older man, was a mine of information; taking a corner with screeching tyres, he pointed to a spot hundreds of feet below where the Caribs had ended up in a mass suicide leap.

'Everyone on this road knows me!' he chuckled, as he whizzed through a village with chickens, cripples, children and dogs leaping for their lives.

It was a long hot trip and after a spell of particularly eccentric driving during which Charlie Bedwell, for such was his name, had zig-zagged slowly down the centre of a stretch of perfectly straight road, Stani leaned forward and asked for clarification.

'Sleep is stealing me away' he explained.

Mr. Benevides was the manager of the hotel. From his black face blue eyes blazed, the legacy of a Portuguese great-grandfather . . . 'many Asaphians have them'. He led them to their bungalow, one of eight surrounding the main hotel complex of lobby, dining room and various comfortable verandahs. With the exception of the lobby which was protected on one side, there were no walls. The hotel was cooled by the gentle trade winds sighing in from the sea a few yards away.

Their bungalow, the nearest to the pink beach, was approached by a door in its surrounding wall. Inside was a patio and a small fresh water pool. The single room was a high-ceilinged, well-cupboarded affair with a large sliding window on one side. The bed was huge and the adjacent bathroom attractive. Large drops of rain began to fall; the shower was short, sharp and heavy. Mr. Benevides looked at the sky and smiled.

'Every afternoon about this time! Clouds form and rain comes to cool the Island – it's very convenient!'

After the rain, the frog orchestra tuned up for an evening performance, deep croaks from fat crapauds on the ground and shrill whistles from tiny tree frogs overhead; Stani and Pandora took their first swim in the crystal clear sea. On the beach elegant coconut palms swayed gently in the breeze, mangroves and sea-grape fringed the shore line, the water was as soft as velvet. The warm air dried their bodies when they wandered hand in hand across lush grass to their bungalow inhaling the fragrance of the frangipani trees and drinking in the beauty of the flamboyants, the jacarandas, the great banks of bougainvillea and of course the poincianas. Pandora squeezed Stani's hand.

359

'Thank you my darling for bringing me here ... it's so beautiful it hurts.'

The hotel could accommodate forty people, but apart from a family of Venezuelans and a pair of elderly Canadians, it was empty. 'This is our slack season,' Mr. Benevides explained. They were sipping a delicious punch of St. Asaph rum and watching the cumulus turn from pink to pale grey in the reflected sunset. They enquired about fishing on the coral reefs.

'Madame does not allow underwater guns of any sort. I'll lend you my spear if you like. The fish are so beautiful and so unafraid, you'll find you won't want to kill them, but it's good to have something in your hand in case a shark or a big barracuda comes along. I'll fix you up tomorrow with snorkels and flippers.'

Pandora shuddered. 'Sharks!'

'Very rare inside the reef, and they're not hungry – just bang them on the nose and they go away!'

Armed with Mr. Benevides' spear they spent hours each day far out on the reefs revelling in the colours of the coral formations, the deep blue grottos and the abundance of fish of every design, from innocent-faced pale blue angel-fish to green or red parrot fish, multi-coloured wrasses, yellow goatfish, blue-striped grunt and huge-eyed squirrel fish. With the spear they teased the bad tempered puffers till they swelled with rage and swam away like spike-covered balloons. They also learned how to provoke big moray eels into darting out of their holes and snapping their alarming teeth against the steel. They saw no sharks, but Pandora rounded a coral outcrop and came face to face with thousand pound giant sea bass: with its hideous head, a mouth of incredible ferocity, and magnified by her face plate, it looked as formidable as a submarine. They stared at each other with mutual terror till Stani gently pricked the great harmless fish in the side and with a convulsion of its tail it swirled away in high dudgeon. On another occasion, busy poking about below him, he felt a tug at his foot and turned in time to see a six foot barracuda making off with a sizeable chunk of one of his bright blue flippers.

In the cool of the evening they liked to take bicycles to explore the rain forest and the surprisingly neat little villages of thatched huts nestling in plantations of guava, paw-paw, nutmeg, clove and vanilla. Waves and smiles followed them wherever they went.

'Hollywood seems so far away' Pandora sighed. '. . . Let's stay here for ever!'

Stani laughed. 'It's all too perfect, I wonder what it's *really* like. Tomorrow I'm going to start using the camera, maybe it will turn up some ugliness somewhere.'

In Port Llangollen, a place of solid little houses of coral blocks painted in pastel shades, one policeman was controlling donkey carts, bicycles and an occasional truckful of sugar cane. Stani photographed the scene and asked him about crime on the island. The arm of the law roared with laughter, displaying one gold tooth among the ivory.

'Ah! Look you, sir, Madame built us a beautiful jail, but we have no prisoners! Never! No crime on this island, sir, sometimes a murder but nothing bad. Everyone happy here. Anyone sick, neighbours look after them, anyone hungry neighbours bring food, anyone does something bad, neighbours all know, nowhere to hide on this island, sir . . . all happy here!'

At a waterfront table over a snack of roti, water melon and rum they asked the owner, a desiccated individual of French extraction, to recommend subjects for photography. He pointed across the bay.

'Try the alligator farm, they breed thousands of them over there.'

'What do they do with them?'

'Parts of 'em they eat . . . the tail, it tastes like fishy chicken.' He turned down his mouth and shrugged with Gallic distaste. 'The rest gets used up, the teeth go to Trinidad, the tourists think they come from sharks, the skins go to Italy to be made into ladies' shoes, and rich men's wallets . . . you won't enjoy the alligators, they are not photogenic . . . they smell and they spend their time half submerged: like most human beings they are only interesting when they're making love! I find them *extrêmement désagréables*'.

When Stani asked who was 'Madame' who built the beautiful jail and protected the beautiful fish, the Frenchman checked to see if they were being overheard before he answered.

'Ask Benevides at your hotel to arrange a meeting with her. He's one of her courtiers, but I doubt if he dare ask her. Or send

361

a note up there to The Plantation . . . it might get through.' He pointed to a green plateau half way up the mountain. A white house was visible among the trees – 'That's where the Mongomerys have been since the middle of the seventeenth century when they arrived with their armed slaves, massacred the Carib Indians and took over the Island. They say that Madame has never left it.'

Mr. Benevides smiled but achieved nothing so with one week remaining of their holiday they dispatched a reluctant Charlie Bedwell with a note to The Plantation. For three days there was no response and with diminishing enthusiasm, it must be admitted, they continued to lie on pink beaches, to poke about on coral reefs, and to photograph water buffaloes in rice paddies, market ladies in huge hats selling baskets, small sloops with immense sails boiling home with the day's catch of flying fish. The very beauty of the place was beginning to pall.

They talked endlessly and inconclusively of future plans. Pandora watched a small sand crab struggling out of its hole and sighed.

'Hollywood's such a transient thing, but it's a great challenge . . . the trouble is I'm not sure that I still find it all that fascinating now that I've poked my head round the door . . . I don't really know how badly I want it any more.'

'You don't have to decide now . . . take your time.'

She dusted the fine sand off his shoulder and kissed the brown skin.

'I've made one moderate film and tottered away from a disaster on television!'. . . I'm not Rita Hayworth . . . I still have to do what I'm told . . .'

'Just take your time . . . Something'll come along that'll make up your mind for you.'

'Like a shark?' Pandora laughed and stretched out her arms. 'Take me for a swim.'

When they came out of the water a young Asaphian in a white uniform was waiting with an envelope. In the background Mr. Benevides was hovering beneath a tulip tree.

The note was written in an elegant, swooping hand that would have delighted an expert on 18th century calligraphy. 'It will afford me great pleasure to receive you tomorrow at afternoon tea which I take at five o'clock. Benevides will instruct you. Salutations, Gwenneth Montgomery.'

The young man spoke shyly.

'I am to take back an answer, Fine Gentleman.'

'Oh yes! Of course, we will be delighted.'

When they were alone Stani nudged Pandora.

'Did you get that? Fine Gentleman? . . . I hope you're impressed!'

'I am indeed. That's Elizabethan English, how odd.'

Before they left for their rendezvous Mr. Benevides ensured that they were properly dressed, skirt and stockings for Pandora, jacket and tie for Stani. Charlie Bedwell and his taxi had also been spruced up for the occasion. If The Plantation had once been well named there was now no sign of regimented growth except for a row of royal palms and hundreds of white, yellow and pink hibiscus bushes, on either side of the long driveway. The house a rambling affair, had obviously been much added-to, but the position was wonderfully chosen with views of a great arc of mountains and rain forest, the aquamarine bay of Port Llangollen and a series of surf-pounded headlands.

The plateau upon which the house stood was carpeted with lush green grass and ablaze with flamboyants and jacarandas; all was dominated by a huge solitary oak.

A white suited major domo led them through cool rooms to a shady patio so full of orchids that they did not see the old lady nestling among the cattleyas and the dendrobiums until she spoke.

'How nice it is when people are punctual – especially young people!'

Although obviously of great age, such was the calm beauty of her face, the high cut of her bodice and the careful Edwardian arrangement of her hair that Mrs. Montgomery reminded Pandora of one of Monet's young ladies sitting in a boat surrounded by water lilies.

To Stani she was reminiscent of a dictatorial great-aunt who had kept a herd of bison in the Bialowieza Forest.

The conversation followed upon easy but probing lines and the guests soon discovered that having married her cousin and produced no heirs their hostess was the last of the Montgomerys of St. Asaph.

'My husband is buried high in the rain forest' she said, 'one day I will be beside him . . . and that will be the end of it.'

The old lady tinkled a silver bell.

'Philomena may serve tea' she told the major domo. When an exquisite walnut trolley was wheeled in bearing silver tea pot, tiny sandwiches of cucumber or 'Gentleman's Relish', scones, butter, strawberry jam and a selection of sponge cakes, Pandora was delighted, but her eyes widened with surprise upon closer inspection of Philomena.

The elderly negress was dressed like a Victorian parlour-maid, a garment of shiny black bombazine was topped by a starched white apron which started at her chest and ended in a huge bow in the small of her back. Detachable shiny white cuffs were at her wrists, on her head reposed a frilly white bonnet tied in a bow beneath her chin.

White gloves covered her hands and upon her face lay a thick layer of white powder which gave her a very unhealthy complexion of pearl grey.

Stani mentioned the policeman's claim of an empty jail in St. Asaph.

'Which policeman?' the old lady asked with some asperity.

'Er, the fat one with the gold tooth.'

'Ah yes . . . Gomez, he talks too much. I shall have a word with him. *Of course* we have crime, but we deal with it much more simply than by locking people up in cages.'

'Stealing for example?' Stani asked. Mrs. Montgomery carefully bisected a scone and buttered it.

'A trinket of mine – a little brooch of gold and pearls – disappeared a week ago from a drawer in my dressing table. I summoned the entire staff including the gardeners and told them I expected it to be returned the next day. It wasn't. I summoned them again and showed them a black doll. I explained that the doll represented the thief, then I stuck a pin in the doll's foot. I told them that the day after I would put a pin in the calf, the next day in the thigh, then in the stomach until on the seventh day I would put one through the doll's heart. Today is the seventh day. Last night the brooch was back in my dressing table.' She poured more tea. 'The people of St. Asaph are children with the instincts of children, good and bad. We try hard to keep them happy but progress too often pollutes and it is very difficult. Jamaica, Trinidad and Barbados are jungles nowadays, crime everywhere, no birth control, unemployment, and where once there was happiness sullen people now watch ill-mannered tourists living off the fat of *their* land. Here they believe in their old ways and respect their old beliefs. The Montgomerys have always nurtured that . . .' The old lady sighed, '. . . When I am gone there will be those who will seek to change this Paradise, to make unnecessary alliances with other Islands or with the so-called Great Powers who can't even live with each other. But we have a very good school system here, the main lesson the boys and girls learn is that we are one family on this Island. A very happy family. If anyone is not happy they are free to leave and we will help them to do so, but we may not want them back.'

'Tourists?' Pandora asked.

'The greatest pollution of all,' said the old lady firmly. She rang for Philomena to remove the tea things, then she turned to Pandora.

'I have seen your eyes looking with pleasure at what you see here, are you interested in such things?'

'I was terrified of dropping one of your Crown Derby plates!' Pandora laughed '. . . and coming through the house I thought I saw a lovely satinwood bookcase and some gorgeous 18th-Century chairs.'

'Very observant, my dear. Yes, my great-grandfather who built the original house had all the furniture sent straight from the workshops of Mr. Sheraton in Soho and Mr. Hepplewhite in Cripplegate, the mirrors and mantleshelves he ordered from Mr. Adam in Scotland, the voyage took many months in those days!'

Stani had left his camera in Charlie Bedwell's car but when they moved to a terrace to enjoy the sunset he found it impossible to ask permission to use it. Mrs. Montgomery was obviously captivated by Pandora and insisted that she visit the Hospital the next day.

'We have splendid doctors trained in Canada – all Asaphians.'

'Forgive me for being so inquisitive, but how can this little Island support schools and hospitals – who pays the taxes?'

365

Mrs. Montgomery stared out over the purple sea.

'In the seventeenth century my ancestor Llewellyn Montgomery was in the . . . shall we say "shipping business" with Captain Henry Morgan! The Montgomery Foundation is very rich indeed and very well run, when the Oak Tree falls . . . everything will belong to St. Asaph.'

'The Oak Tree?' Pandora asked.

'Yes, my dear, Llewellyn planted it by the front door, the Islanders say that when it falls there will be no more Montgomerys.'

When they took their leave of Mrs. Montgomery she held Pandora's hand as they walked through darting fire-flies to Charlie Bedwell's car.

'I have so enjoyed your visit. I hope you will accept, both of you, because I think you will enjoy it, to come to a dance by the light of the full moon, in a village far up in the forest, the day after tomorrow. You will see the Queen of Saints!'

'Oh! we'd love it, wouldn't we darling?' said Pandora.

'I will send the boy down tomorrow with particulars.' She waved as they drove away then moved slowly into the house.

'What an amazing old lady!' said Pandora.'

Aware of Charlie Bedwell's flapping ears Stani whispered 'I think she's raving mad.'

The Montgomery Hospital stood on high ground just before Port Llangollen, three miles down the coast road, so they set off on their bicycles when the heat had gone from the day.

After two miles they crossed a stone bridge over the Gruffydd River, a fast running body of water from the rain forests; a sign pointed up a side road. 'ALLIGATORS ½ MILE'. 'I'd better get some shots for Mulligan,' Stani said. Soon they were passing through rows of 'Breeding Pens', half pond, half grass-covered earth.

'Ugh!' said Pandora. 'I hope those wire fences are strong . . . look at the brutes!'

Half submerged and motionless in the slime of each lay two or three large alligators. In more extensive compounds they saw hundreds of horny backs, baleful eyes and sudden convulsions of flailing, hissing, snapping power.

'Let's go back' said Pandora, 'they terrify me.'

They were turning in front of a hut when a man emerged wearing a gaily flowered shirt.

'Come to see my babies?' he asked. 'You're the first visitors I've had this week!'

They allowed him to display his incubators and in tanks admired his 'babies', slithering hordes of bright green miniature monsters.

'Aren't they beautiful? . . . you can take one with you if you like, they make wonderful pets.'

Pandora managed a smile.

'I'm afraid we're leaving the day after tomorrow.'

The man was so obviously delighted to have an audience that they allowed him to conduct a short tour.

'Do they ever get out?' Stani asked.

'The young males still manage to climb over.' He pointed to a larger enclosure. 'All bulls over there . . . Two hundred of 'em, big boys about fourteen feet long . . . they need a lot of room those bulls . . . if they're crowded they start fightin'. . . and killin'.'

Stani was clicking away with his camera. Pandora longed to be on her bike, but she didn't want to hurt the man's feelings.

'What do they eat?'

'Each other if we don't get there quick. Apart from that . . . sharks they enjoy, then we get some nice animal entrails from packin' houses in Venezuela and tons of chicken necks, of course the people here send us delicacies, rats, dead birds, dogs that got run over that sort of thing. They fight a lot so there's plenty of alligator meat too – they like that.'

'What happens if someone falls into one of those pens?' Stani asked.

'Nothing much for a while but if one takes a bite they all join in – they're very jealous – don't like others having something they haven't got.

'I got bitten once on a farm in Louisiana, they sent me there to learn 'gator farming . . . collecting the eggs that's the most dangerous time, the females don't like it. She took me by the leg. They got me to hospital real quick . . . they eat so much rotten food that the poison on their teeth's worse than the bite . . . like to see the scars?'

'We really must be going' said Pandora.

367

The man was informative to the end.

'Know what a lot of 'em suffer from? . . . Gout! . . . from over-eating!!'

Back on the coast road they found the Hospital entrance and pushed their bikes up a short hill. A young doctor showed them round and they were amazed; small, modern, with the very latest in equipment and operating rooms, it was light and airy with shady balconies for convalescents overlooking the Bay.

'A Canadian architect designed it,' he told them. 'All of us got our diplomas in Canada or the U.S.'

They were invited to take coffee with the Matron. Stani clicked off a roll of film and they departed enormously impressed.

Higher up the hill, half-hidden by cedar trees and flowering shrubs they spied a little church. Built of honey-coloured coral blocks, it was pure Georgian and perfectly proportioned; the door and windows were open, blue and red birds flashed in and out.

Inside it might have been the place of worship of a small village in Britain except that although the altar, the wooden pews, the stone font all looked cared for, it felt somehow neglected. On the walls plaques of mahogany carried inscriptions in memory of members of the Montgomery family. Pandora and Stani knelt together in prayer then sat in silence for a while. The place gave out an aura of loneliness, they felt sorry for the little church and before they left decided to decorate the altar with branches from the flowering shrubs.

'I think we have a helper!' said Stani.

A beautiful little brown girl of five or six stood watching, in her hand was a bunch of flowers as blue as her eyes, her hair was in two plaits and apart from a broad plastic bracelet of iridescent green on each wrist she was naked.

'Hello!' said Pandora. '. . . What's your name?'

'Isabella,' said the child and thrust the flowers into her hand '. . . to make God's house pretty.'

For half an hour Isabella helped with the decorations. 'I work at the Hospital' she said proudly, 'I'm nurse like my Mama.'

When they said goodbye to the little girl she shook her head solemnly and admonished them in her Island sing-song: 'No!

lady and genman . . . don't *never* say goodbye . . .'

On the way back they stopped on a headland, the cumulus were riding higher than usual and, for the first time far above them, cirrus turned pink, rose, gold, even green, as the last rays touched them. It was the most spectacular sunset they had ever seen.

They mentioned this to Mr. Benevides.

'It might mean a little wind tomorrow' he said and gave them their instructions for the following evening.

On the morning of their last day Stani was awakened by the sound of Pandora splashing about in the little patio pool.

'You're up early,' he mumbled when she appeared.

'I couldn't sleep . . . I just can't make up my mind about Hollywood.'

'Don't try, you've plenty of time. I brought you down here so you wouldn't decide everything in a rush. When we get back to New York you'll be able to sniff the wind, and if you go back to California it'll be easier to judge things from there; talk to Chuck and other people you trust and get some good advice.'

Pandora towelled herself.

'I'm terribly torn,' she said.

Stani grunted.

'Remember what you said on the boat coming over? "Let's give it a year, maybe two, if it doesn't work by then – fly away"? *That* made great sense. Now come back to bed.'

She snuggled up against him and murmured 'You haven't asked me to marry you for ages!'

He stroked her satiny skin.

'I'll have a word with my board of directors . . . as far as I remember, the offer has not been withdrawn . . . in the mean-time – I love you!'

After breakfast they swam out to the reef for a farewell look at the coral and the giant sea bass and moray eels which had proved faithful to their 'turfs'. A stronger than usual on-shore breeze swayed the elegant palms, on the horizon the reflection of a slight haze stole some colour from the Prussian blue of the deep water, but the sun was hot and only a few catspaws stroked the limpid surface of the lagoon.

They spent the whole morning poking about with Mr.

369

Benevides' spear but failed to find any of their special friends, in fact fish of all species were preoccupied and busy, not lazing about and nibbling at goodies as usual but hurrying by in small parties like board members late for stockholders' meetings. The reef seemed inhospitable and they were not reluctant to head for shore. After lunch Pandora complained of a headache and Stani, making arrangements for their early morning departure, detected a certain testiness among the normally smiling staff; the morning haze had climbed the sky and the sun's light now filtered down through a yellowish ring; the horizon had turned light grey, an hour later it was the colour of lead.

Charlie Bedwell was ready at seven thirty and said 'better shut your windows when you go to bed, we'll have a storm by morning.'

As they climbed the mountain road the air, instead of cooling off, became sultry and devoid of the slightest movement.

'I feel terribly nervous,' said Pandora. 'Let's not stay long, I'd like to go to bed early.'

Charlie Bedwell refused to be pumped about the Queen of Saints.

'It's a custom, sir, among the mountain folk and many others . . . I know nothing of it.'

The rain forest, still and mysterious was shrouded in mist. They headed for the village along a footpath. Tall trees with broad leaves, and giant ferns, loomed eerily on either side. Charlie Bedwell, declining to come any further, lent them a flashlight for their return.

'Just stay on that path, sir, and keep the drums in front of you.'

A steady African beat was pulsating through the trees, a dank, musty smell rose from the forest floor. After a few minutes walk they noticed a light flickering ahead and at a bend in the path came upon a little pile of fruit, bread and several large bones topped off by a single lighted candle. Before reaching the end of the path they passed several more.

The village, no cluster of dilapidated shanties, consisted of a group of sturdy wooden dwellings with corrugated iron roofs sited round the source of the pounding drums, a rectangular building of white stucco. Waiting to enter were men and

370

women wearing their best clothes, in the fading light their faces seemed paler and more Indian than any they had so far seen on the Island. Stani and Pandora possessed the only white ones and curious glances came their way.

A young man pushed through the throng.

'The Queen of Saints bids you welcome,' he announced solemnly.

Inside, the barn-like place was lit by banks of candles and the heat was stifling; close packed on three sides of the dance floor stood two or three hundred onlookers, in front of them a few wooden chairs had been placed, two had been left empty and to these the young man led them. The floor was of concrete and fifty or sixty dancers, all dressed in white, were shuffling round it with expressionless faces to the steady beat of the drums.

On the fourth side of the dance floor, in one corner, the drummers were located. In the middle, on a row of elaborate chairs, wearing white suits, sat twenty dignified black 'courtiers' of the Queen of Saints, including Mr. Benevides. Above them, on a raised dais, seated on an exquisitely carved gold-painted throne, also clothed in white with a white bandana covering her hair was – Mrs. Montgomery.

They bowed to the Queen of Saints, but received not a flicker of recognition. Mrs Montgomery looked out over the shuffling throng with a smile that never faltered. For almost half an hour the dancers continued their slow swaying progress round the floor to the insistent beat and subtle rhythm changes of the drums, many moved like sleepwalkers with closed eyes. Suddenly there was a scream and a stout woman, bathed in sweat, flung her arms in the air, her eyes rolled up, then out of her mouth came the deep coughing bark of a tiger. The onlookers craned forward eagerly when with incredible agility for one of her bulk she took three or four catlike springs before falling face down on the floor below the Queen of Saints, snarling and clawing at the concrete with her finger nails. The Queen threw some grains of rice in her direction and the woman licked them up; the other dancers with unbroken step eddied round her, totally obsessed by their own involvement except for two who helped her to her feet, bound her loosely with strips of white material, mopped the froth from her lips and put her back on

371

her shuffling course. The rhythm changed again and a young girl shouted loudly with a man's voice, then two more flung themselves shrieking and babbling at the foot of the throne eyes upturned and surrendering themselves completely to whatever or whoever it was that possessed them; the binding process was repeated and the dance continued with unbroken rhythm. Stani found himself with tapping feet sitting forward on the edge of his chair. He looked at Pandora, her head was raised, her eyes were closed, she too was swaying to the beat. With a conscious effort he forced himself not to get involved; the dancers in increasing numbers were now roaring, bellowing, shrieking, crying, baying and falling to the floor before their smiling Queen. The rhythm was ever more persuasive and the onlookers became affected; a man standing immediately behind them raised his arms above his head and emitted a series of long penetrating cries. Stani felt the hair raise up on his scalp, as a little boy he had heard that sound often and it had always terrified him . . . a wolf was howling at the moon. When Pandora swayed to her feet and took a step toward the dancers, he caught her hand and gently pulled her back; she did not notice. He looked at his watch, they had been there two hours. Mr. Benevides approached, moving slowly down the line of wooden chairs offering their privileged occupants a sip from a large mug, his eyes were glazed and when he handed it to Pandora it was as though he had never seen her before.

She raised it to her lips. Stani saw the contents and took it from her before she tasted it. Dark red with a faint aroma of iron – blood. There was a blinding blue flash and an earsplitting CRACK! followed by an explosion of thunder that shook the building, heavy drops of rain rattled on the roof.

The dancers paid no attention but a few of the onlookers drifted towards the door heading for the shelter of their homes before the storm worsened. Stani grabbed the opportunity, returned the cup to Mr. Benevides and steered Pandora outside. The temperature had dropped several degrees.

With the help of the flashlight they found their way back to the taxi; lightning flickered everywhere, the thunder was full of menace and the rain driven by strong gusts of wind. Charlie Bedwell was anxious to be away but he drove with commendable care down the mountain road already slick with mud

372

from the forest.

'It's just a tropical storm . . . they come this time of year . . . tomorrow our Island will be beautiful again.' He reminded them to be ready at seven in the morning to catch the flight to Barbados; when he drove away Stani realized that he still had the flashlight in his hand.

The Poinciana Inn was deserted except for one waiter packing up a box of food in the kitchen.

'Radio announced Hurricane Warning', he said, 'all boys gone home.'

'What are we supposed to do?' Pandora asked.

The waiter shrugged.

'Hurricanes never hit Asaph Lady, not for fifty years. Maybe Mr. Benevides come back soon. Good night Lady and Gentleman.'

'The Venezuelans left yesterday' said Stani 'and I haven't seen those Canadians for a couple of days – I think we're on our own!'

'What fun! I wonder what a hurricane's like? . . . it doesn't look very fierce at the moment!'

'The first thing that goes wrong is the power . . . I read that somewhere, let's find candles and matches and bread and stuff, it might go on all night . . . we'll have a midnight picnic!'

They raided the kitchen and carried their loot to their bungalow. The rain was much heavier by the time they crossed the garden, the drops large and quite painful, several coconuts and fronds had been ripped off the palms, from the darkened beach came the continuous pounding of heavy surf. Blue and purple lightning lit the clouds from within and thunder was crashing over the mountains, so they rolled shut the big sliding glass window and took off their wet clothes.

'Let's go and look at the sea' said Pandora, 'it sounds so exciting!'

They ran naked through the well-lit garden and stopped short in amazement – there was no beach! Built up by some incredible force the sea had advanced twenty yards and the waves, steep, ugly and close together, were booming down at the very feet of the palms and mangroves, several of which had already toppled over; the rest, with tattered leaves were straining in a wind that was now howling alarmingly. Somewhere

373

nearby the rain short-circuited a car battery and the pitiful wail of the horn added to the din. On their return they made a detour by way of the main hotel: the open-sided dining room and the verandahs were flooded, leaves, sodden papers, and cushions filled the corners, tables and chairs were overturned, the rain mixed with spray was whipping horizontally through the lobby. Remembering their nakedness Pandora giggled, 'I *do* hope we meet Mr. Benevides!' When the lights of hotel and garden suddenly went out, they groped their way back along the path and through the door of their protecting wall. They had to push hard to shut it.

'That wind's incredible!' Pandora panted . . . 'it can't get any stronger, can it?'

Stani lit a candle.

'It's about sixty or seventy miles an hour now . . . *could* go to two hundred!'

'This is not funny any longer,' said Pandora.

Stani nodded.

'Thank God we have the patio wall, but if we do get flooded out here, we'll make for the Port, well-built houses there.'

'How long will it last?'

'Hurricanes move very slowly, about ten miles an hour, that's all . . . it'll be several hours before it's gone past.'

When the driving rain found the joins in the sliding glass wall and under the door, they plugged the leaks with towels but the floor was soon awash, so they made a nest of bedclothes in the bathroom, ate a sandwich, put on some clothes and tried to sleep. It was impossible, the storm doubled its force, raindrops no longer existed, they were pulverized by the wind into a solid wall of water. Pandora complained that her ears were blocked 'like before landing in a plane.'

'That's the pressure, darling – we could be near the centre of the bloody thing . . . the Eye.' He had to shout to make himself heard, the thunder, the wind tearing at the roof, ripping trees to pieces and pushing the waves even higher, had combined to produce a continuous and terrifying roar.

Pandora shivered 'I'm getting frightened . . . hold me tight.'

They dozed off. At two in the morning the big glass wall of the bedroom exploded like a bomb, blown into a million lethal fragments. The wind of dreadful ferocity then wrenched off the

374

roof of the bungalow and hurled it, spinning and cartwheeling in the direction of the hotel, water poured in and the roar of the storm increased.

They grabbed the flashlight and made for the patio. The surrounding wall was still standing but the heavy door lay at the bottom of the pool. Such was the wind force at the open entrance that they could only pass through by crawling, breathing like racing swimmers in the protection of their armpits. They groped and slithered their way up to the main road and turned left towards Port Llangollen. The road was well above sea level so except for the brute force of wind and rain there was little danger from that direction; but to their right millions of tons of water were being dumped on the steep mountain sides, flash floods built up and roared down towards the sea carrying mud, rocks, trees, parts of houses and bodies. Twice these dreadful avalanches hurtled down, obliterating stretches of road just behind them.

They made no effort to speak, the blasting roar even swallowed the noise of the thunder; they just concentrated grimly on forging ahead a few yards at a time making use of every inch of cover from the unbelievable power of the hurricane and avoiding all constructions because gutters, tiles and sheets of corrugated iron came scything out of the darkness. To store up energy they rested in mud-filled holes left by uprooted trees; deafened by the noise, they were soon half blinded by pollen from the manzanea trees which, mixed with rain, cut through the air – an infectious paste.

Drained physically by the struggle and battered mentally by the endless shriek of nature gone mad, they stumbled and crawled towards the safety of the Port.

When the first grey hint of dawn filtered through, Stani pointed the flashlight at his watch. Almost two hours had elapsed since they had evacuated the bungalow. Pandora had been gallant in the extreme but she was weakening fast, soon he would have to carry her and they had not yet reached the Gruffydd River. But would his leg be up to it? Already stabs of pain had given warning signals.

Quite suddenly the rain slackened, then the wind lessened its torment and diminished to vicious gusts. Within half an hour both rain and wind were gone altogether. The dreadful roar of the hurricane ceased.

For the first time they heard the noises of people – distant screams of pain, cries for help, the sound of frightened children.

Pandora flung herself on the sodden turf beside the road and began to sob.

'Oh! Thank you, God! . . . Thank you! . . . It's OVER!'

Stani looked up at the low leaden underbelly of the whirling clouds and his heart missed a beat. In a small patch of quickly obliterated clear sky he had caught a glimpse of – a single star. He lay in the mud beside her and broke the news as gently as he could.

'I'm afraid it's not over . . . we're in the Eye.'

Pandora pressed her face to the mud; after a while she spoke. 'What do we do?'

'We keep going as quick as we can now, during the lull. It'll start up again soon. If the bridge is still there we'll make for the Hospital or the Church on the high ground . . . the buildings are strong and it's nearer than the Port. It'll be light in an hour, we're going to be okay. . . . I promise.'

She struggled up and they battled on towards the river. That it had become a raging torrent they could tell a hundred yards away. In the eerie quiet, they heard its swollen rush to the sea and its raging against the bridge; the rain having stopped, the flooding had receded somewhat leaving in the mud at either end the rubbish of decimated cane fields and banana plantations, sections of houses, furniture, mattresses, oil drums and unstable log-jams of trees, telephone poles and bundles of wire fencing. Stani made careful use of the flashlight to ensure that among the dead pigs and dogs Pandora did not see the broken bodies of men, women and children. They attacked the obstacles with care but also with urgency because when the full fury of the storm returned, they knew the log-jams would be swept away to the sea.

By the time they reached the bridge, heavy rain was falling once more and the first gusts of wind heralded the renewal of the onslaught; but the sky was lighter over the sea, the faint outline of the bay was visible and between rain squalls a cluster of lights showed ahead – the hospital, with its emergency generator still operating. Stani pointed it out but her infected eyes were almost completely closed, she was utterly exhausted.

376

'How far?' she whispered.

Stani lied. 'A couple of hundred yards.' It was at least half a mile.

From the far end of the bridge he surveyed the last great hazard before the final climb to the hospital – another log-jam of the same ingredients as before; the water was rising again and some fallen trees were stirring restlessly in the slime. One large palm stripped of its fronds still seemed securely grounded, its fibrous bowl was jammed against the furthest supporting column and its naked top looked fast in the mud a few yards from the bank; trapped along its upstream side were branches, poles and debris of every sort. When he had tested its stability, and measured the depth of the mud with a stick he was fairly confident.

Pandora put her hand in his.

'Just tell me where to put my feet . . . I'll do my best . . . why is the wind coming from the opposite direction?'

'A hurricane spins like a top, we were right in the middle of it.'

He guided her feet to the half-submerged tree, then with a strong arm around her waist he shouted encouragement over the rising wind and they shuffled sideways along its length. Five yards from the safety of the bank the top end of the tree worked free of the mud; somehow he kept his balance, but there was a 'hiss', an expulsion of air and a strange movement beside him. He switched on the flashlight in time to see the armoured back of a monster alligator sliding away in the slime. He swept the beam in all directions. Ahead he saw nothing but mud, downstream only moving flotsam but upstream pairs of round eyes reflected the beam of his light. He did not hesitate, he flung the lighted flashlight towards the eyes, told Pandora to hold him round the neck, lifted her off her feet and jumped into the mud on the downstream side. The slimy muck was heavy and came halfway up his thighs, the bottom was uneven but firm and, taking what seemed an eternity of superhuman effort, he fought his way to the slippery bank and half carried, half dragged her to the top.

They lay on flattened cane till swarms of ants forced them to their feet, then set off on a painful trek across the decimated crop – painful for Stani because his shoes had remained in the mud and among the splintered stalks every step with his bad foot was agony. The wind no longer came rampaging out of the sea whipping the tops off the waves, mixing salt with driving rain. Now it roared down from the mountains, much colder, filling the air with bushes, plants and whirling branches. Pandora, dazed and disturbed by the renewed thunder and the ferocity of the second onslaught, asked again and again, like a child, 'What will happen to all the poor birds?'

When the full blast of the storm had been in their faces they could sense each time a gust was too dangerous and had flung themselves to the ground. The present attacks smashed into them from almost directly behind so they were constantly caught off balance and catapulted forward. When he picked her up after yet another such sprawling fall it was obvious that Pandora had come to the end of her courageous battle. With pain now raging up his leg, he hoisted her over his shoulders in a 'fireman's lift' and staggered on past the shattered remains of a cluster of plantation workers' dwellings. Every now and then that terrifying wind would select a fallen plank, a door, a chair, or a shutter, pick it up as a dog might a toy and toss it spinning into the howling dawn.

At the foot of the hospital hill something slammed into them, almost wrenching Stani's arm out of its socket and knocking him unconscious: he never saw what hit him. How long he lay there he never knew. Slowly his head cleared of a blood-red mist, then the damage to his shoulder, to the side of his head and to his foot forced gasps of pain from his lungs. Face down and able to use his right arm only with the agony of torn muscles, ligaments and tendons he tried to move his legs; he couldn't and the thought of paralysis assailed him till he realized that Pandora was lying across them. He called to her, but she did not answer. Choking with the dread of what he might find he managed to wriggle out from beneath her.

With the rain sluicing over her she lay on her back, her face as calm and beautiful as a camellia; but when he saw the ugly gash and the swelling above her ear his stomach contracted with fear. Frantically he listened for the beat of her heart but the roar of the hurricane forbade it. He thought he could feel a faint pulse on her wrist but with the throb inside his own head he could not be sure. She was very cold.

378

The side of the hill was waterlogged and treacherous, his whole body shrieked with pain but with Pandora sometimes over his shoulders, sometimes in his arms and occasionally on her back being pulled up the slippery slope, he finally reached the shelter of the hospital.

He found a small group huddled in the lee of the main building staring ahead, their faces blasted of all expression, their eyes flat and dead, like shell-shocked soldiers; the wounded among them, moaning or crying out, were being attended to by a nurse; close-packed a few yards away lay others who would never again utter a sound.

When the nurse saw Stani she helped him carry Pandora inside and lower her onto a trolley.

A doctor in a blood-stained surgical gown examined her and she was wheeled away. Stani's head wound was cleaned and stitched, his damaged foot heavily bandaged, pain-killers were injected into his arm, then, numb with apprehension, he waited for news. The doctor returned.

'She has a fracture of the skull . . . she is in coma.'

His world collapsed but he forced himself to ask the question.

'We don't know,' the doctor answered. 'Probably she will live, she is young and strong but it is not good to be too long in coma . . .'

A nurse tugged urgently at the doctor's sleeve. He touched Stani's arm.

'We will do our best. When she wakes we will know if the brain is damaged. Come every day for news . . . something terrible has happened to our Island; even the Oak Tree has fallen.'

By ten o'clock the hurricane had left St. Asaph, not suddenly; over a period of two hours the wind, the rain, the lightning and the thunder had gradually diminished until there was silence; and the sun shone. For days Stani hobbled about volunteering for anything to help the stream of battered survivors who toiled up the hill. The death toll was in the hundreds, the suffering dreadful to see. Pandora lay in a cot in a corridor as pale and still as alabaster.

Protected in the curve of the question mark of the Island, the little town of Port Llangollen had not suffered greatly but, looking down upon the bay, Stani was reminded of the end of a children's party. The whirling centre of the storm had sucked up an area of sea which the power of the wind had sent hurtling shorewards – a foaming tidal wave; dockside buildings looked like trampled matchboxes, fishing boats and trading schooners, some a hundred yards from the sea, lay on their sides or were piled, smashed to pieces, on top of one another. Cars and trucks were among them, houses seemingly intact stood at curious angles and diagonally across the road lay a coaster. A French warship, probably from Martinique, stood offshore unloading medical supplies, Red Cross teams, food and tents. Inland great tracts of low lying land were still flooded, crops of every kind obliterated, and all vegetation left standing was turning brown as the hot sun burned salt-encrusted leaves.

Every morning and every evening Stani dragged himself to the little church; its coral blocks had survived the ordeal, but most of the roof had gone; the rain and the hundreds who had sheltered there had made a sorry mess of the interior. The Minister, a woebegone expression on his face, said with little enthusiasm that it was 'God's will' and knelt beside Stani in the rubbish. For nine days Pandora lay in coma: on the tenth the exhausted surgeon told him that all indications were that a blood clot had formed.

'If you develop a bruise anywhere else on your body' he explained, 'it swells up and gets better but a bruise which develops on the brain cannot swell because it is trapped inside the skull, pressure builds and the result can be very bad indeed.'

Stani felt weak with helplessness.

'What can you do?'

'We must operate to relieve the pressure. We think we have located the clot; now we must bore holes in her skull to let it out. They are shaving her head and preparing her now.'

Stani wandered about in a daze – this *couldn't* be happening . . . a trip to an island paradise suggested as casually as a walk in Central Park because they were worried about a movie career . . . boring holes in her skull? . . . Who was this exhausted man with Pandora's life in his hands? . . . Operating on the brain! *Anything* could go wrong! Suppose it did? . . . Suppose she came out of that operation but could never walk again? Or speak again? Suppose she . . .'

380

He cursed the day he had heard of St. Asaph. 'My beautiful Pandora . . . what have I done to you?'

The Matron of the little hospital was gaunt from strain and lack of sleep but she paused to comfort him.

'Doctor Boaz is very clever, he will take care of her. Get away from this place for a couple of hours – there's nothing more you can do. You brought her here . . . that was the important thing.'

For two hours of torture Stani forced himself to stay outside the buildings, then he took up a position from which he could see the door to the operating theatre. From time to time a nurse wearing a surgical mask came out to fetch something, once in a great hurry she disappeared inside pushing a cylinder of oxygen.

After three hours he had almost given up hope, he had longed to see the trolley emerge, now he dreaded it.

Slowly he dragged himself up the hill towards the little church: some help, or comfort might be found among the fallen timbers, the broken glass and the upturned pews. The stout oak door was padlocked, on it was a notice:

'CLOSED FOR REPAIRS'.

He knelt on the step, pressed his forehead to the cool wood, and prayed for Pandora as he had once prayed in a rubber dinghy in the North Atlantic . . . with heart, soul and his entire being.

He sensed that he was no longer alone among the uprooted trees and splintered headstones. Behind him stood Isabella, the graceful little brown girl with green plastic bracelets on her wrists. She put her hand in his.

'My Mama say you come back now – lady finished.'

A clutch of terror seized him and oblivious to the pain in his foot he raced back to the hospital.

'It *can't* have happened,' he told himself over and over . . . 'Please God let her *live* . . . no matter what her brain may bring her . . . I'll look after her. Just let her *live*.'

In the passage no doctor was waiting at her bedside. Pandora lay as still as marble, her face below a turban of bandages as beautiful and peaceful as a flower. He fell to his knees beside her bed. People stepped over his heels.

When a hand touched his shoulder he looked up. The surgeon's brown face was so drawn with fatigue that Stani hardly recognized him.

'She will live,' he smiled. 'The operation went well . . . the pressure on the brain is gone.' He looked at Pandora. 'She sleeps now, she has been very restless which is a good sign, soon she will come out of her coma. She is very near the surface.'

Stani stood to swamp him with inadequate words of gratitude but with the major hope of his prayers already answered, his face still betrayed his anxiety for Pandora's future.

'Fortunately she is young and healthy,' said the surgeon. 'She has already been moving her head and her limbs so, when she comes out of her coma, if she remembers things that happended or words that were said shortly before the accident, then the chances that she will be restored to you completely and with no ill effects will be very great indeed. I am very happy for you.'

For two days and two nights Stani sat on a wooden chair beside Pandora's bed watching her sleeping at peace or moving ever more urgently: on the evening of the second day she lifted her head off the pillow and mumbled a few words. As dawn was breaking on the third day she opened her eyes, looked up at Stani's face with puzzlement at first, next with wonder and lastly with pure joy. Then she reached for his hand, held it against her cheek, smiled, and whispered:

'What *did* happen to all the poor birds?'